Prologue

June 17, 1624

THE SEA IS A HARSH AND UNFORGIVING MISTRESS...

Bartolome Vargas, King Philip of Spain's most trusted and decorated naval officer, knew this better than most.

Twas the sea that conjured up the early season hurricane that had overtaken the armada and his beloved ship. Twas the sea that forced him to scuttle the grandest galleon in the Spanish fleet on this speck of reef and sand. And twas the sea that was now making the salvage of the Santa Cristina's cargo so difficult.

He scanned the horizon, where whitecaps danced and fizzed in that small, incandescent space between water and sky. For days now, strong winds had teased the ocean into a tizzy, stirring up silt and sediment, forcing his men to work blind.

His men...

Raising his spyglass, Bartolome watched as they toiled tirelessly under the relentless subtropical sun. Only thirty-six of the Santa Cristina's original 224 crew members had survived her wreck. Thirty-six brave souls who, in the most unfavorable of conditions—running on what scarce food they managed to drag from the ocean and what little rainwater they could catch in the unbroken barrels that had washed ashore after the hurricane—continued to dive down on the sunken remains of the ship. Without complaint, and through sheer force of will, they were slowly hauling up the riches of the New World.

"Five, maybe six more days if the wind continues like this." A familiar voice.

Bartolome glanced over his shoulder to find Rosario, his loyal midshipman, standing nearby. The man's eyes were trained on the crew laboring just beyond the reef.

"Five or six more days," Bartolome echoed.

But then what? He shuddered to consider it. Rescuing the treasure from the waterlogged remains of the Santa Cristina was damned difficult. What he planned to do with the riches next would be absolutely backbreaking.

"Have you chosen where to bury it, Capitán?" Rosario smiled at the growing piles of chests and leather satchels accumulating on the beach. The immense treasure King Philip needed to fund his fight against those who would see Spain's might reduced to meekness was a sight to behold.

"We cannot bury the treasure on the island," Bartolome told Rosario.

"No?" His midshipman's deeply tanned forehead wrinkled.

"The ocean is crawling with our enemies. When the water clears, no doubt one of them will stumble across the Santa Cristina's skeleton. First thing they will do after diving down to find we have liberated her cargo is scour this island for newly turned earth. No." He shook his head. "We must—"

Movement out of the corner of his eye stopped him mid-sentence. He scanned the sea and… There!

Holy Madré Maria! Why had not Pablo whistled an alert?

Swinging his spyglass toward a palm at the edge of the beach, Bartolome answered his own question.

Pablo had suffered an injury to his flank during the wreck. Though Bartolome had assigned him the simplest of jobs on the island—lookout in a hastily constructed crow's nest—exposure, hunger, and rot had finally gotten the better of poor Pablo. The man's arms hung limply along the sides of the tree, his head rested back against his shoulders, and his mouth gaped, attracting a cloud of buzzing gnats.

Had Bartolome time to send up a prayer for the man's soul, he would. As it was, he broke into a desperate run up the beach and through the trees, only slowing once he reached the edge of the mangrove forest.

"Capitán?" Rosario panted when he caught up. "What is it?"

"Perhaps 'tis our deliverance." Bartolome wheezed painfully, grabbing his side where his broken ribs had only recently begun to reknit themselves. Gingerly, he lowered himself until he lay flat in the sand. Then motioned for Rosario to join him and added solemnly, "Or perhaps 'tis something to be dealt with quickly and violently."

Hitching his chin toward the vast, endless blue, he did not need to say more. The brown hull of the approaching vessel was easily visible. So was the faded yellow of the mainsail as it flapped drunkenly in the breeze.

His midshipman frowned, licking cracked lips as he glanced over his shoulder at the crow's nest. Upon spotting Pablo, he winced and whispered, "Poor bastard." Then, he turned back and asked, "Could she be Spanish, Capitán? Can you see what flags she flies?"

Bartolome peered through the spyglass. "No flags. She looks to be a fishing vessel."

"All the way out here?" Rosario's tone was skeptical.

"'Tis rough shape she is in." Through the magnified lens, Bartolome watched the lone figure on board frantically toss a bucket of seawater over the side. "Taking on water," he added.

"Likely the sorry sod was caught in the storm," Rosario surmised. "Could have been drifting for weeks. Lucky for him, he happened this way."

How lucky or unlucky the man is remains to be seen, Bartolome thought coldly.

This side of the island was unprotected by the reef. At high tide, the surf reached all the way to the leggy roots of the trees. But now, at low tide, a narrow ribbon of sand was revealed. On it lived sand fleas. The tiny bugs skittered away from their exhaled breaths only to come crawling back once they inhaled.

In and out. Back and forth. Like the sea herself.

Bartolome paid the creatures little heed. His entire focus was fixed on the boat's prow as it plowed onto the thin stretch of beach, hissing its arrival as it made contact with the sand.

The lone crewman jumped onto dry land, immediately falling to his knees and kissing the ground beneath him. When he straightened, he raised his arms toward the cloudless sky and yelled, "Praise you, oh Lord!"

Rosario sucked in a ragged breath. With a curl of his lip, he spat one word. "Englishman."

"Stay here," Bartolome commanded after curling his fingers around the conch shell half-buried in the sand beside him and jumping to his feet. He headed in the direction of the island's newest arrival.

Bedraggled and sporting many days' growth of beard, the fisherman blinked and rubbed his eyes when he saw Bartolome striding his way. After he convinced himself he was not seeing things, he pushed to a stand. A huge smile spread across his face.

A softer man might have been swayed by that smile. But years in the armada had successfully killed any softness that might have once resided inside Bartolome.

"Hello!" The fisherman lifted a grubby hand in greeting. "I thought for certain this island was uninhabited. But I am so pleased to discover it—"

Bartolome saw the instant the man realized his intent. It was the instant before he brought the conch shell down on the fisherman's temple.

Whack! The sound was both solid and oddly wet-sounding.

Bartolome half expected the shell to shatter in his fist and did not relish the thought of finishing the task with his bare hands. But, thankfully, the conch remained intact.

Despite his wounds and weeks of starvation, he still had the strength to drive the man to his knees with his first strike. Whack! His second split the fisherman's skull clean open.

With a startled gasp, the newcomer tipped sideways, spilling a portion of his head's contents onto the sand, twitching once, twice, three times, and then falling still. Bartolome waited until the last light drained from the man's eyes before hoisting the corpse over his shoulder and closing his nose to the smell of damp flesh and urine. The instant the fisherman's soul had left his body, his bladder had released.

Death is such an indignity, Bartolome thought as he hastily tossed the body into the boat.

A cursory inspection showed that, indeed, there was a small hole in the hull. There was also fishing gear and a few other odds and ends that could be quite useful. But he resisted the temptation to seize them.

The presence of new supplies would raise too many questions among the crew.

Instead, he used the last of his strength to push the little vessel back into the surf. The waves tugged at his ankles, then his knees, then his waist. The salty water angered the still-healing wound on his thigh.

When he was chest deep, he sent the boat into the currents, grateful the tide was still going out. It caught the craft and tugged it back in the direction from which it had come. Bartolome knew it would stay afloat long enough for the sea to carry it to deep water. There, it would breathe its last of clear, bright air before slowly sinking into the cold, dark heart of the ocean.

"No!" Rosario splashed into the surf beside him. "Capitán! I know he had to die. We do not have enough food to feed ourselves, much less an English dog. But we could have used his boat. We could have repaired it. We could have sailed it to Havana and—"

"No." Bartolome shook his head. "We would never make it with so many pirates and privateers looking for us. We would surely be discovered. And how long do you think any of us would last if our enemies keelhauled information from us?"

"The men will not be happy." Rosario's expression was mournful. "What if that was our only chance to make it off this godforsaken island?"

Exactly why Bartolome had not kept the little boat for future use. His men were loyal and true, but desperation could make even the best of them lose sight of their ultimate purpose. No doubt, at some point, the boat would have proved too great a temptation.

"The men will not know of this." Bartolome's tone brooked no argument. When he lowered his chin to stare meaningfully at his midshipman, he saw the light dawn in Rosario's eyes.

Yes, Bartolome Vargas would do anything to ensure the Santa Cristina's treasure remained hidden from their enemies. Even if it meant his death.

Even if it meant all their deaths…

Chapter 1

Present day
7:05 a.m.

MASON MCCARTHY HAD A PROBLEM.

His problem was five feet tall. Had curly red hair that was only 50 percent tamed under the best of conditions, and 100 percent out of control this early in the morning. And she was sitting at a table by the window watching the multicolored ships of the shrimp fleet as they rocked precariously with the wave action out near the horizon while her fingers absently fiddled with the corner of a book.

Oh, and she was also studiously ignoring him.

She was wicked good at that last part. Was making a frickin' hobby of it, as a matter of fact. Not that he could blame her, considering what she'd offered him.

And what he'd turned down.

Her name was Alexandra Merriweather. Alex for short, which was a ridiculously masculine moniker for such a tiny wisp of a woman. One with skin like porcelain, eyes the color of Colombian emeralds, and a laugh as sweet and tinkling as a music box.

She was his problem because…well…he liked her. Like, *liked* her liked her. And if his cheating ho of a wife—scratch that, rewind: that would be his cheating ho of an *ex*-wife—had taught him anything, it was that he wasn't fit to like a woman like Alex.

Not anymore.

All the years schlepping his ass through countless missions, maiming and killing in the name of the flag, had turned him into something…not normal.

That was the phrase Sarah had used when he came home early to surprise her for her birthday, but instead found her screwing his ex-best friend in their marriage bed. *Surprise!*

"What d'you expect, Mason?" Sarah's expression had been so sincere. *"You're gone all the time, and when you're here, you're not normal."*

Copy that. When it came to a life of violence, the effects were biological, physiological, and psychological. It was the price of being a warrior.

So even though he'd been heartbroken by her betrayal, he'd never worked up much anger over it. Then and now, there was no way to deny the truth. Mason McCarthy was no longer capable of living an ordinary life with the house, the wife, and the two-point-three kids.

The only reason he was sitting in this hotel bar now, a bona fide civilian, was because of a deathbed promise he and the rest of his teammates had made to Rusty Lawrence, the eighth man in their SEAL unit. Barring that, Mason figured he would've kept on running and gunning until he found the bullet with his name on it.

With a fingertip, he traced the scrolling black letters inked on the inside of his left forearm. *For RL* they read. Picturing Rusty's craggy face, he tried to determine whether to curse the sorry sonofabitch or thank him for forcing them all to make that vow and wave their fond farewells to the navy.

A call of "G'morning, asshole!" cut into his thoughts. Turning, he found Ray "Wolf" Roanhorse standing behind him.

Since he'd yet to determine how good the morning was or wasn't, Mason grunted his reply. Wolf, used to Mason's wordless responses, bent to scratch Meat's exposed belly.

The fat English bulldog slept on his back beside Mason's barstool, dick and balls on display for the entire breakfast crowd, and his snores nearly drowning out the cries of the seagulls coming in through the hotel's open windows.

Meat was the only thing Mason had taken from the divorce. He'd let Sarah have their restored three-decker in Southie, along with the furniture and all the minutia that went with a "normal" life. But Meat? Well, not to put too fine a point on it, but he'd have crossed hell with nothing but a bucket of ice water before he'd have let her keep his dog.

"A wise woman once said, 'If you risk nothin', you risk everythin.'" With the unaffected ease that came with being supremely fit, Wolf settled himself onto the barstool next to Mason's.

The two of them had become instant friends when they'd been teamed up as swim partners way back in BUD/S—Basic Underwater Demolition/SEAL— training. And through all the intervening years, Wolf had never run out of inspirational quotes. He fancied himself a scholar of the world's philosophers and religions.

There were times, including this one, when that could get damned annoying.

Instead of answering, Mason kept quiet. He hoped his silence conveyed his wish for more coffee and less talk.

"I *said*," Wolf said louder, "a wise woman once—"

"First off," Mason muttered irritably, "what part of this face"—he pointed to his scowling mug—"makes you think I'm in the mood for morning convo?"

"You're *never* in the mood for conversation," Wolf drawled, his Oklahoma accent making the words sound twice as long as they normally would. "Don't matter what time of day it is."

"Second off," Mason went on as if Wolf hadn't spoken, "what's that supposed to mean, anyway? *If you risk nothing, you risk everything?*"

"It means you should pull your head from your ass and go for it. Take her up on what she's offerin.'" Wolf stuck a cocktail straw between his teeth and hailed the bartender to put in an order for a Bloody Mary. Hitching his chin toward Alex's table, he added, "Come on, man. You know you want to."

Mason hadn't been kidding when he said he wasn't in the mood to talk. But he sure as shit wasn't in the mood to talk about Alex and her heart-stopping offer. "Anyone ever told you you're a board-certified fuck-ace who should mind his own damned business?"

"Sure." Wolf's onyx eyes flashed with humor, proving he was impervious to Mason's insults. "You tell me all the time. That don't change the fact that every time you see Alex's wild, windswept curls and wide, green eyes, you start scoutin' the area for horizontal surfaces."

"For fuck's sake." Mason snorted. "Tell me you haven't taken up writing poetry too. That'll be the straw that breaks this camel's back."

Wolf shrugged. "Reckoned that was nicer than sayin' you're pantin' after her because she's sexy in a girl-next-door way that makes most men dream about doin' extremely naughty things to her." ·

Mason felt his expression turn sinister.

"Whoa there, brother." Wolf lifted his hands. "Not sayin' *I'm* one of those men."

"I don't pant." Mason truly *hated* this conversation. "'Cause I'm not a dog. And I'm only interested in her for her brain and its ability to help us find the *Santa Cristina*. If anything's sexy, it's her frontal lobe."

Wolf curled his lip. "Gross."

"Ya-huh," Mason admitted. "Sounded better in my head."

"Most self-delusion does," Wolf quipped, and before Mason could tell his former swim partner to go eat a big, steaming pile of unseasoned shit, Wolf added, " Look, man, you want Alex. You know it. I know it. Anyone with eyes in their head knows it."

So much for my whole stony-faced fighting-man persona, Mason thought crossly.

"So why don't you do us all a favor," Wolf went on, "and quit pretendin' otherwise?"

Why indeed? Mason could think of at least a dozen

reasons. But he pretended the question was rhetorical and, instead of answering, let his gaze roam around the room.

Like most establishments on this island at the end of the Florida Keys, the bar—with its kitschy ship's wheel and cheap, strong drinks—was filled with two kinds of people. Those nursing a hangover from the night before. And those who were bright-eyed and bushy-tailed, eagerly discussing their plans for the day while partaking of the hotel's complimentary breakfast buffet.

Key West was unique in that it attracted, in equal measure, fun-seeking tourists and those looking to fall off the map at the end of the road. It wasn't at all odd to see a cheery-cheeked suburban-mom-on-vacation sitting next to a grizzled old barefoot sea dog.

Just one of the things Mason liked about it. Reminded him of his hometown. In the Hub of the Universe, the Ivy Leaguers could often be found rubbing elbows with the tough crowd from the Lower End, especially when they were all rooting for the Sox or the B's.

"That wasn't rhetorical," Wolf said, and Mason imagined how gratifying it would feel to plant a fist in his friend's mouth.

But the better angels of his nature won out, and instead of inflicting bodily harm, he said, "You know after what happened with Sarah, I've sworn off the fairer sex."

"Please." Wolf snorted. "You may have the others fooled into thinkin' you're runnin' some sort of one-man masturbation marathon, but I know you get your wick dipped every time we come to town. You're just secretive about it. Why is that?" Wolf leaned back to study him.

"Worried we'll scare off your potential bed partners by tellin' them about your itty-bitty baby penis?"

Something to understand about Navy SEALs—or *retired* Navy SEALs as was their case—was that their job forced them to make really big, really *adult* decisions on a daily basis. When it came to their humor, as an escape from all those really big, really adult decisions, they tended to harken back to their middle school years. The size of another man's dick being a favorite butt of their jokes.

"See," Mason said with a laconic shrug, happy to be off the topic of Alex, "I might be offended, but *I* know that *you* know that's just not true. You've seen it."

Wolf faked a shudder. "Don't remind me. Ugliest damn thing ever housed behind a zipper."

Mason smirked. "Like most things, they're cute when they're small. But when they're big? I mean *really* big?"

Wolf laughed and clapped him on the back.

After a while, Mason added, "And it's not *every* time we come to Key West. Besides, what I have with Donna is different from what Alex is proposing I have with her."

Alex...

Damn. And just like that, they were back on his least favorite subject.

"Donna, huh? That's her name?" Wolf chewed thoughtfully on his cocktail straw. "Okie dokie, so I'll bite. Why is what you have with the mysterious Donna different from what you could have with Alex?"

"'Cause Donna's fine with what I'm offering—a mutual scratching of itches when I'm here, and radio silence when I'm not. She's not after anything permanent."

A line appeared between Wolf's eyebrows. "What makes you think Alex is?"

The look Mason sent Wolf broadcast just how silly he thought the question was. "She's twenty-seven years old and still a virgin."

Virgin... Saying the word aloud made it resonate within his skull like the *booms* heard around Boston Common when the Ancient and Honorable Artillery Company of Massachusetts held their annual change of command ceremony and set off simulated cannon shots. He found himself shaking his head for the hundredth time because... *How the fuck is it possible to be a twenty-seven-year-old virgin in today's day and age?*

The bartender set a sweating glass of vodka and Bloody Mary mix in front of Wolf. The cocktail perfumed the air with the scent of hot sauce and celery salt. And it came with so many garnishes, Mason decided Wolf could skip the breakfast buffet.

"Alex isn't still a virgin by choice," Wolf said easily, as if they were talking about the woman's penchant for smearing her cute-as-a-button nose with zinc oxide instead of the intact state of her hymen. "She was a late bloomer. Then she was nose-deep in her studies in college and not payin' the datin' scene much mind. By the time she looked up from postgraduate school, she was closin' in on the end of her third decade and no man wanted to take her on because, like you, they all thought a twenty-seven-year-old virgin was on the hunt for a white dress and a big, sparkly diamond."

It took every ounce of self-control Mason possessed

to keep his jaw from unhinging. "How the fuck you know all that?"

"She told me." Wolf pulled a strip of bacon from his drink. That was all it took to awaken Meat from his dead sleep. With a grunt, the house walrus jumped into a seated position, deep-brown eyes laser-focused on the salted pork.

"Why'd she go and do that?" Mason managed to grit from between his teeth. His jaw had no chance of unhinging now. The muscles had locked down tight. In fact, everything inside him had locked down. Well, except for his blood pressure. That had skyrocketed. "She proposition you too?"

He shouldn't care if Alex offered up her virginity to Wolf. After all, Wolf was a good man. The best. The kind that would be gentle and tender and considerate.

And yet...Mason did care.

He cared very much.

"So what if she did?" Wolf eyed him closely.

Mason couldn't answer. He couldn't blink. As the moment dragged on, he began to wonder if he could breathe. A weird *buzz* sounded in his ears, and his vision went white-hot and crackled around the edges.

Eventually Wolf laughed and shook his head. "Relax, asshole. She didn't proposition me. The woman just isn't one to keep what's in her head from spillin' out of her mouth."

That was true. Mason had never met someone who could prattle on the way Alex could. When her nose wasn't buried in a book, she was talking. And given his love for peace and quiet, he found it fascinating that he never tired of listening to her.

Or maybe he just found *her* fascinating.

Ya-huh, that was probably it.

Okay, that was *definitely* it.

Deciding there was no time like the present to change the subject once and for all, he seized on the Bloody Mary lifted to Wolf's lips. "It's not even oh-seven-thirty. Kinda early to start drinking."

Wolf popped an olive into his mouth and grinned around it. "Start? What makes you think I ever stopped? That was some party last night. LT and Olivia sure know how to celebrate."

Mason thought back on the ripper from the night before when their former commanding officer, Leo "The Lion" Anderson, otherwise known as LT, had leg-shackled himself to an ex-CIA officer. Actually, LT and Olivia had gone to a justice of the peace weeks before to do the deed, but last night they'd finally bowed to pressure and had a reception.

"You thought about how with Olivia and LT off to Greece, and with Bran in Houston, there'll be no one around to do the cookin'?" Wolf gave him the once-over.

After leaving the CIA, Olivia Mortier had found a new passion in baking. She'd traded dropping bombs for whipping up brownies—much to Mason's delight because, number one, he had himself a pretty large sweet tooth, and number two, he also suffered from hollow-leg syndrome. Then there was Brando "Bran" Pallidino. Bran was the only one of their former SEAL team members/current

partners in Deep Six Salvage who could navigate his way
around a stove. And since plans to continue the search
for the *Santa Cristina* had been put on hold while LT and
Olivia celebrated their honeymoon, Bran had decided
to bite the bullet and use the downtime to finally go face
the music—"the music" being an introduction to his girl-
friend's four older brothers and oil tycoon of a father.

Mason did *not* envy poor Bran the experience. But
more than that, he didn't envy the piss-poor state of his
stomach in the coming week.

"Been trying my best *not* to think about it," he admitted testily.

"Guess it'll be PB and J's and strawberry Pop-Tarts for
us all." Wolf shrugged.

Pop-Tarts... Mason gritted his jaw. The sugary breakfast treats were Alex's standard go-to.

He glanced over his shoulder at her. But his view was
blocked by the wide chest of Spiro "Romeo" Delgado.

"G'morning, assholes!" Romeo boomed their standard a.m. greeting before snagging a stool on the other
side of Wolf and quickly ordering a coffee from the bartender. "Make it so strong it walks into the cup on its
own, eh?"

Like so many from East LA, Romeo retained a trace
of his homeboy accent. And when he got worked up?
There was more than just a trace.

Wolf took one look at Romeo's face and whistled.
"Man, you look like warmed-over cow pies."

Romeo's grin was downright devilish. "Didn't get
much sleep last night."

Wolf nodded in understanding. "Did she do all the things you wanted?"

"And came up with a few others I didn't even know I liked." Romeo waggled his eyebrows. Then he pretended to pout. "Alas, she left me early this morning to catch a flight to Miami. No note. No number. Just a love bite above my left nipple to remember her by."

Wolf winked. "What happens in Key West stays in Key West, am I right?"

Romeo's coffee arrived, and he lifted his steaming mug in salute before returning Wolf's wink. "Carpe diem, my friends."

Wolf laughed and clinked his Bloody Mary against Romeo's mug.

"What are we lifting a glass to?" Alex asked, having walked up behind them.

Mason instantly lost the ability to breathe.

It happened when she got within three feet. Up close, he could count the freckles across the bridge of her nose. He could smell her clean, no-nonsense soap-and-deodorant scent. And for some inexplicable reason, both things paralyzed his lungs.

He took a swift sip of his own coffee to disguise his discomfort.

"Celebratin' life and seizin' the day and all that jazz," Wolf told her.

"Ah." Alex nodded in understanding. "So just a regular day in Key West."

A small smile played on her face. The woman had one of those damn Kewpie doll mouths, where her top lip formed a near-perfect heart shape. Mason had to look away or risk doing something stupendously dumb. You know, like rubbing his thumb over that lip to see if it was as smooth and cushiony as it looked.

As soon as he turned back to face the liquor bottles lined up behind the bar, however, the short hairs on the back of his neck stood on end. He knew the feeling all too well, because all too often he'd found himself in the middle of some asshole's crosshairs.

Forgetting Alex and her proximity to him…

Okay, so not *forgetting*. There was no way to forget when every cell in his body strained toward her like she was a magnet and he was metal. But now he had something to focus on besides repeating the *Don't get a boner* mantra that was on a loop inside his head anytime she got near.

Letting his gaze take a casual journey around the room, he stopped on a man with a black stare who quickly looked away when their eyes met.

For a few seconds, Mason made no bones about glaring at the guy, his SEAL brain cataloging the man's age—*twenty-one, maybe twenty-two*. His bone structure—*angular and pronounced*. The clothes he wore—*nice without being ostentatious*. And his body language…

Jittery. Like a kid caught with his hand in the candy jar.

Mason cocked his head, wondering, waiting, watching to see what his observer would do next. But as time ticked by, he convinced himself the man probably hadn't been watching *him* at all. Had likely been watching *Alex* because, despite her baggy shorts and T-shirt that read

Well-behaved women don't make history, she was unmistakably pretty. Like a fairy princess had popped out from under a toadstool and flittered into their world.

Maybe I should get my head examined. I'm seeing threats where none exist.

Not normal… His ex-wife's voice seemed to drift on the wind, and his heart clenched into a hard fist.

Chapter 2

ALEXANDRA MERRIWEATHER HAD JUST HAD AN epiphany.

She loved it when that happened.

But before she told the guys about it, first she glanced back and forth between Mason and Wolf. "What were you two talking about earlier?" She was fairly certain she'd caught them glancing her way.

"If it's about my offer to let Mason smash my front door in," she continued, "forget it. Changed my mind. Not wasting my good boob-and-butt years waiting for some guy"—she hooked a thumb toward Mason who was choking on his coffee—"to pull the stick out of his ass and realize he's making a mountain out of a molehill."

"Smash your front door in?" Wolf's dark eyes sparkled with humor.

"You know what I mean."

"Yes," he nodded, biting the inside of his cheek. "Just never heard it referred to quite so…uh…eloquently."

Mason wheezed and blinked at her with tears in his eyes, so she added for his benefit, "Packed up any non-platonic thoughts I had about you into a box I labeled *Do Not Open*. Covered that sucker in crime-scene tape. Then I chucked it into the farthest reaches of my mind." She stuffed her current read—a fairly dry account of modern marine-salvage practices—under her arm so she could dust off her hands. "So there."

"I–I don't—" Mason managed, still choking.

She considered letting him drown in his coffee. But her softer sensibilities won out. She whacked him on the back with perhaps a *bit* more force than was necessary.

After a couple of good hits, he caught her wrist. The look on his face said *You looking to punch a hole through my back or what?*

She refrained from telling him *It'd serve you right, you big butthead.* But just barely.

Truth was, she was embarrassed the men of Deep Six Salvage—the group who'd hired her for her expertise at reading old Spanish scripts and then let her stay on because she was using the hunt for the *Santa Cristina* as the subject of her doctoral dissertation—knew of her humiliation.

Never mind that they knew because she'd told them.

Why'd I do that again? She snapped imaginary fingers. *Oh yeah. Because I thought maybe they'd talk some sense into Mason.*

Mason… Yes, this was all his fault.

A pox on his penis, she thought uncharitably. *May he grow boils, sprout hair from his ears, and get fat and flabby.*

As soon as she finished the curse, she immediately took it back. It would be a crime to wish ill on someone as good-looking at Mason.

Not good-looking in the tall, low body fat, super-model sense. But good-looking in the big, burly, looks-like-he-could-chop-down-a-redwood-with-a-hatchet sense. Good-looking in the black-haired, blue-eyed, chip-off-the-old-Roman-god sense.

You know, if you went for that sort of thing.

Which apparently she did.

From the first moment she saw him, she'd wanted to lock him in a room for a week, during which time she imagined she'd spend the majority of the hours on her back. Or on her side. Or on her front. And maybe up against a wall.

But it was not to be. He had soundly rejected the offer of her virginity. *Harrumph!*

"So?" She turned to Wolf expectantly, dragging her wrist from Mason's grasp, because *wowza!* The touch of his callused fingers made every single cell in her body focus with a capital F. "What were you two whispering about?"

"Guy stuff," Wolf said succinctly.

She cocked her head. "*Sports Illustrated Swimsuit Issue*, beer, and testicles?"

Wolf's grin grew until it split his handsome face. "Pretty much."

"I do love the smell of testosterone in the morning." To prove her point, she breathed deeply and then immediately wished she hadn't because…there it was.

Underneath the scent of sea and suntan lotion was that delicious aroma that was all Mason. It was warm and woodsy. Something she immediately recognized anytime he was near, and then couldn't quite conjure up in her imagination when he wasn't.

Lust unfolded in her belly like the pages of an old history book. It filled her up, from the roots of her hair to the tips of her toes.

Thankfully, she was distracted by Romeo calling out, "Morning, Chrissy! Didn't think it was possible you could look hotter than in a skintight wet suit, but I was wrong. Those shorts, eh?" Romeo made a face and bit his bottom lip. "Damn, woman."

"Save your perfect smile for the tourists." Chrissy motioned with her chin toward two bikinied ladies near the end of the bar who were batting their eyes in Romeo's direction. "It doesn't work on me."

"You sure about that?" Romeo ran a seductive finger down Chrissy's bare bicep when she stopped next to him.

Chrissy rolled her eyes, but there was no heat in her voice when she grumbled, "You've got some balls on you."

Everyone knew Romeo flirted with anything that walked and sported double-X chromosomes. But while other guys might come off as smarmy and gross, Romeo managed to remain charming.

Alex supposed it was because he genuinely *enjoyed* women. All shapes and colors and sizes. When it came to flirting and seduction, he believed in equal opportunities for everyone, and never told any lies to get a woman into bed. He was the epitome of sex positivity, and it attracted the ladies like an argument about the rate of economic growth during the Industrial Revolution would attract a gaggle of historians.

Plus, it helps that he looks like Mario Lopez and Jay Hernandez got together and made a baby.

"Just two balls at last count." His teeth flashed white against his black goatee when he grinned at Chrissy. "But I'd be happy to get your second opinion."

That got a laugh from Chrissy before she hopped onto the barstool beside him. "From what I've seen, you get more beaver than a mountain stream." Unlike Alex, who tended to have a staccato-quick rhythm to her speech—due in no small part to her need to convey information as quickly as humanly possible—Chrissy talked like an islander. Slowly. Softly. Taking the Key West vibe, that whole *We do less by Friday than most people do by 6:00 p.m.* thing to heart. "Which means you don't need to go hunting mine," Chrissy finished.

Alex chuckled. She liked Christina Szareck. The woman was tough and tenacious, not to mention blond and long-legged enough to prove her Polish surname wasn't for show.

And, yeah, okay. So maybe that makes me a little envious.

As a runt of a redhead, Alex had always dreamed of being tall and tanned. To have men turn and stare when she walked into a room. To go through life without being slathered in copious amounts of sunscreen and hair conditioner.

Of course, it helped the envy that Chrissy didn't seem to know or care how pretty she was. Chrissy's hair was always in a ponytail, and she seemed to sport a perpetual pair of flip-flops when she wasn't wearing swim fins. In fact, the first time Alex could remember seeing Chrissy wear makeup was at last night's reception.

Chrissy owned a dive shop on Key West and made her living taking tourists out to the reefs. Although recently she'd teamed up with Seaplane Charters and Deep Six Salvage to bring groups of day-trippers out to Wayfarer Island—the small speck of sand Alex and all the rest of the guys lived on, thanks to a land-lease deal one of LT's ancestors had made with the U.S. government.

Chrissy got to charge more for the excursions because people could scuba dive on any reef anywhere. But treasure hunt for the world's most famous ghost galleon? That was a unique experience. The guys who ran Seaplane Charters got some guaranteed butts in the seats for their flights. And Deep Six Salvage got a whole lot of free eyes looking for their prize.

It was a win-win-win for all those involved.

Unfortunately, except for a few trinkets and some old iron ship's fastenings—none of which had been conclusively tied to the *Santa Cristina*—they'd yet to find the grand old ship. There was an expression treasure hunters liked to use. *You miss by an inch, you miss by a mile.* Meaning, it could be right under your nose, but if you don't land on top of it, you might never find it.

Alex had been mulling over this depressing thought when she'd had her epiphany.

"Spit it out," Wolf said now, eyeing her curiously.

"Hmm?" She blinked at him, bending to scratch behind Meat's floppy ears when he *woofed* at her.

She liked to think the bulldog loved her because she was such a super-duper, top-notch human being. But she feared the truth of the matter was that she was usually eating something and she wasn't averse to sharing. The way to Meat's heart was definitely through his stomach.

"The thing spinnin' around in that pretty head of yours." Wolf tapped a finger against her temple.

It was hard not to preen under the compliment. Wolf was a gorgeous man, after all. But unlike Mason, his male appeal tended toward the beautiful. Like, if he ever decided treasure hunting wasn't for him, he could easily land a job modeling expensive cologne—à la David Gandy.

It was *also* hard not to turn to Mason and stick out her tongue. *Nanner, nanner! See? He thinks I'm pretty. Maybe I should have propositioned* him*!*

Instead of doing either of those things, however, she told Wolf, "It's spooky when you do that."

"Do what?" He quirked a jet-black eyebrow.

"Read people's minds."

That elicited a snort and a head shake. "No mind reading needed. Your body language is screamin.'"

"Yeah," Chrissy piped up. "I can vouch that Wolf has zero ability to read minds."

Wolf glared at the blond bombshell. "Damn it, woman! How many times I got to apologize for that? It was an honest mistake."

"Honest?" Chrissy's voice lifted an octave. "You thinking dragging a woman into—"

"It was *dark*," Wolf interrupted, a muscle going crazy on the side of his square jaw. "I couldn't see. I was goin' on feel. And besides, I didn't hear you complainin'!"

"Ooh-ooh!" Chrissy sputtered. If the look on her face was anything to go by, she was two seconds away from tearing into the soft bits between Wolf's legs.

"Children, children." Romeo patted the air. "Either come clean with what happened, or let it go. Because I'm tired of trying to put the pieces together, eh? And if I wanted to break up fights between five-year-olds, I'd become a kindergarten teacher." He glanced back and forth between them. "So which is it going to be?"

Alex leaned forward, hoping they would finally reveal what had happened to make them go from kind of, maybe, sort of flirting with each other a couple of months ago to taking every opportunity they could find to rip strips out of each other's hides.

Unfortunately, if their thinned lips and locked jaws were anything to go by, neither of them was going to be confessing anytime soon.

With a dramatic sigh, she turned to Romeo. "Guess it'll remain one of those impenetrable mysteries."

Deep dimples appeared in Romeo's cheeks. "In my experience, *nothing* is impenetrable."

"Ew!" Chrissy punched Romeo's shoulder at the same time Alex made gagging noises.

"So?" Wolf prompted Alex. "What's got you so fidgety?"

"That second helping of biscuits and gravy is partly to blame," she admitted dolefully, pressing a hand to her chest where the first warning signs of heartburn were threatening.

Or maybe that's just my body's reaction to being this close to Mason.

Wolf shook his head. "Between you and Mason, I swear."

That had her chin jerking back. She glanced at Mason, but his face revealed about as much as a blank page. His no-talking game was on point. But it was nothing compared to his no-expression game. Which was singularly annoying since most times she'd give her left boob to know what he was thinking.

"Between me and Mason what?" she asked Wolf.

"Y'all are the only two people I know who ask what's for lunch when you're still eatin' breakfast. Peas in a pod and—"

"Keeping you people on topic is like herding cats," Mason quickly cut in, his thick Boston accent apparent in every syllable.

What *wasn't* apparent was his frown. It was tiny. Fractional even. But Alex saw it and knew its source. It was that whole *peas in a pod* thing.

Since she'd offered him her V-card, he'd been touchy about any and all conversations involving the two of them.

"Monsieur Monosyllable speaks!" She threw her hands in the air. "Hallelujah!"

Glaring at her—and really, the man could glare with the best of them—he ground from between clenched teeth, "Only when I got something important to say."

She didn't have to feign affront. Her affront was Grade A prime. "And what's *that* supposed to mean? That I go around spewing verbal diarrhea? I'll have you know a study showed that a person speaks about 16,000 words a day on average. So *I'm* not the weird one. *You* are."

"Children, children!" Romeo patted the air again,

looking exasperated. "What did I just say about breaking up fights between five-year-olds?"

Mason continued to stare at Alex. She tried to hold his gaze, but it made all her girl parts giggle. So she did the mature thing and stuck her tongue out at him.

He looked so startled, she had to laugh. That just made him glower all the harder.

"Oh-ho!" She pointed at his face. "Look how grumpy you are. Do you need me to get you a lollipop?"

"Does your level of joy go up in direct proportion to my blood pressure?" he growled at her, his accent making the end of the sentence sound more like *prahpawtion to my blood preshah*.

"No." She didn't know what possessed her, but she threw an arm around his massive shoulders and gave them a squeeze. "It's just that being a smart-ass is how I hug."

When she pulled back, she expected to see a *you annoy me* expression wallpapered over his face. So she was shocked to see something darkly hungry instead.

Was Kate Upton standing behind her?

She glanced over her shoulder. Nope. No Kate. *Huh.* But when she turned back, she found his hungry look gone and was left wondering if it'd ever been there at all. A second later, she decided that even if it *had* been there, she'd probably been mistaken about what it meant.

Maybe he *was* hungry. Or gassy. Or simply bored. Maybe he had a headache. A backache. Or was day-dreaming about piles of BLT sandwiches.

It was just a look, she convinced herself. *I'm not going*

to be the girl who reads a million and one emotions and moti-
vations into a look.

And…okay…truth time. She'd lied when she told him she'd packed away all her nonplatonic feelings. In fact, right at the moment, she could easily envision him wearing nothing but a sheen of sweat, a smile, and—

"Alex?" When Wolf snapped his fingers in front of her eyes, she realized she'd momentarily forgotten where she was.

"Right." She had to clear her throat. "As I was having that second helping of biscuits and gravy, it occurred to me we might be thinking about Captain Vargas and the *Santa Cristina* all wrong."

Romeo's brow wrinkled. "What do you mean?"

"According to the evidence we copied from the archives in Seville, Captain Vargas's plan was to sail back to Havana. Barring that, he was supposed to take shelter behind Wayfarer Island."

"Right." Wolf nodded. "Which is where LT and Olivia found the hilt of Vargas's cutlass."

"The hilt that gave me a total history-nerd boner," Alex agreed. "Which is why we've been killing ourselves mapping and excavating the area. All to no avail. So what if that cutlass ended up stuck back there on that little reef because of currents or wave action? What if the captain even threw it back there?"

"Why would he do a thing like that?" Romeo asked.

She rolled her eyes. "How would I know? I've given up trying to figure out why you men do anything. But stick with me here. All this time, we've been assuming

Vargas did what he said he was going to do. What if he didn't?" She looked around at the faces staring back at her. "Or what if he couldn't?"

The more she laid out the argument, the more she knew she was on to something. There was a feeling in her bones. The same feeling she'd had when she realized the "ringed island" mentioned in the old texts was, in fact, Wayfarer Island and not the Marquesas.

"Imagine you're Captain Bartolome Vargas," she continued. "You've been tasked by your king, your holy monarch, a man you revere only slightly less than God, to bring back a ship full of riches unlike anything the Old World has seen."

In her mind an image of the ghost galleon bloomed, and her heart rate kicked up. Of course, with Mason so close, she couldn't be sure if her excitement was due to the wreck and the mystery of the *Santa Cristina* or to him.

"Riches that would pay for your country's military might and continued expansion into the New World. And now imagine you're caught in a terrible hurricane. You can't make it back to home port. And for whatever reason, you don't think you have time to sail around to the leeward side of the island. What do you do?"

The three men exchanged a knowing look. But it was Romeo who said, "Scuttle her. Somewhere shallow enough to make salvage possible."

"Bingo." Alex's nod was quick as she pointed a finger at Romeo's nose. "And where on Wayfarer Island would that be?"

For a couple of seconds, no one said a word, and the

air inside the room grew heavy with expectation. Alex could see the answer slowly dawning in their eyes.

"The reef beyond the lagoon." Mason's deep voice made the fine hairs on her arms stand up. Anytime he opened his mouth, she imagined him dressed in muck boots and hauling lobster pots from the sea.

"Got it in one." She winked at him.

"Cut that out," he grumbled irritably.

"What?" She cocked her head.

"The tongue. The hugs. The winking. Don't waste your flirting on me."

"Ugh." She rolled her eyes. "If your ego gets any bigger, you might need to have it surgically removed."

For one long moment, they glared at each other. Then, a corner of his lips twitched and he gifted her with a little chuckle.

Just that easily, her rancor leached out of her.

Why did he have to have such a wonderful laugh? All deep and seductive and so rare that when she managed to pull even the tiniest chortle from him, she felt like she'd won the lottery?

Now her girl parts weren't just giggling; they were howling and singing "Let's Get It On" at the tops of their lungs.

Chapter 3

"DID YOU GET A LOOK AT HIM?" IZAD ASKED, AND then watched the face of his youngest son, his only *living* son, contort around an expression of disgust.

"Yes," Kazem spat out. "He is overgrown, smug, and entitled. Like all of them."

"English, please," the American said in that long, lazy drawl that reminded Izad of America's forty-third president. Good old George W. Bush. The cowboy who ran into Iraq, guns blazing, looking for WMDs that were never there when his true enemy, al-Qaeda, was being funded by a country he considered his ally.

Izad could have told George the Saudis were not to be trusted. That they would stab a man in his back as easily as they would shake his hand.

That one rash decision George made had led to incalculable pain and death in the Middle East. It had brought about the rise of ISIS. Which had created the conflict in Syria. Which had morphed into the terrible and bloody proxy war between Izad's homeland and Saudi Arabia, both nations vying to be the ultimate power in the region.

But Izad cared little for the machinations of nations now. Following the senseless deaths of his older sons, he had resigned his post as commodore in the Islamic

Republic of Iran Navy and focused on one thing and one thing only.

Revenge.

There had been many years of dead ends and wrong turns, but it looked as if he might *finally* get what he was after.

Anticipation fizzed in his stomach, giving him a giddy feeling he hadn't experienced since his boys had been blown into pieces so tiny there was nothing left for him to bury in accordance with his beliefs. Not since he had lost his beloved wife, Hettie.

It was grief that had killed her. A heart so broken that barely three months after the fateful day they lost their boys, she'd followed them into the afterlife.

"I said he looks like a corn-fed sack of shit just like the rest of you," Kazem snarled in English for the American's benefit. "That is the phrase you like to use, yes?"

"Which one?" The American remained impassive in the face of Kazem's animosity. "'Sack of shit' or 'corn-fed'?"

Kazem didn't answer. Instead, he looked to Izad. "I overhead them say they are leaving soon, Father. McCarthy will sail the catamaran back to the island with two women and the one they call Wolf. It is better than we could have hoped for."

When Izad hesitated, Kazem marched over to where he leaned against the edge of the hotel suite's desk. Kazem's eyes sparked with bloodlust as he placed his hands on Izad's shoulders. "In the name of my brothers, I *will* rain vengeance on the head of Mason McCarthy. He will die at sea as they did, nothing but the fishes to comfort his remains."

So eager, thought Izad. *But that is my own fault.* All his talk of how brave Kazem's brothers had been made Kazem feel the need to prove himself their equals.

Kazem had been a late-in-life blessing for Izad and Hettie. They had considered themselves lucky to have two sons, never imagining a third would come years later. A *change-of-life baby* Hettie had called Kazem, who had been six days past his tenth birthday when his older brothers were killed.

No. Not killed. *Murdered.*

"Are you certain you do not want me to come with you?" Izad grasped Kazem's forearm, feeling his boy's youthful muscles bunch beneath his touch. He was old and feeble where Kazem was tall and strong. But he was long schooled in the ways of war. Kazem was not.

Kazem shook his head. "This journey has been long and difficult." Izad knew his son spoke as much about the journey to find the man responsible for his brothers' deaths as he did the weeks it had taken their group to make their way to America through multiple Caribbean ports, using false identities and forged papers. "You stay here. Rest. I will see it finished."

Izad glanced at the sliding glass doors leading to the balcony. Outside, two of his most trusted men smoked and leaned against the railing. Both were well seasoned. Izad comforted himself knowing that what Kazem lacked in experience, those two made up for ten times over.

"Can I state for the record"—the American, sprawled so casually on the sofa, lifted a finger—"that I think it's a bad idea to send only three guys after them?"

"Why?" Kazem frowned. "The odds are in our favor. Three to two."

"Uh…" The America made a show of counting on his fingers. "By my count that's three to four."

Kazem snorted. "Surely you do not think the women factor into this?"

The American shrugged. "Maybe not. But I've had some experience with these guys. You might be better served to send in the entire kit and caboodle." He twirled a finger at the four men standing at attention at their various posts inside the room. Izad's personal security detail.

Kazem didn't bother to hide his annoyance. "Do not listen to him, Father. Like all Americans, he believes in overkill. Especially when the thing he values most, his paycheck, is on the line."

"You will be cautious?" Izad asked. "You will do as Turan and Mahmoud instruct?"

"I will not miss a word."

"Very well." Izad turned to the American. "Show them where you have stashed the weapons."

After a breathy exhale, the American stood from the sofa. "Fine. But don't say I didn't warn you."

The worm of unease Izad had suffered all morning grew into a writhing serpent. But he told himself Kazem was right. The American was…well…an American. If a firecracker would do the job, he would still choose to use an H-bomb.

Besides, Kazem needed this. It was the only way he would ever truly consider himself worthy of his family name.

As if to prove Izad's point, Kazem squeezed Izad's shoulders and kissed Izad's cheeks. "I will make you proud, Father," he whispered.

"Oh, my son." Izad embraced his boy, hugging him against his heart. "I am already proud."

Then he watched as his youngest set off after the American, chin high, shoulders back, impatient to end the man who had done so much unspeakable damage to their family.

———

10:41 a.m.

"You watching him that way is giving him a face like a smacked ass."

Alex came out of her daydream to find Chrissy standing above her. Lifting a hand against the glare of the morning sun, she squinted up at the woman. "A what?"

"Here." Chrissy took off her Clubmaster-style sunglasses and handed them over. "They're polarized. Put them on and take a look."

Frowning, Alex slipped the shades over her glasses and looked toward the pilothouse where Mason was doing a bang-up job of captaining the catamaran against the wind and currents. Also doing a bang-up job of conjuring a million-and-one fantasies of her joining him there and slowly pulling off his swim trunks so she could do the things to his boy parts that she'd studied up on while staying at the hotel the last two nights.

Since there was no cellular service on Wayfarer Island, and since they tried to limit their internet activity to save the generator juice for powering the refrigerator and the few lights in the beach house, Alex had taken advantage of her time on Key West to fire up her iPad, go online, and watch some videos.

When and if a man ever got up the gumption to help her get rid of her virginity, she wanted to be sure he found the exercise worth it. And after spending one entire evening having fallen down the rabbit hole of strange fetishes—Diaper bondage? Pedal pumping? Extreme feeding? These were things? Who knew?—last night she'd settled on the basics. Hand jobs. Blow jobs. And something called *edging*.

After loading up the catamaran for the sail to Wayfarer Island, the memory of what she'd learned and the need to study Mason had been too much. It had been a deep, carnal pull from within. Or without. Or somewhere, and she'd decided—despite his remark about her needing to stop flirting with him—to give in to it.

Plus, she figured her observation of him would go unnoticed. After all, she'd been using her book as a prop, pretending to read the mind-numbingly dull prose of one J. J. Robertson, marine salvor extraordinaire. And with the tinted windows to the pilothouse closed, Mason had been nothing but a silhouette to her. So she figured she'd be nothing but a silhouette to him.

But with the polarized lenses, she could see straight to the captain's chair. And all those dirty thoughts that had been in her head must have been plastered over her face, because Mason's cheeks were tinged with every shade of red from the color wheel.

"Damn," she muttered, embarrassment making her own cheeks burn. She snapped the book closed and tossed it aside. "I thought I was being discreet."

That got a chuckle from Chrissy. "A little hard to be discreet when the view is that way." Chrissy pointed toward the front of the boat where the morning sun gleamed over the water, chasing the whitecaps and making them dance as they spread out over the cerulean surface.

"That's true," Alex allowed, handing the sunglasses back to Chrissy and turning so her feet pointed toward the sea instead of the pilothouse.

It had been decided that, contrary to the original plan of taking a break from the hunt for the *Santa Cristina* while LT and Olivia were on their honeymoon, the rest of the crew—excluding Bran and Maddy who had caught the first flight to Houston—would begin diving on the lagoon reef.

Alex could just imagine LT and Olivia's faces when they returned to Wayfarer Island in seven days to… *Surprise! We've found the mother lode!*

In fact, the idea of such an epic wedding present got everyone so excited that even Chrissy had agreed to join in the fun, leaving Winston, her business partner, to oversee the dive shop and the tourists for the next week. Romeo and Doc, the latter of whom was also a partner in Deep Six Salvage, had eschewed sailing back with them on the catamaran. Instead, they'd opted to stay one more night on Key West—likely because both of them had found a cute tourist to bounce around; *lucky tourists!*— and then fly to Wayfarer Island with John, LT's grizzled old uncle, first thing in the morning.

But after that? Let the games begin!

Alex's blood bubbled with anticipation. She was right about turning their attention to the reef surrounding the lagoon. She could *feel* it.

"Mind if I join you?" Chrissy waved to the knotted polyethylene netting strung up between the twin hulls of the catamaran.

"Be my guest." Alex laced her hands behind her head. The netting—affectionately called "the trampoline"—was her favorite spot. She loved to lie there and listen to the sound of the sea hissing against the sailboat and breathe in the smell of the water. Watch as the wind pushed against the carbon-fiber sails and taste the salt on the breeze.

She'd never considered herself much of an ocean or beach person before moving to Wayfarer Island. Blame it on her fair skin and a natural aversion to sand. *I mean, the stuff gets everywhere.* But in the last few months, she'd come to love the sea almost as much as she loved the dim quiet of a good library.

The open water's beauty, its vastness, how quickly it could go from calm to chaotic had cast a spell over her. She was enchanted by it.

And maybe that's what attracted her to Mason too. His natural dichotomy.

He was huge and powerful. Could break a person's neck in two with little more than a flick of his wrist. But he also had a bulldog he doted on. Like, *doted* on. So much so that the man should buy stock in baby wipes, because he went through a container a day cleaning Meat's copious wrinkles to ensure none of them chafed or developed yeast infections. And he painted. With watercolors. Sitting on a stool with a little easel and everything.

Just like the sea, he was a crazy mishmash of strong and gentle, calm yet capable of meting out great violence should the need arise.

She shuddered as she remembered that night on Garden Key when a group of armed men in the employ of a desperate oilman stormed the island, bent on kidnapping the teenage girls who were camping there and selling them to some lecherous desert sultan in exchange for fixed crude prices. Goose bumps broke out over Alex's arms when she thought back on how Mason and Bran had come to the rescue like the heroic mother-effin' Navy SEALs they were.

Knowing the men she worked for were retired spec-ops badasses was one thing. Seeing them *employing* their badassery had been something else altogether.

In fact, she hoped never to see them doing it again. Because talk about Scary. As. *Hell.*

She still had the occasional nightmare about Garden Key. Although, the times when the bad dreams came to torture her were growing fewer and farther between. Thanks to Doc.

Snatching the pack of strawberry Pop-Tarts she'd pilfered from the galley, she tore open the wrapper and slid one of the sweet-tasting pastries from within. She offered the remaining treat to Chrissy, who waved her away with a "No thanks" and then added, "How the heck do you stay so skinny, eating the way you do?"

"Hobbit blood," Alex declared around a mouthful of sugary goodness. "This here"—she waved the Pop-Tart in the air—"is what my people like to call elevenses."

Chrissy laughed and then laced her hands behind her head. For a while, she was quiet. Then she said, "I get it, you know."

"Get what?" Alex asked around another bite of Pop-Tart.

"Why you can't stop staring at Mason. He's one steely eyed man of the sea. Plus, he's got thighs like tree trunks and arms like Vin Diesel. I bet you could have sex with him without ever touching the ground."

Alex snorted. "I'd love to put your theory to the test. But in case it wasn't obvious, he wants nothing to do with me." And yet more than once she'd wondered if it might be possible to run through the house naked and— *whoopsie!*—fall on his penis.

Chrissy rolled onto her side and propped her head in her hand. "I find that hard to believe."

Alex frowned. "Why? You heard him back at the hotel bar, getting his panties in a twist when he thought I was flirting with him."

"You *were* flirting with him."

Busted. "Fat lot of good it does me," Alex grumbled.

"Oh, I'm not so sure about that. I've seen the way he looks at you."

Alex felt her brow beetle. "What do you mean?"

"It's the same way you look at him. Like you'd like to

cover each other in chocolate syrup and lick each other clean."

The imagery was enough to make Alex shiver despite the warm sea air that washed over her arms and teased the hem of her shorts. "How long has it been since you went to the eye doctor?" she asked skeptically.

Chrissy frowned. "Are you saying I'm blind?"

"That or seeing things that aren't there. But even if what you say is true, which it's *not*, it doesn't matter. Because despite how many times I've told Mason that all I want from him is a little of the old in-and-out, he doesn't believe me. He's convinced himself that what I'm truly after is a happily ever after. I think the distance between my lips and his ears is just too vast."

"And because he's convinced himself you're after a happily ever after, he's doing his level best to stay hell and gone from you," Chrissy surmised, rolling onto her back and stretching out her long, tan legs. "Can't say I'm surprised. Most of the men I've known are serial monogamists at best or commitment phobics at worst."

Alex nodded and found herself turning things over in her mind. Replaying every word she and Mason had ever spoken. Reliving every look. Every touch.

She couldn't help but wonder…

Is Mason using the whole virgin-on-the-prowl-for-a-husband as an excuse? Would he give me a different answer if I looked like Chrissy?

Glancing down at her pale arms, she admitted she had no hope of that. She didn't tan; she burned. And every time she burned, she developed a dozen new freckles.

Which reminded her...

It had been nearly two hours since they'd left the docks at Key West. And the instructions on her SPF said to reapply every ninety minutes.

Finishing the last of her Pop-Tart, she dusted off her hands and snagged the bottle of sunscreen lying next to her book. She was in the middle of slathering her arms when Chrissy asked, "But why?"

"Huh?" Alex scrunched up her nose. "Why what?"

"Why has Mason convinced himself you're after a veil and some vows if you've specifically told him you're *not*?"

"Oh." Alex took a deep breath. Unfortunately, it was long on discomfort and short on actual air. She admitted this next part with all the enthusiasm she'd give a mud pie. "Because I'm still a virgin."

"Wait. What?" Chrissy jolted upright. "How old are you?"

"Twenty-seven."

And there they are, Alex thought with a frown. *The bug eyes.*

"Did you grow up in Utah?" Chrissy asked carefully.

"I'm not Mormon," Alex grumbled, quickly explaining how it had come to pass that she was closing in on the end of her third decade and still in full possession of her, ahem, *flower*. She finished with "So it's not like I've been *saving* it. I got to third base with Tommy Wilson my senior year in high school. We made plans to go all the way, but then his dad got a job in Seattle. Before we could do the deed, he moved away. Then there was the night in undergrad when I swore off my studies and went to a frat party. One of the Lambda Chi Alphas took me up to his room. He managed to get on the condom, but then passed out before he could finish the job. So now my damned virginity is an albatross around my neck. I just want to *do it* already and be done with it."

"Hmm." Chrissy rubbed a finger over her lips in consideration. "And you didn't think to hit up Romeo first? Healthy, consensual sex between adults is his favorite pastime. He'd have happily had you on your back in ten seconds flat."

"Ew." Alex curled her lip. "He's like a brother to me. They *all* are."

"All except for Mason," Chrissy countered.

"Right." Alex's shoulders drooped dejectedly as she rubbed more sunscreen between her hands. "Except for Mason, because he's like…" Her voice trailed off. "I don't know. There's something about him. A steadiness. A… *calmness*. My entire life, my brain has buzzed nonstop. But when I'm near him, even when he's grumbling and growling at me, everything slows down. Maybe that's why I propositioned him. Because when he's near, I can focus on one thing, *the* thing, instead of the million other thoughts and ideas I'm usually dealing with." Chrissy was watching her closely, so she hurried to add, "Plus, you know, it helps that he's hubba-hubba *hot*."

"They're *all* hubba-hubba hot," Chrissy muttered. "It's like opening up a damned *GQ* magazine every time I come out to Wayfarer Island. If they don't manage to find the *Santa Cristina*, they can always join the exotic dancers of Chippendales."

"One problem with that." Alex lifted a finger. "Have you seen LT dance?"

Chrissy shuddered. "He looked like he'd broken his leg on the dance floor last night."

Alex marveled at how a man with so much natural athleticism and coordination couldn't seem to keep a beat. "But what he lacks in skill, he makes up for with enthusiasm."

"It's something that once seen can't be unseen," Chrissy agreed, and they broke into a fit of giggles.

Sobering, Alex returned to their previous topic. "You're right about Romeo, though. He would've been the smarter choice."

Chrissy lifted one shoulder. "Sometimes what our loins want makes no sense at all. That doesn't stop us from following their lead anyway. And Mason does have that whole tough, gruff, ultra-alpha thing going for him."

Alex sighed. "Which makes it doubly irritating that he refuses to believe me when I tell him all I'm after is a little theme-park-level fun in the sun. Or under the moon. Or, heck, I'd settle for out behind a dumpster at this point."

Chrissy laughed. "What about Tinder? You put up a profile, and I guarantee you'll be missing a maidenhead by midnight."

Alex's expression was one of disgust. "Come on! It's my first time. At the very least I'd like to know the guy's real name."

"There is that," Chrissy agreed.

Tired of being the subject at hand, Alex slid Chrissy a considering look. "Speaking of sex and alpha men, what's up between you and Wolf?"

Chrissy frowned. "Nice segue."

"It's proven that a person's ability to steer a conversation is directly proportional to their IQ."

"Or the fact that they're a Nosy Nancy."

"That too." Alex admitted freely. "But I mean, there for a while, I thought maybe you two might hook up and—"

"Yeah, me too." Chrissy cut her off. "I mean, how could I *not* have wanted that? The man is six-plus feet of steely muscles and smooth, dark skin. Not to mention his cheekbones. Have you seen them? They could cut glass. Then again, looks aren't everything. And besides, it's worked out. With all the new business I'm getting by teaming up with Deep Six, I don't have time for penis-sporting humans."

Alex snorted. "Yeah, but that won't stop the penis-sporting humans from making time for you. You're smart. You're funny. And you can rock a tank top."

She eyed Chrissy's cleavage with envy. What she wouldn't give to have C cups. But she was firmly and decidedly only a B. And without the help of a skilled plastic surgeon, she'd had to give up hoping for further growth.

"You're really not going to tell me what happened between you two, are you?" she asked after she finished coating her legs with SPF 50 and recapping the sunscreen.

"No way." Chrissy shook her head. "It's too embarrassing."

"Embarrassing?" Alex huffed. "I admitted that no one has ever punched a hole in my V-card! Nothing could be more—"

"Hold that thought." Chrissy pointed a finger over Alex's shoulder.

When Alex turned, she found Mason was no longer in the pilothouse. A quick glance assured her Wolf had taken over captaining duties. Now, Mason stood at the edge of the trampoline, looking all brown and brawny and…to steal a line from the Campbell's Soup commercials…*mmm-mmm good.*

He should never wear anything but swim trunks, she decided. All those gleaming muscles? All that delicious skin? All that crinkly, black man hair that bloomed across his pectoral muscles and arrowed down his corrugated belly to disappear beneath his waistband? It should be proudly displayed.

Always.

"Alex." Lordy, she loved the way he grumbled her name. "Can I get a word with ya?" His accent made it sound more like *Cannah getta word witya?*

She exchanged a glance with Chrissy and gave a nearly imperceptible shake of her head. She felt too vulnerable to be left alone with Mason. She might say or do something highly embarrassing. You know, like tackle him onto the netting and forcibly sit on his face.

Chrissy swallowed noisily before sputtering, "I have to…um…go vote." And then she jumped from the trampoline and disappeared inside the cabin so quickly Alex felt the breeze of her departure.

Here she'd thought their heart-to-heart had forged between them the strong bonds of sisterhood. Apparently not. Chrissy had cut and run right when Alex needed her most.

The traitor.

Chapter 4

"I'M CALLING A TRUCE."

Chrissy's sexy voice, speaking in that slow island-life way, slid inside Wolf's blood like brandy, delicious and smooth. Not that he was a big drinker, but a good brandy was his weakness.

Kind of like *she* was his weakness.

Glancing away from his study of the currents, he found her standing in the doorway to the pilothouse. Sunlight streamed in, creating a halo around her. But it was superfluous. Because Christina Szareck was a beacon all on her own. So bright he was surprised she didn't draw in flying insects after dark.

I was certainly drawn to her from the beginnin'. Too bad I had to go and screw it up.

An ache bloomed behind his breastbone. He rubbed at it. He coughed. But nothing seemed to make it go away. So he asked, "A truce? Which means you admit we're at war?"

She straightened from giving Meat a quick scratch behind the ears. The shameless mongrel had wiggled over to her the instant she appeared. Meat knew all it took to find himself on the receiving end of a treat or a good petting was one flash of his ridiculous underbite.

To have been born a bulldog, Wolf thought, remembering what it was like to have Chrissy's fingers on *him*.

The woman didn't have soft hands. Not by a long shot. They were strong and callused from hauling equipment and fixing scuba tanks. But her fingers were long and slim, so very feminine. And she knew just the right amount of pressure to—

"It's not a war," Chrissy countered. "It's a mutual dislike brought on because *one* of us, I'm not saying who"—she pointed directly at him—"was a complete and total dillhole."

"It was a damned misunderstandin', woman!" he insisted for the ten billionth time. "And for the record, you might dislike me, but I don't dislike you. Never have. Never will."

"Whatever." She waved a hand, unwilling to let the import of his last statement sink in. "The point is, we need to team up to get Alex and Mason together."

He grunted. "Good luck with that. Mason isn't only built like a boulder, he *is* one once his mind's made up. The man's immovable."

"Nothing's immovable. You just have to find the right leverage."

Wolf might agree with Chrissy that Alex Merriweather, with her sunny smile and eager mind, was exactly what Mason needed to pull him out of the funk he'd been in since his divorce. But Wolf wasn't one to go sticking his nose into other people's affairs.

Okay. That wasn't *exactly* true. He had a huge passel of relatives back in Oklahoma, and everyone knew everything about everyone else. But that was different. That was family. When it came to his friends, his teammates, his business partners? He'd learned to keep his opinions to himself.

Or else couch them in someone else's words of wisdom.

"Ever heard it said that minding your own business will take you far in life?" he asked.

She pursed her lips—those wonderful lips he knew could be soft and warm, so giving and greedy—and declared with a finger in the air, "I'm imposing a ban here and now. No more sounding like a fortune cookie when I'm around."

"Fine." He shifted slightly in the captain's chair because thoughts of her mouth made him hard. "Put simply, you go muckin' around in their love lives, you're lookin' for trouble."

"I don't want to muck. I just want to afford them as many opportunities as possible to be alone." She pointed out the window to where Mason and Alex sat side by side on the trampoline. "Mother Nature will take care of the rest."

Unconvinced but willing to play along, he said, "Just to be clear, you're suggestin' we team up in helpin' Mason and Alex take a trip to Boner City?"

"Please." She rolled her eyes. "Let's remain adults about this. It's Pound Town."

Despite the tension vibrating in the air like a downed power line, he couldn't stop the laugh that burst from him. And yet his humor was short-lived. "I might agree with your plan in theory, but I wouldn't get my hopes up if I were you. Like I said, Mason is one tough nut to crack."

"Since we've already established that when it comes to burgeoning romance you have the emotional IQ of a dumbass ant, how about you worry about your own hopes and leave mine well enough alone?" She smiled cattily, then quickly spun on her heel.

Before she could reach the door, however, he stopped her. "How many times I got to apologize before you forgive me?"

Turning, she offered him a one-shouldered shrug. "Who knows? I'll tell you once you get there."

Then she was gone, and all the air that had been sucked out of the room to make space for her presence rushed back in, making him light-headed.

10:53 a.m.

Mason sat a foot away from the only person on the planet he thought about day and night, and it was a lesson in torture.

And the silence is deafening, he thought uneasily.

But it wasn't an empty silence. It was filled with all the words he needed to say but couldn't. It was a charged silence that skimmed over his skin like electric fingers. It was a heavy silence that pushed down on his shoulders until they ached.

It was a silence that Alex had apparently had enough of, because she looked over at him and blurted out, "For your information, when you tell someone you need to talk to them, that usually requires you to open your mouth and form actual words. I know that's sort of akin to getting blood from a stone with you, but still…spit it out. The longer we sit here, the twitchier I feel. And it's been proven that stress hormones can cause all sorts of adverse effects on the body."

"I…" He tried, but his throat was as tight as the crowds around Fenway Park on game day. Her words back in the hotel had been bold and full of bravado, but he'd heard the underlying pain in her voice. His rejection hurt her. He had to make that right. "I owe you an apology, Alex," he finally managed.

Surprise flashed in her eyes. But she recovered quickly and made a rolling motion with her hand. "Proceed."

Despite his discomfort, he felt one corner of his mouth twitch.

She was funny. And smart. And wickedly sexy.

Although she seemed completely oblivious to that last thing.

He supposed her obliviousness was a big part of the allure for him. It would've been easy to reject her had she been all vampy and vixeny. But her earnestness, her sincerity called to the part of him that wanted to trust in someone again, that wanted to *believe* in someone again.

And yet… *You're not normal.* There was that voice. That *truth.* And he had to spare Alex. For her own sake.

"When you…uh…" He pushed an agitated hand

through his hair. He wasn't good with words. Not like her. And he wanted to make sure he did this right. *Said* this right. "When you made me that…uh…*offer*…"

"You mean the offer of my virginity?" She made a face. "Come on. Let's not dance around the thing. We're both adults."

He dipped his chin in agreement. They *were* both adults. He was *way* adult at the ripe old age of thirty-five. But talking about a woman's virginal state made him feel all of thirteen again. "When you offered to let me take your virginity, I—"

"And that's another thing," she interrupted. "I don't like that phrasing. You wouldn't be *taking* anything. I'd be *giving* it to you. With full agency and consent."

He gave her a stern look, telling her without words to keep her mouth shut.

She pantomimed zipping her lips, locking them shut, and tossing the key over her shoulder.

"When you offered to give me your virginity," he said and she smiled, satisfied with his choice of words, "I was a total tool and didn't respond like I shoulda."

Apparently her zipped lips were for show, because she chimed in with "If memory serves, you told me I was clearly looking for something more than you were willing to give. That you'd been there. Done that. And burned the T-shirt."

"Right." He shifted uncomfortably against the netting. "What I *shoulda* said was 'thank you.'"

Her eyebrows tried to disappear into her hairline.

He'd been fascinated by them from the start. Partly

because they were ever mobile. But mostly because they looked smooth and soft, making him want to reach out and touch. Making him want to trace them with his fingertips and then his lips.

"Thank you for choosing me for such an honor." He pushed ahead before he could get even *more* distracted. Or, you know, spring a boner. "Thank you for wanting to entrust me with such a gift and—"

"Ugh." She rolled her eyes and pointed at his nose. "See? That right there. All those flowery words—*honor*, *gift*—show you haven't been listening to me and are attaching too much importance to this thing. Are your ears purely decorative?"

When she let her hand fall back into her lap, he covered it with one of his own. He was immediately struck by the disparity of sizes. Where he was broad-palmed and thick-fingered, she was soft and small and delicate.

Her skin was baby soft and cool beneath his touch. But it warmed up quickly, as if her blood raced to the surface to be closer to him. Or maybe his blood was hot enough to warm them both.

She used her free hand to push her glasses higher on the bridge of her nose and stared at him in surprise. Touching her was something he had rarely allowed himself to do before her proposal. And something he'd avoided altogether since.

But he wanted her to know how sincere he was now. He wanted her to understand that he meant every single word with every single fiber of his being.

Of course, it was a catch-22. Because when he was

touching her, it was nearly impossible to remember *any* words.

"And you're not attaching *enough* importance to it," he told her quietly, pulling his hand away and settling it back into his own lap. "Which is why I can't do what you want me to do despite the fact that my sixteen-year-old self is calling me a frickin' *idjit* and punching me in the dick."

"You know," she mused, staring out at the waves so that he was gifted with a view of her delicate profile, "when someone says 'It isn't you, it's me,' what they really mean is 'It's you.'"

"No." He shook his head. "It really *is* me. I respect you too much to—"

"Oh, please." She huffed after turning back to him. "Just admit the truth. I'm a big girl. I can handle it."

He blinked in confusion. "Truth about what?"

"About not wanting me that way. About not being attracted to me."

That was so far beyond the truth—like in an entirely different galaxy—that he couldn't help but laugh.

"Damn it, Mason! This isn't funny!" Her scrunched-up nose drew his eyes to the sprinkling of freckles across her high cheekbones. He wanted to lean forward and kiss each and every one of them.

Instead, he sobered and said, "Alex, you gotta know I think you're wicked smart and killer funny even when you're not trying to be."

"You're the only person I know who can insult me while complimenting me." Her mouth flattened into a straight line.

He added, "And you have a natural beauty that makes me wanna paint your portrait every time I look atcha."

"Yeah," she snorted. "Paint my portrait but not diddle me until I'm dizzy."

The thought of doing exactly that was enough to make his dick swell inside his swim trunks. "Bullshit, woman. You're off-the-charts fuckable."

The way she shook her head made her wild hair fly. She wasn't buying what he was selling. "If that's true, why aren't we knocking boots belowdecks right now?"

He regarded her for a full ten-second count, wondering how much to reveal. Then he figured, *Fuck it.* "Maybe 'cause once we started, I wouldn't wanna stop."

Her unblinking stare glued itself to his face. And for the first time in her life, it appeared Alexandra Merriweather was at a loss for words.

Chapter 5

TALK ABOUT BAD TIMING.

Chrissy had walked up behind Mason and Alex at the exact right moment to hear Mason's last statement. And boy, what a statement it was. Her own heart did a little flutter, and her mouth hung open for so long she feared a seagull might decide to fly in and take up roost.

She resisted shooting a fist in the air, because...*I was right! I was right! I was right!* She wanted to sing it like Adele. Rap it like Snoop Dogg.

Deciding the speedboat could wait, she spun on her heel, hoping to slink back into the cabin unobserved.

"Chrissy?" Mason's deep voice stopped her in her tracks. She winced hard enough to hurt her cheekbones.

Lifting her hand, she waved over her shoulder without turning. "Sorry for the interruption. Please go back to your regularly scheduled programming."

"We're finished here," Mason said and that had her hesitantly glancing over her shoulder.

From behind the lenses of her glasses, Alex stared at Mason with eyes the size of monkfishes. And even though her mouth was open and her throat was working, no sound emerged.

Then she shook her head and picked up her book

so she could whack Mason's arm with it. "No, we most certainly are *not* finished! If you think you can say something like that and then just walk away, you're out of your chowder-eating mind!"

"Chrissy." Mason ignored Alex and pointed to the binoculars Chrissy had clutched in her hand. "You sure everything's okay?" His thick New England accent made the word *sure* sound more like *shah*.

She grimaced at Alex, her expression saying *I suck! I know!*

The look Alex sent in return said she was imagining setting Chrissy's right eyebrow on fire with nothing more than the power of her mind.

Chrissy mouthed *sorry* before answering Mason. "It's probably nothing. But there's a speedboat following in our wake. I thought it was…you know…weird."

After her conversation with Wolf, she'd taken herself out to the swim deck at the back of the boat to try to untangle the many feelings she had surrounding his admission that he *liked* her. Apparently it was a day for confessions… *Yay, team!* But before she could do that, she'd become distracted by tiny plumes of white in the distance.

A quick glance through the binoculars brought the plumes into sharper focus. The boat creating them was too far away to make out clearly, but she recognized the rooster-tail effect.

A speedboat.

She'd lived in the Florida Keys her whole life. She could name every kind of shell there was, could identify which way the currents were running just by studying the wave action at the surface, and could recognize a good cluster of oysters from a bad one. She *also* knew that sailboats, ocean liners, and cargo ships were built for the open sea. Speedboats, on the other hand? Thanks to their shallow hulls and relatively small fuel tanks, they fared better in the calm waters around the islands.

For one of them to be this far out was like finding an Easter egg under your Christmas tree. In a word, *strange*.

Her first instinct had been to go to Wolf with her concern. But she hadn't been ready to face him again so soon after their tête-à-tête. She could only be around him for short periods of time before she forgot why they weren't permanently attached at the mouth. She supposed that was partly due to the fact that, like everyone else on the islands, he ran around in shorts and tank tops that showed off all those lovely muscles and all that lovely tanned skin. But it was also because his eyes were strangely intense, so dark and shiny that every time she looked at him, they threatened to suck her in. Like a black hole.

He was a black hole. And it was better to stay hell and gone from him, because she knew if she ever allowed herself to get sucked inside his gravitational pull, she was done for. Finished. He'd crush her like one of the eggs the feral chickens of Key West seemed to lay around the island willy-nilly.

She'd decided getting Mason's opinion on the speedboat was the safer option.

But the look in Alex's eyes told her she should've stuck with door number one.

Sorry, she mouthed again when Mason stood. Given his bulk, it was amazing he could move with such grace.

"Let's go get a look." He motioned for her to pass him the binoculars.

She hesitated, thinking maybe she could convince him to sit back down and say more lovely, sweet, flowery things to Alex. But then he frowned—and truly, he had one hell of a frown—and stared at her with those shocking blue eyes. Her arms turned traitorous. They handed him the binoculars of their own volition.

Alex jumped to her feet then, too, dropping her book onto the trampoline before quickly falling in step behind Mason when he made his way around the cabin and headed for the stern.

"See," Chrissy said under her breath, giving Alex a poke in the small of her back. "I *told* you."

When Alex glanced over her shoulder, her expression said she still hoped for a way to singe Chrissy's eyebrows off. "Told me *what*?"

"Chocolate syrup." She gave Alex a knowing wink.

Alex opened her mouth to respond, but quickly closed it again because they'd made it to the swim deck and Mason immediately lifted the binoculars to his eyes. His massive biceps bulged, and Chrissy thought she heard Alex swallow noisily. When she turned to look, sure enough, Alex was staring at Mason like he was an all-you-can-eat shrimp boil.

It was an expression Chrissy recognized well. She'd seen it on her mother's face often enough, and it had usually resulted in a ring and a trip to the justice of the peace.

Josephine Szareck had fallen in love as easily and as often as Chrissy filled her scuba tanks.

Unfortunately, the *men* Josephine had fallen in love with weren't the faithful-until-death-do-us-part types, so Josephine had fallen *out* of love easily too. Chrissy suspected if her mother hadn't gotten sick, she'd have been on husband number seven or maybe even eight by now.

"Well?" Alex prompted Mason, her voice a little scratchy. "What do you think?"

He didn't immediately answer. And the apprehension Chrissy had felt when she first saw the rooster-tails began to sneak back in, raising the baby hairs on the back of her neck.

That apprehension quickly morphed into stone-cold fear when he turned to them, his expression like a hurricane. "Call in a Mayday to the Coasties. Tell 'em we got three unfriendlies packing assault weapons and headed our way in a speedboat."

"What?" Chrissy squeaked. Now it wasn't only the hairs on the back of her neck standing stick-straight. It was every hair on her body.

She snatched the binoculars from Mason and held them to her eyes. It took her a moment to locate the speedboat amid the vast expanse of sea and sky. When the boat snapped into view, it was still so far back she could barely make out the figures on board. "How do you know they have guns?"

"See that black swatch across the chest of the one who's piloting?" Mason asked.

She decided if she held her mouth just right, she could *possibly* see what he was talking about. "Sort of."

"That's a full auto."

She lowered the binoculars, her eyebrows knitting together. "Maybe you were right," she told Alex. "Maybe I need to get my eyes checked."

"Nothing wrong with your eyes," Mason assured her. "Just gotta lotta practice identifying weapons and hostiles. Both are on our tail."

"Oh god. Not again," Alex murmured.

"*Again?*" Chrissy stared hard at the woman. "When has this happened bef—" She cut herself off and answered her own question. "Garden Key," she whispered and pointed toward the white plumes in the distance. "You think they have something to do with that?"

"Not a fucking clue." Mason shook his head. Like most folks from Boston, he had a rare affinity for the f-bomb in all its variations.

She opened her mouth to say…she wasn't sure what. Her mind raced and was completely empty at the same time. How was that even possible?

"Go!" Mason bellowed. "Now!"

It was as though she and Alex had been buzzed by an electric eel. They jumped into action so quickly Chrissy didn't remember skirting the side of the boat or climbing the steps to the pilothouse. But suddenly, she was standing beside Wolf.

The look on her face must've said it all. He took one hand off the big wheel to grab her forearm. "Chrissy? What is it?"

His palm was warm against her skin, making her realize that, despite the heat of the day, she was ice cold. Was it possible to feel your own flesh turning blue?

What had Mason called the people in the speedboat? She couldn't remember. The only phrase that stuck in her head was *assault weapons*.

"Coast Guard," she managed to wheeze despite her heart having jumped out of her chest to hover in the corner of the ceiling.

Wolf's forehead wrinkled in confusion.

Well, of course it did.

Squaring her shoulders, she opened her mouth to try again. But Alex beat her to the punch.

"I need the marine radio." Alex reached past Wolf. "Mayday. Mayday," she barked after finding the Coast Guard channel. "This is the catamaran *Second Wind* at—"

Alex rattled off their coordinates, speed, and heading, and Chrissy dragged in a deep breath, willing her heart to come back inside her chest. But she was quickly distracted by Wolf's expression. It morphed from concerned and curious to dangerous and deadly when Alex added, "We have a speedboat with three unfriendlies riding in our wake."

Unfriendlies. That's what Mason had called them, and Chrissy understood why she'd had trouble remembering the term.

An old man yelling at kids to get off his lawn was unfriendly. The people who worked at the DMV were unfriendly. But a boatful of bad guys carrying assault-style weapons? They were a lot more than unfriendly.

Wolf released her arm to stomp toward the back of the pilothouse. It was then Chrissy realized she'd been using him for support, because without him, her sea legs failed her and she stumbled.

"Easy, darlin'." He put a steadying hand on her shoulder even as he squinted at the jets of water in the distance.

Alex continued to answer the Coast Guard's questions, and Chrissy squeezed her eyes shut. Unfortunately, the truth of the speedboat and its occupants didn't disappear just because she wasn't looking at them. When she opened her eyes again, it was to find Mason standing next to her.

"Jeez!" She jumped so far out of her skin she was surprised she didn't land back in Key West. Oh, how she would *love* to be back in Key West. "How are you so big and so quiet at the same time? You move like a Prius!"

Mason didn't answer. Instead, he shrugged two gnarly-looking machine guns off his shoulders and onto the back console. Then, from the pockets of his swim trunks, he pulled out a matte-black handgun and a knife with a rubber grip handle and a shiny silver blade.

Once a SEAL, always a SEAL, Chrissy supposed, staring goggle-eyed at the weapons.

She forgot all about that night two months ago and what had happened between her and Wolf. She forgot she'd convinced herself that no way, no how was she allowing herself to like him again. She forgot everything except for how comforting it was to touch him.

Slipping her hand into his, she swallowed a shaky breath of gratitude when he unhesitatingly curled his long, strong fingers around hers.

Chapter 6

EVERY TIME I THINK I'M DONE WITH KILLING, Mason thought as he press-checked the chamber on his pistol, *something happens to prove killing isn't done with me.*

"What the hell's goin' on?" Wolf demanded, grabbing his Colt M4 A1 rifle off the console with one hand and holding tight to Chrissy with the other.

They'd taken the weapons with them after bugging out of the navy. Not because the Colts were souvenirs. More because they were old friends, and because their commander had agreed to look the other way.

The 5.56 NATO round-firing motherfuckers had seen them through some serious shit.

Looks like they'll hafta see us through some serious shit again, Mason thought tightly, reminded of the old SEAL axiom that said *The only easy day is yesterday.*

He'd thought that would stop being true once he was a civilian.

What a joke.

"Not a clue," he told Wolf. "But I recognize an ambush when I see one headed my way."

Wolf squeezed Chrissy's fingers and, in a soothing voice, said, "Chrissy, we'll need you to captain the catamaran."

For a second, Mason wondered if Chrissy heard. She remained frozen in place, her mouth hanging open while she watched Wolf eject, check, and then slam home a full magazine. Just when Mason thought Wolf would have to repeat himself, she came out of her daze. Snapping her mouth shut, she squared her shoulders and dipped her chin in determination.

"Attagirl." Wolf praised her when she took up the captain's seat. Turning back to Mason, there was dark purpose in his eyes. "Alex said there's three of them?"

Mason nodded. "The odds aren't in our favor."

"Yeah." Wolf's grin was intentionally wry. "What else is new?"

"Different day. Same old song and dance."

"Mind if I take a look?" Wolf gestured to the field glasses hanging around Mason's neck.

After handing over the binoculars, Mason watched Wolf scan the seas behind the boat. "Think I recognize that blue shirt," Wolf muttered. "Pretty sure the guy on the left was at the hotel this mornin'."

Foreboding tightened the skin across Mason's shoulders. He snatched the binocs out of Wolf's hands, and sure as shit. The blue shirt *did* look familiar, but at this distance that was only because there was an unmistakable yellow emblem over the breast pocket.

The cocksucker watching me at breakfast.

A spurt of relief hit his blood. So he *hadn't* been imagining things. He supposed there was comfort in that. *Cold* comfort. But comfort all the same.

Hearing Alex sign off with the Coast Guard, he turned

to find her so pale that her cheeks and chin matched the zinc oxide on her pert nose. But his chest swelled with pride to hear her voice was steady. "There's a cutter forty minutes out."

"Damn." Wolf said aloud what Mason was thinking. Forty minutes was too long. Whatever this was, it would be over and done long before that. "They couldn't get a chopper to us quicker?"

Alex shook her head. "They said the one on base in Key West is down for repairs. And the one out of Miami wouldn't be able to reach us before the cutter."

Wolf turned to Mason. "How long you think we got?"

Mason did some quick math in his head. "Fifteen, *maybe* twenty minutes before they're close enough to fire."

"What if we engaged the engines?" Alex asked, having found the *Webster's Dictionary*–size owner's manual for the catamaran sitting beneath a box of Uncle John's rolling papers. She flipped through the pages. No doubt looking for some helpful bit of information about the boat or its capabilities.

Her insatiable mind *always* turned to a book when she was fishing for answers. Usually, Mason found the trait oddly endearing. In this case, he knew nothing would help them but good old-fashioned bull's-eye shooting.

"We're already runnin' close to hull speed," Wolf said after walking over to study the instruments on the console, "but every little bit helps."

Chrissy didn't hesitate to crank over the two Volvo diesel engines. They grumbled to well-tuned life and the boat jerked forward. Alex—a landlubber through and through—was thrown off-balance. She whooped like a longshoreman on payday, dropped the manual onto the decking, and stumbled into Mason's arms.

For just a moment, he felt the warmth of her breath at the base of her neck, the softness of her breasts against his chest. Once again, there was movement behind his fly, and he decided it'd probably take a nuclear bomb to keep his body from reacting to her nearness.

"Sorry." She quickly pushed away, and he immediately missed her sweet feminine heat. She used one finger to shove her glasses higher on the bridge of her nose, and that's when he saw her hand was shaking.

She wasn't as cucumber-cool as she'd have him believe. Knowing that made him want to pull her back into his arms and promise her everything would be all right.

The problem with that scenario—beyond the obvious, which was that once he had her in his arms, he wasn't sure he'd be able to let her go—was he never made a promise he couldn't keep.

On a scale of one to oh-my-fucking-god, the amount of trouble they were in sat right around shit-on-a-stick. The only thing that kept them from going all the way up the scale to oh-my-fucking-god was that he and Wolf had been trained by the best of the best and had spent the better part of their adult lives in places where angels feared to tread, doing what only devils dared to do.

"What do you think they want?" Alex's eyes implored him to explain how the hell she'd found herself in a situation where madmen were gunning for her. *Again.*

"To kill us," Wolf answered for him.

"How can you be sure?" Chrissy asked, keeping both hands on the wheel and one eye on the sea. Despite the shit storm headed their way, she was doing a damn good job of captaining the catamaran. She could navigate the wind and currents better than any of them.

"Because you don't show up to dinner without an appetite," Wolf declared.

Chrissy glared, annoyed by his cryptic answer.

Wolf capitulated. "A speedboat way out here? Three guys with weapons more suited to sorties than sailin'? They got ill intentions. No doubt about it." He turned to Mason, his black eyes narrowed. "What now?"

"Take down the sails. We're gonna need Chrissy to be able to navigate the catamaran more easily."

"Roger that." Wolf turned back to Chrissy, his voice low and steady. "This is goin' to be a high-stakes game of cat and mouse with an opponent faster than we are. But I'm hopin' your know-how can make up for some of that disadvantage. You up for this?"

Chrissy's eyes were each the size of Boston Common, but she swallowed and jerked her chin doggedly.

"Attagirl." Wolf praised her again, squeezing her shoulder, and then refocused on Mason. "Once they get within firin' range…"

Mason finished Wolf's thought. "We blast some rays of sunshine through their frickin' skulls."

He could've couched his words for the ladies' sakes. Sometimes SEALs were all about finesse. But other times they were the bluntest instrument in Uncle Sam's arsenal, and when things went pear-shaped, he tended toward the latter.

"Right." Wolf ran a loving finger over the barrel of his Colt and said something to the weapon in his native language. As a proud member of the Cherokee Nation, he harkened back to his ancestors anytime battle loomed large.

"What about me?" Alex's face was the picture of somber courage.

"What about you?" Mason wrinkled his brow.

"You two will be dodging bullets. Chrissy will be engaged in a high-speed, high-seas boat chase. What should I do?"

"You stay up here in the pilothouse." He didn't add *where it's safe*, because nowhere on the boat was safe from three goons who were locked, stocked, and ready to rock. But the pilothouse was as close to safe as it would get.

"Like hell I will." There was steel in her voice. "Give me that." She motioned toward the pistol in his hand. "Show me how to use it and we can even the odds."

The mere suggestion made a cold fingernail of horror scrape up his spine. "The fuck we can. You're crazy on a cracker if you think you can help in a gunfight when you've never even fired a gun."

There was an old military axiom that said *No plan survives first contact with the enemy*. In laymen's terms, that meant once the bullets started flying, all bets were off. The last thing he needed to worry about on top of that uncomfortable truth was *Alex* throwing herself into the mix.

"And you're crazy on a cracker if you think I'll sit here and do nothing." Her glare challenged him to naysay her again.

Another time, he might have seen the humor in the situation. After all, it was like a teacup poodle asking to be thrown into the middle of a heavyweight fight. As it stood, he had no time to appreciate her desire to engage in ill-conceived feats of derring-do.

The clock was ticking. By his count, they had less than fifteen minutes before first contact.

"Take Meat belowdecks while Wolf and I lower the sails," he told her.

"Fine. Good." She nodded. "Then what?"

"Then come back up here to the pilothouse and keep your head down!"

"Do I need to get 'Like hell I will' tattooed across my ass?" Her chin set at a mulish angle.

Something somersaulted low in his belly. He wanted to blame it on the adrenaline coursing through his bloodstream. But he figured it probably had more to do with the thought of seeing her naked ass, tattooed or not.

"Alex…" he began in exasperation.

She pointed to his nose. "Stop looking at me in that tone of voice."

He could've pointed out that he wasn't sure how a person could *look* at another person in a tone of voice, but…again…*ticktock*.

"Give her the pistol," Wolf said.

Mason swung around to gape at his former swim partner. "You can't be serious."

"What if we're not able to stop them?" Wolf's words had Mason's blood turning as cold as glacier water. "If we're boarded, the women will need a way to defend themselves."

Mason indulged in a three-second curse-fest before finally gritting from between his teeth, "Fine. Go take care of the sails. I'll give Little Miss Weaponless a quick, dirty lesson in firearms and hope like hell she doesn't end up shooting off her own face."

"That's *Miss* Weaponless to you. I'll thank you to avoid aspersions about my size," Alex muttered with a teasing gleam in her eye, proving she had more spec-ops soldier in her than he could have imagined.

For the forty billionth time, he was tempted to pull her into his embrace. In fact, he glanced down and found his hand reaching for her. But to his great relief, Wolf distracted him by asking Chrissy, "If I say 'I'm sorry' one more time, will you forgive me?"

Not taking her eyes off the low waves slapping against the hulls, Chrissy frowned. "This is no time to—"

Wolf cut her off. "Will you?"

She spared him an exasperated glance. "Considering the dire straits we're in, and the fact that you're about to go risk your neck in an attempt to save mine, this feels a bit like extortion."

"Chrissy." There was genuine entreaty in Wolf's voice. "*Will* you?"

Mason saw the instant Chrissy gave in. She took one hand off the wheel to shoo Wolf away. "Yes. Fine. You're forgiven. Go lower those sails."

"See?" Wolf winked at her. "Knew I'd win you over if I just kept at it."

She harrumphed before turning back to the wheel and the water. After Wolf exited the pilothouse, Mason motioned Alex close so he could go over the mechanics of his pistol. How to thumb off the safety. How to eject the clip and reload. How to squeeze the trigger and not jerk it.

It felt sacrilegious. Alex was a historian, for fuck's sake. She should be nose-deep in one of her books, not learning how to kill. And if he ever needed proof his life wasn't normal, that *he* wasn't normal, this was it.

What should have been a beautiful, sunny sail back to Wayfarer Island showed every indication of turning into a bloodbath. He just hoped like hell it wouldn't be *their* bloodbath.

And *that* was the only thing that kept him talking, kept him explaining. The thought that maybe, just maybe, Alex could use the information he was giving her to save herself.

If it came to that.

Of course, he'd do every single damned thing within his power to make sure it didn't come to that.

"You don't happen to have the owner's manual for this thing handy, do you?" Alex asked, weighing the weapon. It looked massive in her small hand.

"You won't need it. It's real simple, just point and pull. And if worse comes to worst, don't hesitate. Put a hole through whichever cocksucker comes through that door as easily as you'd eat a Girl Scout cookie."

"Which flavor?" Her green eyes blinked up at him.

"What?"

"Which flavor? Because if you're talking about Samoas, I tend to savor them. But Peanut Butter Patties? Oh, I can't help myself. I think I actually forget to chew."

He was smiling. He couldn't believe it, but he was. "There you go being a smart-ass again. Is this your way of hugging me?"

"Do you need a hug?" He thought maybe he heard a hopeful note in her voice.

"Do *you* need a hug?" he countered.

"Maybe," she admitted with a twist of her lips. There was fear in her eyes. But there was also the sharp glimmer of provocation. "My heart is pounding a mile a minute. Want to feel?"

If he lived to be a hundred years old, he would remember the way she stood in front in him right now. So brave. So beautiful. So damned tempting he could almost forget they were minutes away from discovering whether this day would end in life or death.

"I think you're gonna have enough excitement today without me adding to it," he told her.

She feigned a pout. "Spoilsport."

"Mmm" was all he allowed before asking her to show him what she'd learned.

She went through the motions without missing a beat. If someone had told him she'd spent her life handling weapons, he wouldn't have argued with them. Her hands were steady, her actions sure.

Sharp as a tack, he thought admiringly, admitting that the only truly foolish thing she'd ever done was set her sights on *him*.

Then, it was time to teach her to aim. "Turn 'round," he told her. "Step back."

She pressed her back against his chest, her round, tight butt hitting just below his crotch. He had to grit his jaw and silently recite the Red Sox 2004 World Series roster to keep from displaying his *own* loaded gun while he showed her how to extend her firing arm and use her other hand to support her aim.

It was only as she practiced lining up a target that he allowed himself to close his eyes and revel in the unqualified pleasure of finally, *finally* experiencing what he'd been wanting to experience all day. All week. Ever since she set foot on Wayfarer Island.

He had the tiny, terrifying Alexandra Merriweather bound in the circle of his arms. And if it happened to be the last bit of pleasure he ever experienced in this world? Well then, he might die a happy man.

Chapter 7

11:15 a.m.

"How the hell are you so calm," Chrissy asked.

Alex made a rude noise beneath her breath. "If my outsides look calm, it's a facade. My insides are pure chaos."

Chrissy let loose with a windy breath. "Thank goodness. I thought maybe it was just me."

After depositing Meat belowdecks, Alex had raced back to the pilothouse to take up a position by the back windows. Chrissy was keeping them on a straight path that would, hopefully, intercept with the Coast Guard cutter sooner rather than later. And Mason and Wolf were lying on the swim deck below, assault rifles up and at the ready for the moment when the quickly approaching speedboat got within firing range.

Seeing them so exposed had a fist twisting in Alex's guts. It took everything she had not to lose her breakfast and her last strawberry Pop-Tart all over the pilothouse's teakwood decking.

Some time ago, she'd heard someone say *Family is where you find it*. Who'd have ever thought she'd find hers with a group of grizzled Navy SEALs turned treasure hunters?

Oh, not to give the impression that her own parents

were unloving or anything. They actually adored her. It's just that they were always...*distracted*.

As academics, they were far more interested in discussing possible alternative forms of energy than asking Alex what was happening in her life. Dinner-table conversations tended toward topics like how the perception of "art" differed between cultures as opposed to how Alex was feeling about finishing her schooling and stepping out into the real world.

In fact, the first time she could remember someone showing a true interest in the inner workings of Alexandra Merriweather was her third night on Wayfarer Island. The entire crew had been gathered around a beach bonfire, listening to the crackle and pop of burning driftwood and enjoying the sea breeze, when Romeo leaned over and whispered, "What's your favorite childhood memory? Who's the one person you look up to the most? If you could choose to live anywhere in the world, where would it be? Tell me everything, Alex. I want to know all about you."

And he'd *meant* it.

It had been Doc who'd found her at the end of the pier, knees tucked under her chin, rocking slightly in an effort to push away the horrifying images of that night on Garden Key. He'd tossed a warm arm around her shoulders and let her cry out her terror, softly murmuring assurances that the memories would fade with time, and promising that anytime she felt them closing in, she could always come to him to talk.

And she had. Many times over.

Then there was Bran. After declaring "A woman cannot live on Pop Tarts alone," he'd endeavored to teach her to cook. With patience and more than a little good-natured ribbing, he'd taught her how to make an omelet, whip up some macaroni and cheese that didn't come from a box, and grill a hamburger.

It wasn't much. Her go-to meals still tended to come out of packages, but she loved all the time spent in the kitchen with him, exchanging movie quotes, singing songs, and dissecting the differences in the way they'd been raised.

Yes, the men of Deep Six Salvage had come to mean the world to her. Now two of them were gearing up to get shot at. So it was a pretty safe bet the dead *last* thing she was feeling was calm and—

Chrissy sat up straighter. For a blessed minute, Alex thought maybe she'd spotted the Coast Guard cutter. Then Chrissy's grip on the wheel went white-knuckled, and that was the only warning Alex had before the catamaran took a rogue wave broadside.

It wasn't much in terms of what the sea could conjure when she was really trying. The crest was only three or four feet high. But it was enough to make the boat list precariously.

Alex forgot the first rule of sailing: *Keep your feet planted shoulder-width apart.* She lost her balance, and the only thing that saved her from getting a face full of decking was her hip hitting the back console with enough force to make her teeth clack together. Mason's pistol slipped from her grip and clattered to the floor. Skidding across the decking, it came to rest in the corner, barrel out, malevolent black eye blinking at her.

Her heart jumped into her throat. She expected to feel the deep, burning pain of a bullet slamming into her leg, because that's how it happened in the movies, right? The dropped gun went off and maimed the dumbass who'd mishandled it?

But to her great relief, there was no bark of discharge. No stab of searing agony. Thank goodness she hadn't proved Mason right by accidentally shooting herself.

"Sea's getting rougher." Chrissy's voice was sandpaper. "You all right?"

"Fine," Alex assured her. The adrenaline coursing through her system saved her from feeling the pain in her hip, even though she knew she'd be sporting one hell of a bruise in the morning.

If you live that long, an insidious little voice whispered at the back of her head.

She'd been doing her best to keep herself from even *considering* that option, evidenced by her fire-eyed demand that Mason give her a job. She knew from that night on Garden Key that when she was left to twiddle her thumbs, nothing but worst-case scenarios swept through her brain.

She bent to retrieve Mason's pistol, and the menacing weight of it, the lethal promise of its purpose, traveled from her palm into her arm. She felt as if a part of him was with her.

Had there ever been a man born who was warmer or more solid than Mason? If so, she'd yet to meet him.

That's how I'll get through this, she decided. *By imagining him beside me, lending me his strength.*

"How much longer you figure we have?" Chrissy cut into her thoughts.

"Not sure." Alex was dismayed to see the speedboat closer still. Close enough that she could make out the features of the men on board. "Not much longer, because I—"

That's all she managed before the evil sound of gunfire punched through the air.

11:19 a.m.

"Looks like our newfound friends are anxious to get the party started!" Wolf shouted above the roar of the catamaran's diesel engines and the *ping, ping, ping* of nearly spent rounds ricocheting off its twin hulls.

Whizzing bullets would have most guys pissing in their pants. But Mason and Wolf weren't most guys. Fifteen years in the navy had inured them to itchy-trigger-finger syndrome. Unlike their attackers, they would wait until the speedboat was close enough to make each shot count.

As the seconds ticked by, Mason's gut filled up with a tight, hot emotion he recognized as fury. Pure and simple, he was wickedly...nay, *righteously* pissed.

This isn't supposed to be my life!

Not anymore.

And it sure as shit wasn't supposed to be Alex's life.

The thought of her up in that pilothouse with a gun in her hand was enough to make him want to hurl. She was all things soft and gentle, and this, whatever the hell this was, promised to be anything but.

"You were right!" Wolf called. "They haven't seen us yet!" Obvious because their assailants hadn't aimed rounds their way. Instead, the fuckfaces on the speed-boat concentrated their fire at the spot on the deck above where the inboard engines chugged.

Mason had decided they should take up a position on the swim platform not only because it afforded them unencumbered views out the back of the catamaran, but also because the dingy and its pulley system offered some cover from anyone approaching from the rear.

But that wouldn't last long. Sooner rather than later, their assailants would spot them. Mason just hoped he and Wolf had time to take out a couple of the bastards before that happened.

Sucking in a slow breath, he exhaled for a count of ten, numbered his heartbeats, and focused on matching the bank and sway of his weapon to the bank and sway of the catamaran.

"I'll take out the pilot!" Wolf yelled, one eye to his Colt's scope. "You go for Red Shirt!"

Mason didn't ask why Wolf didn't mention the dude from the hotel bar. It was obvious from the way the cheese-dick fired his weapon that he was the least sea-soned of the three. Which meant he'd be saved for last.

First rule of combat. Take out the motherfuckers who know what they're doing.

"You ready?" Wolf yelled.

Mason's grip on the stock of his M4 tightened. The metal of his trigger was worn smooth by years of action and the thousands of rounds it'd sent downrange. His reply was a curt nod of his head.

"On the count of three! One! Two! Three!" Wolf roared and…*Bam!*…Mason squeezed off a shot, barely feeling the impact of the Colt's recoil. He was too busy watching his target through his scope.

There was a sweet spot at the base of the skull called an "apricot." Snipers aimed for it because it meant instant lights-out.

Mason wasn't sure he'd hit his target's apricot, but he'd scored a head shot. Pink blood sprayed from Red Shirt's cranium a second before the man tumbled backward into the bottom of the speedboat.

Later, Mason would find a quiet spot to consider the weight of having snuffed out another life, but right then he didn't give it a rat's ass of a second thought. He immediately turned his weapon on the douche canoe from the hotel.

Unfortunately, before he could line up a shot, a bullet found one of the inboard engines. The catamaran let loose with a mighty groan, and the deck shuddered beneath them. Black, acrid smoke poured from the back of the boat, burning Mason's throat and stinging his eyes. It effectively ruined any chance he had of getting a clear bead on the speedboat.

Without the aid of both engines, the catamaran veered off course. Waves splashed over the swim deck, dousing everything in fuel-tinged water. Up in the pilothouse,

Chrissy quickly adjusted to the new normal, wrestling the boat back on track until the twins bows once again matched the direction of the following seas.

Good girl, Mason thought at the same time Wolf used a hand signal to indicate they should make for the portside. The wind pushed the smoke starboard. So the left side of the catamaran was the last/best option for finding a bettering firing position.

"Mine's down!" he yelled to Wolf as they crouch-ran across the deck. "Yours?"

"Dunno!" Wolf blinked back tears brought on by the foul smoke. "Engine blew before I could confirm and... Damn it! Starboard! Starboard!"

Mason swung his Colt around in time to see the nose of the speedboat edging past the back end of the catamaran. The blown engine meant they'd lost speed quickly. Their pursuers had overtaken them.

Mason only had time to squeeze off one round before...*Bwaaaarrr!*...a barrage of bullets blasted across the boat. He and Wolf were forced to hit the deck.

Fuck! was his first thought as he pancaked. His second thought was *Fuck, fuck,* fuck! Because the door to the pilothouse burst open, and a tiny white hand holding a big black gun appeared in the void.

"Alex, no!" he bellowed, wondering if was possible to shit his own heart. But he was too late. She got off a shot, and immediately the bastards in the speedboat turned their fire her way. *Rat-a-tat-tat! Rat-a-tat-tat!* Mason watched in horror as the pilothouse took on the look of a cheese grater.

"No!" he yelled again, but he couldn't afford to waste time on having the stroke he so richly deserved. He had to take advantage of the opening Alex had given him.

Wolf didn't hesitate either. He jumped to his feet, lifted his Colt, and beat Mason in getting off a round. Fire blinked from the end of his rifle, and Mason saw a hole open up in the side of the speedboat pilot's face a split second before the man went flying overboard.

Two down, he thought grimly, turning to aim at Hotel Guy, the last man standing.

Mason took his shot, but he couldn't be sure he hit his mark. The pilotless speedboat was on a collision course with the crippled catamaran, and he had to spin toward the pilothouse and bellow, "Bang a U-ey!" No sooner were the words out of his mouth than he realized Chrissy probably didn't speak Bostonese. "Port! Turn to port!"

The catamaran banked hard left, and Wolf slammed into him, taking them both to the deck. Mason's knees hit the teakwood hard, but he barely felt it. He was too busy scrambling back to his feet and yelling Alex's name.

He wasn't a praying man, but he found himself silently imploring, *Please, God. Let her be okay and I promise I'll—* That's all he managed before the uncaptained speedboat blazed by them with a deafening roar, narrowly missing the limping catamaran and dousing the deck with a deluge of seawater.

Mason squeegeed the saltiness from his eyes in time to see Hotel Guy fall overboard, narrowly missing the speedboat's screaming engines as it careened wildly across the water, heading for the horizon.

"Alex!" Mason yelled, his chest caught in a vise of fear so tight no oxygen entered his lungs. He couldn't feel his bare feet slamming across the decking as he made a bee-line for the steps to the pilothouse.

The last engine on the catamaran chose that moment to give up the ghost. It sputtered and died, leaving an eerie silence behind that made Mason's quickly indrawn breath of relief sound as loud as a cannon shot when Alex's red head appeared in the open doorway.

Her voice sounded like it had been put through a paper shredder, but it was still the sweetest noise he'd ever heard. "I'm okay." She waved a shaky hand.

He'd never had his legs give out on him before. Not when they'd busted ass over the Ogo Mountains in Somalia, outrunning an entire army of al-Shabaab militants. Not even when their transport chopper crash-landed them in the middle of a Taliban-operated opium field on the edge of the Registan Desert. So he was more than a little surprised when he had to take a knee on the second-to-last tread.

"Chrissy?" Wolf's cry was a bullhorn in his ear. His old swim partner was right on his ass.

"She's fine too," Alex assured them.

When Wolf grabbed the handrail and leaned heavily against it, Mason could sympathize. He couldn't remember having been in any gun battle he would call easy. But this one felt like it had been worse than most.

Maybe because they were out of practice. But more likely because they had so much more than themselves to lose.

"Holy shit. They almost had us." Wolf scrubbed a weary hand over his face. "If Alex hadn't opened fire when she did…" He didn't finish the sentence.

Mason grunted. It was all he could manage because the image of Alex throwing open that pilothouse door was clear in his mind's eye and he was concentrating very hard on keeping his stomach from emptying its contents.

She's lucky she didn't get herself killed! he thought sickly.

In fact, looking at the state of the pilothouse, he wasn't sure how either of the women had managed to come out unscathed and—

A cry from somewhere in the water stopped his thoughts. Squinting against the glare of the sun and leaning from side to side because the smoke leaking form the back of the catamaran obscured his view, he finally located the source of the wailing.

Hotel Guy. Apparently, Mason's last shot had ranged wide, because the asshat was still alive and bobbing like a cork about fifty yards back.

The fury he'd felt earlier returned in full force. "This fucking guy," he growled.

"Let him drown." Wolf lifted his M4 so he could get a better look through his scope.

"That's some blue-sky thinking. We needa find out who he is and why the fuck he tried to kill us."

Wolf grunted his displeasure. "Catamaran's a dead stick. Dinghy's our only hope of reachin' him."

Mason wearily pushed to his feet, trudging toward the back of the boat. After a slapdash repair job on two bullet holes, they had the little rubber dingy in the water.

Mason was about to step on board when pale fingers landed on his forearm.

"Mason?" Alex's voice made his skin tingle. Or maybe that was her baby-soft touch. "Where are you going?"

He turned to explain about the survivor, but the blood trickling down the side of her face had him yelling, "Damn it, Alex! You said you were okay!"

"Bumped my head against the console when Chrissy swerved to miss the speedboat," she told him. "It's nothing. No need to get all spun up, tater tot."

Ignoring her attempt at levity, he framed her pale cheeks with his hands, brushed unruly curls back from her brow, and leaned close to inspect the wound.

He hated the thought of anything marring her perfect skin. But, thankfully, the cut was only about an inch long. And it wasn't very deep.

"You'll live," he told her, inviting oxygen back into his lungs.

"What a relief." Her mouth twisted around a wry grin. But it quickly morphed into a frown. Then her eyes grew big and shiny.

Before he could think better of it, he pulled her against him, allowing himself the hug he'd wanted earlier. "It's okay." He smoothed a hand over her hair, amazed at how it could look completely wild and yet still feel silky soft. "You're okay. We're all okay."

When her arms curled around him, so did her feminine heat. Every cell in his body began to vibrate. "The smoke is making my eyes water," she insisted.

A bald-faced lie, but he didn't call her on it.

So brave. Too brave, he thought, hugging her tighter just to assure himself that, yes, she really was okay. Still living. Still breathing.

Still likely to make his life a misery.

"I swear to God, woman," he told her gruffly, "you gotta be my penance for...*something*."

"Penance? More like a prize." Despite everything, despite what she'd just seen and done, despite the feel of her pulse pounding beneath her skin everywhere he touched her, there was mischief in her voice.

As much as he didn't want to, as much as he'd have loved to stand there all day with her safe and secure in the circle of his arms, he had to step back. Number one, springing a boner while trying to comfort someone after a hair-raising firefight was something only assholes did, and he'd tried his whole life not to be an asshole. Number two, if she felt it, she'd never let him hear the end of it. And number three, there was still the hotel prick to deal with.

Pointing a finger at her nose, he told her in his sternest of voices, "Next time you involve yourself in a gun battle, I swear to Christ I'll tan your ass."

"You promise?" She batted her lashes.

He was saved from sputtering like a fool when Wolf told him, "If you want some answers from that bag of dicks, we better get a move on. The current is takin' him fast."

"When you get back, we need to finish that conversation we started before all hell broke loose," Alex told him, her tone definitive.

Mason felt a scowl darken his features when he stepped into the dinghy. "Told you we were done with that."

"And *I* told *you* you're out of your chowder-eating mind if you think that's true."

"Not all Bostonians like chowder," he grumbled, apropos of nothing. It was the best he could come up with since his brain was busy trying to devise a way for him to never, ever, *ever* have to repeat what he'd told her earlier.

She batted his assertion away. "Lies. The next thing you know, you'll be telling me not all Bostonians like Dunkin' Donuts."

He grabbed his chest as if she'd shot him. "Shut your mouth, woman! Disparaging Dunkies is fighting words."

She blinked myopically. "Did you just make a joke?"

"It's the adrenaline," he deadpanned. "Or maybe wishful thinking on your part."

Her eyes roamed over his dripping form. It might as well have been her fingers, the way his muscles quivered. When her gaze returned to his face, she gave him an arch look. "I'll have a towel waiting for you when you get back. Or we could always use friction to get you dry."

Aaannnddd it happened again. She'd tied his tongue into one hundred knots.

Knowing he didn't have (a) the wherewithal or the vocabulary to outwit her after something like that, or (b) the time, he simply turned his eyes skyward and prayed for salvation. Then he settled himself into the dinghy without looking back at her.

He and Wolf were headed toward the speedboat's lone survivor, salt water spraying up behind the outboard engine, when Wolf gave him a considering look. "You okay, man?"

For a moment, Mason thought Wolf was asking if he was okay with what'd happened during the gunfight. Which was weird. In all the battles they'd fought, Wolf had never checked in on Mason's emotional state. In fact, one of the ways they'd learned to handle their roles as death-dealers was to go on as if nothing had happened.

The human brain has an amazing capacity for compartmentalization.

Then Wolf's considering look melted into a smirk, and pointing to his own face, he added, "You got a little sweat on your upper lip there."

Mason pretended he didn't hear and focused on piloting the dinghy around a larger-than-usual wave.

"I *said*"—Wolf lifted his voice above the sound of the engine and the sea shushing against the rubber hull— "you got a—"

"I'm *fine*," Mason muttered. Which wasn't exactly true, because he was still in the process of cooling the fire in his blood caused by that titillating little exchange with Alex. "It's hot out here."

"Right." Wolf snorted. "It's the weather that's got you steaming, not the fact that it's takin' everything you have not to haul Alex's ashes."

Mason gave Wolf his best scowl. "Haven't we been through these waters before? Just this morning, in fact? Alex is *not* for me. And her pressing the issue is gonna drive me to drink!"

"Because it's every man's worst nightmare to be chased

down by a horny virgin hell-bent on his manhood," Wolf scoffed.

Mason studied Wolf's face and tried to decide if his fist would look better firmly planted in the man's left eye socket or his right one. "Every time I reject her, I hurt her," he insisted, rubbing at the deep ache in his belly. "I *hate* hurting her."

"So stop rejectin' her," Wolf said, as if it were that easy. "And before you try to explain again in that emotionally crippled way of yours why—"

"I'm not emotionally crippled!" Now Mason was tempted to plant his fists in *both* of Wolf's eyes.

"Please." Wolf rolled his eyes. "I've never seen anyone more tainted by the dark stain of D-I-V-O-R-C-E than you. You've spent the last five years doin' your best to bury all your emotions in a grave so deep I bet you can't even see the bottom of it. And if you want my opinion—"

"I *don't*," Mason assured him.

"I think it'd do you a whole hell of a lot of good"—Wolf pressed on as if Mason hadn't spoken—"to let Alex have her way. It'd make her happy. It'd make *you* happy. You deserve a little happiness, man. We all do, and—" Wolf jerked his chin. "Better slow down or you'll run over our friend there."

"Fuck!" Mason pulled back on the throttle and yanked the tiller hard right. He narrowly avoided plowing into the human buoy bobbing in the middle of the sea.

"Take over," he told Wolf. "I wanna be the one to haul his sorry ass out of the drink. And if I happen to accidentally punch him in the face while doing it…" He shrugged. "Oops-a-daisy."

One corner of Wolf's mouth twitched. "Did you just say 'oops-a-daisy'?"

Mason shot him a burning glare. "Ya-huh. And I'm owning it."

Wolf took over piloting duties and expertly motored the little craft next to the man who had left off calling for help because he was in the process of coughing up a lungful of seawater.

The tinge of pink in the ocean told Mason that while his last shot hadn't managed to kill the bastard, it'd still done some damage. There was satisfaction in that.

"Who the fuck are you?" He swung his M4 around to his back so he could grab the man under the armpits and haul him aboard. But he'd barely lifted Hotel Guy's torso out of the water when he felt the cold bite of steel.

A second later, a sharp report cleaved the air in two and Hotel Guy's head exploded in a cloud of blood and brains. Mason glanced over his shoulder to see the end of Wolf's Colt silently smoking.

"Don't pull it out!" Wolf barked, his complexion ashen.

That's when Mason realized his hand had instinctively gone to the hilt of the hunting knife protruding from his flank.

Chapter 8

1:30 p.m.

THE EDGES OF CHRISSY'S THOUGHTS WERE JAGGED and cutting, and she felt like she was moments from bleeding out mentally.

So far today, she'd been involved in a high-speed boat chase, shot at by machine-gun-toting strangers, and stranded on a crippled catamaran surrounded by dead bodies. Oh, and she'd watched in horror as a man she admired and respected took a knife to the gut.

Luckily, the Coast Guard had arrived not long after that and the captain had hustled the four of them on board the cutter. Unluckily, Chrissy had no idea how Mason was faring because he and Alex had been taken belowdecks to the ship's medic. Wolf had followed the captain up to the bridge, and Chrissy and Meat had been escorted to a small cabin by a young man who looked barely old enough to shave, much less wear a uniform.

He'd introduced himself as Ensign Watts and had been kind enough to fetch her a steaming cup of coffee despite it being eighty-five degrees out.

After settling herself at the cabin's small built-in desk, she'd tried to take a fortifying sip. But she'd nearly spilled the cup's entire contents down the front of her shirt because poor Meat, who'd been traumatized by the gunfire and the smell of his master's blood, chose that moment to prop all fifty-five pounds of himself against her legs and whine up at her pitifully.

She'd reached down to give him a reassuring pat, and that's when she'd realized the nearly spilled coffee might not have been entirely Meat's fault. Her hands had been shaking so hard it looked like she'd touched an underwater high-voltage power line.

How long ago had that been?

Her java was long gone. Meat was sprawled at her feet, only letting out a snuffle of unhappiness every few minutes. And if she wasn't mistaken, it sounded like the ship's big engines were gearing down.

Are we back to Key West already?

She took out her cell phone and blinked in astonishment when she saw she had cell reception and then realized two hours had passed since the shootout.

Shootout, she thought a little crazily. *Makes it sound like we were at the OK Corral and—*

"Sorry!" Wolf burst through the door, his face contorted in a grimace.

Meat jumped to his feet with a growl. Then, seeing it was Wolf, the dog belly-crawled toward his master's best friend, seeking comfort.

Wolf obliged, rubbing Meat's rotund little belly. And only when Meat seemed sufficiently placated did he return his attention to Chrissy.

"Sorry," he said again, straightening to lean a hip against the desktop. "Time got away from me."

Everything in the little cabin went out of focus when he

bent to take her hand in his. Well, everything except him. He was crystal clear and filling up her entire visual field.

"It took longer than I'd hoped to lay out the timeline of events for the captain," he explained. "Then I called the authorities on Key West. They're goin' to meet us at the docks and take our statements. I also checked on Mason and Alex to—"

"How are they?" Chrissy cut in, glad for something to focus on other than the feel of his warm flesh against her own. She was acutely aware they were *alone*. In a tiny room. With a bed not two feet away.

Would it really be so bad to let him lay her down and make her forget this wretched day? If she asked him to, he wouldn't hesitate.

The problem would be what happened afterward.

Because she was fairly confident that if she gave him her body, her heart would blithely follow. She had enough of her mother in her to recognize the warning signs. And he'd proved beyond a shadow of a doubt that while he was exactly what a gal needed if she was looking for some afternoon delight, he wasn't a man who could be depended upon to offer much more than that.

Not that Chrissy was looking for anything serious per se. But neither was she looking for a heartbreak. And that's what Wolf was. Walking heartbreak.

"They're fine," he assured her. "Alex has a couple of butterfly bandages. Mason has eight stitches and what will surely be one badass scar."

"Eight stitches. That's *it*?" Chrissy was incredulous. "After losing all that blood?"

She and Alex had both been standing on the catamaran's swim deck, absently waving away the weak wisps of smoke floating up from the burned-out engines, when Wolf and Mason reached the man in the water.

The scene replayed itself in Chrissy's mind in slow motion. The way Mason's back muscles bunched when he bent to lift the shooter from the sea. The way their assailant reminded Chrissy of a Gorgon, rising up all dark and menacing, his eyes filled with so much hatred that, even from a distance, he managed to turn her heart to stone. The way the Gorgon lifted a blade that flashed silver in the sunlight and, with a stark cry of fury, sank it deep into Mason's side.

Chrissy hadn't been able to breathe. She hadn't been able to move. She'd been so stunned by the unexpected violence that she might have stayed a living statue forever, glued to the spot, if it hadn't been for the horrible sound issuing from the back of Alex's throat.

It was the noise a dying animal might make. And it had been enough to break the spell holding Chrissy in place.

She'd put a steadying arm around Alex's shoulders, feeling the shudders going through the woman. And in that moment, she'd known that what Alex felt for Mason went a whole lot deeper than lust.

Whether *Alex* realized that, Chrissy couldn't say. What she *could* say was that Alex didn't leave Mason's side. Not after Wolf brought him back to the battered catamaran. Not while the three of them worked to stanch the blood with towels from the galley. Not even after the Coasties arrived.

"It wasn't all that much blood," Wolf said now.

She eyed him askance. "If that wasn't a lot of blood, I'd hate to see what is."

"The onboard doc said the knife missed everything vital. To steal a phrase from Monty Python, 'It's just a flesh wound.'" He grinned and hitched a shoulder. It drew her attention to the contrast between the baby blue of his tank top and the deep, delicious hue of his skin. Then, his expression grew serious. "You did everything right today, Chrissy." His thumb traced circles in her palm. He meant the gesture to be comforting. Instead, it made her burn for things she knew were impossible. "I'm crazy proud of you, woman. You should be crazy proud of yourself."

"Trying to find something good in anything that happened today feels a little like searching for a pearl in pig shit," she whispered.

"I do love your way with words." His voice was so low she would swear she heard it with something other than her ears, something decidedly *south* of her head.

It was high time she let go of his hand.

Regrettably, the moment she wasn't distracted by his touch, all those jagged, cutting thoughts took over again.

Wolf must've recognized the look that came over her face, because he squatted in front of her. "I know what you saw today was awful. And I know you have to be thinkin'—"

"About the wanton uselessness of it all?" she cut in. "Three men are dead and I can't understand it. Why did they do it? Why did they come after us?"

He shook his head and the sun shining through the

porthole created a halo effect behind him. He looked almost angelic. But she knew firsthand how devilish he could be.

"Don't know," he admitted. "I'm hopin' the authorities will be able to answer that."

She nodded, and for a while they were both quiet. Then, picking at the frayed hem of her shorts, she asked, "It's not like in the movies, is it? In real life, gunshots are so much messier."

"It's not always like that. The M4s we use are..." He seemed to search for the right words. "Serious pieces of machinery. Military grade."

And there was something in his voice, a slight waver, that had her glancing into his eyes. Those beautiful, black eyes that had seen too much destruction.

For the first time all day, she wondered how *he* was doing. He'd been the one forced to mete out those gruesome gunshots. And no matter how much practice or training he had, that couldn't be an easy weight to bear.

"Are *you* okay?" She went to brush the ink-black hair away from his brow, and then thought better of it. Acting as if it had been her intention all along, she tucked a stray strand of her own hair behind her ear.

"Sure." He shrugged. "Not like I haven't done it before."

"Even so, I don't suspect it's something you get used to."

"No." His Adam's apple bobbed in the tanned column of his throat. As with the rest of him, she found it strangely fascinating. "But men who live by the sword die by it."

The air inside the room was heavy with something Chrissy couldn't name. And the tight skin over Wolf's razor-blade cheekbones told her he wasn't as unmoved by what had happened as he'd like her to believe.

Making sure her expression was appropriately teasing, she hoped to defuse the tension. "Didn't we agree you'd stop sounding like a fortune cookie when I was around?"

The tightness in Wolf's shoulders loosened. A small smile played at his mouth—that wonderful, full mouth that knew exactly how she liked to be kissed. And that's all it took for her to think, *Lordy, I've got to get him out of here, or I'll be throwing myself on him in two seconds flat.*

In fact, she wasn't sure how she'd refrained as long as she had.

"Okay," she told him. "You've officially checked in with me. I know you probably have other things to attend to, so…" She made a shooing motion with her hand. "Fly away, Batman."

"Pretty sure Batman didn't fly. Pretty sure it was Superman who—"

"Don't get technical with me."

"You're right, darlin'. Today's not the day for technicalities."

The endearment had her silly heart tripping over itself again. "That's the second time you've done that."

"Done what?" His eyebrows knit together.

"Called me darlin.'"

"Sorry." He looked genuinely contrite. "Don't mean no offense. I'm not tryin' to infantilize you or—"

She cut him off. "It's okay. I mean, sure, the feminist in me might be screaming and shaking her fist. But the rest of me kind of likes it."

She instantly regretted admitting as much because he lifted one eyebrow, his expression going dark and seductive.

"But don't take that as an invitation to pick up where we left off two months ago." She pointed a finger at his nose.

"Why not? You said you forgave me."

"Forgiven and forgotten are two entirely different things."

He pretended to pout, and it was disconcerting how he could look like a warrior ripped from the pages of a history book one minute and an earnest schoolboy the next. And, holy moly, would she have loved to fall for his particular brand of charm.

But she knew what kind of man he was. And she'd be damned before she ended up like her mother.

———

1:48 p.m.

"Well?" Izad asked the head of his security after Navid clicked off from his call and shoved his cellular phone into his hip pocket. "What did he say?"

"The Coast Guard ship is pulling into port now. Omid and Cas are positioning themselves to see anyone disembarking from the vessel. They will call us as soon as they know something."

"Yes. Good. That is good." Izad nodded, telling himself to be patient even as he resumed his pacing.

He was surprised he hadn't worn a hole through the hotel suite's carpeting. He'd been at his back-and-forth vigil ever since they heard the *Second Wind* put out a Mayday call over the marine channels. Which, of course, they'd expected. What they had *not* expected was for the Coast Guard to report, less than an hour later, that they'd rescued survivors from the *Second Wind* and were bringing them back to Key West.

"Survivors." Izad mumbled the sickening word to himself now.

"Please, sir." Navid placed a gentle hand on his superior's elbow and steered him toward the sofa. "You are tiring yourself unnecessarily. Sit and rest."

"What does that mean that there are survivors?" Izad grabbed Navid's forearms. He knew his expression matched his tone. Both were desperate.

"It could mean many things," Navid assured him, softly insisting he sit.

It was only after Izad settled into the sofa's cushions that he realized Navid was right. His muscles twitched from overexertion. His bones ached.

"Perhaps after Kazem killed McCarthy, he did not have time to kill the others because the Coast Guard got there too quickly," Navid said. "Or perhaps Kazem *thought* he had killed them all, but had only wounded a couple of them. We will have our answers soon enough."

"Should not Kazem have called by now?" Izad looked at his watch.

The plan had been for Kazem and the others to kill those on board the *Second Wind*, then race to Cuba where like-minded friends were waiting to spirit them back to Iran. But first, Kazem was supposed to call Izad and tell him they could rest easy knowing their vengeance had been achieved. Knowing their loved ones had finally been vindicated.

"Not necessarily." Navid's tone was reassuring. "The journey may be taking longer than anticipated. The National Weather Service's marine forecasts say the waters of the Florida Straits are rough today."

From the corner of his eye, Izad saw the American shake his head. The gesture instantly ignited Izad's pique. "What?" he demanded with a snarl.

"I told you it was a bad plan."

Red crept into Izad's vision, but it was Navid who stomped over and bent to growl in the American's face. "You know nothing more than we do, so it would behoove you to shut your mouth."

"I know since there are survivors, things must've gone at least a *little* sideways out there," the American persisted. "I know Mason McCarthy is one tough sonofabitch and you underestimate him at your own peril. And if I were the betting sort, I'd lay down ten-to-one odds that at least one of those survivors the Coasties are bringing in is the man himself."

The thought turned Izad's already roiling stomach into a cauldron of acid.

He knew little about the American. Not his name, not his age, not even his real hair color—because the dark, listless hue he sported atop his head had obviously come from a bottle. But it was clear the man had some military training. It was there in the way he carried himself, in the vernacular he used. And he had to have connections inside the government.

For ten years, Izad's offer of one million U.S. dollars to anyone who could help him uncover the name of the person or persons responsible for his sons' deaths had gone unclaimed. For ten years, his network of underground informants and spies had come up with nothing, unable to hack into the records of the U.S. Navy to give him the answers he sought.

And then, four weeks ago, the American had contacted him out of the blue.

At first, Izad had thought the man was a gift from God. Now, he wondered if the American was the devil himself. He seemed to enjoy sowing discord and spreading doubt at every turn.

"You had better pray you are wrong. Because if you are right"—Izad's words dripped like venom from his tongue—"you will come away from this with absolutely nothing."

Chapter 9

WHAT FRESH HELL IS THIS? ALEX THOUGHT WHEN THE door to the conference room she'd been sequestered in for the last—she checked the clock on the wall—*seven hours* opened a crack and low voices sounded outside.

As soon at the Coast Guard cutter docked in Key West, she'd been separated from the others and whisked into the bowels of the Coast Guard station—a building she knew well because this was where she'd been questioned by an FBI agent named Tomlinson after those horrendous events on Garden Key.

This time, however, she'd been grilled by the local authorities, the state police, *and* the FBI.

Apparently, there was an issue of jurisdiction when it came to crimes committed on the high seas. Everyone was vying for the case. And you would think that after having given her statement so many times, the events of the day would have cemented themselves in her mind.

Just the opposite was true, however. As the hours wore on, exhaustion set in, making everything feel like a dream. Her memories had become fuzzy and faded, like ancient words on sun-damaged parchment paper.

She wasn't sure she was up for more tonight. At least not on an empty stomach.

"Hey!" she called to whoever was behind the door. "If you're coming to ask me more questions, you better bring a pizza with you. That ham sandwich you fed me three hours ago has long since digested. And according to an article I recently read in the *New England Journal of*—"

She snapped her mouth shut when the door fully opened to reveal Chrissy, Wolf, Mason, and Meat standing outside. Each and every one of them—yes, including the dog—looked about as bad as she felt, but she didn't think she'd ever seen any four more beautiful beings.

"Sorry." Chrissy made a face. "I'm fresh out of pizza."

Alex jumped from the uncomfortable metal folding chair—which she thought for sure must bear a permanent imprint of her ass—and ran around the conference table to drop to her knees and enfold Meat in a hug.

He *woofed* softly and snuffled in her hair as his chubby hind end wiggled side to side.

"I love you too," she told him, hiding her face in his many neck wrinkles and giving herself a few moments to camouflage the strain in her expression and plaster on her game face. "Even if your breath does smell like unwashed balls," she added.

"No wonder." Chrissy harrumphed, and then went on in that slow island cadence, "I've seen him working on the suckers morning, noon, and night."

Alex chuckled. And, *oh*, it felt good to laugh. Then she was on her feet and gathering Chrissy into a bear hug.

"So this is what we're doing now?" Chrissy asked drolly, patting her on the back.

"After what we've been through today, I'd say a round of hugs are definitely in order." When Alex stepped back, she tried to offer Chrissy a wide grin. But it was so brittle it made her cheeks hurt. "Man, it's good to see a friendly face."

Chrissy pointed to herself. "You call this friendly? I feel like twenty pounds of shit shoved in a ten-pound bag."

"You and me both, sister," Alex agreed. Now that she was back among her people, she could almost forget how scared she'd been all day long. "I'm officially past my sell-by date. In fact, I'm afraid the only thing holding me together right now are my clothes. When I take them off later, I might ooze into a puddle like a stinky cheese."

"Great," Wolf muttered. "Now I'll have *that* imagery in my head when I'm tryin' to get to sleep tonight."

"You're welcome." Alex went up on tiptoe to hug his neck.

It was weird. She'd never been the touchy-feely sort before moving to Wayfarer Island. But Romeo always rubbed her neck. Doc always tossed an arm around her shoulders. And Wolf gave the best hugs. Like, he really committed, with lots of pressure and a little lift off the ground.

When he set her back on her feet, he hooked a finger under her chin. "How'd you hold up under questionin', kiddo?"

"Pretty good," she admitted with a kick of pride. Then she winced and added, "That is until Special Agent Albus Fazzle came in. I thought Agent Tomlinson was bad. But Fazzle has all the charm of a broken Slinky. I may or may not have told him at one point that I wouldn't be the least bit sad if his dick got stuck in a blender."

Wolf chuckled. Then his expression morphed into one of commiseration. "Just so you know, I think they make those federal boys hand over their senses of humor before they'll agree to train them up there in Quantico."

"Do they also give them really dumb names? I mean, Albus Fazzle?" Alex blinked. "Is he serious?"

Wolf shook his head. "Leastways *you* were able to hold on to your sense of humor through all this."

"What was my other option? Draw a warm bath and plug in the nearest toaster?"

Chrissy grunted. "You were tempted to do that too? I thought it was just me."

Alex frowned at Wolf. "I didn't like his smile either. It was all veneers and arrogance, but there was no real feeling behind it. He reminded me of a crocodile. Plus, he kept asking me about your guns. I mean, three guys in a speedboat tried to kill us. Shouldn't he have been more worried about *that*?"

Wolf rubbed a weary hand over his beard stubble. "That's because we're not supposed to have full autos. It's against this little law called the National Firearms Act."

Alex didn't think it was possible for her empty stomach to feel more hollow. But she was wrong. "You used the same guns on Garden Key that night and no one said a thing."

"Apparently, Fazzle's a stickler."

Alex swallowed incredulously. "He's not going to arrest you, is he?"

She turned to Mason for the first time. She'd avoided doing exactly that because she was afraid one look at his haggard face and she'd lose what little control over herself she still possessed.

She was putting on a good show, but the truth was, for hours she'd been sorely tempted to curl up in a corner. That, or run through the halls screaming his name at the top of her lungs.

She thought she'd been scared that night on Garden Key, but it hadn't compared to the terror she'd felt seeing him take a hunting knife to the flank. Ever since they'd been separated, and despite what that Coast Guard medic had said, she hadn't been able to let go of her worry for him. In fact, then and now, she was shaking with it.

"Never said nothing about bagging us, but the motherfucker threatened to confiscate our weapons," he said in that thick Boston accent that made "motherfucker" sound more like "muthafuckah."

Other than the deep, delicious timbre of his voice being laced with exhaustion, he really did seem okay. A little pale beneath his perpetual tan, maybe. But otherwise fine.

She was able to draw in a full breath for the first time in hours.

"Luckily," Wolf added with a smug grin, "someone above Fazzle's pay grade changed his mind for him."

"Is that your way of saying you have friends in high places?" she asked.

It was Mason who answered. "The highest."

"Lucky you, then," she told him. And she meant it. He was so damn lucky that knife hadn't done more damage.

One nick of an artery, and instead of standing here in front of her in the too-tight T-shirt he'd gotten on loan from one of the Coasties, he could have been zipped in a body bag. The thought of how close she'd come to losing him forever had her going up on tiptoe to squeeze his neck.

She was careful to avoid his injured side. But she didn't even attempt to avoid pulling that unique smell that was all sea, sun, woods, and *man* deep into her lungs.

Thank heavens he's alive, she thought. *Because even if he is the most relentlessly stubborn man ever born of woman, and even if he has rejected me so many times I've lost count, I can't imagine a world without him in it.*

Where would she be without his scowls and his grumbles and his insistence on keeping his distance?

He wrapped his arms around her and held on tight. A little squeak of gratitude, fatigue, and pent-up fear escaped her. She thought maybe he didn't hear it, *hoped* he didn't hear it. She didn't want to ruin all the hard work she'd put into convincing him she was one tough cookie.

But when she pulled back, the look of remorse on his face told her he hadn't missed a thing. "Sorry this happened." Then he added with a grimace, "*Again.*"

She forced another smile. This one hurt, too, but she kept it in place by sheer dint of will. "Yeah. I suppose I should start wearing a hard hat, huh?"

He cocked a confused eyebrow.

"You know," she said. "Because of all the shit that's come down on my head since I started working for you guys."

Wolf gave a little snort. But the joke fell flat with Mason, and she immediately wished she'd kept her mouth shut.

Mason took things too personally. He'd taken what happened on Garden Key, the danger she'd been in, too personally. And he was taking the danger she'd been in today too personally too.

Looking for a change of subject, she pointed to the side of his T-shirt. Had she mentioned the thing was too small for him? It was as if John Cena had gone shopping in the juniors department.

In any other situation, all of that *maleness* on full, mouthwatering display might've distracted her from what she wanted to ask. But the edges of Mason's bandage were visible beneath the white cotton, and that was more than enough to keep her focused. "How are you feeling?"

He glanced down and this time *he* was the one trying to lighten the mood. "What?" he scoffed. "This little thing? Just a mosquito bite. How about you?" He hitched his chin toward her bandaged forehead.

Two can play this game, she thought.

"Any other woman would be strapped to a gurney and screaming for pain meds," she told him, mimicking his macho-man stance. "But I barely feel a thing."

And then it happened.

The mighty Mason McCarthy offered up one of his rare smiles.

Something to understand about Mason... He looked like the kind of guy you wouldn't want to meet in a dark alley. His brow was heavy and usually slammed into a scowl—especially when she was around. And then there was his nose. It was wide and listed a little to the side like maybe he'd been a boxer in his youth, or otherwise just a kid who'd gotten into more than his fair share of scrapes. And his jaw looked like it could withstand a hammer strike and come back all Oliver Twist style. *Please, sir. I want some more.*

But when he smiled?

Oh, when he smiled, it transformed his face the way the spring sun transforms the earth after a hard winter. His bluer-than-blue eyes lit up from within. His wide mouth curved into an arc so perfect, it looked like it'd been formed by a master sculptor. And all that was hard and unyielding about him seemed to fall away, revealing a softness that made everything inside Alex want to...

Something.

Sing, maybe? Dance? Whoop and holler?

In short, Mason McCarthy's smile was a wonderful gift.

"So I guess that means we're a coupla badasses, huh?" He looked so yummy smiling at her that she wanted to hug him again. Hug him and kiss him and...*other* things.

And never mind all of his objections.

"Or it means we're crazier than wax bananas." She made a face.

Mason's shoulders shook when he chuckled.

A smile and a chuckle? A banner day, indeed!

"So what now?" Chrissy asked. "I wasn't given any instructions when I was shown to this room." She circled a finger to indicate the conference room, otherwise known as Alex's Least Favorite Place on the Planet. "Are we good to go or what?"

"Go?" Alex asked dubiously. "You want to go before we have any answers? Or did all those uniformed types mention to you guys who the A-holes on the speedboat were? Or why they wanted to kill us? Or if they have any friends who will try to finish the job once they find out we're still alive and kicking?"

Chrissy stumbled like the thought made her knees go weak. She reached to brace a hand on one of the metal folding chairs, but Wolf was there to offer her support as she lifted a hand to her head. "Holy shit. I hadn't considered that."

"From what the local boys told me"—Wolf eyed Chrissy—"they're workin' off the assumption the crew that hit it us are the same guys who've been robbin' fishin' boats in the Straits for the last six weeks."

Alex's skepticism showed on her face. "The Baitfish Bandits?"

Wolf's right eyebrow arched. "Is that what they're called?"

"That's what the editor at the *Key West Citizen* dubbed them because they approach the vessels under the guise of selling baitfish. But I thought that was two guys with pistols. And none of the fisherman who've been robbed reported actually being shot at."

Wolf lifted a hand and let it fall. "The cops are thinkin' maybe these assholes brought in a third partner and the new guy upped their game."

"I suppose that could be true," Alex allowed, still not completely convinced.

"We'll find out soon enough," Wolf said. "While you and Mason were belowdecks gettin' fixed up by the doc, the Coasties were fishin' two of the bodies out of the water. I'm sure they're runnin' the men's prints and dental records through the databases as we speak."

"Not sure how much dental work will be left on that one guy." Alex's empty stomach filled up with bile at the memory of Wolf making a head shot at close range.

"If nothin' pops on the prints or the dental work," Wolf continued, "then hopefully the cops can get a hit on their DNA."

"So that brings me back to my original question." Chrissy looked around the group expectantly. "What now?"

Wolf scrubbed a hand over his face. "Now, we find a place to lay our heads for the night. And cross our fingers that by tomorrow mornin' we have some answers."

Chapter 10

"Hey." Wolf placed a hand on Chrissy's arm. She'd taken off like a shot as soon as they exited the large government building near the docks. He was having to jog to keep up with her. "Is there some sort of invisible race we're runnin'?"

"No," she answered stiffly. "You just have short legs."

"I'm over six feet tall," he scoffed. "And most of that is—" That's as far as he got before he saw who was waiting for them on the other side of the chain-link fence. The ham sandwich the local cops had fed him during his questioning instantly petrified at the bottom of his stomach. "Oh, hell," he groaned.

That was enough to have Chrissy slowing down. "What?" She glanced from him to the quartet gathered near the parking-lot gate and back again. "Am I missing something?"

It was one of those perfect subtropical nights. The moon was high and full. The sky was a black sheet dusted with silvery specks of starlight. And the breeze played with the palm trees, making them cackle in delight.

But all of this was lost on Wolf, because he knew—call it instinct or, hell, call it experience—that the brunette standing between Doc and Romeo was none other than Mason's itch-scratcher, a.k.a. the mysterious Donna.

This is bad.

"I think the brunette is Mason's…uh…occasional workout partner," Wolf murmured from the side of his mouth, loud enough for Chrissy to hear, but hopefully not loud enough for Alex and Mason to hear since they were a dozen paces behind, waiting for Meat to make his slow, waddling way across the lot.

"His workout partner?" Chrissy's face showed confusion a split second before realization dawned. "Oh." Her mouth rounded, right along with her blue eyes. "So *that's* why he rejected Alex."

Wolf didn't comment that there was more than a cute, curvy brunette keeping Mason from agreeing to Alex's offer. Instead, he glanced surreptitiously over his shoulder, wondering if Mason realized Donna was on the scene, and quickly discovering the sorry sod was too busy shooting fleeting—*And might I add longing?*—glances at Alex to have clued in to what lay in store for him beyond the fence.

"This is goin' to go bad for him," Wolf muttered, and winced in commiseration with his old swim partner.

Chrissy crossed her arms and grumbled, "He deserves whatever comes his way."

"Mmph" was all Wolf was willing to allow.

"Mmph? What's that supposed to mean?" Her full mouth pulled down in a frown. Chrissy had one of those classic faces that, no matter the decade or era, was always considered beautiful. Such perfect proportions. Such symmetry and harmony. Wolf could've spent the rest of the night staring at it, using the moonlight to catalog the different striations of blue in her irises, or count every hair in the perfect arches of her eyebrows, but he was going to have to file that under Another Damn Time because things were about to get dicey.

"It's complicated" was all he said as he searched for a way to warn Mason that—

"Mason!" Donna squealed.

Too late, Wolf thought as Donna's shriek hit his ears like grinding metal. *Cue the drama.*

Donna skirted the gate in a flash of Daisy Duke shorts, long hair, and bouncing body parts. Wolf thought it a wonder she didn't come out of her halter top when she jumped on Mason, wrapping her arms around his neck and her shapely legs around his waist.

She planted a loud, smacking kiss beside his ear before saying in a single, urgent breath, "The island is buzzing with news of what happened. And when I found out you were involved, I ran straight over here. I'm so *happy* you're okay."

"Donna," Mason wheezed, sounding like he'd swallowed a tea towel. *Looking* like he wanted the sky to open up and flash down a thunderbolt to strike him dead.

Meat growled low in the back of his throat, and Donna, still stuck to Mason like a cocklebur, laughed at the dog. "Jealous as always, huh, Meaty?"

"Damn it, damn it, *damn it*," Wolf hissed to Chrissy. "Look at Alex's face."

Alex's eyes, usually filled with mirth and mischief, were as brittle as green glass. And her expression, usually so open and earnest, was contorted into a mask of disbelief and… Yup. He was pretty sure that was hurt.

"I'll kill him," Chrissy muttered, hands planted on her hips Wonder Woman style. Her stare was sharp enough to cut glass as it sliced violently in Mason's direction.

Alex did that to people. Brought out their protective streaks. Probably because she was so friendly, so eager and sincere in everything she did.

Everyone who knew Alex grew to love her. And to a man—and a woman, given the deadly smile that crept over Chrissy's face; like, seriously, it was the kind of smile that ended in a body bag—they would defend her honor as if she were a medieval maiden.

"Hi!" Donna, completely obvious to the chaos she was creating, held out a hand to Alex. "I'm Donna Crestone. Pleased to meet you."

Alex looked at the woman's hand and blinked as if it didn't make any sense. Then she clenched her jaw as if she were girding herself and firmly shook Donna's hand. "Pleased to meet you, Donna," she said in a voice so flat that had Wolf not been watching her lips move, he'd have sworn up and down the sentence hadn't come from her. "I'm Alex."

"Alex!" Donna squealed. "I've heard so much about you!"

Wolf could tell by Alex's face that she was holding back from saying *Well, that makes one of us*.

"Donna." Mason squeezed the woman's firm thigh. Wolf saw Chrissy's right hand clench into a fist and knew she was envisioning planting it into Mason's nose. "Hop down. I had a wicked-sharp hunting knife sticking out of me not ten hours ago."

"Oh my god!" Donna unwrapped her tan legs from Mason's waist and gaped at the bandage visible beneath his shirt. Then she cooed "Oh, baby!" and grabbed his face so she could pepper his jaw with more tiny kisses. "Are you okay? I'm so sorry. I had no idea."

Alex looked like she might throw up.

"Time to kick some ass." Chrissy took a step in Mason's direction.

"Don't bother." Wolf hitched his chin toward Doc, who was quickly striding Alex's way. "The cavalry has arrived."

"Alex!" Doc boomed in his deep Montana-boy bass. His muscular arms were open wide. "Come to Papa, Baby Bear!"

Doc and Alex had been spending a lot of time together since the shit went down on Garden Key. No doubt because Doc, who'd joined the Navy SEALs when he was a mere three months away from completing his medical residency to become a doctor, knew a thing or two about helping people cope with the aftermath of trauma.

"Doc!" Alex broke into a run and threw herself into Doc's arms. One of Doc's big, work-worn hands came up to cup her head. The other splayed firmly against the small of her back. His wide palm completely spanned the width of her waist.

A look of surprise—and creeping fury—slid over Mason's features. Wolf felt vindicated on Alex's behalf, and just a little bit disloyal to his old swim partner.

"Ah, baby girl," Doc bent to murmur in Alex's ear, "I heard you had one hell of a day."

At six and a half feet, Dalton "Doc" Simmons was the tallest of any of the Deep Six partners. With shaggy hair, sea-green eyes, and a lean, mean face that'd been carved by the Mission Mountains wind, he was the kind of man other men called *sir*, and the kind of man women tripped over themselves to get near.

"That'll teach Mason." Chrissy made a sound at the back of her throat that was damn near diabolical. "Talk about a big, steaming pile of quid pro quo."

Before Wolf could respond, Uncle John and Romeo walked up behind him, each of them clapping a hand on his shoulder. "That's the last time I trust you to take my boat out." Uncle John's tone was teasing.

Technically, John was only LT's blood relative. But everyone who lived on Wayfarer Island called him "uncle." John liked to tell people it was an honorary title, like "your grace" or "your lordship."

Wolf turned to offer Uncle John an apologetic shake of his chin. "I'm sorry as hell about the catamaran."

John, decked out as always in an eye-bleeding hula shirt, cargo shorts, and flip-flops, shook his full head of thick gray hair and ran a hand over his Hemingway beard. "Bah. Just shittin' you. My insurance company already sent out a boat to tow her back in. Nothin' a little patch, some antifoulin' paint, and a couple of new engines won't fix. I'm just happy everyone's okay."

"Donna's right," Romeo broke in. "The news is all over the island. You think it was really the Baitfish Bandits?"

"Your guess is as good as mine. I'm hopin' we know somethin' solid tomorrow mornin' after all the uniforms do their thing." Wolf suddenly felt every single one of the hours of the day and every single drop of the adrenaline that'd coursed through his system. His eyes were gritty in their sockets.

"We reserved some rooms back at the hotel," Uncle John told him. "Reckoned after the day you've had, you'd want a beer, a bath, and a bed."

"You read my mind." And when a pair of taxicabs pulled up next to the fencing—their rides back to the hotel, no doubt—Wolf added, "Come here and let me kiss you."

"Try it"—Uncle John held up a hand—"and you'll be walkin' funny for a week."

"My house is on the way to the hotel." Chrissy's tone sounded as weary as Wolf felt. "Can I share a ride with you guys?"

"Whoa." Wolf turned to her with a frown. "There's no way you're goin' home alone."

"Excuse me?" She huffed out a breath of indignation.

"We don't know what today was about. We don't know who those guys were or *what* they were about. No way in hell I'm leavin' you by yourself until we have some answers."

When she smiled, it was all teeth. "Not even if I tell you that the reason I was beating feet a few minutes ago was because I need a break from your tender charms?"

His chin jerked back. "Me? What'd *I* do?"

"You mean besides coercing me into granting you my forgiveness when I thought we were all about to die?"

"Here we go again," Romeo grumbled.

"Fifty bucks on Chrissy," Uncle John muttered,

glancing back and forth between Wolf and Chrissy. If he'd had popcorn handy, he'd have been chewing with avid interest.

"No deal." Romeo shook his head. "Women always win. Didn't your mamma teach you that?"

Wolf ignored them both, pasting on his most contrite expression. "You're right, Chrissy. That isn't how I should've done it. My only excuse is I didn't want to slip off into the great beyond with you hatin' my guts." He swallowed uncomfortably. "*Do* you hate my guts?"

"Maybe." She let her eyes roam over him. "But it's hard to know for sure since the package they come in is pretty okay."

Never had he been more happy to hear the phrase "pretty okay" in reference to himself. Also, he recognized an olive branch when it was extended his way, and decided to extend one of his own.

"You can take your forgiveness back if you want to." He waited for her response with bated breath.

"No." She grabbed her face, her thumb and forefingers rubbing her temples. "Today put things into perspective. I don't want to waste any more time harboring resentments. What happened that night happened."

He blew out a windy sigh of relief.

"What *did* happen?" Uncle John asked. "We'd all like to know."

Chrissy went on as if John hadn't spoken. "Neither of us can do anything to change it. But I *can* do something to change the way I smell. Fear-sweat and seven hours in a hot, humid interrogation room is not a good odor on me." She dropped her hand. "I just want a shower, some-thing to eat that isn't a ham sandwich, and my own bed."

"We can make the first two happen. But that last one is a no-go." Wolf shook his head, trying to couch his dic-tatorial decision with a gentle tone.

"Don't you think the police would've assigned us a security detail if they thought we were still in danger?"

She had a point. The truth was, whatever today had been about, whether it was the Baitfish Bandits or some-thing else, all the bad guys were dead. The danger was probably a done deal.

It was the *probably* part that stuck in Wolf's craw.

"The police have been known to make mistakes." His eyes implored her to understand.

He *would* get his way. He could be the most stubborn, domineering bastard ever born when he set his mind to it. But he hoped she'd see reason and not make him go there.

"Fine." The look she gave him was tired and defeated. Then she turned to Romeo. "You didn't happen to reserve a room at the hotel for me, too, did you?"

"*Mi amada.*" Romeo waggled his eyebrows. When they found themselves in the middle of a shit sandwich or when he was wooing a woman, Romeo often slipped in a word or two of Spanish. "You can bunk with me. I know just what you need to forget this day."

Wolf heard himself declare "Over my dead body" in a voice he barely recognized.

Chrissy blinked, as shocked by his deadly tone as he was. He opened his mouth to say... He wasn't sure what. But he was interrupted by the sound of a honking horn.

One of the taxi drivers hung out the window and yelled, "Hey! Y'all coming or what? I got an airport run scheduled in twenty minutes!"

"We're coming!" Uncle John hollered back. Then, in a quieter voice, he told the group, "Let's go, children. I think we've all had enough fun for one day."

Chrissy followed after John, so much weariness in her steps that Wolf wanted to scoop her up and carry her the rest of the way. But she wouldn't welcome the gesture. The woman prided herself on being as tough as Teflon.

"If you try to use Chrissy's exhaustion and vulnerability as excuses to seduce her, I promise a slow, painful death," he said when Romeo fell into step beside him. Each of his words was hard enough to make his jaw hurt.

Instead of looking properly cowed, Romeo grinned that stupid grin that was all perfect white teeth and swarthy swagger. "Handguns or hunting knives?"

"Hand *grenades*." Wolf fixed him with his blackest scowl.

Romeo snorted. "That'd be painful. But I'm not sure it would be all that slow."

"You're *not* sharin' your room with Chrissy." It wasn't a question.

"She can have the room I reserved for you, and you can shack up with me. I can make you forget this day too." Romeo hooked an arm around Wolf's neck and gave him a noogie as if they were thirteen instead of in their thirties.

Wolf had just had a very, very bad day.

He feared a night stuck in a hotel room with Romeo might be worse.

Chapter 11

"YES, I UNDERSTAND. I WILL LET HIM KNOW." NAVID disconnected his call and was quiet for what seemed to Izad to be an eternity.

He tried to be patient. He truly did. His head of security was a thoughtful man, never jumping to conclusions or making snap judgments. But eventually Izad couldn't take it a second longer.

"Well?" he demanded, raking in a deep breath that smelled of the hotel room service they'd ordered for dinner.

More to the point, the hotel room service the *others* had ordered for dinner. Izad had been too nervous to partake. But even if he *had* been able to keep anything down, nothing on the menu suited him.

American fare was so salty and greasy. They didn't know how to season their foods with herbs and spices and so added flavor with oil and sodium.

Oh, how he longed for some *baghali polo* or *Fesenjan*.

How he longed for *home*.

If he closed his eyes, he could almost smell the saffron in the air, see Kazem's winning smile as the winds from Mount Tochal ruffled his son's black hair.

And speaking of his son...

The wait to hear from Kazem had been—and continued to be—interminable. As was the wait to hear back from Omid or Cas as to who the survivors were.

Unfortunately, his men had been too late getting into position to see who had exited the Coast Guard's ship. And the hours since had ticked by like years.

Izad felt ancient. And exhausted.

"Omid has confirmed it." Navid's expression was carefully neutral. "Mason McCarthy is alive."

Izad had stood from the hotel sofa when Navid's cell phone jangled. Now, he sank back into the cushions, lifting a hand to his pounding temples.

From the other end of the sofa, the American mumbled, "Told you this would happen."

Ignoring him, Izad beseeched his head of security. "There is more, Navid. I can see it on your face."

"According to Omid," Navid said slowly, "all those aboard the catamaran survived the assault. They appear unharmed and have been released after questioning by the authorities."

"So." Izad swallowed the bile that burned the back of his throat. "Kazem failed."

He felt that failure as keenly as if it were his own. *Worse.* Because his son would be devastated by it. And anything that hurt Kazem hurt Izad ten times over.

"What a disaster," the American spat out.

"Shut your mouth," Izad snarled, having reached his limit. "Or I will have my men shut it for you."

The American glanced between Navid and Jamshid, the two of Izad's security detail who had stayed behind, and proved that he was indeed smarter than he looked. He clamped his mouth shut. The only indication of what it cost him to do so was the muscle ticking spastically in the side of his jaw.

"One other thing," Navid said with a grimace.

Izad felt his heart cave in on itself under the weight of the fear that spread through his chest. He could not draw breath for words. All he could manage was a nod of his head.

"The authorities are attempting to identify two bodies they pulled from the sea."

Anguish had a sound Izad had not heard since the death of his wife issuing from the back of his throat. Then the import of Navid's statement sank in and a small spark of hope ignited. "Only two?"

"It would seem from everything that Omid and Cas can gather, the authorities have yet to find the speedboat or the third man involved."

"So Kazem could still be alive." Izad clung to the possibility as a man lost at sea would cling to a life ring. "We will assume he is and that, even now, he is trying to get word back to us." Determination hardened his jaw. "Which means now we must turn our attention to Mason McCarthy and how we plan to finish the job Kazem started."

———

9:53 p.m.

"Stupid, nonexistent water pressure." Alex cursed the hotel showerhead and turned up the heat until what it lacked in adequate water supply, it made up for with steam. As she lathered herself, hot vapor curled around her, opening her pores. What rushed in was anger.

Pure.

Unencumbered.

White-hot.

Damn Mason for first telling her he wouldn't sleep with her because he was convinced she was after a husband and no way, no how was he up for *that*. Double damn him for going back on that and telling her the real reason he wouldn't sleep with her was because he was worried that once he started, he wouldn't want to stop. And triple dog damn him for getting her hopes up because…

Lies! Lies! Lies!

In truth, he didn't want to sleep with her because he was already sleeping with someone else. Donna of the dark hair and doe eyes. Donna of the sultry laugh and pouty lips and skin that didn't appear to sport one single, solitary freckle.

Ooohhh! He could have told me the truth!

Anger gave her the wild-eyed, lock-jawed determination to do what must be done. Namely, killing off once and for all any tender feelings she had toward one Mason McCarthy.

"A pox on his penis!" she growled into the steam. "May he grow boils, sprout hair from his ears, and get fat and flabby!"

This time, she didn't call back the curse. She let it sit out there, hoping some higher power would hear it and grant her every wish.

Stepping from the shower, she used the rough hotel

towel to give her body a vigorous drying, feeling a little drunk on the rage running through her blood. Like most intoxicated people, she wanted to share her buzz. Maybe folks could get a contact high just by being around her.

Wouldn't that be nice for them?

After dragging a comb through her wet hair and watching the curls spring into loose spirals, she slathered on some lotion, taped fresh Band-Aids to her forehead, and slipped on her glasses.

A quick peek at her reflection showed her eyes were bright and flashing, her lips were deep pink from the heat of the shower, and her jaw was set at an obstinate angle. The months spent on Wayfarer Island had given her pale skin a faint, rosy glow. No access to a regular stylist meant her hair was longer than it'd ever been in her life, reaching past her shoulder blades, and if she wasn't mistaken, those were actual muscles in her arms.

She flexed and was surprised to see definition. All the swimming and diving and digging in the sand had done her some good. She'd never have Michelle Obama arms, but hers would do in a pinch.

Except for the bandages, she thought she looked… decent. She wasn't going to win any beauty contests, but that was the case any day of the week.

She exited the room after throwing on the hotel's complimentary robe and slipping into her flip-flops. All her clean clothes were in her bag on the catamaran, so she'd sent the dirty clothes she'd been wearing to the hotel laundry with a note pleading with them to get everything washed and back by tomorrow morning.

She hoped everyone would simply assume she was wearing a swimsuit under her robe. After all, this was Key West. People tended to run around robed when hopping from their rooms to the pool to the beach.

Once she was in the hallway, she turned toward the elevator. She had one destination in mind. The downstairs bar.

Number one, she could use a stiff drink. Number two, she was starving. And if memory served, the kitchen stayed open 'til midnight.

As she waited impatiently for the elevator to arrive, she ticked off on her fingers the events of the day. She'd gone all gooey over a guy who was a big fat liar, had learned to shoot a handgun, had *shot* a handgun, had been shot *at*, had seen three men die violently, had watched the big fat liar get stabbed, had hitched a ride for the second time in her life on a Coast Guard cutter, had been questioned to exhaustion by local, state, and federal authorities, *and* had stood by helplessly as all her hopes and dreams of the big fat liar had died an instant death.

She laughed a little hysterically and thought, *What will I do tomorrow for an encore?*

Then the elevator arrived. When it opened, she made sure her expression was appropriately *un*neurotic looking. She didn't want to frighten the elderly couple who moved aside to make room for her.

Her theory about the robe/swimsuit combo proved correct when the man, who bore a striking resemblance to George Burns, said, "It's a beautiful night for a swim."

"Mmm," Alex hummed noncommittally. She didn't

want to be rude, but it was difficult to speak when she was busy chewing nails.

"Just be careful of those bandages, dearie. I'm sure you're not supposed to get them wet," added the man's… wife?…sister?…friend?…lover? Alex wasn't an ageist, sexist, or traditionalist; she didn't want to make any assumptions.

Since she figured what would come next was a question about how she'd injured herself, since she didn't currently have the wherewithal to think up a good lie, and since she *sure* as heck couldn't tell them the truth, she forced herself to spit out the nails, paste on a passive smile, and ask, "Is this your first time to Key West?"

"Oh no, dearie." The woman chuckled. Alex couldn't tell if her eyes were gray or just clouded by cataracts. "We come every year to celebrate our anniversary." The woman patted George Burns's arm. "Yesterday marked fifty-eight years of marriage."

"Wow! Happy anniversary." Alex wondered if *she* would ever find someone who would love her for fifty-eight years.

Judging by her current trajectory, the odds weren't looking good.

"I bet you want to know the secret, huh?" The man winked at Alex. Since the lenses of his round glasses magnified his eyes to about three times their normal size, the experience was a little startling.

"Do tell," Alex enthused, surprised she didn't have to fake it. The little couple was just too cute. It was impossible to hold on to her pique around them.

"Find someone whose favorite breakfast cereal is different from yours."

The man's wife nodded enthusiastically. "That way, you never start the day with a fight over who gets the last bowl."

Alex smiled. "That's all it takes?"

"Oh, no, dearie." The woman grinned. "But if we had the true secret to making a marriage last, we'd be millionaires and celebrating our anniversary in Fiji."

Ding!

Alex was chuckling when the elevator hit the ground floor. She waved affectionately at the couple before stepping into the lobby.

A quick right took her to the bar, which was filled to capacity with sunburned tourists and leather-skinned locals. The air was heavy with the smell of suntan lotion and booze. And the Rolling Stones blasted from the speakers in the corners—good ol' Mick lamenting how he couldn't get no satisfaction.

You and me both, brother, Alex thought as she headed toward the bar, her steps quickening when she saw the tall, spare man seated on a stool at one end.

Doc Simmons didn't have an ounce of wasted flesh on him. And his handsome face and devil-may-care hair usually meant he was surrounded by a bevy of female admirers. Tonight, however, he appeared to be drinking alone.

"Doc!" She pushed through the crowd toward him.

She would be forever grateful to him for coming to her rescue at the docks earlier. Seeing Mason with

Donna—Mason with that body and those eyes and that smile turned toward someone else—had been too much. Alex had needed to run and...find shelter from the vicious thing eating at her insides. Doc had provided all of that when he hollered her name and opened his arms.

"Hey, Baby Bear." He used the nickname he'd adopted for her one day after Bran called them into the kitchen to taste test his latest homemade lasagna.

Doc, a true westerner with little tolerance for spice, had declared the lasagna too hot. Alex, on the other hand, had pronounced it just right. Bran had made a "Goldilocks and the Three Bears" joke, and from then on, Doc was Papa Bear and she was Baby Bear.

"Headed to the pool?" Doc eyed her robe now.

"That's what I'm hoping everyone thinks," she said above the sound of music and laughter. "Truth is, all my clothes are in the wash."

Doc was in the middle of sucking on his beer and lowered it to the bar with a *thud*. "You're telling me you're in the raw under there?" His jaw hung open just a bit.

The man who was sitting on the stool next to Doc craned his head around and gave Alex a considering once-over. Then he smiled flirtatiously, and Alex instinctively grinned in return. When the guy swung back around, it was to find Doc frowning at him loudly enough to strip the paint from the walls. "Time to call it a night?" Doc asked him, or rather *growled*.

The man made a strangled sound, dropped a five-spot on the bar for the bartender, and quickly hopped up to disappear into the crowd.

"Well, how about that?" Doc patted the empty stool beside him. "A seat just opened up."

"Poor guy," Alex mused as she snagged the vacated spot. "He'll probably see you in his nightmares for weeks."

Doc ignored her, hitching his chin toward her robe instead. "Better keep that thing cinched tight. Don't want you falling out and then me having to fight off a crowd of horny men."

"Please." Alex rolled her eyes, snagging a menu from behind the bar. "I don't see anyone with magnifying glasses in here. So even if I fell out, I'd be safe from unwanted advances."

Doc eyed her quizzically. "In case you didn't know it, a boob is a boob is a boob. We men like them all. And I'm sure yours are nicer than most."

Alex folded down the menu and gave Doc her most winning smile. "Why, Doc, that might be the nicest thing anyone has ever said to me."

He snorted and pointed the neck of his beer bottle at her. "If that's true, you need to get out more."

"I've been *trying*." She huffed at the same moment the bartender appeared in front of her. "Do you recommend the cheeseburger or the patty melt?" she asked the short, stout gentleman wearing a Hawaiian shirt and a straw fedora. "I'm so hungry I could eat the ass out of a low-flying buzzard."

When the bartender blinked, Doc offered an explanation. "You'll have to excuse her. I'm pretty sure she suffers from low blood sugar."

"The cheeseburger gives you more bang for your buck." The bartender tossed a bar towel over his shoulder.

"Great." Alex nodded. "I'll take a cheeseburger with a side of fries. And a bourbon. Neat. On second thought, make it a double. I've had myself a day."

The bartender poured her drink and then scurried off to put in her food order. After he was gone, Doc said, "You can tell me to mind my own damn business, but what's giving you the most fits? What happened out on the water? Or what happened this evening with Mason and Donna?"

"The latter. Definitely the latter." Then visions of the former flipped through her mind like a movie reel and she clapped a hand over her mouth. To her dismay, a little bleating sound escaped her throat and she shook her head. "Or maybe I'm lying. Maybe being mad at Mason is easier than thinking about what happened this morning."

Doc nodded in understanding and picked at the label on his beer bottle with his thumbnail. "When you're ready to think about it, I'm here for you."

She squeezed his arm in gratitude. "I know, Doc. And thank you for coming to my rescue with that whole Donna"—she choked on the woman's name—"thing. That could've been humiliating. Not that it *wasn't* humiliating, given how I've been throwing myself at Mason like cheap confetti. But, you know, it could've been even *more* humiliating."

He regarded her kindly. "When she showed up out of nowhere, I knew there'd be a scene."

Alex traced a finger over the top of her bourbon glass. "Did you know about her? Before tonight, I mean?"

She liked to think that if the Deep Six Salvage guys

had known about Donna, they would've given her a little warning. But maybe she was wrong. Maybe the bonds of brotherhood were stronger than the bonds of any friendship they'd formed with her.

"I..." Doc began and then hesitated. "There were a few times Mason and I did supply runs together and he disappeared on me," he finally admitted. Alex grimaced at the thought of what Mason was doing during those hours. "So, sure. I suspected he was seeing someone. But I never got the impression it was anything serious enough to keep him from taking you up on what you're offering. Sorry, Baby Bear. Maybe I *should* have seen it. It's just that Mason... He's..." Doc frowned as if searching for the right word.

"A asshole of gargantuan proportions?" she supplied helpfully.

"Private," he finally finished. Then he slanted her a look. "But that's no excuse for him hurting you the way he has."

"He hasn't hurt me, per se. But he has made me look like a fool." Doc didn't say anything to that, so she added, "As frustrating as he can be sometimes...okay, *most* times...I thought he liked me. I thought he respected me. I thought at the very least we were friends. I can't understand why he didn't just tell me the truth from the get-go."

"Maybe because the truth is more complicated than you think. And you know Mason isn't one for explanations when a grunt will do."

Alex let loose with a grunt herself, and then they both

fell silent. Doc slowly drinking his beer. Her staring into her bourbon, trying hard not to imagine Mason upstairs with Donna of the bubbly personality and winning smile.

Green Day came through the speakers now. Billie Joe Armstrong singing about walking down a boulevard of broken dreams.

It's like someone made a playlist for my life, she thought dejectedly.

Laying her head on Doc's shoulder, she sighed. "I don't suppose *you'd* be willing to help me out, would you?"

Doc got very still.

She shoved away from him and found his eyes laser-focused on hers, his expression… What was that look exactly? Stricken?

"Help you with what?" he asked slowly.

"Never mind." She waved a hand. "It was a joke anyway, so you can stop looking at me like I asked you to go out and kick a dog."

"Alex." He deep voice was achingly tender, and it made her own throat feel full. "If I thought you really meant it, I'd take you upstairs this minute, peel off that robe, and show you everything you've been missing."

Now her throat wasn't just full, it was dry too. Her tongue stuck to the roof of her mouth when she said, "Don't bullshit a bullshitter, Doc."

"Alexandra Merriweather, you are many things, but a bullshitter isn't one of them. In fact, you're so earnest it's almost painful." She felt her chin wobble and he was quick to add, "It's one of your best qualities. Never lose it."

Snagging one of her curls, he pulled it straight. Then he let it go and watched it spring back into a spiral. His green eyes darkened, and it seemed as if he chose his next words carefully.

"You're a lovely woman." When she opened her mouth to object, he lifted a finger and placed it over her lips. "Hush. Let me finish."

She swallowed thickly and nodded for him to go on.

"I know you don't see it because you feel like you were an ugly duckling growing up. And maybe you were. Who am I to say? But just like the story, you've turned into a swan. And if you keep going around offering yourself up to men, one of them is going to take you up on it."

"That's the whole point." She crossed her arms irritably. "There are forty million unmarried men over the age of eighteen in the United States. I'm hoping at least one of them will agree to *do* me."

"I know you think it doesn't matter." He shook his head. "That it's not a big deal as long as it's a done deal, but it can be beautiful if you wait and do it with the right person. It *should* be beautiful and done with the right person."

"Ugh!" She blew out an exasperated breath. "I live on an island with a bunch of men who act as if life is one giant bachelor party. But when it comes to me and my virginity, they get all flowery and virtuous."

Doc didn't respond to that. Instead he said, "Can I ask you a question?" His visage seemed…something. Not troubled exactly. Maybe *puzzled* was the word she was looking for.

"Go for it." She made a rolling motion with her hand. "I'll answer, because you know me. Miss Earnest."

"Why Mason?"

"Ha!" That made her laugh. "That's the million-dollar question, isn't it? I've asked myself that so many times I've lost count."

"What answer did you come up with?"

"I don't know exactly." She shrugged. "I like him. Or *liked* him." She glowered at the bar, running her fingernail over a scratch on the wooden surface. "And it felt right to ask him to be the one."

Her food arrived. But for the first time in her life, she'd lost her appetite.

"Can I close out my tab and get this to go?" she asked the bartender. Wincing, she added, "Sorry to be a bother."

"No trouble at all," the bartender assured her because being courteous to pain-in-the-ass customers was part of his job description.

After he whisked her food away to box it up, Doc asked her quietly, "Do you want my opinion?"

"Of course, Papa Bear. That's why I come talk to you. You have the rare ability to cultivate clarity."

He smiled slightly, and Alex saw the blond at the other end of the bar stare lustfully. There was something about Doc—aside from his big, lean body and ruggedly handsome face. It was a...*sadness*, Alex decided.

There was a tragedy in Doc's past. Grief was written all over him, and it was a vulnerability women couldn't resist.

"Things that feel right don't happen very often." His

tone was soft, his voice not much more than a whisper. "In fact, they're damned rare. Don't give up on Mason. Not yet."

"I hate to contradict you." She shook her head. "Especially since you're sort of my guru. But I've offered myself to Mason McCarthy for the last time. I won't let him make a fool of me again."

Despite what she'd told Doc, seeing Mason with Donna *had* hurt. She felt the ache in her bones. Deeper. In her marrow. But she refused to dwell on why that should be. Why she should even care if all she'd wanted from him was a little slam-bam-thank-you-sir.

It was easier and far more satisfying just to be mad at him.

"Speak of the devil and he shall appear," Doc said in a stage whisper.

She followed his line of sight and saw Mason standing in the doorway. When his eyes landed on them, his face took on the mien of a storm cloud.

Correction. That would be a storm cloud on *legs* because he pushed through the crowd with determination, each step eating up what seemed like miles of distance.

Alex's hands and feet tingled with the urge to run when he came to a stop directly behind Doc's stool. His stance was wide and hostile-looking, punctuated by his huge arms crossed over his massive chest. His brows knitted together, turning his face into a mask of... Was that anger?

He was mad at *her*?

Oh, this is rich!

"Shoulda known I'd find the two of you together," he growled. His accent made it sound more like *the two a yas tahgethah.*

"Oh yeah?" Doc arched an eyebrow. "Why's that?"

"Well, after that little display dockside…" Mason didn't finish the sentence, simply let it die at the end.

Alex opened her mouth, but words failed her and she was reduced to an indignant sputter.

Once again, Doc showed mercy by answering for her. "You mean that little display where you had a brunette hanging off you like a dog tick?"

"Yeah!" Alex found her voice. "If anyone was making a scene, it was *you*." She glanced over Mason's shoulder. "Where is Donna, by the way? Waiting on you to come back to your room with chocolate and champagne? Are you too cheap to spring for room service?"

Mason had the good sense to loosen his stance and look a little conscience-stricken. "She went home," he mumbled.

Alex made a show of checking the time on her nonexistent watch. "Already? Wow! Who'd have figured you for a two-pump chump?" She turned to Doc while hooking a thumb toward Mason. "Guess I really dodged a bullet with that one, huh?"

Now it was Mason's turn to sputter. And in a rare gift of perfect timing, Alex's to-go ordered arrived, along with the check. After peeking at the total, she pulled a wad of cash from the pocket of her robe, slapped it on the bar, and tossed back her double shot of bourbon.

She willed herself not to collapse into a fit of coughs, which would most assuredly ruin her exit. Grabbing her food, she hopped from the stool and strode toward the lobby without ever looking back.

Chapter 12

10:22 p.m.

MASON WATCHED ALEX DISAPPEAR INTO THE CROWD and had to will his legs not to stomp after her.

Because...then what? What the hell would he say to her? He had no idea. What the hell would he do with her? He had a few *hundred* ideas but none of them were in any way advisable.

What he *was* sure of was that he had a thing or two to discuss with Doc. And even though he wasn't much for words, more than a few choice ones came to mind as he snagged the stool Alex had vacated.

"I don't like you sniffing around her." He blasted Doc with his chilliest stare, surprised when the man didn't reach up to check if his face had turned into a block of ice.

Ever since the scene by the docks, Mason had been imagining little Alex in bed with the giant from Montana, and he'd grown more furious with each passing second. It'd only gotten worse when, after Donna left, he stopped by Doc's room and found it empty. His rage had reached a boiling point by the time he knocked on Alex's door, sure he would find them together.

Truth to tell, however, he hadn't been precisely sure who he was mad at. Maybe himself for caring when he wasn't supposed to. Maybe himself for being so relieved when he discovered Alex's room empty too.

Of course, now, with Doc so close and looking so tall and self-righteous, Mason decided that, no, the person he was mad at was Doc. Because Doc had no business with Alex.

He wasn't the only one feeling ill will toward an old friend, though. Doc stared at Mason's nose for so long that Mason got the distinct impression Doc was imagining using his knuckles to smash it in.

Then Doc's face turned impassive, and he drawled lazily, "Jesus, man. You make me sound like an anteater. I don't sniff. Much."

That "much" was said with a hint of a smile. Suddenly, Mason was tempted to put a hitch in Doc's Sam Elliott swagger.

"You can't give her what she needs," Mason said through gritted teeth.

Doc choked on his beer. Unfortunately, he didn't expire from it. "Are you questioning my ability to please a woman in bed?"

"No, you tool. I'm saying she deserves someone who'll share more than his body with her. She deserves someone who'll give her a piece of his heart. And we all know you gave yours away years ago."

For a moment, Doc said nothing. Then he shrugged. "From what I gather, she's not after a piece of my heart. She's after my d—"

"Not," Mason cut in, that single syllable heavy with barely controlled violence. "Another. Word."

Doc took a slow sip of his beer. After he swallowed—again, *slowly*—he said, "Why the hell do you care, man? You don't want her. So why not let someone else step up to the plate?"

"'Cause she's *Alex*!" Mason realized he was shouting when the people around them stopped their conversations to turn and stare. Clearing his throat, he added more calmly, "She's smart and sweet and…and…all things good. She needs someone who'll appreciate the gift she's offering."

"To hear her tell it, she doesn't see it as a gift. She sees it as a burden."

Mason didn't want to know the answer to his next question, but he heard himself asking anyway, "Did she proposition you?"

"Sure enough."

Once again, Mason was considering visiting violence upon the head of one of his closest friends. Red edged around his vision.

What the fuck was wrong with him?

Oh, right. Alex. Alex is what's wrong with me!

He would lose his mind if she kept going around offering up her virginity to every Tom, Dick, and Harry.

"But she didn't mean it," Doc added. "She's not really interested in an old warhorse like me."

Mason grimaced. "He says with false humility while the blond at the end of the bar tries to eat him alive with her eyes."

Doc's lips twitched, and he tipped his beer toward the blond in a little salute. Mason thought she might've orgasmed on the spot. Her lips fell open and her eyes went half-lidded.

Then Doc returned to the subject. "It's not like that between me and Alex."

"Coulda fooled me. I saw the way she ran to you in the parking lot."

"That's because I've become her touchstone when things are tough. I've been helping her work through some of her feelings from that night on Garden Key, some of the fears and worries she's had."

Mason felt something inside him shrivel up. He thought maybe it was his heart. "She has fears and worries? I–I didn't know."

"No shit, man. You've been doing your best to avoid her since then."

He had. Because she was so fucking tempting. Because he couldn't trust himself around her. But he should have known she'd need someone to confide in. Someone who could offer her a shoulder to lean on, to cry on.

That shoulder should've been his. *He* should've become her touchstone.

He'd been there, after all. On Garden Key. He'd seen and heard and suffered all the same things she had. Which meant he was in the unique position to commiserate, to comfort.

He tried to swallow down the guilt and self-recrimination, but they both stayed stuck in his throat. When the bartender came over to ask after his drink order, he waved the man away. He was too busy thinking to drink.

Thinking about Alex and all the ways he'd let her down. Wondering if there was something he could do to make it up to her.

"You need to talk to her." Doc cut into his thoughts.

"Not very good at that," Mason admitted miserably. "You're probably better when it comes to—"

"I'm not talking about what happened on Garden Key, dipshit." Doc's tone was exasperated. "She's already worked her way through most of that. I'm saying you need to talk to her about why you're holding yourself back from what she's offering. Admit what you're truly feeling. What you're truly afraid of."

"I *did*," Mason insisted. "Told her this morning on the catamaran that if we started up something, I probably wouldn't wanna stop."

Doc's eyes widened. "So you *do* want her?"

Want her? That was too tame a phrase. Mason didn't want Alex. He *craved* her.

All of her. Above him. Beneath him. Around him. Inside of him.

He craved her so much it terrified him. Especially because he couldn't have her. Or he knew he *shouldn't* have her.

He didn't say any of this aloud, however. What he said was, "What red-blooded man wouldn't?"

For a long time, Doc was quiet. Contemplative. But eventually he murmured, "So it's what happened with Sarah that's keeping you from taking another chance?"

"No." Mason shook his head. Then he reconsidered. "Maybe. Fuck, I dunno. I think it has more to do with the *other* shit in my life. The stuff that's changed me, hardened me."

Alex deserved a man who didn't need to sit with his back to the wall in a restaurant so he could watch the entrance without worrying about his six. She deserved someone who didn't feel naked without a weapon strapped to his body. She deserved someone who wasn't plagued by nightmares of the people he'd killed or the friends he'd lost.

She deserved *normal*.

Of their own accord, his fingers strayed to the tattoo on his arm. Doc saw the move and said softly, "We all have ghosts, you know. The trick is to let them haunt you and not possess you."

Mason snorted. "You been hanging around Wolf too long. Careful, or you'll be spouting Plato and Buddha next."

"The truth is the truth no matter who says it."

Mason let loose with an irritated exhale. He'd had about all of Doc's Mr. Miyagi he could stand. "Can you just sit there and be quiet so I can try to figure out a way to like you again?"

Doc clutched his heart. "You wound me, sir. Oh, how you wound me."

"I'm considering it," Mason mumbled, a million and one thoughts bouncing around in his head like the pinball machines at the Boston Bowl in Dorchester.

Was Doc right? *Should* he go talk to Alex again? Try to better explain his position?

"I think my work here is done." Doc stood. "Now, I need to go see a woman about a horse."

With that, Doc headed in the blond's direction, leaving Mason to stew in his own uncomfortable juices.

10:48 p.m.

Alex stared at her carton of french fries, trying to decide if there was a way to regain her appetite before they got soggy, when a hard knock sounded at her door.

Oh, thank goodness.

It was Doc coming to see if she was okay.

She *wasn't*. Not by a long shot if her lack of hunger pangs were anything to go by.

She couldn't decide what was making her more nauseous. That awful run-in with Mason at the bar when she'd taken the low road and insulted him instead of just being honest and explaining how he'd hurt her and how he should've told her the truth from the beginning? Or the images of the morning that'd instantly assaulted her the moment she stepped into the cold, dark, far-too-big-and-empty hotel room?

At some point over the past few months, she'd stopped being good at being alone. She'd grown accustomed to her little daybed on the screened-in porch of the Wayfarer Island beach house. People coming and going. Meat barking. Li'l Bastard—their resident rooster—crowing. And Uncle John blaring Jimmy Buffett or Bob Marley from his eighties-style boom box.

Once upon a time, silence and solitude had brought

her comfort. Now they only made her nervous. Twitchy. She *liked* being part of a big, rambunctious, noisy family.

Securely cinching her robe, she threw open the door with a gushing "How do you always know when I need—" As soon as she saw who was standing in the hall, the last word came out accusatory. "*You!*"

Her heart gave a little jolt at the sight of Mason. She reminded the recalcitrant organ he was currently persona non grata.

For a full tèn-second count, he stared at her with those damned eyes of his that were the clearest, richest blue. Eyes ringed by lashes so thick and dark they made him look like he was wearing mascara and—

"Did you need something?" She blank-slated her expression and wasn't surprised when his reply was one of his patented grunts. "Yes." She nodded as if he'd spoken actual words. "Very articulate. Now, if there's nothing else, I'm going to enjoy my cheeseburger before it gets cold."

She went to shut the door, but was thwarted when he smacked his palm against the wood. She gave him another ten-second count—okay, so this one was probably closer to five seconds—before sighing with exasperation.

"You understand that whole 'Silence is golden' thing doesn't apply to a woman who has been lied to, shot at, and questioned for hours in a hot tin-can of a room, right?" she asked tiredly. "Just say whatever it is you came to say so I can eat my food and go to bed."

His brow wrinkled, which drew her attention to the hair that'd flopped over his forehead. It was long and wavy, in need of a cut. The little curls that wrapped around the tops of his ears seemed to be shouting out an invitation to touch.

She fisted her hands inside the pockets of her robe.

"For the love of living!" she exclaimed when he continued to stand there, all big and bulky and disturbingly male.

And mute! Let's not forget the mute part!

A flicker of doubt crossed his eyes. But it was quickly replaced with steely determination. "Came to apologize," he mumbled.

"Huh?" She cupped her hand around her ear, the devil in her fiendishly delighting in making him repeat himself.

"I *said*," he ground out from between clenched teeth, "I came to apologize."

"Oh." She nodded. "That's what I thought you said. But I couldn't be sure I wasn't suffering déjà vu. Didn't we do this on the catamaran? And has no one ever told you the way to keep from having to apologize to someone over and over again is to stop doing things you need to apologize for? Now, thank you for saying you're sorry. *Again.* I accept. Good night."

"Wait!" He pushed the door wide. "Dontcha wanna know what I came to apologize for?" As a fast talker herself, she appreciated the swiftness with which he spoke. But unlike her, he accomplished the feat by leaving out consonants. *Want to* became *wanna. How are you* became *hahwahya*. It was a winsome trait.

As if he needs more of those, she thought testily.

"I assumed it was a blanket apology for all your lies

and for having spent the last few weeks making a complete and utter fool of me," she told him with a lift of her chin.

"Never meant to make a fool of you. I just…" He blinked, and a scowl once again possessed his face. "Wait. What lies?"

"Oh, I don't know." She tapped her lips sarcastically. "I suppose number one"—she held up a finger—"would be when you told me the reason you wouldn't sleep with me was because you'd convinced yourself, despite my many assurances otherwise, that I was after a couple of 'I do's.' Two"—a second finger joined the first—"would be when you changed your story and said the *real* reason you wouldn't sleep with me was because you were afraid if you did, you might not want to stop. That was my favorite, by the way, because I almost fell for it. And three"— now three fingers were standing at attention like the spines of books on a library shelf—"would be when you decided to keep the lovely Donna, the *real* reason behind your rejections, a secret."

"Hang on a frickin' minute." Two red patches stained his cheekbones. "You may be right about that first thing. I *was* using that bullshit about husband hunting as an excuse. But what I said on the catamaran was true. And Donna? Never so much as mentioned her name, so how could I lie about—"

"A lie by omission is still a lie." Her gaze was cool as she gave him the once-over. "And that's the gospel according to Alex."

For a moment, she thought he would argue, and she

watched in fascination as a muscle twitched beside his right eye.

He was nearing his limit. But his limit of what? Patience? Penitence? His ability to withstand any more slices from her glib tongue before responding in kind?

Lordy, how she'd love to see him lose that stony composure. But to her annoyance, he took a deep breath, wiped his expression clean, and said, "Didn't say anything about Donna 'cause there's nothing to say. We're friends." Her disbelief must've showed on her face. He quickly added, "What I mean is, we aren't exclusive."

She hadn't realized there was a vise around her heart until his words loosened it. It took everything she had to keep the relief from showing on her face. "Fine. Good. Whatever. Now…" She made a shooing motion with her fingers.

"Look"—he ran an agitated hand through his hair—"can I come in? Standing out here in this fucking hall makes me feel like a naked penis at a petting zoo." *A nekkid penis atta pettin zoo.*

His accent, combined with the imagery, tickled her funny bone. But through sheer force of will, she managed to keep a grin from tilting her lips. With a put-upon sigh, she stepped aside and motioned for him to enter.

He started forward with steps that were…not hesitant. But they weren't exactly determined either. It was as if, now that he had her permission, he was having second thoughts.

What? she wondered acerbically. *Does he think I'll tackle him to the floor and have my way with him?*

Come to think of it, the idea had merit.

After closing the door, she watched him stop at the foot of the bed, his stance uncomfortable. Then he moved on to the desk. Placing a hand on the back of the chair, he asked, "Do you mind?"

"Be my guest." She waved magnanimously, perching on the edge of the mattress and crossing her legs.

She realized her robe had gaped open over her thighs when, after settling his bulk into the rolling chair, his gaze latched onto her bare legs. That muscle beside his right eye went to town again. She considered leaving the robe exactly as it was. It obviously made him uncomfortable. And she figured, rather uncharitably, he was due a little of that given how uncomfortable *he'd* made *her* earlier.

Unfortunately, his distraction with her legs made *her* distracted too. And more than a little breathless. Which most decidedly would *not* do.

After she covered her legs, he seemed to relax. His big shoulders dropped a full three inches. His fingers loosened on the arms of the chair.

She took a moment to study his hands. They were broad and tanned, knobby-knuckled and sporting more than a few scars. A working man's hands. A fighting man's hands. Hands she'd dreamed of nearly every night for the last few months.

Hands that'd been around Donna's waist barely two hours ago.

She suddenly had the overwhelming desire—nay, it was a *need*—to strangle him.

Homicide is legal in the Keys, isn't it? No? Well, it should be.

He finally opened his mouth. But he proved ever vexing when his words weren't anything she expected to hear. "You thought it was Doc at your door, didn't you?"

Her brow furrowed. "Yeah. So?"

He rubbed a hand over his face, looking so tired her traitorous heart softened toward him. Of their own accord, her eyes roamed to the bandage beneath his T-shirt.

She would *not* give him the upper hand by asking how he was feeling. She would *not*.

"How are you feeling?" *Damn it!*

"Huh?" He saw the direction of her gaze, and glanced down. "Oh. You know. Feels like I got stabbed. But that's not why I'm here. Alex, look. Doc…he…uh…told me you been having some trouble since that night on Garden Key. I shoulda known. I shoulda—"

"*That's* what you came to apologize for?" she asked incredulously.

"Partly." His heavy-lidded gaze would've had her swooning under other circumstances. But disbelief made her immune to his usual charms.

Partly? Right. Well, she supposed she was *partly* placated.

"What happened on Garden Key wasn't your fault," she told him, refraining from adding *But there are a lot of other things that* are!

"Shoulda known you'd have trouble," he insisted.

"Like I said. Not your fault. So if we're done here…" She let the sentence hang. "It's been a day."

She expected him to make his exit, but instead he regarded her french fries, which sat on the desk next to her cheeseburger. If her eyes weren't mistaken, his fingers twitched in their direction.

"Touch one and you're dead," she warned him. "I need every bit of grease in those suckers to soak up the bourbon in my belly."

And there it was again. That leg-melting smile of his.

Thank goodness I'm sitting down.

But then his expression sobered and he stared at her with startling frankness. "You got no idea what it's like having sex with someone. Especially if it's good sex. And us?" He flicked a thick finger back and forth between them. "It'd be good, Alex. It'd be really good."

H-h-holy crap.

The bed tried to buck her off. The only thing that kept her seated was the death grip she had on the comforter.

"Good sex sends a rush of hormones through your body," he continued, oblivious to the blood pounding in her ears. "If you're not experienced, it's easy to get hooked on that high. It's easy to..." He cleared his voice. "To fall in love. And since we already like each other—"

"We do?" The two words croaked from her constricted throat. She couldn't see her reflection in the mirror above the desk, but she was sure her eyes bugged from her head.

"Don't we?" He frowned. "Guess I shouldn't speak for you. Can only speak for myself. And I'm telling you, I like you. So, so much. Fuck, I probably like you more than anyone I know."

Alex wanted to say something witty. Or maybe something seductive. But her sharp mind failed her. And she suspected that was due to lack of oxygen.

Chapter 13

MASON WAS A FIRM BELIEVER THAT SOME THINGS—fuck it, *most* things—were better left unsaid.

But all of his partial explanations for declining Alex's offer had only hurt and confused her. So he'd decided to come clean with as much of the truth as he could.

For one thing, she deserved it. For another thing, sometimes a Hail Mary was the only Mary a guy had left. And he didn't think he could live with himself if he saw another flicker of pain cross her eyes and knew he was the cause of it.

He wasn't sure what he expected her response to his confession to be, but it certainly wasn't the slamming of her eyebrows over her nose. She said something that sounded a lot like "Completely, totally, utterly vexing."

"Huh?" He sat forward, clasping his hands tightly between his knees to keep from touching her legs.

Her robe had fallen open again, revealing inch upon inch of silky, soft skin. It was taking everything he had not to stare. And drool. If he touched, there would be no hope for him.

She blew out a breath, and he would swear he felt it moving over his body. Just like that he was hard.

Alex had done that to him from the start. Turned him

into a fourteen-year-old boy with no control over what happened in his pants.

"You make it impossible to stay mad at you," she grumbled, but he was pleased to note her normal expression, one of good humor, played around the edges of her face.

"Is that a bad thing?"

"*Yes!*" She tossed exasperated hands in the air. "I *want* to be mad at you."

He jerked back his chin. "Why?"

"Because..." She started and stopped and tried again. "Because..." This time when she stopped, she scrunched up her nose in frustration. Finally, she staunchly declared, "Because!"

"Right." He used her own words against her. "Very articulate."

She blinked and he was sorely tempted to remove her glasses so he could stare into her eyes until...well, until he got tired of it, which he thought might be never. "Did you just make a joke?"

He shrugged. "Two in one day. Must be some sorta record."

"Oh my god. A joke followed by sarcasm." A delicate hand landed on her chest. "Who are you? And what have you done with the real Mason?"

His lips twitched. Sparring with Alex always made him a bit giddy. "So glad you're enjoying yourself at my expense."

"Is it just my imagination, or have you decided to pull the stick from your ass?"

"Maybe." He waited a tick before adding, "So I can beat you with it."

"Three! *Three* jokes in a day!" She laughed, and it was a sweet, tinkling sound that burrowed under his skin. Her smile was enchanting and so guileless. Just like the woman herself.

What must it be like to live life so free and open? To have nothing to hide? To not couch every word or worry about every move for fear one slip would tell the world just how abnormal you really were?

"Let me see if I have this straight," she said. "You think if we sleep together, it'll be so good we'll be flooded with hormones. Which will either (a) have you falling in love with me." Her quirked brow could only be described as coquettish. "An outcome I could definitely see. Because even though I haven't done it before, I've been studying up. I think, given a little practice, I can master most of the skills. You'd be putty in my hands."

He refused to let his mind dwell on what she meant by *studying up.*

Or at least he *tried* not to let his mind dwell.

Against his will, images of her flipping through the pages of a sexy novel or glued to a screen watching X-rated videos flashed through his head.

Putty? Shhyeah. If by "putty" she means "painfully, achingly hard."

"*Or* (b) it'll have *me* falling in love with *you*," she continued, oblivious to his brain having spontaneously exploded to leak gray matter from his ears. "Which is probably a little *less* likely. Because while I think you're an exquisite example of male prowess, you talk too little. You're alone too much. And you have the most annoying habit of leaving dental floss half-dangling out of the bathroom trash can. I mean, seriously? Why can't you get the whole piece of string in?"

One of the many drawbacks of living at the beach house was there were only two bathrooms. Privacy wasn't a concept anyone on Wayfarer Island held dear. At least not if they wanted to keep their sanity.

Mason opened his mouth to point out that good oral hygiene should be applauded, not berated. But she went on before he could get a word in.

"But regardless of who falls in love with whom, I'm assuming your contention is that the other party will end up hurt. And you'd rather head that eventuality off at the pass. However, what you've failed to account for is what would happen if we fell in love with *each other*."

Someone shot a cannonball into his throat. The sucker lodged directly beneath his Adam's apple, so his voice was barely a whisper. "That'd be the worst outcome of all."

She blinked in confusion.

"Then we'd *both* end up hurt," he explained.

For a couple of seconds, she said nothing. Then she shook her head like Meat shaking off water after having gone in for his daily dose of seaweed. The stupid mutt loved to eat the stuff. Then he liked to barf it back up on the wooden floorboards of the porch.

"Sorry." Her voice was flat. "Are you speaking Martian? Nothing about that makes any sense. Why would we both end up hurt if we loved each other?"

He dropped his eyes to his clasped hands. They were hard and scarred, proof of the life he'd lived. The life that'd made him what he was. *Who* he was.

"You wanna get married someday?" he asked gently. "You wanna have kids and make a family and do that whole American pie thing?"

She didn't answer immediately, forcing him to lift his gaze to her face. He wouldn't have thought it possible, but she was even more beautiful in the glow of the bedside lamps. They caught the honey-blond strands in her hair and made them shine like spun gold.

"I'm a little leery of the institution, if you want the truth," she admitted. "But I think a lot of modern women are. I read an article recently that attributed the decline in the marriage rate to the uptick of women entering the workforce, but still being restricted by traditional gender roles. Basically, the author's point was not only are women supposed to bring home the bacon, but they're also supposed to fry it up, get the kids ready for bed, and make sure the laundry is folded." She lifted a finger. "*Another* article I read—"

Mason watched the play of emotions over her face as she delved into the subject. Her eyes were bright. Her cheeks flushed a lovely pink. And her Kewpie-doll mouth wrapped itself around the words.

When he realized he'd stopped listening, he gave himself a mental slap and once more attended to her monologue.

"Modern woman is the most dissatisfied woman in history. But that's not to say I don't want a life partner.

I'm a romantic at heart. I like the idea of finding some-one who'll wake up and choose me every day. Someone I'll wake up and choose every day. But I don't think that requires a legal document."

·He opened his mouth to press home his point, but she lifted her finger again and kept at it.

"Although, there *are* financial incentives to making it legal. Tax benefits and whatnot. Did you know it behooves couples to have large income disparities? The spouse making less money can pull the spouse making more money into a lower tax bracket. And it certainly benefits them to have dependents. Which brings me around to the second part of your question. Kids? I think I want some someday. Or maybe just one." She pushed her glasses higher on the bridge of her nose. "The birth rate is declining right along with the marriage rate. People still use that whole two-point-three statistic when they're talking about the American family. But as of 2018, that number has decreased to one-point-eight." She cocked her head. "What are you smiling at?"

"You," he admitted. "Not sure I ever heard someone say that many words without taking a breath."

She grimaced. "Yes. A boy in high school used to call me Gabby McGabberson. Which I'm pretty sure he meant to be an insult. However!" Up went her finger for the third time. "The joke was on him. *His* name was Richard Johnson."

When Mason frowned, she explained. "Dick Johnson? He was a penis no matter which way you sliced him."

A wicked little smile pulled her lips tight, and Mason

felt his own twitching in response. Then he cleared his throat, determined to circle back around to the subject.

"I'll never have a wife or a life partner or a family." He watched unhappily as her smile faded and her eyes darkened.

For a long moment she said nothing. Finally, her voice too soft, she murmured, "Your first marriage really did a number on you, huh?"

His tone was dark when he told her, "This has nothing to do with Sarah. I promise you that." *After all,* he thought, *it wasn't Sarah's fault I became who I am.* "Can't you and I agree to be friends and leave it at that?"

"Friends like you and Donna are friends?"

The question—and the imagery that came with it—caused renewed movement behind his fly. *Don't get a boner. Don't get a boner.*

He opened his mouth, but she must've read the look on his face. Before he could say anything, she blurted out, "Okay, I'll agree to be friends, just friends, if you'll agree to do one of the following two things."

Girding himself, he grunted for her to continue.

"Option one"—up went her finger again; Alex talked with her hands so much he was surprised he didn't get motion sickness watching them—"you tell me *why* you don't want to get remarried or have a family."

"What's the other option?" he asked, embarrassed to admit that his teammates seemed to have no problem going from SEALs to civilians, but he was forever changed by his life in the navy.

It was an innate weakness in him. A deficiency. One he'd just as soon keep to himself.

"Option two." Up went a second finger. In that moment, with her hair falling around her shoulders, and the breeze from the open window playing with the ends of her curls, she'd never looked more tempting. "Kiss me."

"What?" he choked. "Why?"

"Because you said you and Donna aren't exclusive and I—"

He shook his head, cutting her off. "Never mind. Doesn't matter. The answer is no."

"Which means you've chosen option one. So spill."

He felt trapped. Desperate. There had to be a third option, but for the life of him, he couldn't think of it. She turned his brain to mush.

"Why would you wanna kiss me?" His voice was so low and harsh it sounded like someone stood on his throat. He *felt* like someone stood on his throat.

"I want to do a lot *more* than kiss you. But I think a kiss is a good compromise. Neither of us will get everything we're after, but both of us will get something we want. I'll get to see what it's like to taste you, which I've been wanting to do since day one. And afterward, you'll go on your merry way and I'll never proposition you again."

He shook his head the whole time she was talking. Now, he put words to the gesture. Granted, they weren't terribly intelligible words. But they were words. And that was saying something considering...she wanted to *taste* him?

For fuck's sake! Who says stuff like that?

Alex.

Alex, that's who.

"No. That's just… I just… I can't," he managed.

She tilted her head. It made one long curl come to rest in the dark hollow between her robe's lapels. "So were you lying when you said you thought I was off-the-charts fuckable? If you don't like me like that, if you don't *want* me like that, I wish you'd—"

"I *like* you like that, Alex!" he roared so she'd shut up. Her words were coming so hard and fast he could. Not. *Think.*

She blinked. "You do?"

"*Yes.*"

She broke into a happy dance while sitting on the end of the bed. An actual *happy dance.* And all her gyrating and twisting and finger-gun shooting caused her robe to fall open above the belt.

He was suddenly witness to the creamy inner curves of her breasts and an expanse of lickable skin that stretched from her neck all the way down to her navel.

Is she naked *under there?*

It was a good thing he was still seated. Otherwise, his legs would've given out on him and his ass would've been on the floor.

From somewhere, he wasn't sure where, he found the strength to say, "Stop it." When she didn't, he hitched his chin toward her gaping robe and added breathlessly, "If you don't stop, you'll be stark naked in two seconds."

Not that he would mind.

Or maybe he would. Because how the *hell* would he ever withstand her advances if she was wearing nothing but God's pajamas?

"What?" She glanced down. "Oh!" Blushing slightly, she pulled the halves of her robe together and tugged the belt tight.

He was able to breathe again. There was no hope for his raging hard-on, however. The thing had a mind of its own, and that mind kept replaying the sight of all that skin and that exquisite little belly button that was a perfect oval and just the right size for the tip of a man's tongue.

She shot one of her finger guns at his nose and grinned in triumph. "To steal a line from Gracie Hart, Sandra Bullock's character in *Miss Congeniality*, 'You think I'm gorgeous. You want to kiss me. You want to hug me. You want to—'"

Jesus H. Christ. This was his greatest fantasy and biggest nightmare rolled into one. Alex, being all demanding and adorable. Him, knowing he had to resist her but not having the first clue how he was supposed to accomplish that.

"Anyone ever told you you're forthright to a fault?" he wheezed, his heart trying its best to beat its way out of his chest. Undoubtedly in a bid to get closer to her.

"Sure." She shrugged unconcernedly. "All the time. But I take issue with it because how can forthrightness ever be considered a fault?"

He pinned his hardest scowl on her and pushed up from the desk chair. He'd found it! Option three! "Gotta go."

Unfortunately, his injury slowed him down and Alex beat him to the door. She stood with her back against it, her arms and legs spread wide, barring his exit.

He glanced longingly out the window, wondering how badly he'd hurt himself if he jumped.

Broken ankle or leg at the worst. It might be worth it.

"You're hopeless." He ran an agitated hand through his hair.

"Nope." She shook her head. "Shameless, maybe. But never hopeless. Now, choose. Option one or option two?"

"You got no idea the position you're putting me in," he mumbled.

"Sure I do. If I can't put you in the missionary position, then I'll settle for this one. Option one or option two?"

Something broke inside him. His restraint? Certainly. His ability to think? Most definitely.

With a growl of…what? Impatience? Defeat? Who the fuck knew?…he stomped toward her. As he closed the distance, she became his entire world. Or maybe she'd been that since the moment she landed on Wayfarer Island.

Then he was on her.

She squealed slightly when, with a hand at her waist, he pushed her hard against the door. Stepping close, he eliminated any space between their bodies.

Her eyes rounded when she felt him hard and throbbing against her belly. Her mouth fell open, and he took advantage of her unwitting invitation.

When his lips landed on hers, he wasn't gentle. He wasn't rough either. It was more like he was a starving man. Devouring her. Consuming her.

He thought perhaps his abruptness, his lack of finesse, would frightened her. Quite the contrary. Her hands speared into his hair. Her tongue darted into his mouth. And the most erotic-sounding little moan he'd ever heard issued from the back of her throat.

She tasted like something he'd been missing his whole life but hadn't known it until right that very second. She smelled like sincerity itself, so clean and fresh.

Never dreamed it could be like this, he thought a little desperately.

But that was a lie. He'd dreamed. He'd dreamed every damn night. Except not one of those dreams had come close to this. The reality of her. The reality of *them*.

She kissed stardust into his mouth. It sparkled. It burned. He wasn't sure if she flew him to heaven or tossed him into hell.

He *was* sure that as the moment stretched out, as her unrestrained fingers and tongue and hips moved against him, desire stole away what little control he had.

He'd come to her room to put an end to the idea of them sharing anything more than friendship. But what was he doing instead?

He was kissing her.

And just as he'd feared, now that he'd started, he couldn't make himself stop.

In the end, he thought, *maybe it was inevitable.*

Chapter 14

MASON'S LIPS WERE LIKE THE REST OF HIM. A dichotomy. Both soft and strong. Tender and tough. And he used them so expertly, Alex ached in a way she never had before.

This wasn't like when she was reading a romance novel or watching a rom-com and felt a squeezing sensation low in her belly. Heck, it wasn't even like when she was studying up using adult websites and felt beads of sweat form on her brow.

The squeezing sensation was throughout her entire body. Every inch of her skin was dewed.

She hadn't expected him to kiss her. In fact, she would've put down ten-to-one odds he'd choose to come clean about why he was so adamant he would never marry or have a family.

She wasn't accustomed to being wrong. But she couldn't honestly say she was upset at having been wrong about this. Maybe she would be later. Maybe after he left her and she was forced to stop her pursuit of him, she'd wish he'd explained himself instead.

Right now, though? All she could think about was the here. The now. And the low, hungry animal noise that sounded at the back of his throat.

"Mason," she groaned when he let her up for air. "Please."

She wasn't sure what she begged for. Or maybe she *was*. Maybe she begged him not to stop. Never to stop.

It felt so good. Too good. She wanted to get away and get closer at the same time. She wanted blessed relief and for the delicious ache to last forever.

God, he smelled right. Felt right. *Tasted* right. It was a thing her body had known long before her head caught up.

"Alex." Her name was a growl. "You taste so fucking good."

As if to prove his point, his lips skimmed her jaw and then latched onto her earlobe. His mouth was hot. His tongue was wet. When he sucked on her lobe, she would swear she felt the sensation much lower in her body.

Then his lips were on her throat, covering her pulse point.

Could he feel her heart racing? Could he sense the heat of her blood?

Her response was unintelligible, even to her own ears. Her words simply syllables of sensation. Syllables of need.

"Alex," he said again, shoving her robe down over one shoulder so his mouth could continue its journey south.

"Mason," she moaned again. Her voice dazed and dreamy. Not her own at all. "Please."

This time she knew what she begged for. She begged for help with the sharp ache between her legs. She begged for the kind of pleasure she'd only ever dreamed of.

Maybe it was his vast experience, or maybe it was the

way she writhed against him, her hips thrusting, seeking the smallest amount of friction, but whatever the reason, he knew. He knew what she needed and he obliged, the magnificent, *marvelous* man.

Nudging her knees apart, he found the slit in her robe and pressed his thigh high and tight against the junction of her legs.

She gasped at first contact. The material of his swim trunks wasn't as rough as she would've liked. But she was so worked up, she knew it would do the trick.

Pulling his mouth back to hers, she welcomed the silky, hot glide of his tongue and reveled when he groaned, low and deep. One of his hands splayed wide over her hip, assisting her in her subtle but desperate thrusts against his leg.

She ground hard, the material of his trunks growing wet with her desire. Then the material pushed up and it was nothing but skin on skin. Hers was swollen and slick. His was hot and hairy. And *this!* This was the kind of friction she needed.

Just like that, she was close. She could feel it in her toes. Taste it on the tip of her tongue. That tingling, sparkling precursor to release.

"Fuck me, you're wet," he growled against her lips. "And hot." His accent made the last word sound like *hawt*.

She could no longer speak. She'd been reduced to little mewling sounds as her body wound tighter and tighter. Higher and higher. As she squeezed her eyes shut and gave herself up to that singular sort of pleasure she'd only ever experienced alone.

This was so much better. Because she was sharing it with someone she cared about. Someone who knew how to kiss her. Knew how to touch her. Knew just what she needed.

She felt the instant he bared her right breast. The cool air in the room made her nipple furl so tightly, she hissed at the pleasure-pain of it.

"You're beautiful, Alexandra." There was reverence in his voice.

Without warning, he bent and sucked her nipple into the heated haven that was his mouth.

That was all it took.

A nuclear bomb went off inside her. She contracted. She expanded. She burned red hot and yet goose bumps erupted over her skin.

Pulsing white lights flashed behind her squeezed-tight eyelids. They quickly turned into multicolored fireworks that flowered and sparked as wave after wave of pleasure washed through her. Washed over her. Lifting her up and pushing her down in an ever-slowing rhythm.

And then…it was over.

Not all of a sudden. But gradually her body became her own.

She could breathe.

She could think.

She could *see*.

When she opened her eyes, it was to find Mason's gaze latched onto her face, his baby blues blazing with unquenched desire. The insistent pulse of him against her hip was proof positive she was the only one to have floated upon the blessed tides of release.

Undoubtedly, that was because she was new at this. She'd yet to learn how to stave off the inevitable.

She couldn't make herself regret it, though. Especially because she was still a little drunk from it. Her bones liquid. Her brain a snarl of fried synapses. Her womb a shivery mass of remembered bliss.

In her drunkenness, she decided the world looked different from her current position, loomed over, caged by, overwhelmed with a man who was so close she felt as if they might be sharing the same skin. It was darker there. More mysterious. And yet more exiting.

Strangely enough, instead of feeling vulnerable, she felt powerful. Powerful because he wanted her.

As he held her gaze with lethal steadiness, a muscle twitched beside his eye, and his voice was hoarse when he said, "You came."

"Yeah. Uh." She made a face. "That probably screamed virgin, huh? I probably wasn't supposed to do that. But I can assure you, I'm a quick learner. With a little practice, I know I'll be able to hold off until—"

"For fuck's sake, Alex. Be quiet."

Her jaw snapped shut so quickly her teeth clacked together. She searched his eyes, looking for... She wasn't exactly sure what.

When he pulled away an inch, it felt like a mile. Desperation had her grabbing his hand.

She recognized a flight risk when it was staring at her. Especially *this* flight risk whose expression was grim and whose lips—those wonderful lips that'd been taking her to the highest peaks such a short time ago—were now set in a straight line.

His breaths came hard and fast. If he clenched his jaw any harder, she feared his molars might shatter.

"Mason?" She placed a gentle hand on his shoulder, feeling the muscles tense at her touch. "Should I not have—"

"Hush, woman." He pressed a finger over her lips. She was tempted to kiss it, but didn't know if he'd welcome the gesture.

"You were..." His voice was guttural. She'd never really thought about what *guttural* sounded like. But now she knew it was a mix between a groan and a growl. It was low, rough words gritted out between clenched teeth. "You were the most beautiful fucking thing I've ever seen. But you needa be quiet now. And stay very still so I can catch my breath. So I can *think*. So I don't rip that fucking robe off and—"

Mention of the robe had his gaze sliding south. He squeezed his eyes shut and cursed a blue streak so hot and filthy it blistered Alex's ears.

When she glanced down, she saw her breast was still exposed. Not only was her nipple hard, but it was wet and shiny from his mouth. A new warmth spread through her belly.

"So you don't rip my fucking robe off and *what*, Mason?"

Whoa. Was that low, sultry, come-and-get-me-big-boy voice really hers? If so, she was going to like postorgasm Alex. Postorgasm Alex sounded like a temptress from those old black-and-white films.

His eyes blinked open, and he quickly pulled her robe back onto her shoulder. She couldn't tell if regret or relief flashed across his face once her breast was covered.

"And toss you onto that bed and fuck you 'til you scream," he snarled.

She knew he was trying to shock her. Good thing she didn't shock easily.

In fact, his words titillated her. Excited her. Those telltale prickles of arousal were making very specific places on her body tingle anew.

"Please explain to me again *why* I wouldn't want you to do that?" She cocked her head, gratified when his eyes followed one curl as it slipped over her shoulder and fell into the valley between her breasts.

"Fuckin' A, Alex!"

He wrenched out of her grasp so quickly she stumbled. Chills erupted up her arms. But they weren't the good kind of chills, the ones brought on by intense pleasure. These were the kind of chills that occurred when the most delightful heat source she'd ever encountered suddenly put five feet of distance between them.

"Gotta go," he declared with an adamant dip of his square jaw.

"Wait." She crossed her arms in an attempt to hold in some of his heat. "Wha—"

That's all she managed before he picked her up and set her aside as if she weighed no more than one of her favorite history books. He threw open the door and was through it before she could blink.

Running into the hall, she whispered his name. Not loud enough for him to hear. But somehow he did.

He swung around and was back to her in three determined strides. Gazing up into his face, she felt her bottom lip tremble. She hated it for doing that.

She *also* hated that she was the reason for the tortured look on his face.

What have I done? she thought desperately. Because in all the time she'd known him, she'd never known him to look like *this*. The stark pain in his face found an echo in her heart.

He'd kissed her. She'd come. And now he regretted the whole thing.

She should never have insisted on that kiss, even if she *had* assumed he would choose confessing instead. In fact, she'd thought it the perfect plan. A way to force him to reveal a bit of the mystery that was Mason McCarthy.

But apparently, he was willing to do almost anything to keep from exposing the truths about himself.

"I'm sorry," she whispered.

"No." He shook his head. "*I'm* sorry. I'm sorry I can't be what you want me to be. And I'm sorry I can't do what you want me to do."

Then, with one last regretful look, he turned on his heel and disappeared down the hall.

Alex's heart grew so heavy she was surprised it didn't sink down to her soles and bust a hole through the floor. She had no idea how long she stood there. It could've been ten seconds or ten minutes. But eventually, she turned and slunk back into her empty hotel room.

She'd just sat down at the desk, watching the grease from her burger congeal into an unappetizing blob on the wax paper, when a hard knock sounded at the door.

She was across the room in a flash. A hiccup of happiness lodged in her throat, because... *He came back!*

His name was on her lips when she threw the door wide. But her smile melted when, instead of Mason, she saw Romeo standing on the threshold.

"Mason told me you could use a little company tonight, eh?" His East LA accent sounded thicker than usual.

She blinked in astonishment. Mason sent *Romeo* to her? To do...*what*? Finish the job he started?

"Why are you looking at me like that?" Romeo frowned. "Do I have something stuck in my teeth?" He pulled back his lips, revealing a set of straight white chompers.

"Sorry." Alex shook her head, trying to sound calm even though her insides roiled. "Uh, thanks for offering to, uh, step in. But I'll pass for now. No offense to you," she was quick to add. "Honestly, you're probably the smarter choice. But I kind of had my head and maybe even my heart set on something else, and now I need time to regroup."

The look on Romeo's face said she'd just sprouted a third ear on her forehead. "What are you talking about? Do you want Meat for the night or not?"

Meat, who must've been sitting between Romeo's feet all along, licked his underbite and let out a little *woof*.

"Meatball!" she cried, dropping to her knees so she could bury her face in the bulldog's copious wrinkles.

He smelled like he'd gotten into spoiled vegetables, but she didn't care. She was so glad for his warmth and his wiggles and his wet kisses.

"I'll take that as a yes." Romeo turned down the hall. Before he rounded the corner, he threw a "G'night, Alex!" over his shoulder.

"Good night, Romeo!" she called back. But as soon as he was gone, she sighed and whispered, "Oh, Mason."

Standing and holding the door wide to allow Meat to waddle inside her hotel room, she thought, *Who can resist a man who sends his dog to comfort a woman in need?*

Certainly not me.

Chapter 15

11:48 p.m.

"IT'S WEIRD," ROMEO SAID, STANDING IN THE DOORWAY to the hotel bathroom in nothing but a pair of red boxer briefs with pink hearts on them. He towel-dried his hair.

"What's weird?" Wolf asked from his squatted position in front of their room's mini fridge. He contemplated the selection of beers inside, but after glancing at the little card listing the prices and discovering that twelve ounces of domestic brew was coming in at a cool fifteen bucks, he slammed the door closed. "Highway robbery," he muttered.

"I always thought I'd die a SEAL." Romeo dropped his wet towel onto the floor. "But in the shower just now, it occurred to me I might live to a ripe old age and die of some horrible wasting disease." He shuddered. "The horror, man. Think I prefer a bullet, eh?"

"I usually sing when I'm in the shower," Wolf told him dryly. "Keeps me from thinkin' too much. You might give it a try next time."

Former fighting men generally came in two categories. Those who spent an inordinate amount of time alone with their thoughts. Like Mason. And those who avoided time alone with their thoughts, because chances were their minds would go to places and people better left dead and buried.

Wolf endeavored to be part of that second group. Unlike some of the others who had never hoped to live long enough to see a civilian life, he'd *always* wanted a chance at something beyond the navy. A chance to raise a family. To build something he could call his own.

"I'm serious," Romeo insisted. "Have you thought about how you'd like it all to end?"

"Sure." Wolf pushed to his feet and took a seat on one of the two queen-size beds. "Peacefully. In my sleep. Like most folks, I reckon."

"Not me, man." Romeo shook his head. "I want Alicia Vikander to choke me out with her thighs."

Before Wolf could do more than snort, a soft knock sounded at the door.

"If that's Mason with another errand, I might have to pull his lungs out through his nose," Romeo grumbled. "What's so hard about taking Meat to Alex that he couldn't do it himself?"

"Probably didn't trust himself to be that close to her and a hotel bed," Wolf speculated.

Romeo placed a finger beside his nose and then pointed it at Wolf.

Bang! Bang! Bang!

Whoever was on the other side of the door had lost their patience.

"Yeah! All right, already!" Romeo called, throwing open the door.

When Wolf saw who was standing on the other side, he jumped from the bed so quickly he got dizzy.

Catching sight of Chrissy was always a gut punch.

Catching sight of her dressed in a hotel robe, fresh from a shower with her long, blond hair falling around her shoulders in damp waves, nearly had him taking a knee.

He'd always been a sucker for a woman in her natural state. No perfume. No hair gel. No makeup. Just clean skin and a smile.

Although Chrissy was missing the latter. In fact, her mouth hung open as her eyes set out on a journey down the length of Romeo's nearly naked body.

"Take your time," Romeo had the audacity to drawl, crossing his arms and leaning lazily against the doorjamb. "I know there's a lot to take in."

Wolf wasn't the jealous sort, but he had the sudden urge to wrap his hands around Romeo's throat and squeeze until the man's pretty little eyes popped right out of his pretty little head. That he was able to refrain from doing exactly that surely had him in the running for sainthood.

Chrissy blinked before glancing over Romeo's shoulder to spy Wolf. He offered her a smile she didn't return. Instead, she said unsteadily, "I…uh…I…" Stopping to gather herself, she lifted her chin and tried again. "I don't want to sleep alone tonight."

He'd been wrong before about that whole nearly taking a knee thing. *Now* he was nearly taking a knee.

"Ah, sweetheart." Romeo's voice dropped low. His accent thickened. "Thought you'd never ask."

Before Wolf could think, he was across the room. He bent to grab the corner of the wet towel Romeo stood on, and yanked it with all his might.

Romeo went down in a slew of curse words, arms flailing comically along the way. Wolf barely saw him hit the tiles before he stole Romeo's spot in the doorway.

"*Wolf!*" Chrissy's eyes rounded as she craned her neck to check on Romeo. "Why in heaven's name did you do that?"

Behind him, Romeo said, "So it's like that, eh?"

Wolf decided it was best not to answer either of them. Instead, he said, "I'm the man for that job."

Chrissy's expression was...not terribly encouraging. Her words were even less so. "I've long suspected the males of the species were idiots. I think now I'm certain."

"Hey!" Romeo lumbered to a stand, dusting himself off like he'd fallen into a sandpit instead of onto a perfectly clean floor. "What'd *I* do?"

"Let me make myself perfectly clear." Chrissy's stare was level. "I have no intention of having *sex* with anyone. But every time I close my eyes, what happened out there on the water replays itself on the backs of my eyelids, and I know I won't get any sleep if I'm alone."

"I'm the man for the job," Wolf reiterated at the same time Romeo said, "Wolf's the man for that job."

Chrissy frowned at Romeo. "Whatever happened to good old-fashioned chivalry? I thought you military types were supposed to jump at playing the gentleman?"

"I'm not saying I couldn't spend the night with you and not keep my hands to myself." Romeo lifted a finger. "I'm saying I've been told I can seduce an ice cream cone just by walking into the parlor, so I'm saving *you* from not being able to keep *your* hands off of *me*. If what you're after is some platonic spooning"—Romeo hitched his chin toward Wolf—"then Wolf's your man."

"Am I insulted or flattered? I can't tell," Wolf muttered, feeling more the former.

"You realize you have an ego the size of a whale shark. Right, Romeo?" Chrissy asked.

Romeo waggled his eyebrows. "It's not the only thing on me that's oversize."

"Oh, for crying out loud," Wolf grumbled.

Chrissy shook her head and then turned her sea-blue eyes on him. Right on cue, his stomach squeezed painfully and his blood ran hot. "Are you ready, then? Or do you need to grab a toothbrush or something?"

"We're headed back to your room?" His voice came out like the wind over the plains, dry and crackling.

"You didn't think I'd stay in there"—she jerked her chin toward the room behind him—"with both of you. That would be"—she curled her upper lip and landed on—"*weird.*"

"No." He shook his head. Although, the truth was he hadn't been thinking much of anything besides *Me! Me! Pick me!* "I already brushed my teeth. I'm good to go."

"I'm sure you are." Romeo smirked.

Wolf responded by stepping into the hall and slamming the door in Romeo's face.

As Chrissy made her way down the hall to her room, Wolf kept close beside her, studying her pretty profile. There was a skip in his step, and a lightness to his heart that'd been missing since that night he went and screwed everything up. He couldn't stop the happy smile that curved his lips.

"Have you ever wondered," she began and then did a double take when she saw his face. "Why are you looking at me like that?"

"Have I ever wondered what?" he asked.

"Nope." She shook her head, which caused a lock of hair to fall over one eye. He lifted his hand to tuck it behind her ear. Unfortunately, she beat him to it. "*Why* are you looking at me like that?" she demanded.

"Don't know." He shrugged. "Just happy, I guess."

Her eyes narrowed. "We are *not* having sex."

"I know."

"Do you?"

"*Yes*. Can't a man be happy about spendin' a sexless night with a woman he likes and admires?" He waited a few seconds before adding, "After all, snugglin' is nice too."

She was in the middle of swiping her keycard in the lock, and her spine snapped straight. "We're not snuggling either."

"Fine." He lifted his hands. "Sleepin' in the same bed with a pillow fort built between us."

She searched his eyes, and he tried his best to look innocent. He wasn't sure if he succeeded, because she harrumphed. But she *did* open the door, and then…

He was in! Inside her hotel room! For. The. *Duration*.

He would never have guessed when it started that this would turn out to be the best night of his life.

11:50 p.m.

A knock on the door had Izad jumping to his feet, his heart a wild thing in his chest. His mind silently screaming one word. One name. *Kazem!*

Was it possible his son had returned to Key West? Had he lost his burner phone in the melee, and that's why he didn't call them once he got within cellular tower coverage?

Hope was a flame inside Izad's heart. It burned as brightly as the fires at the festival of Sadeh. But it guttered and died when Nazim opened the door, and instead of Kazem standing on the threshold, it was Omid.

Not that it wasn't nice to see a loyal member of his security team, but Izad wanted only one thing now. His boy. His precious, precious son.

Well, *two* things. His son and Mason McCarthy's head on a platter.

He did not wait for Omid to finish pouring himself a glass of water before demanding, "Well? What can you tell us?"

Omid thirstily drained the water, and it took every bit of restraint Izad possessed not to slap the glass from the man's hands. Gritting his teeth, he reminded himself that Omid had spent hours in the wind and the sun, watching and gathering information.

Wiping the back of his hand over his mouth, Omid finally said, "Cas has gone to the morgue where the authorities have taken the bodies. He'll wait until the wee hours to slip inside to make an identification."

Izad refused to allow his mind to even touch on the notion that one of the bodies might be Kazem's. No. His son was still on the missing speedboat. Kazem was alive. He *had* to be. Izad could not lose everything. Every*one*.

"In the meantime," Omid continued, "You should know that McCarthy is staying here at the hotel. I followed his group from the docks and I know which room is his."

Izad let his head fall back on his neck. Closing his eyes, he lifted his hands in silent prayer. When he lowered his chin, he voice was steely. "So we do it here. Now. Tonight."

In Kazem's name. In Hettie's name. In the names of all my sons.

"Whoa. Whoa. Wait a damn minute." The American quickly stood from the sofa. "It's one thing to plan an attack out on the open ocean. But killing a man in a hotel is something else entirely. There are security cameras inside and out. The instant his body is found, the cops will comb through the footage and they'll find you. They'll find *all* of you. They'll find me too."

"We will be long gone by then," Izad assured him.

"You *hope*. But even if McCarthy's crew doesn't notice he's missing until, say, oh-nine-hundred tomorrow morning, that's still only a handful of hours for us to get the hell out of the country."

"Sit down and shut up," Izad snarled. "I am sick of your bellyaching."

All the man ever did was spout worst-case scenarios. If Izad had cowered in the face of what *could* happen every time he came up against adversity, he would never had risen to the rank of commodore. Bravery, quick decisions, and the fortitude to see a thing through, *that* was what made a man.

The American closed his mouth, but refused to sit.

Izad was tempted to give Navid a nod. His head of security wouldn't hesitate to swiftly kick the backs of the American's knees and *force* him to sit, which Izad would find immensely satisfying. However, *another* thing that made a man was the ability to focus on the important things. And right now, what was important was Mason McCarthy and the fact that he still drew breath.

"Thoughts on how we should do it?" he asked the men gathered around him.

"Hell, no." The American made for the door. "It's too risky. I didn't sign up for this."

This time, Izad *did* nod at Navid, who stepped in front of the American, a staying hand pressed firmly against the man's chest.

The American glanced down at Navid's hand, and then up at Izad. There was anger in his eyes. But also fear.

"We cannot let you leave," Izad told him, his tone sinister. "You know too much for us to trust you not to go to the authorities."

The American's jaw unhinged. "And tell them *what*? Anything I have on you would implicate me."

Izad shrugged. "Surely you have heard of an anonymous tip."

"I w-wouldn't do that," the American sputtered. "I

want him dead as much as you do for what he and his friends did to my men."

"Ah." Izad nodded. "So it *is* personal with you. I had wondered if you were motivated by more than greed. Now," he turned to his security team, "let us discuss our plan to end Mason McCarthy this very night."

Chapter 16

11:58 p.m.

CHRISSY SEEMED TO HAVE TWO EMOTIONAL SETTINGS when it came to Wolf. The first was annoyance. The second was extreme hyperawareness.

As she watched him build the agreed-upon pillow fort in the center of the king-size bed, she was sorry to say she was currently stuck on the second setting.

He wore the same cargo shorts and tank top from that morning—when the Coast Guard arrived at the catamaran, the last thing any of them had thought about was going belowdecks to grab their overnight bags. But he'd taken a shower. That much was obvious. She could smell the hotel soap on his skin as he moved around.

His skin…

Her eyes hungrily drank in inch upon inch of deeply tanned flesh. Flesh that was so smooth she had to shove her fists into the pockets of the hotel robe to keep from reaching out to run a finger down his arm to see if it was as firm and warm as it looked.

He wasn't packed with muscle like Mason. Or as heavily built as Romeo. No, his body was made for stamina, big-boned but leanly muscled. She thought for sure he must be able to go for days, be that swimming or running or—*gulp*—other activities.

His dark eyes always flashed with intelligence and humor. And his hair was thick and jet black. He kept it short, but she wondered what it would look like if he let it grow long. No doubt it would be stick-straight and so shiny it would hurt to look at it.

But of all the parts that made up his delicious whole, it was his mouth she found the most distracting. His lips were classically beautiful, full and well-defined around the edges. It didn't help matters that she remembered the feel of them moving over her own.

So hot. So hungry. So…damn…*talented*.

Because he's had a lot of practice, she reminded herself. *Because he's got that natural charm and charisma that means he's never had to work for a woman. Because he's one of those guys.*

A man like him should come with a warning label. It should say *Stop! Don't fall for that smile and that charm and that quick wit! He'll use it to win your heart, and then he won't know how to treat it once he has it. He'll hurt you so badly you'll wish you'd never met him!*

Maybe that was a little long-winded for a warning label. Perhaps all he needed was a forehead tattoo that read *Stop! He'll hurt your heart!*

"Uh-oh." He finished building the pillow barrier and caught her frowning fiercely at his back. "The look on your face is about as invitin' as a rabid porcupine. Are you havin' second thoughts?"

"Gee." She flattened her mouth into a straight line. "Careful with all that flowery talk. I just might swoon."

"Chrissy, if you're not comfortable with this, I'll leave. Just say the word and I'll—"

"No," she interrupted. She was suffering the after-effects of all the violence. Being tormented by a hangover from all the adrenaline.

Sleep was the ticket. A few blessed hours where she wouldn't have to relive this awful, terrible, *horrible* day. A few blessed hours where her mind could relax and restore itself to its factory setting—which she liked to think was pretty even-keeled.

"Like I said, I'll be better tomorrow." Lord, she hoped that was true. "But for tonight, I just… I just need some-one to stay with me."

"I could take you to Alex's room. She's got Meat with her. I'm sure the three of you could—"

"No." Again she cut him off and had to force herself to spit out the truth, because it wanted to stay stuck in her throat. "I want it to be you."

He tried not to smile. And failed.

"I wouldn't look so happy about it." She crawled into bed in her robe. She'd washed her clothes in the sink, and they were drying in the bathroom. "It's not because I like you better than Alex. It's because you're more likely to engage in hand-to-hand combat should a bad guy come bursting through the door. Which will give me enough time to escape. I plan to sacrifice you to save myself."

His tone was dry. "I appreciate the vote of confidence in my fightin' prowess, but I can assure you, the chances of a bad guy burstin' through that door are pretty slim."

His weight depressed the mattress when he climbed into bed. It caused her to slide toward the line of pillows.

She'd purposefully turned her back to him. But she would swear, even with the barrier between them, she could feel his heat.

Her blood rose and she pushed a bare leg out from beneath the comforter, hoping the hotel room's air would also cool the heated images that ran through her mind because...you know...Ray "Wolf" Roanhorse was next to her. In *bed*.

"I bet this morning you would've said the chances of running into three men on a speedboat who were armed to the teeth were pretty slim too," she told him, turning her pillow over to the cool side and punching a divot in the center to make room for her head. "And look how *that* turned out."

He switched off his bedside lamp. Instantly, the room took on a golden glow, lit by the single lamp burning on her nightstand. It looked suspiciously like mood lighting. Which made her long to reach out and switch off her lamp too. But the idea of complete darkness...

She shuddered. All of her heated thoughts were once again replaced by icy visions of violence, and she pulled her leg back beneath the comforter.

Wolf changed positions and the mattress bounced. To her surprise, his hand curled around her shoulder. It was wide-palmed and warm.

She hadn't realized how tightly she was wound until his touch loosened her muscles. The simple weight of his hand, the feel of his fingers giving her a comforting squeeze, had the strain of the day leaking out of her as easily as if she were a human sieve.

"This okay?" His voice sounded close. He spooned the pillow barrier.

"Yes," she whispered.

Wolf might need to come with a warning label, cautioning all females to protect their hearts. But when it came to needing someone to protect their *bodies*, there was no one better than him. Put simply, he was a warrior. And she could relax knowing he was beside her.

"Wolf?" she said as she clicked off her own lamp. She was no longer scared of the dark.

"Yeah, darlin'?"

There it was, that endearment that should've piqued her annoyance but didn't. She'd have to think long and hard about why that should be. But she'd leave it for tomorrow. Tonight, she was too tired.

"Thank you for this." She scooted her foot under the pillows until her toes found his warm shin. She waited to see if he would pull away, and was relieved when he didn't. Settling more comfortably into the mattress, she closed her eyes and was gratified when no terrible scene bloomed with Technicolor clarity on the backs of her lids.

Then his voice sounded in the darkness. "Of course, Chrissy. And I know I told you earlier, but it bears repeatin'. I'm crazy proud of how you handled things today. You were one iron-spined marvel behind the wheel of that catamaran."

She snorted sleepily, oblivion trying its best to tug her under. "I was scared shitless."

"Courage isn't about bein' unafraid." His voice was

hypnotic in the cool blackness of the room. "Courage is about bein' afraid and still doin' what needs to be done."

"I thought we talked about that whole fortune cookie thing." Her yawn was so wide her jaw cracked.

She thought she heard him chuckle, but couldn't be sure. Sleep had taken her.

9:02 a.m.

Alex climbed out of the cab and waited for Meat to join her on the sidewalk. He took his sweet time, disembarking from the vehicle like a little hippo slowly sliding into a river. Once he was safely sitting on the ground by her feet, she lifted a hand against the glare of the morning sun and scanned the tarmac, visible through the chain-link fence.

There was the de Havilland Otter, the single-engine amphibious plane that was Romeo's pride and joy. And there was Romeo right along with Wolf, Doc, and Uncle John.

But where was Mason?

She'd asked that question so many times, she was beginning to sound like a broken record.

She'd asked it around 5:00 a.m. when she'd been jolted awake by Meat horking up a gut full of water weeds. After cleaning up the mess—all while trying not to hork herself—she'd tiptoed to Mason's door, hoping there was something she could give Meat to soothe his belly. But Mason hadn't answered, and she'd assumed he was already down at the hotel gym.

The man loved his early-hour workouts. She suspected all that lifting and pressing of iron was a way to exorcise his demons—she knew he had a few. Probably *more* than a few. But the times she'd tried to ask him about them, she'd been met with a grunt and a stony stare.

The second time she asked the "Where's Mason?" question had been at breakfast. The entire Wayfarer Island crew had been eagerly partaking of the hotel's buffet and listening to Wolf explain what he'd learned during his a.m. phone call to Special Agent Albus Fazzle.

"The FBI doesn't know any more than they did last night," he'd said while slathering jelly onto a biscuit. "There were no matches for the prints or dental records in the databases. Fazzle says the feds are still workin' the angle that it was the Baitfish Bandits."

"What about the third guy in the speedboat?" Doc had asked.

"Coasties are sendin' out drones to scout the seas around where the assault occurred. Fazzle hopes maybe somethin' will pop on the boat or the third body once they locate it. Barrin' that, we'll have to wait for the DNA results to come back before gettin' any real answers," Wolf had finished around a mouthful. "Fazzle says it's safe for us to get back to our lives and chalk this whole thing up to a case of bein' in the wrong place at the wrong time with the right weapons and the right kind of luck."

"That's it?" Chrissy's face had been full of disbelief. "We act as if nothing happened?"

"Pretty much."

Alex had heard most of this as an aside, her mind strictly focused on one thing, one *man*. And when there had been a lull in the conversation, she'd demanded, "Where's Mason?"

"Who knows with that one." Wolf had shrugged unconcernedly. "We said last night we'd leave for the airport at oh-eight-thirty. He'll meet us in the lobby when it's time to go."

Then, before Alex could sputter any objections, the conversation had turned to the details for their trip to Wayfarer Island, and she'd been left to chew on her tongue.

The *third* time she'd asked the question was when the men were climbing into one taxi while she, Chrissy, and Meat hailed a second.

Chrissy had wanted to stop by her house to pack another overnight bag. The men, having no interest in waiting around and "twiddling their dicks" as Uncle John had oh-so-eloquently put it, had decided to head to the airport early to get the floatplane loaded up with the extra supplies.

Romeo had been the one to answer her that time. He'd simply shrugged in the middle of stepping into the cab to say, "You know how he is. The man values his alone time. He's probably planning to meet us at the airport, eh?"

At that point, Alex had wanted to scream with frustration that no one but her had seemed concerned that Mason was MIA. Then again, she'd thought maybe they were right. Mason *was* the private sort, not at all the type to alert others to his comings and goings.

Of course now, having arrived at the airport to find

him *still* missing, all the little dings of apprehension she'd felt became klaxons of alarm.

Where the hell *is he?*

As she, Chrissy, and Meat made their way through the little terminal and out onto the tarmac—the best thing about flying privately was skipping the security lines—she lamented that Wayfarer Island lacked cell service. It meant those who lived there had canceled their plans. The logic being why pay for something they wouldn't be able to use 90 percent of the time?

Living a simple life in the modern world was nice. Romantic, even. But right then she'd have given up a body part to be able to shoot Mason a text.

"It's like we've time-traveled back to the eighties or something," she muttered while coaxing a waddling Meat toward the waiting plane. "Next thing you know, I'll be teasing my bangs and wearing jelly bracelets."

"What?" Chrissy shot her a curious look, shrugging her overnight bag higher on her shoulder.

"Nothing." Alex waved her off, raking in a deep breath that she hoped would ease some of her anxiety. It was only partially successful, since along with the pleasant aromas of sand and surf, there was also the decidedly *un*pleasant smell of jet fuel.

Deciding what she really needed was a change of subject, she slid Chrissy a sly look. "You had sex with Wolf, didn't you?"

Chrissy sputtered like Alex's old American history professor when a student had argued the New Deal was the beginning of the end for capitalist America.

"Why would you think that?" Chrissy demanded, coming to a halt on the blacktop and shoving her sunglasses to the top of her head.

"Because I saw him come out of your room this morning. And then at breakfast, he was whistling and humming and in the best mood I've ever seen him in."

"Ah, yes. And sex with me would definitely explain the change in him." Chrissy flicked her sunglasses back onto her face and resumed walking. "What it *wouldn't* explain"—her tone was peevish—"is why I'm not currently curled in the fetal position and weeping from self-disgust."

Alex did a double take. "You don't think Wolf is gorgeous?"

"Oh, yes." Chrissy nodded emphatically. "He's handsome as hell if you're into that whole tall, dark, and dangerous thing."

Alex snorted. "I hate to be the one to tell you this, sis, but there's not a woman on the planet who isn't into that whole tall, dark, and dangerous thing."

Chrissy didn't say anything to that, and Alex frowned. "I don't know what he did to make you hate him, but I'm sure whatever it was, it was a mistake. Wolf is solid gold. He's one of the good ones."

"I don't hate him," Chrissy insisted. "And I know he's one of the good ones. I mean, he came and slept in my room last night—just *slept*," she insisted when she saw the prurient gleam that entered Alex's eyes, "because I asked him to. But good guys can still be bad news."

Before Alex could comment on that, Chrissy turned

the tables. "Enough about me. What about *you*? I see Mason loaned you his dog for the night. Did he happen to loan you anything *else*?" She bobbed her eyebrows above the frames of her sunglasses. "Like, say, his *penis*?"

"Alas, no." Alex sighed. "I agreed to stop hounding him to help me lose my virginity and satisfy myself with simply being his friend. Of course, that was after I trapped him in my hotel room and kissed the bejesus out of him."

Chrissy choked. "Holy shit, woman. You got a *big* old set of brass balls, don't you? So? How was it?"

How was it?

Amazing. Beautiful. Transcendent. *Transformative.* Alex didn't get the opportunity to say any of that aloud, because they'd made it to the plane, and Romeo was in the middle of doing something to the propeller. Beside him, Doc asked, "How'd it go with that dark-haired beauty you were hitting on at the end of the night?"

"Her name was Gina," Romeo said, bending toward his task. "After last call, she told me she had an early flight to catch and needed to get some sleep. So I was left to jack my own beanstalk."

"Poor baby," Chrissy crooned and both men jolted around, looking as guilty as teenage boys caught flipping through a girlie magazine.

Alex couldn't hide her chuckle.

Her humor dried up quickly, however, when she heard Wolf, who'd been helping Uncle John arrange supplies in the cargo hold, shout, "It's about damn time, man! Ten more minutes and we were sendin' out a search party!"

Spinning around, she scanned the tarmac. There he was. The man of the hour.

No mistaking him, really. Not with those shoulders that blocked out the sun.

His hair was wet from a recent shower, and his face sported the dark shadow of a full day without the touch of a razor. Seeing his walk, it was obvious he'd been in the military. There was a marching quality to the way he carried himself.

Alex was tempted to break into a run, anxious to confront him about where the hell he'd been and tell him she'd been worried sick. But her feet glued themselves to the ground because, just over his shoulder and beyond the fence surrounding the airport, she saw a Smurf-blue scooter. The brunette sitting atop it was none other than Donna.

Something hard and sharp lodged under Alex's lungs, nicking the organs until every breath hurt. She suddenly understood what Chrissy meant when she said even good guys could be bad news.

Never mind that Alex had *made* him kiss her. Never mind that he'd regretted it immediately. Never mind that Donna had a prior claim to him. And never mind that Alex had promised to be his friend.

How could he have locked lips with *Alex*, getting all hot and bothered in the process, and then go to spend the night with Donna?

Honestly, Alex didn't know who she was more upset for, herself or Donna.

Donna, she quickly decided. *Because no woman should be forced to slake a lust inspired by another.*

Any guilt she'd felt for the look on Mason's face outside her hotel room disappeared quicker than a signed copy of *The Wealth of Nations* at a historical society event.

His eyes lasered across the distance separating them, stopping once he found her angry gaze. Despite her pique, being the sole subject of his attention was still like being hit by a thunderbolt from the clear blue sky. She caught her breath. Every nerve in her body fired at once.

Chrissy spied Donna as she motored away and said, "Oh hell."

Oh hell is right, Alex thought. *As in, oh hell, who would have thought Mason McCarthy would turn out to be a total asshole?*

Mason continued to make a beeline toward her, and Chrissy took the opportunity to lean over and whisper in her ear, "I'll walk over there. Far enough away to give you some privacy, but not so far away that I can't eavesdrop."

Alex paid her little mind because suddenly Mason was in front of her. "Good morning, Alex," he said so calmly that the spark of hostility that had ignited inside of her when she saw him arrive with Donna grew into a conflagration.

She thought she heard Chrissy mutter, "Oh, no he didn't," but she couldn't be sure. The blood rushing in her ears was so loud it reminded her of the time her parents had done a lecture at the University of Buffalo and afterward had taken her to see Niagara Falls. The pounding and power of that big water was something she would never forget.

Just like she would never forget this moment when

the man of her dreams fell straight off the pedestal she'd put him on only to land flat on his ass.

"Looks like it was a good morning for *you*." She tried, but she couldn't keep the frostiness from her tone. "I was going to thank you for lending me your dog for the night. But now I realize it was less of a loan and more of a dog-sitting assignment."

Mason shook his head. "I'm sorry?"

"Yeah," she quickly agreed. "You've been saying that a lot lately."

Behind her, Romeo asked Doc, "Is that Wolf calling us?" No doubt he wanted to skedaddle before the situation got even *more* awkward.

"I'm staying put," Doc muttered.

"No." Alex gave Doc a grateful nod. "I got this. Go on."

Doc looked hesitant, but jerked his chin in acceptance before slowly making his way to the other side of the plane. Romeo, on the other hand, moved so quickly he lost a flip-flop. He had to hop back to retrieve it before running to catch up with Doc.

Mason frowned after his friends and then turned his attention back to her. "Am I missing something?" She couldn't tell if the confusion in his eyes was feigned or genuine.

Before she could call him on being a complete and total asshat, Uncle John yelled, "Everybody load up!"

Chrissy scurried over to wrap an arm around Alex's waist. "Let's go. The look on your face says you're about to punch him in the dick, and I think you might regret that later."

"I'd just add it to my long list of regrets," Alex grumbled, wondering why she'd ever thought Mason was so great.

Chrissy hustled her onto the small plane, pushed her to the front row, directly behind the pilot's chair, and made sure to grab the seat next to her so no one else could take it.

That no one else being one Mason McCarthy, of course.

The plane rocked slightly while the others boarded. Alex knew the instant Mason climbed aboard. Even without looking back, she could feel his energy. The throbbing heat of him. That ephemeral *something* that always called to her.

His previous rejections hadn't been enough to make her give up hope. But this? This had done it. This proved he wasn't the man she thought he was.

It's over, a voice in her head whispered, and all her anger turned into sadness. The finality of giving up on her dream of Mason made her bones ache like they were missing marrow.

But why? Why should she care so much?

Because you fell in love with him, that stupid voice answered. To her utter dismay, she admitted it was right. She *had* fallen for him. Like the inexperienced ingenue she was.

Barf!

Romeo made his way to the pilot's seat and slipped on his headset. With a push of a button, he started the plane and the big propeller on the nose spun to life. The dull roar of the engine was a blessing since Alex was pretty sure a pitiful little sigh escaped her.

Biting her lip, she turned toward the window and watched the lone man who worked as the ground crew use hand signals to give Romeo the go-ahead to taxi to the end of the runway. When the plane began to move, she pressed her forehead against the window and battled the aggravating urge to cry.

Chapter 17

9:13 a.m.

IZAD GLANCED AT HIS REFLECTION IN THE BATHROOM mirror and tried to see the young man he once was.

It was impossible.

Years of grief had taken their toll, wiping away any vestiges of his virility. But if there was one thing he could be grateful for, it was that with age came wisdom. Wisdom and patience.

He understood that just because McCarthy had thwarted his plans by disappearing from the hotel, that did *not* mean McCarthy would thwart his plans forever.

Age had *not* stolen Izad's relentlessness. If anything, it had only strengthened it.

"Sir?" Navid's voice was accompanied by a soft knock at the door. "Cas has returned from the morgue."

"One moment, please." Izad's voice sounded weary, even to his own ears.

He gave himself one last look in the mirror before turning for the door. His hand shook on the knob. His knees were shakier still as he exited the bathroom and glanced first at Navid and then at Cas.

He knew what Cas had discovered without the man saying the words. Horror was written over Cas's face.

A heavy shadow fell over Izad's heart, blanketing his

spirit and driving him to his knees. The pain was familiar, and yet it was impossible to put into words. Unless one had lost a child, one could never understand the magnitude, the limitless breadth and depth of the grief that came with it. The imagination failed in its ability to conjure such agony.

He knelt on the cold tiles, his throat full, but the tears…they would not come. It was like the punch of a bullet or the slice of a knife. The flesh was so shocked it could not process the injury. Even though his mind now had the horrific, bloody truth, his body could not accept it.

"Tell me." His voice was barely above a whisper.

"I gained access to the morgue during the shift change." Cas's throat was thick with grief. "I identified Kazem and Mahmoud."

Though Izad had been expecting them, the words still stung like a thousand angry hornets. Bile burned the back of his throat. "Was it quick?"

Cas nodded. "A headshot."

Izad let out a ragged breath and sent up a prayer of thanks. If there was any peace to be had, it was in knowing his boy had not suffered.

"I am sorry, sir," Navid whispered, wiping at the tears that slipped down his cheeks. Kazem had been a favorite of all the men in Izad's security detail, a blazing light that had brightened their days.

Now, thanks to Mason McCarthy, Kazem's fire had been snuffed out forever.

"Do not be." Izad's jaw clenched so tightly the words

were barely intelligible. His grief would not help him now. But his anger would. He opened himself to it. Letting it fill him. "Just help me *kill* Mason McCarthy."

The American lifted a hand. "Is anyone interested in how *I* think we can accomplish that?"

As much as it infuriated Izad to admit it, the American had been right. About everything. It was time for Izad to heed the man's advice.

Age *also* brought with it humility.

"Go on then," he said with a nod. "Tell us what you have in mind."

9:18 a.m.

Seated as Mason was, across the aisle and one row back from Alex, he was privy to little more than her profile when she finally turned from the window. But that was enough to tell him her face, which was usually in motion—her mouth grinning with devilment, her eyes rounding in excitement—was now completely still.

Closed off.

Blank.

The thought that *he* was the cause of the change had a deep, abiding regret filling him up, pressing against his skin until he thought he might burst from it. But for the life of him, he couldn't understand where he'd gone wrong.

He'd done as she asked. Chosen option A and kissed

her—boy, had he ever; he was *still* reeling from it. Then afterward he'd sent Meat to keep her company for the night because that's what friends do. They lend their lovable animals to those in need of a furry face. And yet the look on her face this morning—

"I'll give you to the count of one to explain yourself." Doc, his seat mate, leaned close to growl in his ear, "And then I'm going to punch you in the balls."

"Huh?" Mason blinked incredulously.

"I know you understand English, cock-holster." Bloodthirstiness gleamed in Doc's green eyes. "It's one of your greatest achievements."

Mason's chin jerked back. "Why the fuck are you treating me like a bleached asshole?"

"Because you hurt Alex. *Again.*" There was a world of accusation in Doc's tone.

All the air leaked from Mason's lungs and left him sagging. "I know," he admitted grievously. "But I dunno what I did!"

"No?" Doc glared at him. "I thought you were headed to her room to explain things. But now I see you went and baked Donna's cake instead."

"I *did* go to Alex's room to explain things, and we made a pact to be nothing more than friends," Mason said defensively. "Also, not that it's any of your frickin' business, but I didn't bake Donna's cake. After I left Alex, I went to Donna's house to break things off with her. But then I fell asleep on her couch. Blame it on the blood loss."

For a while, Doc was quiet. Then, "If you and Alex

made a pact to be friends, why did you kick Donna to the curb?"

"Fuck if I know," Mason admitted wretchedly. "Just felt wrong keeping things going with her when... when..." His voice trailed off.

When *what*?

When what he felt for Alex was so much more than what he'd ever feel for Donna? When his feelings for Alex affected him like he'd never been affected before, even with Sarah? When everything and everyone paled in comparison to Alex, and when the thought of *being* with someone else held absolutely *zero* interest for him?

He closed his eyes and saw Alex. Her head thrown back against the hotel door. Her little pink nipple tight and wet from his mouth.

He hadn't been lying when he told her she was the most beautiful thing he'd ever seen. The sheer magnificence of her in the throes of orgasm had managed to break through the shock he'd felt at watching a woman come so easily.

In his experience, women's bodies were finely made machines that required a patient, knowledgeable hand to coax them to perform at their peaks. But it appeared Alex was more of a bottle rocket.

Light her fuse and watch her go.

"Will you tell Alex you ended things with Donna?" Doc cut into his thoughts.

Mason shook his head. "Despite our pact, she might think I did it 'cause of her, and it won't matter what I say after that. She'll convince herself she should see this as a sign I'm reconsidering her offer. Which I'm *not*."

He wasn't, was he?

No, he was *not*. But he *had* allowed himself to fantasize about it. About taking her out to the secluded beach at the back of Wayfarer Island, laying her down on a soft blanket, and teaching her all the things she was so eager to learn.

Afraid Doc might read in his face what was in his head, he turned toward the window and stared out at the endless turquoise waters below. Every now and then, they were interrupted by a speck of brown and green.

Oh, to be an island, he thought.

So simple. So serene. So *quiet*. No one judged them. No one wanted things from them they couldn't give. No one was *hurt* by them.

"I think it's high time you and I sat crooked and talked straight," Doc said, cutting into his thoughts again. "You say Alex deserves someone who'll appreciate the gift she's offering, and in return, that man should give her a piece of his heart. *I'm* saying that man is *you*."

Mason opened his mouth, but Doc pressed on before he could get a word out. "I don't have time to play the fiddle to your excuses dance. We'll be landing in five minutes, and I'll need every second of that to say what I have to say. Now, here's the way I see it. Sarah burned you. And you've decided you never want to dance close to those flames again. I get it. Love hurts, and who the hell needs that?"

Doc pointed in Alex's direction. "But she's not asking you to jump in the fire with her. She's asking you for one night. You wouldn't be giving her your *whole* heart, you'd just be giving her a *piece* of it. And if you're worried you won't know where to stop, where friendship and lust and affection will end and where love will begin, then lay down some damned ground rules."

Doc made an it's-so-easy gesture with his hands. "Limit it to one time, or two times, or ten times. Then stick with it. She'll get rid of her virginity, and you'll have some fun with a woman you admire and respect and *want*. Maybe it'll be enough to wipe away the hangdog expression you've been wearing for the last five years."

The mere notion had all the oxygen leaving Mason's lungs.

"Fate's hand has been pushing at your back since the moment Alexandra Merriweather set foot on Wayfarer Island," Doc continued. "It's been fun watching you fight it. But for all our sakes, it's time you gave in."

Chapter 18

CHRISSY LOVED WAYFARER ISLAND.

Loved the peaceful waters of the lagoon. The crash of the waves against the reef. The rambling old beach house that, despite its lack of modern amenities like Wi-Fi, reliable electricity, and hot water for showers, still felt like a home.

She even loved how Uncle John blasted music from his boom box at a volume that threatened hearing loss. And how Li'l Bastard, the island's resident rooster, crowed his head off at the slightest provocation.

Case in point: When she cast her line and lure into the water, Li'l Bastard, who'd been strutting around her feet, let loose with a throaty *cock-a-doodle-do*.

"Shoo!" she scolded him, stomping her bare toes in the sand. He squawked in offense before running into the bushes. Off to pillage and plunder the island's insect population, no doubt.

Back at the house, Meat answered the rooster's call with two barks, and Chrissy smiled. She'd known that was coming.

If Meat barked, Li'l Bastard crowed. And vice versa. It was like the animals were caught in a never-ending conversation. And the oddity of their friendship made it all the more adorable, especially come midafternoon when the two of them curled up together to nap in the shade of the porch.

Humming to the sound of Bob Marley crooning about "three little birds" she reeled in her lure, the muscles in her arms attuned to the gentle tug of the current. If something other than the current took her bait, those same muscles would automatically react.

Fishing was her solace.

Her mother's second husband, Doug, had taught her how on her eighth birthday. Two months later, her mother had found Doug in bed with the local manicurist. Doug had disappeared from their lives soon after that, but Chrissy would always be grateful to him for giving her a hobby to last a lifetime.

There was something soothing about the repetitive motion of casting and reeling. It put her body in a meditative state while allowing her mind to float free. In that freeness, she found comfort, satisfaction, even enlightenment.

Her mother used to shake her head and say, *I'll never understand how you can spend so much time alone.*

Chrissy had tried to explain that she couldn't begin to reckon with herself, with her achievements and mistakes, with her strengths and weaknesses, with the knowledge of who she was and who she might become until she found some quiet. Some solitude. And fishing allowed her both.

Josephine had simply thrown her hands in the air and muttered, *My daughter, the philosopher.* And that had been the end of that.

After landing on Wayfarer Island and unloading the plane, the Deep Six Salvage guys had decreed that, given the chaos of the last couple of days, everyone could use some time to decompress. Tomorrow, they would relocate their search grids to the reef circling the lagoon. Today, they would get a little R & R.

Hearing that, Chrissy had wasted no time traipsing out to the wind-stripped wooden shed to grab the fishing equipment stored there.

She needed to think. Needed to understand why last night, when she'd found herself caught in a storm of anguish over the things she'd seen, *Wolf* had been the shelter she ran to.

"Thought I might find you out here." His deep voice with that Oklahoma twang sounded behind her.

Speak of an angel and he'll flap his wings, she thought. Then she quickly decided Wolf was far more devilish than he was divine.

Turning slowly, she watched him heading closer. He was barefoot and wearing fresh swim trunks. His chest was smooth and hairless. Black tribal tattoos wrapped around his biceps.

Feeling like she was getting a sugar rush from so much man-candy, she forced her gaze to his chin. But she quickly decided that was cowardly, and so firmly met his eyes. Those black, fathomless eyes that, when focused on her, were so warm and liquid they made her heart want to melt.

It wasn't really a smile he gave her, more a subtle deepening of the lines on either side of his mouth. But it was enough to have the corners of her own mouth curling down in response.

It'd been easy to resist his advances when all she'd had was the memory of That Night to go on. But now she had so much more.

She had the memory of *last* night. Of how he'd sweetly kept a hand on her shoulder for hours so she could enjoy a deep, dreamless sleep. Of how he'd looked this morning, all warm and lazy as he got out of bed and stretched like a cat. Of how he'd given her the first cup of coffee from the little hotel coffeemaker after adding cream and one sugar. Just as she liked it.

Plus, she had the memory of his bravery on the catamaran. Of his selflessness. His heroism.

"Figured I'd come out here so I didn't inadvertently get cut by the dagger eyes Alex keeps sending Mason's way." She hoped her expression revealed none of the confusion in her head.

Wolf stopped beside her, his face pained. "On a scale of one to smotherin' him in his sleep, how much do you think Alex hates him right now?"

Chrissy shook her head. "She doesn't hate him. She loves him."

A startled look contorted Wolf's face. "Did she tell you that?"

"She didn't have to. If you'd seen her when he got stabbed, if you'd heard the noise she made, you'd know."

"Shit." He ran a hand through his short hair. It made his bicep bunch which, in turn, made Chrissy's stomach bunch.

She sighed. "And it gets worse."

He looked at her expectantly.

"Apparently, last night, Alex made a deal with him to be friends. But that was only *after* she kissed him."

"She *kissed* him?" He blinked, and shook his head in wonder. "That woman has a set of balls on her to do Wesley Warren Jr. proud."

"That's what I told her." Chrissy agreed, then frowned. "Wait, who's Wesley Warren Jr.?"

He shuddered dramatically. "A tragic guy with scrotal elephantiasis."

She decided she'd rather not picture that. "Then Mason went and showed up this morning with Donna."

Wolf's brow wrinkled. "So? I thought you just said Alex and Mason agreed to be friends?"

Chrissy stared at her fishing rod and then stared at his head.

"Don't even think about it." His mouth curved around a knowing smile.

"Are *all* men clueless?" she demanded. "Or is it just those of you who live on an island in the middle of nowhere? He *kissed* Alex and then went and *slept* with someone else."

"Mason didn't have sex with Donna."

She felt her forehead wrinkle. "And how do you know that?"

"He told Doc. Doc told me."

"Even if that's true," she declared with a sniff, Team Alex all the way, "it doesn't excuse his decision to let Donna drive him to the airport this morning. It was like he was rubbing her in Alex's face."

Wolf grimaced. "True. He probably could've been more sensitive." His eyes laser-focused on hers when he said this next part: "But one bad decision does not define a man."

She instantly felt uneasy and refocused her attention on casting her lure into deeper water. "Are we still talking about Alex and Mason?"

"Would you rather we be talkin' about somethin' else?" His voice was soft. "Like why you put your sleepin' bag on the porch next to Alex's daybed instead of in my bedroom?"

"Wh-what?" Her heart grew wings and fluttered like the fins on the pygmy sea horses that liked to latch onto the floating sargassum grasses.

"Ah, come on. Surely, after last night, I proved I can keep my hands to myself. No reason you should sleep on that hard trundle bed when I've got a nice, soft mattress upstairs."

The Wayfarer Island house had seven bedrooms, one for each of the Deep Six Salvage guys and Uncle John. Alex had chosen the daybed on the screened-in porch for her abode. The few times Chrissy had stayed over after a dive session ran late, she'd slept on the trundle.

In short, Wayfarer Island was a bit like summer camp.

"While I'm grateful for last night"—she leveled a direct stare on him—"it was a one-off. Never to be repeated."

A smile flirted with his perfect mouth. "I've learned never to say never."

"Mmph" was all she allowed before feeling a tug on her line. She yanked her rod to set the hook.

"Got one!" Wolf hooted.

"Not a very big one," she grunted, quickly reeling in her catch. It was a red grouper, and after pulling the hook from the fish's bottom lip, she held it up for inspection. "A two-pounder, I'd say. Not big enough to keep."

Wading into the shallows, she released the fish back into the ocean where she hoped it would grow big and strong before being hauled ashore again to end up on someone's grill. Then she lifted her hand to shade her eyes against the sun as she squinted at the waves lapping over the reef.

If Alex was right, the *Santa Cristina* could be right out there. Under their noses all this time.

She got a little chill at the thought. Or maybe it was Wolf's words that caused the goose bumps on her arms and legs.

There was a smile on her face when she returned to the beach and checked the knot on her lure. A good catch and release always made her happy.

"Christina of the Sea." Wolf crossed his arms and grinned at her.

"What?" She turned to him.

"You're so at home out here, miles from anywhere, nothin' but sand and sea. You should've been born a mermaid."

"Oh, believe me"—she cast her line again—"that was my most fervent wish until I was twelve. I used to beg my mother to change my name to Ariel."

He chuckled. "Glad you stuck with Chrissy. It suits you."

She wrinkled her nose. "You think? I don't know. Bobby Joe Cuthbert called me Chrissy the Sissy after I got sick while dissecting a fetal pig in freshman physiology class."

"Bobby Joe Cuthbert sounds like a penis wrinkle of legendary proportions."

She snorted. "He was."

"Chrissy isn't a sissy. She's straightforward. Effortless."

Warmth spread through her at the compliment.

What the hell was she supposed to do with him now that she'd forgiven him? Now that she could look at him without remembering That Night? Now that she was beginning to *like* him again?

"Thank you," she said demurely, and then listened when he began to hum along with Bob Marley, who was still crooning loudly from the boom box on the porch.

The chorus came up and Wolf belted "Cereal! Little darlin'! Cereal!" in a deep, smooth tenor.

She stared at him.

"What?" He blinked. "My *elisi* tells me I have a nice voice." His expression grew pained. "God, is she lying?"

Chrissy endeavored to maintain a straight face. She was pretty sure she failed. "First of all, what or who is an *elisi*?"

"My grandmother."

"Right." She nodded. "So then second of all, do you really think the late, great Bob Marley wrote a song about breakfast food?"

His brow furrowed. Then a self-deprecating grin tugged at his lips. "Don't tell me I got the lyrics wrong."

She could feel the laughter bubbling inside her. "Bob is telling his little darling to 'stir it up.'"

"Really?" He looked genuinely perplexed. "That Jamaican accent sure makes it sound like he's sayin' 'cereal.'"

She couldn't hold it in any longer. Doubling over, she howled with hilarity. By the time she straightened, she had to wipe tears from her eyes.

Wolf crossed his arms. "If you must know," he confessed self-deprecatingly, "those aren't the only lyrics I've mangled. I'm sort of known for mishearin' songs."

She thrilled at the thought of the mighty Ray "Wolf" Roanhorse having such a simple, human foible. "So what else have you gotten wrong?"

"You just want to make fun of me." The look he gave her was put-upon, but he cleared his throat and asked, "You know that song titled 'Escape'? It goes 'If you like piña coladas'..."

"Yeah." She knew her eyes were sparkling with anticipation.

"So I...uh..." He scratched his chin, and her gaze was momentarily drawn to the tattoo on his forearm. The tattoo she knew was a monument and a testament to his dead teammate. "I thought they were singing about bean enchiladas until one day LT heard me and cleared things up."

She choked. "Oh god, that's good."

"You're probably too young to remember the band Starship. Hell, even *I'm* too young, but I have a whole passel of aunts and uncles who aren't, and they like to pull out their ancient mix tapes anytime the family gets together."

Chrissy imagined Wolf surrounded by aunts, uncles, cousins, and a wrinkly old grandma who loved to hear him sing. She found the image bittersweet. She'd always wanted a large family. But all she'd ever had was her mother. And now...she had no one.

Unaware of the reflective turn of her thoughts, he continued, "Anyway, so Starship had this song titled 'We Built This City.'"

"I know the one." Chrissy put a hand to her mouth, trying and failing to guess how he could've gotten any of *those* lyrics wrong.

"We built this city on 'sausage rolls'..." he sang.

Again, she doubled over with laughter. The kind that made her stomach hurt in the best possible way.

This time when she straightened, she had to hold a hand to the stitch in her side. "What is it with you and food?" she wheezed. "'Cereal' instead of 'stir it up.' 'Bean enchiladas' instead of 'piña coladas.' And, my all-time favorite, 'sausage rolls' instead of 'rock 'n' roll.'"

Saying it aloud sent her into another round of uncontrollable giggling.

He waited until she was finished before screwing up his mouth and conceding, "I never realized it, but you're right. I *do* hear food references in songs."

"A city built on sausage rolls," Chrissy gasped. "Sounds delicious."

"Don't it just?"

She was fascinated by the humor dancing in his eyes.

Then a voice in her head whispered *Be careful*, and she immediately sobered.

Turning back to her fishing line, she frowned because she still didn't have the answers to why it'd been *him* she sought out the night before, and what that meant for how she wanted to handle things with him in the future.

"So," he said at length, having clued in to the change in her mood. "How're you feelin' today?"

"Better," she told him, filling her lungs with the salty air. "Much better." She slid him a long look. "You?"

He hitched one shoulder as he stared out at the waves. "Killin's never easy. But I've never taken a life without cause. There's peace in that."

She nodded solemnly. "I can't imagine what it's like to be a soldier."

"Sailor, in my case. But semantics aside, most military men and women can't imagine life as a civilian. It gets in their blood. In their brains."

"Is it in yours?"

For a long while he didn't answer. Eventually he said, "I'd be lyin' if I said it wasn't. But that don't mean I'd choose to go back to it. I always knew I wanted out someday. That I wanted a normal life."

She snorted. "I don't think you'll find anyone who considers treasure hunting a 'normal life.'" She made air quotes.

"True." A small grin twitched at his lips, and just that easily the gravity of the moment lightened. His tone was a bit too innocent when he added, "So back to the sleepin' situation. I've been thinkin' you *shouldn't* sleep with me in my bed in a totally platonic fashion with a pillow fort built between us."

"No?" She frowned.

"I've decided you should sleep with me in my bed in a totally *non*platonic fashion with nothin' between us."

She dropped her fishing pole and had to bend to retrieve it. All the blood rushed to her head. She blamed that for the squeaky sound of her voice. "*Excuse* me?"

"We should have sex." He enunciated each word.

Oh my god!

Okay, so she could play this one of two ways. She could get all discombobulated and flabbergasted, which was surely what he expected. But she hated being predictable. So she quickly settled on option number two.

"Hmm." She tapped her chin. "Let me think about that. Okay, I've thought about it, and while I concede it's an interesting concept, I don't think you could handle this." She indicated the length of her body. "Do *you* think you could handle it?" She cocked an eyebrow suggestively, hoping *he* was the one to get discombobulated and flabbergasted.

He swallowed convulsively before admitting, "Not sure, to be honest." Then his expression turned lecherous. "But I'd love to give it a try."

She laughed, remembering this was how it'd been between them before That Night.

Easy. Uncomplicated. *Fun.*

They'd been friends. Was it possible they could be friends again?

Is that the answer to how I should deal with him?

The idea had merit. If they were friends, she wouldn't have to worry about losing her heart to him. If they were friends, she could look at all his teasing and flirting as amusing and entertaining without being scared it might turn into something more.

The longer she thought about it, the more she liked the notion.

Friends. Yeah. It could work.

"Haven't you heard?" She slid him a sly smile. "All a man needs is a place to have sex, but a woman needs a *reason*. So, what reason could I possibly have for sleeping with you?"

"Billy Crystal's character in *City Slickers* was the one who said that."

She rolled her eyes. "Of course you'd know where the quote came from."

"And the *reason* we should have sex," he continued, "is simple. Because it would be fun."

"Possibly," she allowed.

"*Definitely*," he countered, waggling his eyebrows.

"But it would also be complicated. And I detest complicated." When her lure popped out of the water, she didn't bother casting it back in. Instead, she propped the handle of the rod into the sand beside her feet. "So I propose an alternative. I propose we let bygones be bygones and agree to be friends."

"Ow!" He grabbed his chest. "Did you get a splinter from driving a wooden stake into my heart?"

She laughed, and it was easy. Nice.

Yes, she thought again. *This could work.* As long as she kept things in perspective. Kept *him* in perspective.

"Come on," she cajoled. "What do you say? Want to be my pal?"

His face looked comically forlorn. "Apparently, agreeing to be friends is somewhat of an epidemic on this island. But I suppose if that's all you're offerin'...." He let the sentence dangle and glanced at her hopefully.

"It is." She nodded decisively.

"Well, I guess I accept." He offered her a hand. She shook it. But when she went to pull back, he held on, the look in his eye having turned from teasing to intense. "On one condition," he added.

Misgiving had her narrowing her eyes.

"At some point, I'm going to ask a favor of you." His voice was low, and it seemed to have an edge. "And when I do, you have to agree to it."

"What kind of favor?" Why was she suddenly breathless?

"That's for me to know and you to find out."

"Mmm-mmm." She shook her head. "Way too broad. I can't agree to something like that. What if you ask me to jump off a bridge or run out and kill a bunch of kittens?"

His mouth flattened. "You really think I'd ever ask you to do either of those things?"

"No. But you see my point." She tried to tug on her hand again, but he held firm. Little electrical pulses of awareness shot up her arm.

For a long time, he said nothing, simply stared at her until she blinked and looked away. When he finally spoke, his voice was lower than usual. "Those are my terms, Christina." No one ever used her full name except for him. And why that should make her feel giddy, she'd never know. "Take it or leave it."

"Fine," she said hoarsely. At the same time, the voice in her head screamed, *Are you crazy? Stop! Turn back! There be dragons ahead!*

Smiling broadly, he tossed an arm around her shoulders. "Good. Now, mind if I grab a pole and join you?"

"Plenty of fish in the sea for both of us," she said, and thought she saw his eyes narrow slightly.

Then he winked and headed for the shed.

Watching him go, she tried to shake off the feeling that she'd just made a deal with Satan himself.

Chapter 19

11:23 a.m.

ALEX WAS A WRECK.

For the first time in her life, she didn't know what to do with herself. What to do with the deep, abiding sense of loss that left a gaping hole at the center of her.

How could I have been so wrong about someone? And worse, how could I have allowed myself to fall head over heels for that same person?

She'd always thought herself a good judge of character. Able to spot a bad penny when it turned up in her path. But apparently, she was blind as a bat if that bad penny happened to sport miles of muscles, raven-black hair, and eyes the color of the blue glass used to make nineteenth-century cobalt medicine bottles.

So what did that say about her?

That she was shallow? That she was no better than a teenager who was a slave to her hormones? That she wasn't as smart as everyone said she was?

None of those possibilities made her feel overly proud. Couple that with the sharp pain that pinched in her chest each time her heart beat, and she'd been battling the urge to cry ever since leaving Key West.

After landing on Wayfarer Island, she would've preferred a distraction. Would've liked to divert her attention away from herself and her heartache by relocating their underwater search grid from the small reef at the back of the island to the large reef at the front. But the guys had declared it a holiday.

Her second thought had been to lose herself in a book. She hadn't finished *The Buccaneers of America*, arguably *the* sourcebook on seventeenth-century piracy. But no matter how hard she'd tried to focus, the words had blurred on the pages. And Mason had been in the kitchen, banging pots and pans, further exasperating any chance she had at concentrating.

So here she was, doing her version of a Disney princess and sweeping the sand off the boards of the wrap-around porch.

Why did all Disney princesses sweep something at some point in their respective movies? Was it a not-so-veiled comment on a woman's place in the world? Or was it simply more fun to sing and dance with a broom in hand?

Hmm. Something to think about.

Although no matter how hard she tried to apply herself to the topic, her traitorous mind kept returning to Mason.

Mason and that kiss.

Mason and all her untenable feelings for him.

Mason in the lovely Donna's arms.

Just keep sweeping, Alex. A body in motion stays in motion. And sometimes a body in motion can stop a mind in motion. So just keep sweeping.

Making her way down the wide wooden steps, she

industriously sent clouds of dust into the yard. When the last tread was clear, she stepped down and wiggled her bare toes in the sand. It was warm and soft. Inexplicably, it felt like home.

Home…

Turning a slow pirouette, she took in the sight of the big clapboard house with its peeling paint and creaky hurricane shutters. Another half turn, and there was the crescent-moon-shaped beach hugging the turquoise waters of the lagoon. Further out was the reef that protected this side of the island from the crash of the ocean, and anchored just beyond it was the big salvage ship they used daily in their search for the *Santa Cristina*.

There was the long dock she liked to sit on and watch the sunset. Above her head were the palm trees that woke her up each day by chattering in the morning breeze. And there was the hammock where she liked to sip sweet tea and read. That is when Uncle John wasn't occupying it for his afternoon siestas.

She dragged in a breath, and it was filled with the warm smells of sand and salty sea, plus the more pungent aroma of Uncle John's infamous chicory coffee as it wafted from inside the house.

Having been born and raised in the Crescent City, John swore his java was the cure for anything from a concussion to the common cold. Of course, John was *also* a vocal proponent of marijuana, claiming he smoked it for his glaucoma, even though Alex was pretty sure his eyes were just fine.

In short, Uncle John enjoyed his substances.

She remembered one evening when he'd found her sitting out on the dock. For nearly thirty minutes while the sun sank into the sea, he'd regaled her with his theory that it was crazy-pants that humans drank the milk of other mammals.

I mean, it's not natural. If it were natural, you'd see a hippo gettin' a gullet full of gazelle milk, right? He'd waved his joint in the air. *Scientifically speakin', we're pretty screwed up as a species.*

When Alex had asked him, *How high are you?* his answer had been, *Yes.* Then he'd grinned and declared, *But see, that's the thing about bein' stoned. It makes you interestin'. Much better than alcohol, which makes you dumb.*

She found herself smiling at the memory, and was surprised because she wouldn't have thought herself capable of smiling. Not today.

Meat ambled by her, stopping to sniff her toes before following his nose around the side of the porch. Li'l Bastard strutted in Meat's wake, clucking contentedly. And once again, that word drifted through her head, as sweet as a lullaby.

Home…

If she couldn't find a way to reconcile her feelings for Mason, what would that mean for her future on the island?

The Deep Six guys needed her. Because even though the colonial Spanish documents pertaining to the sinking of the *Santa Cristina* were written in a language very similar to the one still spoken today, the writing itself had drastically changed over the centuries.

The flowing script, called *procesal*, had rounded symbols connected by long Arabic-like letters. She was one of about twenty people alive who could translate it, thanks to an interest she took in it after doing her undergrad thesis on Mel Fisher's hunt for, and eventual excavation of, the renowned *Atocha*. Afterward, she'd spent a year in Seville, Spain, under the tutelage of a master in *procesal*.

But she could read the old documents for the guys from anywhere. And even though it would break her heart to leave, she didn't know if she could stand staying, what with—

She felt his presence behind her before she heard his footfall.

"Alex?" His deep voice was soft. His tone inquisitive.

She clutched the broom handle tightly and briefly squeezed her eyes shut in an attempt to prepare herself for the visual onslaught that was Mason McCarthy. Turning slowly, she made extra sure what was in her heart didn't show on her face. "Yeah?"

"It's lunchtime."

She wondered what her response should be to this seemingly inane bit of information. *So it is? Bon appétit? Did you know the abbreviation "lunch" is taken from the Northern English word "luncheon," which is itself derived from the Anglo-Saxon word "nuncheon" or "nunchin" meaning "noon drink"?*

For a woman usually brimming with words, she suddenly was at a loss in coming up with anything appropriately frivolous or pithy. Also, a noon drink sounded pretty good right about now.

"I made BLTs," he added.

She nodded hesitantly. "Ohhh-kay. Should I tell everyone to come—"

"No." His eyes were so intent on hers, she couldn't have looked away even if she wanted to. "Only made enough for you and me. Thought we could have a picnic."

Her mouth fell open and a breeze picked up a strand of her hair, depositing it inside. She pulled it out at the same time she croaked, "Why?"

A line appeared between his eyebrows. "'Cause we're friends, right?"

She blinked. *Friends?* He still wanted to be *friends*?

Well, of course he did. Because in his mind, he'd done nothing wrong. In his mind—

"And I didn't sleep with Donna," he added, and her jaw unhinged a second time. The wind saw the move as another invitation.

My right boob for a hair tie! she thought wildly as she yanked a strand of hair from her mouth again. The beach house ate her ponytail holders. That was all she could figure.

He looked away, out toward the beach where Wolf and Chrissy stood fishing. "It didn't hit me 'til I was packing the picnic what you musta thought when I showed up with her at the airport. That's what you meant, right? When I wished you a good morning and you said it musta been a good one for *me*?"

All she could manage was a nod.

His expression turned pained. "I shoulda thought. Shoulda…" He swallowed and shook his head. "Taken a damn cab."

H-h-holy shit!

He hadn't slept with Donna. Note, he hadn't said he *wouldn't* sleep with Donna. Because of course he would. At some point. He and Donna were…well, whatever they were. But he hadn't kissed Alex and then run to get his rocks off with someone else.

Alex knew it was ridiculous to feel delighted about something *not* happening while knowing it likely *would* happen many times in the future. But she *was* happy.

She *hadn't* been wrong about him! He *was* all things good and brave and wonderful!

Considering the raucous nature of her inner celebration, she was surprised—and sort of proud of herself—when her voice came out calm. Dare she say serene?

"While I'm happy you didn't kiss me and then go bounce Donna around, because that would've been skeevy and proved you weren't the guy I thought I knew, you have every right to sleep with her whenever you want. She's your…" She scrunched up her nose. "Whatever you call her. Your *lady friend.* I'm just your regular friend, right?"

Funny, if you'd asked her last night if she could be happy being nothing more than his gal pal, she would've answered with a resounding *no.* But now? After having spent the last couple of hours thinking the worst of him? After thinking she'd never truly *known* him? Not to mention the idea that she might not be able to be around him and would have to leave the home and family she'd made for herself here on the island? Well, now the thought of being his friend sounded just fine. Better than fine. It sounded *great!*

Her love would remain unrequited. But that would be the extent of it.

It was as if a weight had lifted.

"I was with her this morning 'cause I ended things with her," he muttered.

Alex's chin jerked back so quickly she was surprised she didn't give herself whiplash. "Why?"

He frowned as if carefully considering his words. "Our kiss made me realize how wicked good it can be between two people who really care about each other." *Cayah 'bout each awtha.* "I didn't wanna be the reason Donna held herself back from finding that for herself."

Alex's lips parted. For a guy who so rarely strung more than a handful of sentences together, he sure had a way with words when he set his mind to it.

11:45 a.m.

"Did you know Spain called the Florida Keys 'Los Martires'? It means 'the Martyrs.' Why do you think they gave such beautiful places such tragic names?"

For the past ten minutes, Mason and Alex had been hiking through the mangrove forest behind the beach house, past Uncle John's marijuana patch, headed toward the small secluded beach at the back of the island. During each and every one of those minutes, Alex had regaled him with facts.

Truly, she hadn't stopped talking to draw air. And

Mason had been perfectly content listening to her chatter. But now she'd been quiet for a full five seconds, which meant her last question hadn't been rhetorical. She was waiting for him to answer.

"Maybe 'cause they were home to pirates who preyed on the galleons sailing from Central America to the New World."

She stopped in her tracks.

"What?" He frowned back at her.

"How do you know that?" Her eyes were wide behind the lenses of her glasses. "Did you read that book I left on the kitchen table?"

"You were pretty adamant we should, and I quote, 'Educate ourselves on the amazing history that surrounds the place where we live and work.'" He chucked her on the chin and then immediately regretted it because... *soft*. Alex's skin was so frickin' soft.

He curled his hand into a fist and dropped it to his side.

"But I'm *always* leaving books around and telling you guys to read them. I didn't think any of you ever took me seriously."

"I do," he said simply. He took her very, *very* seriously.

"Well, holy hell." She shook her head in wonder.

"I know." He made a face. "The blockhead from Boston can read. Who knew?"

"No." She was quick to correct him. "What I mean is that half of the stuff I've been telling you I got from that book. So you already *know* everything. And yet you let me prattle on. Why didn't you tell me to shut up?"

He continued up the trail. When she fell into step

behind him, he admitted over his shoulder, "'Cause I like hearing you talk."

"Aww. You say the sweetest things." When he glanced back, he found her full lips wrapped around a teasing smile. "I think I'm going to like having you for a friend."

He opened his mouth to say... He wasn't sure what. So he quickly closed it again.

The sad truth was he'd yet to come up with the right words to explain how, after weeks of turning her down, he was now ready to take her up on her offer.

Thanks to Doc, and with conditions attached, of course.

Some very strict, very set-in-stone, cannot-be-broken, hard-and-fast rules.

He hoped he would find the words he was missing during their picnic. With a full belly, and with Alex's penchant for opening her mouth and putting things out into the world unfiltered, he thought for sure an opportunity would arise where he could casually mention *Hey, Alex. I changed my mind. Let's bang.*

Okay, so obviously it wouldn't be *that*. It would be smoother. Sexier.

Or, you know, he could always pounce on her. *That* would get his point across. And it was far more his style. Less talk. More action.

Unfortunately, it would also preclude the laying down of the rules. And that couldn't happen. He had to make it clear to her, before anything physical happened, that this would be a one-time deal.

He wouldn't be able to live with himself if there were any misunderstandings and—

"Mason?" He realized he'd been quiet for too long. "Were you about to say something?"

"Ya-huh." He turned back toward the trail. "I'm starving. Let's hurry."

It wasn't a lie. He *was* hungry. He just happened to be hungry for far more than the BLT sandwiches and brownies he'd packed in the basket.

With images of the two of them naked and sweaty on the picnic blanket, his pace quickened. Fine, it was more like his anticipation had him nearly running.

When he realized she was having difficulty keeping up, he forced himself to slow down. And when he glanced back again, he saw a bead of sweat trickle down her forehead next to the bandage covering her cut. He hated the sight of it. The proof that she'd been in danger. That she'd been hurt.

"I, uh, never thanked you for saving our asses yesterday." He adjusted the picnic basket in his hand.

"Just doing what you taught me." She waved off his gratitude.

"You were *brave*, Alex." He hoped she could read the truth in his face. "Only reason we're standing here now is 'cause of you. You distracted them just when we needed you to."

She chewed her bottom lip. But given the way his body reacted, she might as well have been doing a striptease.

His own lips tingled. They remembered exactly how lush that bottom lip could be. How warm and soft.

Don't get a boner! The old mantra screamed through his mind.

"I wasn't trying to distract them." Something moved behind her eyes. He'd seen that something many times with green recruits who'd gotten their first taste of battle. It was the look of someone who'd come face-to-face with what it truly meant to deal in death. "I was trying to *kill* them. I wanted them dead. I wanted to send them to hell. What's that say about me?"

"That you're human," he assured her. "That you'll fight for your survival and the lives of those you care about."

She nodded. But the funny look on her face told him that while she wanted to believe him, she wasn't sure she did.

"It changes how I see myself." She glanced down to where she drew a circle in the sand with the toe of her flip-flop. "But more than that, it changes how I look at the world." When she glanced at him, her green eyes were overly bright.

It was probably a mistake, but he set the picnic basket on the ground. "Come here." He motioned her forward.

She hesitated. So he grabbed her hand and pulled her tight against him.

Could she hear how quickly she made his heart race? Could she feel how fast she made his blood run? Did she have any idea what she did to him?

"I used to think people were intrinsically good. That life was sweet." Her hot breath seeped through the cotton of his tank top to tickle the skin beneath. "I used to think I was safe as long as I didn't frequent seedy bars or walk down dark, deserted alleyways. But people *aren't* intrinsically good. And I'm *not* safe. The world is dark, Mason. And it's dangerous."

He wished he were more like Wolf. In a moment like this, the sorry bastard would be able to come up with something perfect and profound to help ease her mind. Instead, the only thing Mason could think to tell her was "Sorry, Alex."

She patted his chest, her hand light and warm over his heart. "It's not your fault. It's not anyone's fault. It simply *is*."

She tilted her chin back. "Does it ever get better? Do you ever stop looking over your shoulder, expecting to find monsters creeping up behind you?"

He squeezed his eyelids shut. Partly because he couldn't keep looking down at her without kissing her. But also because Alex was unsettlingly perceptive. If he looked at her now, she would see *him*.

All of him. All the good, bad, and ugly things inside.

"Gets better for some people." His voice was low with solemnity. "They can experience death and violence and put it behind 'em. Move on as if nothing happened. For others"—*Including me*, he silently added—"they're changed. Things from their past overshadow their present."

"What separates one group from the other?" Her tone was as somber as his.

"Wish I knew," he told her. "But I think you're the type who'll be able to forget. It might take time. But I think you'll see the world through rose-colored glasses again."

Her lips twisted. "I take it you don't feel you're the kind to forget and move on?"

He shrugged and stepped away from her. She was traipsing too close to the truth of him. Also, he'd lost the battle with his body when it came to her nearness. The clean, beachy smell of her had gone to his head. The little one decidedly south of his neck.

He retrieved the picnic basket. "I was born and raised in Southie, babe. My rose-colored glasses were gone by the time I was ten."

Chapter 20

ALEX LICKED THE LAST OF THE CHOCOLATE BROWNIE frosting from her fingertips and flopped onto the soft blanket Mason had laid down for the picnic. Folding her hands behind her head, she tried to see shapes in the fluffy, popcorn clouds overhead.

It was something she'd done since she was a child. She loved never knowing what sort of pattern would appear next. A pirate ship perhaps? A pig wearing a top hat?

Beside her, Mason was sprawled out, his shoulder touching hers, one arm folded behind him, pillowing his head. It felt nice. Comfortable. *Friendly* even.

Maybe this will work, she thought optimistically. *I mean, it's okay to be in love with a friend, isn't it? As long as I don't screw things up by telling him?*

When a cloud morphed into a boy holding a baseball, she mused aloud, "Did I ever tell you that the first base-ball game I ever went to was at Fenway Park?"

"No shit?" He turned his head slightly to stare at her.

"Mmm-hmm. My father landed an adjunct professor-ship at Boston College one semester. A colleague gave him some tickets. It was cool."

She smiled at the memory of her father enjoying something outside the world of academia.

"We sat really close to the dugout. I could see the players change gloves and dig into the bubble-gum bucket. And in the eighth inning, this really big guy got up to the plate. He swung that bat so hard I thought for sure the ball would end up outside the ballpark. But he only tipped it, and it *thudded* into the ground at his feet. He picked it up and then, casual as can be, turned and tossed it right to me."

"Which player?"

She frowned. "He was wearing number thirty-four."

Mason sat up so fast, she could feel the wind he displaced. "What year?" Both his tone and his eyes were suddenly intense.

"Mmm. Pretty sure it was 2011."

"Fuck me!" He grabbed his chest like she'd given him a heart attack. "That was David Ortiz. You got a ball touched by Big Papi."

When she blinked in confusion, he said, "Ten-time All-Star? Three-time World Series champ? Seven-time Silver Slugger winner?"

She winced and admitted, "I wasn't much of a baseball fan and—"

"Please tell me you kept it," he interrupted.

"Of course. It's in a box with a bunch of other souvenirs in my parents' basement."

"Listen to me carefully." He pointed at her nose. "Next time you go 'round to see 'em, you find that frickin' ball, take it out of the box, and put it inside a plastic baseball display cube. They're cheap and you can order 'em online."

"Oh-kay…" She was confused about why one dirty baseball was such a big deal. It sounded like this Big Papi guy was special, but it wasn't like he'd *signed* the ball or anything.

Maybe only baseball fans can appreciate its significance, she silently mused.

"*Promise me*," Mason insisted, his eyebrows slammed into a V.

"Cross my heart and hope to die." She used her finger to draw a cross over her chest before lifting her hand in pledge.

That seemed to satisfy him. He nodded and dug into the picnic basket for a brownie. After unwrapping it, he lay beside her and took a giant bite. The fresh smell of chocolate made her stomach rumble.

Or maybe it was the smell of *him*.

She wished she wasn't so aware of him. Wished she didn't notice every time he took a breath or made a sound.

Friends aren't supposed to be so attuned to each other, she admonished herself. *They're not supposed to feel every move the other makes.*

It was something she'd need to work on. Something she'd need to practice *not* doing in the weeks and months to come if she had any hope of keeping her love for him a secret.

Had she mentioned she hated secrets? Was complete crap at keeping them?

Above her, a cloud took on a recognizable shape. "Look." She pointed. "It's a baby elephant."

He slid his head closer to hers so he could follow the direction of her finger. A lock of his hair tickled her cheek.

"Looks more like a baby rhino to me." Hearing his voice so close had an unseen hand tugging at an invisible string attached to the bottom of her belly.

"*Now* it does." Her voice was husky. Did he notice? "The wind cut off its trunk and shortened its ears. Fifteen seconds ago, it was definitely a baby elephant."

"There's a bunny." He pointed and then licked his finger when he saw a speck of chocolate icing stuck to the tip.

The sucking sound had her heart thundering.

"It's called pareidolia," she said, trying to distract herself from the overwhelming urge to jump on top of him and taste the chocolate on his lips.

"What?"

She repeated the word slowly, and he pushed up on an elbow so he could frown down at her. The wind played with the wavy ends of his hair. The beard stubble on his cheeks and chin gave him a charmingly disheveled look.

Is this how he looks after sex? she wondered, then quickly reminded herself that friends didn't contemplate how the other looked postcoitus.

"I mean what does pareidolia *mean*?" He absently wiped a grain of sand from her cheek, and that's all it took for her to lose her breath. "Is it a name for the clouds? Or their shapes?"

"Both," she said, or rather *wheezed*. "Pareidolia is the tendency to interpret known patterns from vague formations. Like when people see Jesus in a piece of burnt toast or human faces on the moon."

One corner of his mouth curled. "You ever overwhelmed with all the stuff stored up there?" He tapped her temple. But given the way her heart leapt, he might as well have leaned down to kiss her.

"All the time." She frowned. "But I've found ways to"—she searched for the right words—"quiet the noise, I guess would be the way to describe it."

"How?" He seemed genuinely interested, so she gave him a genuine answer.

"Like you, I spend a lot of time alone. Away from outside stimulation. I like to sit on the dock. I like to read." At his look of confusion, she conceded, "I know it sounds weird. But my brain is *focused* when it's learning something new. It's quiet. It's concentrating. Also...there's you."

"Me?" A line appeared between his eyebrows.

"For whatever reason, when I'm around you, everything slows down." She wasn't able to meet his eyes for this next part. "I'm not sure why. Maybe it's because you always seem so calm, so deliberate. Everything about you screams *Slow down. Take a breath.* And so...I do." She shrugged.

When she dared glance into his eyes, his expression was oddly intent. She thought she saw a flicker of indecision flash across his face, as if he was working his way around to telling her something or asking her something, but hadn't quite figured out how to do it.

"With a brain like yours, you coulda been anything. A

doctor, an engineer, a rocket scientist. Why'd you choose history?"

She screwed up her mouth. "Because history holds all the answers. Why we have certain customs. Why we use certain words. Why we celebrate certain holidays. History is the beginning and the end of everything. It's the alpha and the omega."

"It's your religion."

She thought about that. "It *is* the thing I put faith in." Tilting her head, she studied all the different striations of blue in his irises. "What would you say is *your* religion?"

He snorted. "I was raised Irish Catholic. Most people don't expect that. They think I should have red hair and freckles. But I assure you, my great-grandparents on both sides came from the land of shamrocks and shillelaghs." She wondered if he realized that his accent thickened anytime he spoke of his origins or upbringing.

"Black Irish." She nodded. "A lot of people believe the darker complexions in Ireland stem from the Spanish Armada that landed there in the 1500s. But most historians agree there were dark-skinned, dark-haired people on the Emerald Isle long before that. The Celts started arriving as far back as 500 BC, and they're known to be darker people." She swallowed when a small grin pulled at his lips. "And there I go with the useless trivia, huh? It's okay if you want to let your eyes glaze over now."

"Nah." He shook his head. "Like I said, I like hearing you talk."

He could say that a million times over and she'd never get tired of hearing it.

She desperately wanted to reach up and trace the shape of his lips, feel his hot breath puff against her skin. Run her fingers over the subtle lines radiating from the corners of his eyes, because each of them was a testament to the life he'd lived. The hard-fought battles he'd won.

Was there a face on the entire planet more fascinating than Mason McCarthy's? If so, she'd yet to see it.

Instead, she asked softly, "You said you were *raised* Irish Catholic. Does that mean you're lapsed?"

One of his shoulders twitched. It wasn't really a shrug. More a gesture of vacillation. "After all the fucked-up stuff I seen in this wide world, it's hard to believe in a benevolent God who loves us and cherishes us."

It was a tender subject. She could see that. And since she didn't want this marvelous day to end, she quickly picked a new topic. "So why the navy?"

His lips twisted. "Kids who grew up where I did had one of two choices. Join the trades or the military." He was quiet for a moment before adding, "I wanted to see the world."

Once again, she thought she saw something strange move behind his eyes. Only this time, it looked suspiciously like regret.

"You wish you'd chosen differently?"

"Sometimes." He shrugged. "All the years of running and gunning changed me. I'm not the same person I was when I left Boston."

This time, she wasn't able to stop her fingers from pushing a lock of hair away from his eye. He instantly stilled, his gaze so sharp she quickly dropped her hand and curled it into a fist.

Stupid, stupid Alex!

He opened his mouth, and she was sure he was going to say it was time to leave. Sure she'd ruined everything by touching him. So when he said, "I wanna accept your offer," her mouth fell open.

Quite a feat considering she was still flat on her back. She wasn't sure how the physics behind that worked.

For a few seconds—or hours? Time no longer held meaning—she turned his words over in her head. They couldn't mean what she thought they meant. Could they?

Nah.

And yet...

Slowly, she pushed into a seated position. "Just to be clear"—her voice was a harsh rasp—"are you talking about the offer of my virginity?"

"Ya-huh."

Ya-huh. Strange how two tiny syllables spoken in a New England accent could make her heart feel so airy and light she thought it was a miracle it didn't float away on the breeze.

"But there are conditions," he added. "Everything I told you is true. We like each other. We respect each other. Heaven knows we *want* each other. It'd be too easy for one of us to let our feelings grow into something more."

Too late.

"Haven't changed my mind, Alex. I don't wanna fall in love again." His eyes implored her to hear what he was saying. "I can't be someone's everything. I'd just disappoint 'em. And I'd disappoint myself."

She tried to listen with an open mind. But she couldn't

shake the thought that if people could choose how and when they fell in love, or who they fell in love *with*, they'd choose not to fall at all.

Falling was scary. And in her experience, it *hurt*.

"To make sure that can't happen, we gotta limit ourselves to one day. *This* day." He glanced down at her hands, and she realized they were fidgeting in her lap.

She tried stilling them by curling them into fists. But that just made her knee jump. "Tomorrow, we wake up and go back to being friends and colleagues." His elusive smile held a hint of bedevilment. "Difference being you won't be a virgin, and we will have scratched this fucking itch we got. What d'you say?"

She couldn't bring herself to meet his eyes. Her own might reveal too much. So she directed her answer to his chin. "Okay."

The word came out hesitant, making her frown.

If she appeared even the slightest bit unsure, he'd call off the whole thing. Then where would she be?

She'd have lost her one chance to make love to the man who held her heart in his hands. And even if he didn't want it, even if he was determined that no one would ever hold his, didn't she *want* that chance? Wasn't something better than nothing?

Squaring her shoulders, she lifted her chin. "Okay," she repeated, sounding far more certain.

That seemed to satisfy him. Because he pulled her into his lap and claimed her lips.

His first kiss made her lose her mind. His second convinced her she'd never need it back.

Chapter 21

THE NICE THING ABOUT LIVING ON AN ISLAND WAS that few clothes were required. It was possible to get naked in about two seconds flat.

Which Alex seemed dead set on doing.

Straddling Mason's lap, she kissed him with a desire that was equal measures sweet and fierce. Between licks and sucks and nips and nibbles, she managed to whip his tank top over his head as well as her own T-shirt. Through it all, she rocked her hips against his hardness in a rhythm guaran-fucking-teed to drive him wild.

One of her hands speared into his hair. The other reached between their bodies, past his waistband, and wrapped tightly around him.

He hissed at the cool, firm feel of her fingers. Every fiber of his being wanted to flip her onto her back, rip off her shorts, and plunge into her.

But he couldn't. He *couldn't*!

The only time he'd been with a virgin, he'd been one himself. If memory served, it'd been quick and sweaty and awkward. Neither of them had known what they were doing, and both of them had come out the other side of the experience feeling they'd missed something important.

It would be different for Alex.

He was her first lover. *Her only lover,* a savagely possessive voice whispered through his head. It was incumbent upon him to do this right. To use everything he'd ever learned from every woman who'd come before to ensure this was everything Alex ever dreamed it would be.

First things first, though, he thought a little desperately. *We gotta slow this way fucking down.*

Her movements in his lap, not to mention her hand around his dick, were becoming frantic. She was making those tiny gasps of pleasure he remembered from the episode against the hotel door.

He knew what came next. Namely, *her.*

If she did, he wouldn't be able to hold back. Seeing her find her release? Watching her rub herself to completion atop him? That would be too much.

He was too excited. Too worked up. He'd wanted her for too fucking long.

"Alex." He ripped his mouth away. "Babe, slow down."

She either didn't hear him or didn't care to heed his instructions. Her little teeth latched onto his earlobe and her pistoning hips didn't miss a beat.

"Alex," he managed even as he felt his balls draw up. Much more and he was done for.

She might not have any experience, but her instincts were spot-fucking-on.

Growling, he jerked her hand from his shorts and flipped her onto her back. Immediately, she reached for him, trying to pull him on top of her. But he caught her wrists in one hand and manacled them above her head.

"*Alex!*" This time she registered her own name. She blinked, her eyes glazed with desire. "Slow down, babe. No need to rush this. Let's take our time."

"What if I don't want to?" Her chest rose and fell with harsh breaths.

He decided there was nothing in the world more captivating than her face when it was flushed with passion. "You do," he assured her. "You just don't know it yet."

She pouted prettily, and he wanted very much to claim her lips and forget what he'd just said. Then her eyes snagged on the bandage on his side and her expression grew horrified. "Oh my god! I wasn't thinking! Did I hurt you when I was—"

"Believe me when I tell you," he quickly put in, "*nothing* on me hurts when I'm with you. Well"—he frowned—"not in a *bad* way."

"Are you sure?" The care in her eyes hit him directly in the heart.

"Never been more sure of anything." And that was the truth. This moment with this woman, it was…right.

He mapped out his next moves in his head, anticipating which would make her moan and which would make her purr. "You trust me?"

She nodded quickly and he removed her glasses, setting them far enough away so they would be safe from what was to come. When he turned back to her, it was to find her eyes blazing.

Her gaze burned him. Singed his soul and ignited his heart. Then she turned her attention to his mouth, her little tongue darting out to wet her lips.

He followed the movement eagerly. Wondering what it would be like to feel her tongue lapping at his nipple. Swirling around his belly button. Gliding over the head of his—

He stopped *that* thought in its tracks and forced himself to take a deep, calming breath. When he had himself in hand, he did something he'd wanted to do since the day they met. He traced the arches of her eyebrows.

They *were* soft. Softer than he'd imagined. Warmer too.

It pleased him very much to watch the skin over her cheeks pinken from little more than the brush of his fingertip. And she looked so small and perfect staring up at him, her eyes full of anticipation. Full of…faith in him.

It made him feel ten feet tall and bulletproof.

"This feel okay?" he whispered gently. He'd let his fingers stray to the butterfly bandages on her forehead.

"Nothing hurts, Mason," she murmured. "Please don't stop."

"Never," he assured her, his blood pounding through his veins in a rhythm as old as time. And yet, he'd never felt this way before. Never experienced this level of awareness. "I'm gonna show you just how good it can be," he swore. "I'm gonna take you to places you've never been before. And we're gonna hit every stop along the way."

He wasn't one for words. But suddenly, he couldn't stop speaking. Vowing. Making promises.

After tucking a wayward curl behind her ear, he kissed the side of her mouth, loving how her lips automatically sought more. "And when you're ready, I'm gonna put myself inside you. Y'okay with that?"

A smile lit up her face and his whole body contracted. It was crazy what she could do to him with just one smile. "Yes, please."

There were certain memories so warm and wonderful that they seated themselves into a man's brain. This was one of those memories. Until his dying day, when he closed his eyes, he would conjure Alex in his mind. How she was right now, so utterly open and honest and beautiful.

Her bra was cotton-candy pink. Simple. Sweet. But it looked sexy as hell cupped around the soft, creamy swells of her breasts. He fingered one strap, arching an eyebrow. "Should we begin?"

"Yes, please."

He bit the inside of his cheek. "For a woman who usually has ten thousand words perched on the tip of her tongue, you're being awfully succinct."

She rolled in her lips—those delicious Kewpie-doll lips. "I figured that was far more expedient than telling you you're pushing on an open door and you're welcome to come on in."

"Well, then." He bent to kiss her shoulder and slide down her bra strap. "Let's get to it."

There was laughter in her voice when she answered, "Yes, please." But it ended in a gasp when he pulled down her bra cup and bared one delectable nipple to the sun dappling through the leaves of the palm overhead.

"You're beautiful, Alex." He brushed the callused pad of his fingertip over the tip of her breast and watched it pucker and pout. "So perfect. So soft." When he pinched the hard little nub, her hips came off the blanket by a foot.

She was a firecracker. No doubt about it. And experience told him it wouldn't take much to shoot her into the sky. But before she did, he wanted to watch her burn.

He wanted to make her beg.

He wanted the pleasure he pressed on her to be so exquisite that this memory, this moment, this *day* would seat itself in *her* mind too.

In the years to come, when she closed her eyes, he wanted her to see him as he was now, feel him as he was now, hot and heavy with desire for her.

Holding her tightly so she couldn't wiggle away, he closed his lips over her nipple and sucked until she squealed.

———————

12:39 p.m.

Alex had never cared for the color of her nipples.

They were too light. Not berry brown or cherry red like the women she'd seen while doing research for this moment. Hers were a pale, baby pink. Sweet. Cute. A far cry from anything she'd consider erotic.

Boy, was I wrong!

Now her nipples were two of her favorite body parts. Because Mason seemed to enjoy them immensely, and in doing so, he'd proved they were *highly* erotic.

When he sucked on them, delicious aching sensations traveled down to her belly. Farther, to pool hot and heavy between her legs. And when he gently caught the ruched nubs between his teeth, flicking the tips with his insanely talented tongue? Well, she nearly came.

"Mason," she moaned, her hips pumping. Twisting. Seeking. "Please, I need—"

"Shh, woman." Her nipple popped free of his mouth, and it was pure torture. Or a reprieve. She couldn't tell which. "I know what you need. You'll get it when I'm ready. When *you're* ready."

"I'm ready *now*." She tried to break free of his merciless grip. But it was useless. He was too strong.

"Good things come to those who wait," he growled, and the sound swirled in her ears. Low. Warm. Shockingly seductive.

"'Come' being the operative word," she insisted.

He blew over her nipple and her areola furled so tightly that she cried out with the pleasure-pain of it. Shocking herself because she'd never heard herself make a sound like that. It was primitive. Wild. Keening.

He awakened something within her that had been dormant her whole life. It was as if it'd been waiting for him. For his touch. For his kiss.

"Let go of my hands," she pleaded. "I want to touch you."

"No." He loomed above her, huge and triumphant.

The wind blew a shock of hair over his forehead, making him look almost boyish. But the expression in his eyes was anything but. It was hot. And wonderfully lecherous.

"When you touch me," he continued, slowly pulling down the other cup of her bra until both her breasts were exposed to the breeze and his ravenous gaze, "I can't think. And I *wanna* think, Alexandra. I wanna see and touch. I wanna feel and taste. All of you. Every sweet inch."

To prove his point, his mouth reclaimed one breast while his free hand cupped and shaped and caressed the other.

She opened her mouth, but no sound emerged. Every wire in her brain crossed and every synapse misfired while he patiently, tirelessly tended to her breasts with his tongue and teeth and fingers.

Mason was a multitasker. He seemed able to do a million things at once.

And he was magic. That's the only way she could explain how her bra was off and crumpled on the blanket beside her head when she couldn't recall him removing it.

His dedicated fingers strayed to the button at the top of her shorts, and when he lifted his head to say, "I'm gonna get you naked now," his expression looked very much like she felt.

Deliciously tormented. Full of aching need.

A line appeared between his eyebrows when she shook her head.

"You don't want me to get you naked?" She thought she heard a hint of desperation in his voice.

"Oh, no. I *definitely* want you to get me naked. But I want *you* naked first."

She thought herself a genius. If he took off his swim trunks, he'd have to release her wrists. Then she'd be able to touch him like she'd been dying to since the first day she saw him sitting shirtless on a little stool in front of his easel.

So many heavy, roping muscles. Such thick slabs of flesh. All that wonderfully crinkly man hair.

He'd been covered in flecks of paint. She remembered how she'd wanted to offer to help him wash them off. With her *tongue*.

For a long moment, he regarded her, obviously seeing through her ploy. She held her breath, wondering if he would appease her anyway. She blew it out when he sat up and whipped off his shorts in one quick movement.

Turning back to her, he eyed the button on *her* shorts, intent on getting her naked as quickly as he'd gotten himself, so he didn't see her eyes fly open so wide that the breeze coming in off the ocean dried them out and made them tear.

H-h-holy shit.

He was glorious. Also…a bit terrifying.

She'd thought her hours of research had prepared her. But it was one thing to see a very large, fully engorged penis on the screen of her iPad. Quite another thing to come face-to-face with one in real life.

She licked suddenly dry lips. "I guess my curse didn't work."

"What?" he asked distractedly, having pulled down the zipper on her shorts. They—along with her panties— were quickly wrenched from her legs.

He's good. I'll give him that, she thought with reluctant admiration, at the same time she couldn't take her eyes off his dick.

It was…impressive. And sort of…*aggressive*-looking. His shaft was straight and thick, roped with angry veins. And the head? Well, it looked like a plum. Round. Shiny.

Will it taste as sweet? she wondered.

If she hadn't been so mesmerized by his nudity, she might have been self-conscious about her own. After all, hers wasn't a figure most men craved.

But apparently, Mason was the exception. Because his eyes roved over her from head to toe, taking pit stops in places that raised her blood. His tone was reverent when he lay down beside her. "You're perfect. Such a delicate pink," he murmured, watching her body's response when he smoothed the callused pad of his thumb over her nipple. Then he hooked a hand behind her knee and bent her leg up and out. Exposing her. Opening her to the warm kiss of the sun.

He took a quick look at the hot, wet center of her. Before she could feel bashful about such blatant appraisal, his gaze turned predatory, and she felt herself growing hotter and wetter still.

"Your sweet pussy is just a shade darker." His accent turned the last word into *dahkah*. "I think rose pink is my new favorite color." *Cahlah.*

Before she could sputter a response, he reclaimed her lips in a kiss that had her forgetting how badly she wanted to touch him. Instead, she dug her nails into the hard, corded brawn of his shoulders and held on for dear life as his mouth consumed hers and his busy, *busy* hands brushed and teased and squeezed. He found curves and valleys she didn't even know she possessed.

Just when she thought he'd touch her where she most wanted to be touched, where she most *needed* to be touched, he stopped. She barely refrained from screaming in frustration.

Opening her eyes, she needed a while to focus. She was dazed and confused by the thrum of unrequited need. But when she *was* able to focus, she found him watching her intently. "What curse?"

"Huh?" She blinked in confusion.

"You said your curse didn't work. What curse?"

"I know I'm new at this, but is there usually this much talking?"

He hitched a shoulder. "We're taking things slow, so I don't see any harm in continuing our conversation. What curse?"

"The one I wished on your penis." She ran one finger over his nipple, delighting when goose bumps broke out across his skin. "Well, it was more of a pox than a curse really." She used the side of her thumbnail to press into the center of the flat, brown disk, and he hissed her name.

Lifting her head, she sucked his nipple into her mouth and he palmed the back of her head, holding her to him. Instinct had her reaching down to fist her hand around his unimaginable hardness. The instant she did, he groaned.

The sound was barbaric. Crude. And completely beautiful to her.

Unfortunately, all too soon, he gripped her wrist and pulled her hand away. At the same time, he forced her flat against the blanket.

Her mouth immediately missed the taste of him. Her fingers immediately missed the feel of him. All that soft, silky flesh encasing a thick rod of tempered steel.

"Ugh." She pouted up at him. "More talking?"

"Why'd you put a pox on my penis?" There was something more than curiosity in his eyes. He looked very serious all of a sudden.

"Well..." She twisted her lips. "The first time was because you refused to use it on me. And the second time was because I found out you were using it on Donna."

When she tried to wrench her wrist from his grasp, he tightened his grip. She blinked at him. "What now?"

"Sorry, Alex." Regret shadowed his eyes. "Never meant to—"

Using her free hand, she shoved a finger over his lips. Those gorgeous lips that should be doing unspeakable things to her instead of, you know, *speaking*. "How about you make it up to me by getting this show on the road?"

Her words must've pleased him. Because a second later, he sucked her finger into his mouth and laved it with his tongue. Then, he claimed her lips and gently palmed her breast, rolling her nipple between his fingers until she gasped with pleasure.

She tried to fist his turgid length again, and again he manacled her wrist to stop her. "Waist up, woman," he grumbled against her mouth. "You got free range there but nowhere else."

"Fine," she muttered, "but please don't think you're restricted to the same area with me."

His answer was a low growl and a return to what he'd been doing.

He used his lips and teeth and tongue and hands on every inch of her. Each part of her seemed to hold some sort of fascination for him, and he took his time exploring. Thoroughly. Very, *very* thoroughly until his warm, callused palm splayed over her lower belly.

If he didn't ease her exquisite misery soon, she was going to do it herself. It was too much. She couldn't take any more.

Just when she was about to reach down to touch herself, the wonderful, talented man placed the heel of his palm directly over the spot where she needed it most. Then he curled his fingers around her. "Fuck me, you're wet. And your little clit is so swollen and hard."

At that point, she could do little more than whimper. When he dragged his hand up and down in a dirty grind, she couldn't even manage that. She was no longer a human woman. She was a wanton mass of flesh and blood and screaming nerve endings.

She *was* her clitoris. It was where she began and ended. And just when she thought it couldn't get better, it did.

He slipped a thick finger inside her and pumped twice before adding a second. Now, along with the jangling of the nerve bundle at the top of her sex, she was deliciously full. Wonderfully stretched. That void at her center mercifully filled.

His tongue stroked into her mouth in a rhythm to match the advance and retreat of his fingers. Then he wiggled them in a come-hither motion, and she disintegrated.

That was the only way to describe it.

She blew into a million pieces and every single one of them pulsed with delight. Over and over and over again. Throbbing. Tumbling. Expanding. Retracting.

She was pleasure. She was pain. She was the universe and she was an atom. Whole in a way she'd never been before and yet nothing at all save for a jumble of exquisite, raw satisfaction.

She couldn't say how much time passed. It could've been ten minutes or ten seconds. But eventually her spasms were reduced to shivers. And she thought she heard him say, "That's one."

One what?

She didn't know. She didn't care. She was too busy basking in the aftereffects of a glorious release.

"Alex?" He rubbed a knuckle down her cheek, coaxing her eyes open. She blinked twice because she'd gone cross-eyed.

"Sorry." She cleared her throat. "Difficult to talk. Vocal cords and body paralyzed by orgasm."

His expression was bemused. "Are they, now? And just think, that's only the first one. How will you feel after the next?"

When she replied, "Can't wait to find out," he chuckled and she became acutely aware of the length of him against her hip. He was weighty and thick.

"Can I venture below the belt now?" she asked when he nuzzled her cheek. Her ear. His breath hot and wickedly moist over her flesh.

"No." He tongued her earlobe.

"Why not?" She pouted. "When's it going to be my turn?"

He nipped at her collarbone. Her nipples seemed to think he was headed their direction, because they sat up and started trying to get his attention.

"After I give you three orgasms, you can do everything, anything you wanna do. In the meantime, I claim the right to do everything and anything *I* wanna do. And right now I wanna taste what I just touched."

Something about his plan seemed inequitable. But she couldn't figure out what it was. Not with his fingers busy at her breast.

After her explosive orgasm, she would have thought she needed time to recover. But apparently not. She was already losing her mind again. Everything inside her squeezing impossibly tight.

He wanted to give her three orgasms before he'd allow her to touch him?

Who was she to argue?

Chapter 22

ALEXANDRA MERRIWEATHER WAS AS CUTE AS A kitten and as sexy as a siren.

Mason had never thought those two things could coexist in one woman, but she proved him wrong. And despite being a virgin, she seemed to understand physical pleasure on a visceral level.

She approached it the same way she approached everything in her life. Headfirst and with gusto. As if it were her due. Which, he supposed, it was. It was *every* woman's.

But Alex made it hot as fuck.

Having kissed his way down her body, reacquainting himself with all the places he'd found in his earlier explorations, he finally made it to his destination. He lay between her legs, his dick pressed firmly against the blanket so the fabric could catch the drops of excitement that slowly leaked from him.

"You ready?" He placed a tender kiss on her hip bone.

"I was born ready."

His chuckle was low and full of lust. Then, he immediately sobered as he thought, *I know just how she feels*. It seemed he'd been put on the planet for this one purpose. To be her first. To guide her. To teach her. To *know* her.

But first…

He wanted—no, he *needed*—to make good on his promise to taste her.

Draping her legs over his shoulders, he sucked in a breath. The view was unreal. So pretty. So pink. So swollen and ready.

The sight had his balls quivering for release. The tangy, clean smell of her arousal made his nostrils flare.

"Please, Mason." Her hips thrust up at him. The most female of invitations.

It was all he needed. He buried his face between her thighs.

She moaned when he licked, whimpered when he sucked, and cried out incoherently when he caught her clitoris between his teeth and stabbed at it with his tongue. Her taste was salty and candied and something more. Something that was uniquely Alex.

He hoarded every sound. Every squirm. Every flavor. Stored every memory so he could conjure them up for future fantasies.

"I need you to—" Her hands were in his hair, her fingers gripping and pulling in frustration because she was close but couldn't quite fall over the edge.

"I know what you need," he growled against her swollen, hungry flesh, sinking two fingers deep into her wet heat.

Wail was really the only word to describe the sound that issued from the back of her throat. Raising her head, she looked down to watch what he was doing. Her eyes collided with his, and that was all it took for her body to go into nuclear meltdown.

He thought it'd been amazing to feel her come apart around his fingers. But nothing compared to this. To the smell of her release. The taste of it. The feel of her thighs clasped tight around his ears.

He decided if he died then and there, he'd be happy. Because... *What a way to go.*

He didn't die, of course. He continued to gently suck and lick until the final tremors tore through her and her legs fell listlessly to the sides.

Pushing into a kneeling position, he never took his eyes off her, wanting to see every last quiver of delight, while at the same time reaching into the picnic basket for the jimmies he'd stored there.

It was the work of an instant to roll one on. But he was so needy, so *ready*, that even the touch of his own hand was enough to make him hiss.

The sound had Alex's eyes fluttering open. The pleasure he saw in them was still crystalline and sharp. But the way she looked at him?

Oh, the way she looked at him made him feel... There was no word for it. *Desirable* and *heroic* to start. But then add in *trusted* and *adored*.

This must be how Superman feels, he thought.

"I can't wait anymore," he told her, his voice raw.

"I don't want you to." She reached for him, but he resisted the haul of her hands against his shoulders. He wanted to see the moment he entered her.

Lifting her leg to make room for himself, he grabbed the base of his cock and placed his swollen head at her entrance, notching inside the barest inch.

"You'll tell me if anything hurts?" A bead of sweat gathered at his temple. Another slipped down the groove of his spine.

She bit her bottom lip and nodded.

That was all the permission he needed. Claiming her mouth, he sank in another inch.

It was heaven. It was hell. And even though every fiber of his being screamed at him to stroke home, to rut and fuck and take her, take her, *take* her, he couldn't.

He had to make every second everything it could be. Every *sensation* everything it could be. But also he had to ensure she was really, truly ready to receive him.

She was very wet, very warm, and very aroused. But she was also very small. And he was...*not.*

With more willpower than he would have thought possible, he continued to sink inside her by tiny, excruciatingly slow increments. She whimpered. She wiggled. But never once did she ask him to stop.

What seemed like a hundred years later, he was finally in. To the hilt. His balls pressed against the sweet curve of her ass. His entire shaft encased and caressed by her tight, silky walls.

They moaned in unison, and it was the song of angels. Or devils. He didn't know which. He just knew this was the sweetest, most amazing sex he'd ever had.

And he hadn't even really begun.

Releasing his lips, she buried her face in the crook of his neck and whispered his name against his skin. Her arms and legs wrapped around him, pulling him so close he knew she was trying to make them one.

He was undone.

A wave of possessiveness washed through him. It was followed by a wave of protection. She was his. And he would move heaven and earth for her.

Except…she was his only for this day. And he didn't need to move heaven and earth for her, he only needed to move himself. Out of her life once this was over.

The thought hurt so much he knew there could be no more pretending he simply liked her and lusted after her.

He loved her. *Loved* her. Like he'd never loved anyone in his whole sorry life. And yet that changed nothing. Because he was still *him*.

When she fell for someone, that person would be sweet and clean. Unfettered by a violent past. Mason would make sure of it.

But first, he would make love to her.

He would put a lifetime of love into this one time.

With that thought wrapped around his heart, and with Alex wrapped around his body, he began to move. Slowly. Softly. Shallow strokes that had a voice in his head growling *mine, mine, mine* with every forward motion of his hips.

Her lips sought his. He obliged. When he plunged his tongue inside her mouth, he swallowed the sound of her moan. Took it into himself so it could knit with the fabric of his being.

Alex, Alex, Alex…

Her name was a silent song that matched his strokes. Her little nipples grazed his chest. One more exquisite sensation on top of the mind-melting sensation of her tight body surrounding him so thoroughly.

Speaking of her tight body…

It grew more accustomed to the intrusion of his own. Every thrust home was a little easier. Every slick slide back was a little more fluid. He stretched her. Smoothed out every fold. Owned every inch he touched.

Picking up the rhythm, he simultaneously lengthened his strokes. The feel of her, all that wet heat sliding against him, sucking at him, had his brain buzzing right along with his balls.

He was drugged by the feel of them together. By the way she sank her teeth into his shoulder, her tongue laving his skin. By the way her hips rose to meet him move for move. By the way she let out a lusty growl when he sank deep and held firm, the tip of his dick smashed hard against the entrance to her womb.

He wanted to see, *needed* to see.

Gently gripping her hip with one hand, he used the other hand to lift himself. She grumbled unhappily and tried to pull him back.

"Shh," he whispered. "I wanna look at us, Alex. I wanna see the point where you stop and I start. And I wanna know we're connected even beyond that."

He did just that, and it was the most erotic sight he'd ever seen. She was so pink. So sweet. So deliciously swollen around him that when he pulled back, her body tried to go with him, her flesh dragging wetly against his shaft.

He was harder than he'd ever been. He looked monstrous and red.

If she hadn't been mewling and squirming, her hands on his hips, urging him forward, he might have thought there was no way he wasn't hurting her. It seemed impossible that—

"Oh my god." Her breath was hot against his chest. She'd lifted her head to see, too, and she obviously found the sight as stimulating as he did because her pupils dilated until they eclipsed her irises. "Move," she whispered. "I want to see us and—Oh my *god*!"

He was already doing as instructed, and truly, it was a wonder he didn't come on the spot. He was *close*. Too close. If he kept watching, he'd get closer still.

Closing his eyes, he pistoned his hips harder. Grinding into her on the downstroke. Hoping he could last even though, with every thrust, his heart beat faster, his breaths came harder, and more and more of his brain cells died.

Not to mention his balls. The hum inside them grew angry. Desperate. They needed release. They'd waited too long. *He'd* waited too long.

"Your pussy's the sweetest thing I've ever felt." He adjusted his angle until the head of his cock rubbed her in just the right spot.

He *knew* it was the right spot because she cried out, fell back against the blanket, and let her eyes roll back in her head.

"Come on, babe," he coaxed as the scent of sex filled his nostrils. "Come with me, Alex." He could feel the telltale ache at the base of his dick.

He tried sneaking a hand between them so he could thumb her little clit and speed her along. But she growled low in the back of her throat, locked her heels behind his knees, and slammed her hips against his hard-riding cock.

"Fuck!" he gasped. "I'm gonna—"

The rest of his words strangled in his throat because right at that moment, her body began to suck greedily at his dick. She screamed his name and her release triggered his own.

It was unlike anything he'd experienced before. *She* was unlike any other woman.

She was sweeter. Hotter. Sexier.

His orgasm was so intense he wasn't sure he hadn't blown the head off his dick. And it lasted forever. Pulse after pulse. Spasm after spasm. Contraction after contraction. The pleasure just went on and on and *on*.

By the time he collapsed on top of her, he was completely, utterly, thoroughly wrung dry. His throat was a desert. He'd come all the moisture from his body, and he couldn't see. Couldn't speak. Couldn't move.

And yet…some small speck of his mind remained.

It told him he was crushing her. But he didn't want to leave her. Didn't want to lose that connection.

So he slipped a hand beneath her and took her with him when he rolled onto his back. She lay atop him, warm and soft and totally languorous, their bodies still gloriously joined.

It felt amazing. Real. *Right.*

He had no concept of time, so he wasn't sure how much passed before she patted his chest and said breathily, "I'm officially no longer a virgin."

"Fuck no you aren't." He chuckled, thinking there may have never been another woman in the history of the world who'd been so completely and so thoroughly devirginized.

She smiled. He could feel the curve of her cheek move against his heart. That heart that had fallen for her even though he'd tried his best not to let it.

"Thank you," she whispered. Then he thought she let out a little snore.

Ducking his chin, he smoothed the hair from her brow.

Sure enough. She was flat-out asleep. Just like that.

He wasn't sure if he should take that as a compliment or an insult.

Closing his eyes, he wrapped his arms around her and snuggled her close. He pretended they could be this way forever. He pretended she was truly his.

Chapter 23

"MASON AND HIS BUDDIES DESERVE EVERYTHING they have coming for what they did to your family and my men." The American stared hard at Izad. "But there are two women and one old man on that island too. They haven't done jack shit to anyone. Y'all ready to kill them too? The only way this plan works is if we leave no witnesses behind. I don't want you or your men getting cold feet when faced with the eyes of an innocent."

"Strange you did not mention this to Kazem before he left. The women were part of the equation then too." Izad matched the American's hard stare and even harder tone, even though saying his son's name left a bitter residue on his tongue and made his heart ache so badly, he nearly collapsed from the pain.

Truly, the only thing that kept him on his feet was the thought that he *must* prevail where Kazem had failed. All of this loss and death and pain couldn't be for naught. It had to *mean* something. Izad had to see it through and make certain of that.

"Kazem was young and idealistic," the American countered. "He didn't understand it's the collateral damage that sticks in a man's mind long after the mission is over. But *you* understand. And I'm assuming your men understand too." He waved a hand to include the four remaining members of Izad's security detail. They were gathered around the hotel suite's dining table, studying the maps of Wayfarer Island the American had downloaded from a government website of federal land-lease deals.

"Everyone here is an experienced soldier or sailor," the American continued. "That can work *against* us in this situation."

"They know the difference between revenge and vengeance," Izad assured him. "Revenge is equitable. But vengeance? Vengeance means killing the enemy no matter the cost. When they followed me here, they understood this was a mission of vengeance. They will not falter."

Again, the American glanced around the table. He must have found what he was looking for in the eyes of Izad's men because he jerked his chin down once and then pointed to the map in front of him. "Okay, so the first step will be to go in at oh-late-thirty. I'm thinking between midnight and one in the morning. We'll approach from the back side of the island—"

As the American laid out his plan, Izad lent him half an ear. The rest of his mind drifted to his wife and children. Their beautiful faces. The sounds of their voices. The smell of their hair.

He *would* prevail in this endeavor. He could not imagine Allah would have it any other way. And yet…a dark foreboding itched at the back of his brain. He was suddenly sure he would *not* survive to see the new dawn. He would die in the process of ending Mason McCarthy.

Just as well, he thought. *I am ready to see my family again…*

———————

2:57 p.m.

Alex had wondered what Mason looked like after sex and now she knew. He looked…pretty much the same.

Big. Bronze. And a little untouchable, even in his sleep.

Those muscles, the tattoos, so much latent strength… it all screamed, *Beware! This man could crush you like a bug!* And yet, she knew just how tender he could be. How truly *touchable* he was.

How his nipples beaded under the sweep of her tongue. How the brush of her fingertips raised goose bumps over his arms. How he hummed with pleasure when she sank her fingers into his hair.

Oh, yes. Mason McCarthy is eminently touchable.

She would like to touch him *now*, but she didn't want to wake him. Not when he looked so peaceful, all the worries wiped from his wide brow. Not when his big chest rose and fell in a deep, even rhythm that told her he was enjoying a dreamless sleep.

Not when she could use the opportunity to study him.

All of him.

When she'd first awoken from the deepest sleep ever, he'd been on his side spooning her, his arms tucked firmly around her, one hairy thigh sandwiched between her own. She'd reveled in the feel of him. The heat of his skin warming her back. The moist puffs of his breath at her neck. The steady hammer of his heartbeat against her backbone. But a cramp in her calf—no doubt brought on from having her toes pointed in sheer ecstasy for so long—forced her to wiggle out of his embrace.

At first, he'd grumbled, his forehead wrinkling in his sleep as if her desertion upset him. But then he'd flipped onto his back and quickly sunk back into oblivion.

She couldn't say she was sorry. The view was...pretty damn spectacular.

She let her eyes wander over him, cataloging all the big details. Like the patch of hair across his chest which, it turned out, was soft to the touch. Like the muscular lines on the inside of his hips, evidence of his manly fitness. Like the curlicue lettering of the tattoo on his forearm, the tribute to a man she'd heard so much about but would never get to meet.

She made note of the small details too. Like the white crescent-shaped scar above his collarbone. Like the little freckle beside his left nipple. Like how his belly button wasn't an innie or an outie, but some delightful combination of both.

Then there was his penis. Normally, she would give it the label of "big detail." But flaccid, it wasn't nearly as aggressive-looking. In fact, it was sort of cute. Like a roll of flesh-toned Play-Doh or—

What would he think if he knew I was comparing him to Play-Doh?

Probably not much, she decided with a giggle.

Men were so sensitive about their penises. Then again, having experienced *his* penis in all its wonder, she could understand what the fuss was about. As far as appendages went, it was pretty darn handy. And amazingly adroit—although that might have more to do with its owner than the organ itself.

Indeed, she couldn't have found a better man or penis to rid her of her virginity had she searched and—

Oh my god! I'm no longer a virgin!

She'd realized it on a surface level directly after the main event, but it wasn't until right at that moment that the knowledge sank deep, hitting her on a cellular level.

It was done. She was rid of it.

I'm no longer a virgin! She rolled the delicious idea around her head.

Yes, indeed. Virginity sucked and sex was wonderful.

She wished she could go back in time and club her younger self over the head for not doing as her peers had done and pursuing it with more interest.

Then again, if she'd done that, Mason wouldn't have been her first. And she was so happy he'd been her first because…well, she loved him. And that had to make it the best it could be, right?

Better if he loved you back, that voice whispered.

Screw you! she silently growled. She had this day. This *one* day. She refused to let anything ruin it. Especially inconvenient truths.

Raising her hand to shield her eyes, she checked the position of the sun. It was making its way across the western sky, proving they'd slept for at least two hours.

When her stomach rumbled, she reached into the picnic basket, fishing around for a second helping of brownies. Her fingers bumped into a strange foil square instead. Grabbing one corner, she pulled out the mystery item and discovered it was a condom.

Not just one. A whole strip.

Five to be exact.

Got a healthy opinion of your sexual prowess, don't you? she thought as she smirked down at Mason. She couldn't wait to put that opinion to the test.

Dropping the condoms back into the basket, she searched some more and pulled out a brownie. Sitting cross-legged, she took a bite. Sweet, sugary delight exploded against her tongue.

Closing her eyes, she wondered if there was anything on the planet more delicious than chocolate. When she reopened her eyes, they snagged on Mason's manhood.

What does that *taste like*, she wondered?

Then she nearly choked on her brownie because the member in question began to lengthen and swell. Watching with avid interest, she saw it go from an innocuous-looking roll of flesh to a long, meaty column of steel. The wide, plummy head touched the hollow of his navel.

"See something you like?"

She jumped at the sound of his voice, nearly dropping the brownie. Heat flooded her cheeks when she realized he'd caught her ogling him.

So what if I was? she told herself. *He's my lover, even if that's only for today. And lovers have free license to gawk.*

"Just appreciating you in all your manly splendor."

He hummed encouragement and ran a hand up her hip. Goose bumps followed in the wake of his touch. Her nipples joined in the party by furling painfully.

An idea bloomed to life in her head. A wonderful, delicious, *diabolical* idea.

With her heart thudding in anticipation, she dipped a finger into the icing atop her brownie and smeared it over his bottom lip.

He went to lick it off and she swatted him. "Uh-uh. Leave it. I have plans for it."

The blue in his irises darkened dangerously.

Another dip of her finger, and this time the icing ended up on his collarbone.

"Hey." He grabbed her wrist, his frown playful. "What're you doing?"

"That's for me to know and you to find out," she assured him.

"Can two play this game?" He reached for the brownie, intent on painting her with icing. She whipped the treat out of his reach.

"Nope. You had your three. Or"—she corrected with a siren's smile—"rather, I had *my* three. Now it's time for you to make good on your promise. You said I could do whatever I wanted to you, and I want—" She transferred some icing onto his nipple, watching with delight as it crinkled. Another dollop went in his belly button. "—to kiss my way from your lips to your chest to your belly and then…"

She didn't finish. She let his mind fill in the blank when she placed a big smear of chocolate on the head of his bobbing dick.

The sound he made at the back of his throat was that of a wild animal.

Feeling powerful in a way she never had before, she straddled him and pressed his hands over his head. "No touching. No fondling. No kissing. It's *my* turn."

"How 'bout breathing?" He blew across her nipples because, in this position, her breasts dangled dangerously close to his face.

Her eyes briefly crossed, but she had the wherewithal to sit up and remove herself from temptation.

"Breathing is totally acceptable," she told him, donning the imperious tone of a schoolmarm.

His pulse hammered in the big veins snaking up each side of his throat. Color flooded his face. What she planned on doing obviously excited him.

It excited her too. The flesh between her thighs grew achy and wet.

"This isn't fair," he complained. "I didn't say you couldn't touch me *at all*. I only said—"

"Shh," she scolded. "My turn. My rules. I expect you to follow them just like I followed yours. Is that understood?" She lifted a haughty eyebrow.

He grumbled something so wonderfully dirty it made her cheeks flame.

"I'll take that as a yes." And then she kissed him. Kissed the chocolate off his bottom lip, sharing it with him by delving her tongue deep inside his mouth.

It wasn't chocolate syrup like Chrissy had said. It was better. Alex far preferred icing.

"I'm not doing this to torture you." She kissed her way

to his ear. "I'm doing this because when you touch me, I can't think. And I *want* to think, Mason. I want to see and touch. I want to feel and *taste*. All of you. Every sweet inch."

She dropped her head to lick his pulse point, loving the feel of his heart hammering against her tongue.

"You stole my line," he accused through gritted teeth.

"It's a good line," she teased, tonguing the chocolate off his collarbone and then quickly making her way to his nipple.

When she closed her mouth over it and sucked, she assumed he was fully on board with her plan because he didn't utter another objection. Instead, he got a better grip on the blanket over his head by balling the fabric between his fingers.

By the time she got to the dollop of chocolate on the head of his penis, he was covered in sweat and trembling. A wicked smile curved her lips when she asked, "Are you ready?"

"I was born ready."

"Now who's stealing lines?" she teased.

His chuckle turned into a deep, desperate gasp when she took him into her mouth, chocolate and all.

Chapter 24

MASON. WAS. CHANGED.

Whatever Alex had done to him, some sort of strange alchemy he'd never experienced before—which, yes, he got the irony considering *he* was the one supposed to be showing *her* all the moves—had re-formed him on a molecular level.

There was the Mason who existed before. There was the Mason who existed after.

After Mason understood pleasure on a whole new level.

When he closed his eyes, he could still see her there, kneeling between his thighs, her hands working his shaft while her cheeks hollowed out from the force of her sucking. She was a savant. Despite her inexperience, she'd known just how to touch him, how to lick him to have his entire sex going nuclear.

And she'd done it over and over and *over* again. Brought him to the brink, and then backed him away until, finally, he'd begged her to take pity on him.

She had, and his orgasm had been... There were no words to describe it. Except to say once again that he was changed.

Turning his head, he found her lying beside him,

propped up on her side watching him. The smile on her face was one of extreme self-satisfaction.

"Where in the *world* did you learn to do that?" His voice sounded like it'd been run over by a tank.

She caught her bottom lip between her teeth. "It's called edging. There are entire websites dedicated to it. I studied up."

Of course she had. Because Alex never took on any task without first educating herself. Later, he knew the thought of her watching dirty videos in an effort to learn ways to blow his fucking mind would make him hard as a rock. But currently, he was more spent than he'd ever been in his life.

"How'd I do?" she asked cheekily.

"Minx, you know damn well how you did." He poked at his thigh. "Right now I'm trying to decide if my legs will ever work again."

Truly, he was completely numb from the waist down. But little tremors of electric delight still played at the base of his spine.

"I'm sure you'll be fine." She patted his shoulder and then pushed to her feet. Grinning down at him, she added, "In time."

When she went to step off the blanket, he snagged her ankle. "Wait. Where are you going?"

"Thought I'd go for a swim and cool off."

"Oh, I see how it is." He pretended affront. "Now that you've had your way with me, the mystery is solved and you've lost interest. You're gonna run off for a swim and leave me here completely spent and utterly alone."

"Ha!" She threw her head back. The breeze tangled in her curls, making them riot. And even though he would have thought there was no chance he could perform for *at least* another month, seeing her standing over him, gloriously nude, her breasts lifting themselves proudly to the sun, he felt a telltale stirring between his legs.

Tugging on her ankle, he cajoled, "Come back down here. I'm assuming I'm free to use my hands again?" When she nodded, his pleading expression morphed into a leer. "Good. Then I'm claiming that right."

"If you insist," she huffed, but he could tell by her secretive little smile that she was delighted by his continued interest.

Curling beside him, she rested her head on his chest, splaying her hand over his heart. He picked up her fingers and began to trace the lines on her palm. His thumb lingered over a thin, white scar near the outer edge.

"Misadventure with Cory Taylor's pocketknife when I was eight," she told him. "Cory bet me I couldn't throw the knife Elektra-style and hit the paper bull's-eye he'd nailed to a tree in his backyard. I *won* that bet," she added proudly. "But I also ended up with six stitches."

"And this one?" He gently ran a finger over the ridge of puckered flesh below her earlobe. He'd noticed it while nuzzling her.

"A Wonder Woman moment gone wrong when I was six." She sighed. "Turns out my Halloween costume didn't bestow upon me the power of flight."

He envisioned little Alex, hair curling crazily around her head, skinny legs, and skinned knees, and felt his heart melt. A vision of another little girl with her red hair and his blue eyes popped into his brain so quickly, he jerked with the impact of it.

Just my mind playing tricks on me, wishing things coulda been different. Wishing I coulda been different.

"A rough and tumble little girl, were you?" he asked Alex.

"The roughest and tumbliest," she assured him. "Much to my mother's horror."

"And still looking for adventure even all these years later."

She chuckled. "Guess so, huh? I mean, a woman would have to be crazy to move onto an island in the middle of nowhere with seven men she's never met." Running a finger over the scar above his collarbone, she added, "Your turn. Where'd you get this?"

He covered her hand with his own, still shaken by the vision of the little girl. "We'll be here all afternoon if you wanna start counting *my* scars."

She pushed up on her elbow, cupping her cheek in her hand so she could look down at him. Her beauty wasn't obvious; it didn't hit you over the head. But it was even more breathtaking *because* it was subtle. Because it grew on you. Because the more you looked, the more you saw.

Mason wished he could look forever.

"You've seen and done so much." Her tone was reverent.

"Seen more than most ever will, and done more than most ever wanna," he agreed. It was an easy way of admitting a hard truth.

Of course, Alex being Alex, she cut through the bull-shit and hit at the heart of his statement. "That's the second thing you've said that makes me wonder if you regret your time in the navy."

"'Regret' isn't the right word." He shook his head. "How could I regret the friendships I made? The broth-erhood I share? It's more of a...what-if, you know? What if I hadn't joined? What would my life be like now? *Who* would I be now? Would I be happier?"

"You said the navy changed you." She twirled her fin-gers in his chest hair. It was such a soothing feeling.

Maybe that's why he was able to talk about this thing he'd been keeping to himself for years. She soothed him. Tamed him. Made the great and terrible truth of him seem...not so great and terrible.

"But *how* did it change you?"

His breath left his lungs on a long exhale. "You ever heard of the 2 percent?"

"No." She brushed a fingertip over the scar above his collarbone again.

"This group of Spanish scientists did a study and found that about 2 percent of the human population are natural-born killers. Spec-ops guys. Mercs. SWAT. Most, if not all, of us fall into the 2 percent."

When her brow wrinkled, he was quick to continue. "I'm not saying that makes us *bad*. We're not psycho kill-ers who indiscriminately murder people. But I'm saying it makes us different from the rest of the population. *Abnormal.*"

He gazed at her then. He wasn't sure why. Wasn't

sure what he was hoping to see in her eyes. Sympathy? Understanding? Repulsion?

Or did he just have the need to look at her? As much as he could, for as long as he could?

"For the sake of argument"—she went back to stroking his chest hair—"let's say I buy this whole 2 percent idea. How does that answer my question of how the navy changed you?"

"Because I didn't *know* I fell into that category before I became a frogman. And maybe I coulda gone my whole life not knowing. Maybe I coulda gone my whole frickin' life thinking I was normal."

He wished he could be different for her. He wished he could be what she needed. He wished—

"You said earlier that for some people, things from their past continue to inform their present. You said you never wanted to fall in love again because you'd be a disappointment. I thought both of those statements alluded to your bad divorce. But it's more than that, isn't it?"

Trust Alex to figure it all out. To figure *him* out.

"Sarah knew me from before I became a SEAL." His voice was low. Hoarse. "She watched the change happen, and she couldn't bear it. Hated it, in fact." He shook his head. "I don't blame her for wanting out of a relationship with a man who was no longer normal."

Alex's eyes narrowed. "I've never met your ex-wife, but when you spoke just then, I got the feeling I was hearing her words. Not yours."

He shrugged. "Doesn't matter who's saying it. It's still the truth."

"Mason, I think—"

"Enough talking," he interrupted because he'd reached his limit. He'd spoken more words in the last two days than he'd spoken in two *years*. Besides, the truth was out of him. She knew the whole of it, and he didn't want to waste one more minute of this day with her. "Let's get back to more important activities."

Just as he was leaning in to claim her mouth, the entirely heinous sound of Doc's voice boomed out of the tree line. "Finish digging sand crabs, you two, and get your asses back to the house—preferably with clothes on! Just got an email from Special Agent Fazzle! He'll be calling us on the satphone in twenty minutes! They found the speedboat and the third body and got a hit on some prints!"

Alex had squealed and pulled the edge of the blanket over herself after hearing the first word out of Doc's mouth. But not before Mason watched her skin blush with so many shades of rose and pink that he was reminded of the dawn. When the sun first sent its warm rays across the sky.

Fucking piss-poor timing, he thought, silently calling Doc a litany of unkind names.

"We're coming!" Alex yelled, and then her cheeks flamed red when Doc chuckled and she realized her double entendre.

Wrinkling her nose, she whispered, "I'm assuming 'digging sand crabs' is another of the colorful euphemisms you guys have come up with for sex?"

While Mason would like to say he had no idea what

she was talking about, the truth was that right behind
dick jokes, the next thing his former teammates and current
business partners enjoyed best was coming up with
creative phrases for the act of procreation.

He avoided answering her by calling out to Doc,
"We'll be right behind you!"

Only after he heard the crunch of Doc's footfalls grow
faint did he stand and offer Alex a hand up.

"A return to reality, huh?" She swiped up her glasses
and slipped them onto her face.

"One way or another," he reluctantly agreed, "it always
creeps back in."

She sighed and bent to retrieve her bra and panties.
The sight of her bare butt, all sweet and plump and heart-
shaped—not to mention the peek he got at her wom-
anhood, still swollen and ripe—had his recently spent
manhood twitching with interest.

*Do we really needa be present during this phone call?
Couldn't we get the information from the others...after?*

Alex saw what was happening between his legs, and
her eyes pinged to his face. His intention must've been
written there in indelible ink.

"Nope." She took a step back when he reached for her.
"As much as I like where your head is at, I need a break.
Every muscle in my body is sore. Including muscles I
didn't even know I had before today. No," she quickly
added when his brow furrowed. "Don't get all troubled
and concerned. I'm fine. I'm better than fine. I'm *great*.
But I'm calling a brief timeout. You need one, too, if the
look of that bandage is anything to go by." Now it was *her*

brow that was furrowed. "Damn it, Mason. Did we pop a stitch?"

He glanced down to see three splotches of red staining the white of his dressing. "It's fine," he hedged when she bent to get a closer look. "Wounds bleed."

She straightened and crossed her arms, eyeing him skeptically. She looked so adorably stern that all he could think of doing was throwing her onto the blanket so he could erase that expression and replace it with one of ecstasy.

Again, what was in his head must've been plastered all over his face, because she took another step back, quickly shrugging into her bra.

He wanted to weep when her lovely breasts disappeared from view.

"Come on," she cajoled, stepping into her panties. "Get dressed. And be quick about it, because if you continue to stand there looking like *that*"—she motioned with her hand up and down his length—"then I might have to practice a few more of my newfound skills on you."

Her words hit his ears, traveled down his spine, and landed inside his cock with a deliciously warm *thunk*. In response, the organ faithfully lifted itself vertical.

Her breath quickened. "No." She waggled her finger. "No, no. I can see you took that as an invitation, but I—"

She jumped away when he lunged for her. Then, to his complete shock, she danced by him and smacked his bare ass hard enough to leave a handprint.

"I've always wanted to do that," she admitted with an impish grin, hastily gathering up her T-shirt and shorts.

When she straightened, she saw the look in his eyes had turned positively predatory, and her own eyes widened in response. "I'll meet you back at the house." She darted passed him into the woods, narrowly escaping his next lunge.

Run, little rabbit, he thought hungrily. *The big, bad wolf will be right on your tail.*

As he finished dressing and packing up the picnic supplies, he found himself smiling. *Really* smiling.

He realized it was because for the first time in a long time, he was happy.

———

4:20 p.m.

Ring, damn you, ring!

Despite Alex's silent pleading, the satellite phone remained aggravatingly mute in the center of the kitchen table. No help whatsoever in diverting the attention of the five sets of eyes that glanced between her and Mason.

An unspoken question hung in the air like a suffocating cloud.

She didn't like being the center of attention. Neither did Mason, judging by his fierce scowl and the agitated bunch of his biceps when he crossed his arms over his chest.

Biceps…

Chest…

She may have called for a hiatus from their amorous

congress, but seeing him across the table from her—so damned big and sexy—made her think perhaps break time was over. The idea must've registered on her face because when Mason caught her looking at him, his eyes darkened in that way she now recognized.

The peanut gallery must've caught on too. She'd swear the back-and-forth glances grew faster. The air grew thicker.

"Oh, for Pete's sake!" She threw exasperated hands in the air. "The answer is *yes*, okay? Mason finally pulled his head out of his ass and accepted my offer. The deed is done, so can we *please* focus on something else?"

"Mazel tov!" Uncle John saluted her with the joint he was in the middle of rolling. "It's about damn time," he added after licking the edge of the hemp paper.

The color over Mason's cheeks deepened about ten shades, and the look he shot Alex succinctly said *What the fuck?*

She shrugged. "Sorry. I was suffocating under the weight of their speculation. Besides, it's not like anything on this island stays a secret for long. They were bound to find out." She looked pointedly at Doc who'd been the one to catch them canoodling naked on the picnic blanket.

"What?" Doc blinked innocently. "I didn't say a word."

Romeo kicked Doc under the table. "You *knew* and you didn't tell?"

Doc rubbed his abused shin. "I was waiting until *after* Fazzle called."

Alex pointed at Doc, but lifted her eyebrows at Mason. "See? Told you."

Mason's expression said he still would've preferred she keep her trap shut, but his eyes promised reprisal. Delicious, dirty reprisal.

Hot blood pooled at the tips of her breasts. Mason noticed the instant her nipples furled, because his eyes darted down to her chest and his pupils dilated.

When he looked back at her, she grinned and made sure *her* expression said she'd see his delicious, dirty reprisal and up the ante with some sexy quid pro quo of her own.

Next to her, Chrissy wiped her arms. "Ew! Stop it, you two! I'm getting splashed by your disgusting eyegasms."

"I don't mind it," Romeo disagreed. "Makes me proud to see my babies all grown up and getting down to business. It's enough to moisten the old peepers."

Mason muttered something under his breath that sounded like he might have called Romeo a *dildo dipped in beard stubble.* But one corner of his mouth twitched. Alex felt her own lips curl in response.

When they were like this, sitting around the table like a family, it was easy to pretend tomorrow would never come. That it would always be just as it was right now.

So natural. So comfortable. So...

Meant to be? that voice in the back of her head singsonged.

Wolf lifted the satphone to his ear when it jangled to life. "Roanhorse here. What do you know?" he asked without preamble.

Agent Fazzle's voice was tinny and crackling on the other end. Alex couldn't make out what the FBI agent said, but the look on Wolf's face didn't bode well. "Give me a minute," he grumbled. "I'll tell the others."

Setting the phone aside, Wolf glanced around. "Two things. Number one"—he lifted a finger—"Fazzle says the speedboat was rented from a local spot in Key West. The name on the rental agreement was Paulie Gatto. Anyone know the guy?"

Heads shook in unison. Well, every head except Uncle John's. He rubbed his beard and stared thoughtfully into the middle distance. "Sounds familiar," he mused, then snapped his fingers. "*The Godfather.*"

"The movie?" Doc's eyebrows made a perfect V.

Uncle John nodded. "Paulie Gatto was the traitor who almost got Don Corleone killed."

"You're right." Wolf pointed at him. "I remember that now."

Chrissy whispered to Alex from the side of her mouth, "What is it with men and that movie?"

Alex's own mouth flattened. "I think they like the excess of testosterone and the story line's exaltation of the patriarchy."

"That's a bald-faced overgeneralization if I ever heard one," Romeo declared with a righteous lift of his chin. "Men love *The Godfather* because it's nuanced and lavishly acted and—"

"Fazzle?" Wolf picked up the phone. "You still there? Yeah, sorry. The wheels tend to fly off the bus when it comes to conversations around here." Something Fazzle said made Wolf chuckle. But then he grew serious. "So Paulie Gatto. Gotta be an alias, right?" He listened for a minute longer and then said to the group, "Fazzle's goin' to see if he can find any CCTV footage of this Paulie guy. If he does, he's hopin' he can use it to make a solid ID."

"What was the second thing?" Uncle John prodded, twisting the end of his newly rolled joint.

"What?" Wolf frowned. Then, "Oh, yeah. The FBI got a hit on the prints they pulled off the body on the speedboat. Turan Jamshidi was the man's name. He was an officer in the Islamic Republic of Iran Navy."

"Those guys were Iranians?" Now Doc's eyebrows were trying to disappear into his hairline. "What the hell?"

In disbelief and growing dread, Alex looked at the faces around her. Iranians? Like, from *Iran*? The place where people shouted *Death to America* in the streets?

"*Please* tell me the FBI, in all its vast wisdom, is now ready to admit the men who attacked us weren't the Baitfish Bandits." Her voice was hoarse. "Or do they think three Iranians would travel halfway around the world to rob fishermen at gunpoint?"

The satphone crackled with the sound of Fazzle's voice. Wolf translated, "Fazzle agrees that, given what we now know, yesterday's attack smells less…uh"—he grimaced—"baitfishy. He would also like to know if any of us did work in Iran or had occasion to have a run-in with the navy of Iran during our time with the SEALs."

Doc glanced pointedly at the phone in Wolf's hand. "Even if we did, we couldn't tell him."

Doc's words reminded Alex who, exactly, she worked with. Men with secrets so dark and dangerous they were obligated to keep them secure even from the Federal Bureau of Investigation.

Men who were dark and dangerous themselves.

A chill snaked up her arms, lifting the fine hairs there. The thought of being attacked by a boatful of local yokels bent on mayhem and murder was bad enough. Knowing they'd been attacked by Iranians bent on…what? Revenge? For what? Well, that was about as bad as it got.

"Ladies, Uncle John." Wolf broke into her thoughts. "Would y'all cover your eyes for a moment?"

"Why?" Chrissy looked alarmed.

"I'm goin' to ask my former SEAL team members a question," Wolf explained. "And they're goin' to give me either a nod of their heads or a shake of their chins. In the interest of national security, we can't have civilians knowing which way they answer."

"Sweet Jesus." Chrissy dutifully covered her eyes with her hands. "I feel like I'm in a bad episode of *The Unit*. Although…" She paused. "I don't think there *were* any bad episodes. I was so sad when that show got canceled."

"Was that the one with Dennis Haysbert?" Alex followed Chrissy's lead and covered her eyes. But her intestines writhed. Her heart danced a fast jig.

"Mmm," Chrissy hummed. "That man has a voice like butter. He could whisper in my ear any day of the week and twice on—"

"That show was a crock of crap," Doc interjected. "They got almost everything wrong. And the things they got right were overdramatized."

"It's *fiction*," Chrissy insisted. "And *entertainment*.

Don't rain on the parade of those of us who happen to enjoy some—"

"Damn it, people!" Wolf slammed something on the table, making Alex jump. She thought maybe it was the palm of his hand. "Can we *please* keep the wheels on the damn bus for once?" When silence met his demand, he cleared his throat and continued, "Good. Thank you. Now, the question on the table is this… Did any of us have any occasion to come across Iranians durin' our time with the navy?"

The silence that followed his question was so thick you could cut it with a jelly knife. Curiosity made Alex want to peek through her fingers. But respect for the privacy of the men of Deep Six Salvage and the oaths they'd sworn upon entering and exiting the navy kept her eyes firmly shut.

Eventually, Wolf muttered, "That's what I thought." Louder, he added, "Fazzle, you're barkin' up the wrong tree if you think this is some sort of revenge plot for an op we were involved in."

A relieved breath leaked out of Alex's lungs. They hadn't been attacked because some Iranian cleric had issued a fatwa calling for their heads. That was something.

Then again, as silver linings went, it wasn't as shiny and sparkly as she would've liked. Because it also meant they were no closer to figuring out *why* yesterday happened.

"You think we can open our eyes now?" Chrissy whispered close to her ear.

"No clue." Alex shook her head.

Mason, who'd been true to character and silent

throughout the entire conversation, suddenly spoke. His words were quiet, but in Alex's not-so-humble opinion, his deep voice could compete with Dennis Haysbert's any day. "Open your eyes."

She did as instructed and found his blue gaze laser-focused on her.

Most days she forgot he was a Navy SEAL. The Mason McCarthy she knew and loved was the guy who doted on his dog and painted scenes of the island in watercolors. He was the guy who had shockingly neat handwriting for a man and a charming loyalty to all things Beantown, including the Bruins, the Sox, and a good Boston lager.

He's the guy who gently, tenderly, and expertly introduced me to the world of passion, she thought, warmth once again stealing into her blood.

And yet, he was also a SEAL. That part of him had been there that night on Garden Key. It had been there yesterday morning on the catamaran. It was in his eyes now. In the steely expression on his face.

He and the others might never have had any dealings with the Iranians, but she could tell he believed yesterday's attack must have *something* to do with their work in the navy. And he blamed himself for the danger they'd been in. The danger they might *still* be in.

She felt her own expression soften, and reached for his hand. But before she could grab his fingers, Wolf distracted her by ending the call with Fazzle and running a weary hand over his face. "Fazzle will call us tomorrow with any additional information."

"And until then, we do what?" Chrissy asked. "Cross

our fingers and hope, like Alex said back on the docks, that those guys in the boat don't have friends looking to finish the job? Why isn't Fazzle flying us all to a safe house? Why aren't we running to the nearest—"

"Chrissy, darlin,'" Wolf gently interrupted her. "We don't know enough yet to set the alarm bells ringin.'"

"Excuse me"—her chin was set at a mulish angle—"but unlike you, I'm not used to being shot at by men who rent boats under aliases they got off *The Godfather*. This is so far outside the realm of normal that my alarm bells aren't ringing, they're blaring and—"

She choked when Wolf grabbed her hand and gave her fingers a reassuring squeeze. "I'll die before I ever let anyone hurt you."

Beneath the table, Mason scooted his foot next to Alex's, applying gentle pressure. His curt nod told her he echoed Wolf's sentiments.

Chills spread across Alex's back and down her legs. While she appreciated the thought, the mere idea of losing him was unthinkable. Unbearable.

He was her North Star. Without him, she'd be left to scramble around directionless.

And yet you will lose him, that damnable voice whispered. *No matter what happens tonight, tomorrow he stops being yours.*

Chapter 25

"IS IT SERIOUS BETWEEN YOU TWO?"

Chrissy's voice was soft in the darkness. Alex could barely hear her over the noise of night insects and Meat's deep, satisfied snores.

Mason was on watch duty at the back of the island, and Meat had chosen Chrissy to bless with his presence. He was flat on his back at the bottom of her trundle bed, airing his junk while he slept.

Alex envied the dog his oblivion. Even though she and Chrissy had turned in early, the sandman refused to visit them. Probably because, unlike Meat, they weren't blind to what was happening on the island.

They'd swallowed their alarm while the men of Deep Six Salvage debated the merits of staying versus loading up the floatplane and heading back to Key West. They'd kept their opinions to themselves when the guys decided the island was safer and "far more defensible"—*gulp*—than any place else. They'd watched in dismay while weapons were oiled and press-checked and loaded. And they'd listened with their hearts in their throats while the men drew up a schedule for sentinel duty. Then they'd grumbled about the patriarchy when their help had been refused.

"I mean, seriously," Alex had said at the time. "It doesn't take six weeks of BUD/S training to use a pair of binoculars."

"BUD/S training lasts twenty-four weeks," Mason had informed her, and she'd thought, *Sweet lord! What could they possibly be teaching them all that time? Oh, right. How to jump out of airplanes. How to dive to unimaginable depths. How to stealthily kill people.*

He'd added, "And it's less about using a set of field glasses than it is knowing what to look for."

"Duh." She'd rolled her eyes. "Anything that shouldn't be there. Like a boat or a plane or a raft or—"

"Will you be able to make a visual assessment of the craft's speed and trajectory so you can gauge how much time you have and warn the others?"

She'd glowered at him because…he'd had her there. Obviously, she needed to study up on how to calculate the speed and trajectory of an approaching watercraft. *Do you suppose there's a YouTube video on that?*

That was the last time they'd had a chance to speak. He'd been too busy conferring with the guys the rest of the afternoon. And then in the evening, when she took him a paper plate heaped with the mac and cheese she'd made for dinner—she'd needed *something* to keep her mind and body busy—he'd barely dropped the binoculars to thank her for the food.

Mason took sentry duty as seriously as he took everything in life, giving it 100 percent of his concentration. Not that she was complaining. Because when that concentration was focused on her? *Whew, boy!*

"You can totally tell me to mind my own business." Chrissy broke into her thoughts. "I won't take offense."

"Is it serious between us?" Alex pondered the question. "I guess you could call it that. Or maybe 'terminal' is a better word for it."

Chrissy rolled onto her side and propped her cheek in her hand. Meat voiced his disapproval at being jostled by grunting loudly and smacking his floppy lips. Then he immediately went back to snoring.

In answer, Li'l Bastard, who roosted on the porch railing just beyond the screen, clucked contentedly. The happy noise mixed with the clacking of palm fronds as they were tickled by a warm sea breeze.

"Why terminal?" Chrissy asked. "Because you're in love with him?"

"More because he's *not* in love with *me*," Alex admitted wretchedly. The knowledge made something hard and sharp poke at the backs of her eyes.

"Give him time." Chrissy's tone was certain.

Alex made a rude noise. "See, that's the one thing I don't have."

The moonlight streaming in under the roofline caught in Chrissy's hair and made it shine when she shook her head. "I don't understand."

"All Mason agreed to was one day. Today. Tomorrow we go back to being friends and pretending today never happened." Saying the words aloud increased the sharpness of the pressure behind her eyes. "I thought something was better than nothing, you know? But now I'm not so sure. It's killing me thinking of living and working next to him without being able to touch him or hug him or kiss him."

"Why would he insist on something like that?" Even in the low light, Alex could see the deep line that appeared between Chrissy's eyebrows. "Like I said, I've seen the way he looks at you, and it's a far cry from a one-night stand and then let's-be-friends."

Alex didn't tell her what Mason had said about never wanting to fall in love or have a family. She didn't explain that he thought the navy had changed him, made him unfit to lead a regular life. Neither did she reveal her suspicions that some, or maybe *all*, of that had something to do with his ex-wife.

She thought, perhaps, she might have been the first person he'd ever shared those secrets with. She wouldn't break his confidence.

Instead, she said, "Speaking of the way a man looks at a woman, you and Wolf seem to be getting along better."

Chrissy's eyes narrowed. She was no fool. She hadn't missed Alex's swift change of subject. But she shrugged. "Like you and Mason, we've agreed to be friends. I guess it's contagious."

Alex frowned. They said misery loved company, but she wished with her whole heart that it could be different for Wolf and Chrissy. Mostly because Alex loved Wolf like a brother, and she particularly loved how Chrissy walking into a room made his whole face light up.

"It's like licking honey from a thorn," she mumbled. "Sweet and painful at the same time."

Chrissy cocked her head. "What is?"

"Being in love with a man you can't have."

"Oh, no." Chrissy shook her head. "That's were our two paths diverge. I'm not in love with Wolf. And I plan to keep it that way, despite his charm and that damnably pretty face of his."

"Does it work that way? Can you choose whether to fall in love?" Alex genuinely wanted to know. In her experience, it did *not*. Nothing she'd done in the past could have kept her from loving Mason. And she couldn't imagine anything she could do in the future that would change that.

He was under her skin. In her blood. Deep in her marrow.

Her body had been born with a Mason-shaped piece missing. The day she met him, she'd been made whole.

"Of course it works that way," Chrissy declared. "We might not get to choose who touches our hearts. But we can *definitely* choose who we allow to hold them."

Before Alex could reply, the screen door banged open. Meat flipped onto his stomach and let out a testy *woof*. Then he relaxed when Wolf walked onto the porch.

"Headed to the back of the island to take over from Mason." He stretched his arms toward the porch's roof. He looked long and sleek in the moonlight, like a dark jungle cat. Alex thought she heard Chrissy suck in an involuntary breath.

"You ladies doin' okay out here?" He included Alex in his inquiry, but she knew the only answer he truly cared about was Chrissy's.

"Fine. Stay safe out there." Chrissy's tone was curt. No doubt an overreaction to her unintentional gasp upon seeing his magnificence.

Wolf offered her a mock salute.

In return, Chrissy stuck out her tongue.

"Careful." His voice dropped an octave. "Some men might take that as an invitation."

"Guess it's a good thing you're not *some men*," she shot back cheekily.

"You're right. Do me a favor and remind yourself of that as often as possible."

Chrissy sputtered. But before she could come up with a reply, Wolf descended the porch steps and disappeared into the night. He was swallowed up by the blackness of the trees so quickly, Alex might have thought he'd *truly* disappeared if not for the crackling sound of the walkie-talkie on his hip.

The guys were exchanging information.

Or telling bawdy jokes?

She thought she heard a faint *What did one butt cheek say to the other?*

"Have a good night," she told Chrissy when Wolf's walkie-talkie grew too faint for her to hear the punch line. Throwing back the covers, she climbed from bed.

"Wait." Chrissy grabbed her wrist. "Where are you going?"

"To Mason's room. He has four hours before he's supposed to relieve Doc from duty." Having decided on three lookout spots, the men had set a schedule that allowed them to rotate. "I plan to make good use of each and every one of them."

10:15 p.m.

The whole time Mason had been on lookout duty, all he'd been able to think about was Alex.

Alex and the way her eyes lit up when she smiled. Alex and the way her voice got high with excitement when she talked about the hunt for the *Santa Cristina*. Alex and the way her cheeks flushed crimson during orgasm.

Alex and the way she was in danger. *Again.*

Maybe. Possibly. Because of him.

Or even if it wasn't his fault *precisely*, it had to be tied to him or his teammates somehow. The men on the speedboat had specifically targeted them. And he didn't delude himself into thinking that was because they were searching for a long-lost ghost galleon.

No. It *had* to be because of their time as SEALs.

It was further proof—*as if I needed it*, he thought—that his was nothing resembling a normal life. That his would *never* be anything that resembled a normal life.

Despite the asinine jokes his partners had been exchanging over the walkies, his heart had grown heavy as the hours wore on. So heavy he wouldn't have thought the organ capable of quick movement. And yet it leapt sky-high when he climbed the beach house's creaky, old stairs, opened the door to his bedroom, and saw Alex sitting cross-legged on the end of his bed.

The moonlight shining through the window made her pale skin luminesce. In fact, she gleamed so brightly that she looked to him as if she'd swallowed the sun.

"Alex," he choked out. He'd intentionally come in through the front door instead of the back, where her daybed was located, so he wouldn't have to see her. So he wouldn't have to look her in the eye and be reminded of how impossible their situation was.

She gave him a shrewd glance over the frames of her glasses. "Mason McCarthy, you look like shit. Ruggedly handsome shit, but shit all the same. You should be recovering from yesterday's blood loss, not traipsing around playing soldier boy."

"Sailor boy," he automatically corrected, shrugging his Colt's strap over his head and leaning the weapon against his bureau. "And don't hold back, Alexandra." He kicked the door shut behind him. "Please, tell me how you really feel."

"Come here." She patted the bed next to her, and his heart rate went through the roof. "Let me rub your shoulders. I give the best massages. They're not too soft. Not too hard. I give Goldilocks massages."

"Just so you know"—he waggled his eyebrows as he stalked toward the bed—"the last thing a man wants rubbed by a beautiful woman are his shoulders."

She rolled her eyes. "How about I *start* there and work my way down?"

Before he could agree—most wholeheartedly—his walkie-talkie crackled to life. "What do you do with a year's worth of used condoms?" This from Romeo. "Melt them into a tire and call it a Goodyear."

Mason winced. Unhooking the walkie-talkie from his swim trunks, he turned the volume down so that the laughter and ribald comebacks were nothing but a low buzz.

After setting the unit atop the bureau, he turned to Alex with a sheepish expression. "Please don't judge me by the company I keep."

She shrugged. "It's a pretty good way to pass the time and keep everyone awake."

He shook his head. "Does nothin' offend you?"

In answer, she patted the bed again. "I'm willing to let you try to figure that out. *After* I work some of that tension from your shoulders."

Who was he to argue?

Plunking heavily onto the end of the mattress, he moaned gratefully when she sank her fingers into his traps. For long minutes, she worked the tendons at the back of his neck, and knuckled the knots between his shoulder blades.

"Fuck me, woman. You should do this for a living." His bones loss their ache. His muscles turned to putty beneath her talented fingers.

"How to give handies and blowies isn't the only thing a girl can pick up off the internet."

Just that easily, he was hard. Of course, having had her hands on him, he'd already been halfway there.

Maybe someday she'll watch those videos with me.

The carnal thought made the head of his dick push against the waistband of his swim trunks. Then the rest of him stiffened when he remembered there would be no "someday." Tonight was all they had.

"You ready for me to start working my way down?"

Her voice was pure innocence. But when he glanced over his shoulder, he found her expression was pure seduction.

"Do I need a answer with words? Or does my raging hard-on speak for itself?" He motioned with his hand toward the pup tent in his lap. Seriously, a whole troop of Boy Scouts could camp beneath it.

Chuckling, she leaned forward and lazily paid homage to his mouth. Claiming it. Worshipping it.

Claiming *him*.

Worshipping *him*.

He withstood her soft, slow ministrations for as long as he could. Then he lunged and had her flat on her back, fitting himself between her thighs and growling his appreciation at the sultry heat he found waiting for him.

He'd never met a woman more naturally amorous than Alex. Her little body was made for love, so soft and wet and warm. His body answered in kind, burning hard and fast and hot.

"No." She pressed at his shoulders. "You're exhausted. Let me be on top this time. I have a few positions I want to try." She began enumerating them on her fingers. "Reverse Cowgirl, the Louise, the Fantastic Elevator, and—"

He rolled her on top of him, wondering if now would be a good time to take off her panties and muzzle her with them. The more sexual positions she named— *Fantastic Elevator? Is she for real?*—the hornier he got. Which didn't bode well for her if she actually wanted him to *last* through all of her experimentation.

"Don't take offense," he told her breathlessly, unable

to stop himself from cupping her breasts through the cotton fabric of her tank top, delighting when her nipples pebbled under the brush of his thumbs. "But it's time for you to shut up and kiss me."

Her smile was one part bemused and two parts sex kitten. "No offense taken," she assured him, removing her glasses to set them aside on the bedside table. "And kissing you would be my pleasure."

This time when she touched her mouth to his, he would swear her lips and tongue plastered over the cracks in his heart. For that one sweet, fleeting moment in time, the organ felt blessedly whole again.

And it beat only for her.

12:21 a.m.

"Sex might be the best invention of all time. I feel like a note of thanks is in order, but who would I send it to?" Alex was sweaty and buzzing and completely content after two more educational bouts of lovemaking.

It was *two* bouts instead of one because when she'd come during Reverse Cowgirl, Mason had shouted her name and followed her over the edge. After catching his breath, he'd apologized.

"For such a small woman, you gotta fucking caboose on you. Watching it bounce up and down on my dick was too much. Gimme fifteen minutes and we'll go again."

For the record, he'd been ready in ten. And *that* time

he'd lasted through every position change she could think of, gently adjusting her angle or increasing her rhythm when something didn't work for her.

Now, two hours and three orgasms later, she was spent. A little delirious. And a whole lot in love with the act of procreation.

Of course, that last thing probably had something to do with her being a whole lot in love with the man she was procreating *with*.

"You could send the letter to me," he said, the sweat on his brow making his deeply tanned skin sparkle in the glow of the moonlight. His accent turned the word *letter* into *lettah*.

She rolled onto her side and propped her head in her hand. "Why? I did all the work."

"*All* of it?" He quirked a brow, and she was reminded of how busy his lips had been. The industriousness of his wide-palmed hands and callused fingertips.

"Okay," she allowed, "maybe not *all*."

Tossing a leg over his thigh, she nestled her head against his chest so she could listen while his heartbeat wound down from a rapid tattoo to a steady thud.

Steady. Strong. Relentless. Just like the man himself.

She went to place a tender kiss over the organ but jerked to a sit when a distant *snap* sounded through the window. "What was that?"

"Dunno." Mason was sitting up and frowning next to her.

Sound traveled far in the middle of the ocean, so it was possible the noise was simply a heavy palm frond falling to the ground on the south side of the island. The guys didn't groom the trees back there, and they were always shedding their dead foliage.

"You think it—"

"Shh," he interrupted, turning his head to listen to his walkie-talkie. But seconds ticked by and the gadget remained mute on his dresser. "Probably a palm frond falling," he said, echoing her own conclusion.

When he fell back into bed, she followed him, pillowing her head on his chest and running her fingers through the hair between his pecs. Crinkly strands wrapped around the tips of her fingers, enchanting her.

She'd never appreciated the difference between men's and women's bodies before. Had always considered them basically the same. Arms. Legs. Organs. Skin. But now she understood what truly made the sexes unique were the subtle variations. The way he was hairy where she was smooth. The way he was hard where she was soft.

"Mason?" She watched his areola contract when she brushed a finger over his nipple.

"Mmm?" he hummed, absently running a hand over her hip, making goose bumps break out under his fingertips.

"If you had one chance for a do-over in life, what would it be?"

He tucked his chin to frown at her. "You always philosophical after sex?"

She made a face as she grabbed her glasses from the nightstand so she could clearly see him. "How would I know? This is only the second time I've done it." Then she scowled in consideration. "Or do you count orgasms? In that case, it's the—"

He hooked a thumb under her chin, lifting her face so he could quickly kiss her mouth. She knew it was to shut her up. Even so, the slow, soft glide of his tongue had her rubbing her nipples over his chest and humming in delight when the sensations at the tips of her breasts echoed through her womb.

He knew what he'd started because he jerked back and groaned. "You're gonna be the death of me, woman."

"Nuh-uh." She nibbled on his warm neck. All he had to do was last a couple more hours. Then he'd take over lookout duties from Doc, the sun would rise, and he'd be safe from her ministrations and machinations. *Forever.*

The knowledge was a stone in the center of her chest. Wasn't it a stone in the center of *his*? Didn't it depress him beyond all reason? Or at least enough to make him want to reconsider their deal?

"So?" She pinned him with a look. "The do-over?"

His mouth curved into a frown. He lifted his hand as if to say, *Dunno. Why are you always asking so many questions?*

"Mine would be spending more time with my maternal grandparents," she told him, figuring he might open up if she went first. "I know Grandpa Gene fought in the Korean War. I know Grandma Iris was a hairdresser. But that's it. I have all these questions now that I'm older, but Gran and Gramps are gone and there's no one to give me answers."

"When we're young, we don't understand the one fundamental truth about life."

Her brow wrinkled. "What's that?"

"Nothing lasts. Including the people we love."

"The people may not last, but the *love* does," she insisted.

He said nothing to that, his face absent of expression.

"So?" She prodded him again by poking him on the shoulder. "The do-over?"

"Fuck, Alex." He let out an aggrieved breath. "Dunno. There are a hundred of them. That's the thing about being a fighting man. I'm plagued by what-ifs. What if I'd been faster to the LZ that time in Afghanistan? Would that chopper gunner still have gotten shot by militants? What if I'd had more Intel during that op in Syria? Would that kid still have gotten killed by an IED? What if I'd waited longer before pulling the trigger? Could that firefight have been avoided?"

"What if you gave us a chance?" she added quickly. "Don't you think it's possible there's more to life than memories and maybes?"

Her words hung in the air like priceless figurines unearthed from a shipwreck. His answer would determine whether she walked away a million times richer or whether those figurines fell to the ground, shattering into tiny pieces that would cut her heart into ribbons.

"Don't do this, Alex." His blue eyes looked brittle in the silvery moonlight.

"I can't help it." Her voice was achingly small. But her heart was the size of a galleon. "I don't want to look back in twenty years and have this moment be one of my what-ifs, one of my do-overs. I love you, Mason."

She put her hand to her mouth. She hadn't meant to tell him. But like so much that was in her head, it just fell out of her mouth.

"Fuck me." He threw back the covers and clambered out of bed to stand with his back to her. The expanse of tan skin and the tattoo on his back—a stylized Celtic cross—looked a mile wide.

He'd only moved three feet away, but it felt more like three hundred yards. A chill replaced the space where his big body had been next to her in bed. She shivered and pulled the sheet over her breasts.

"I know you care about me too," she insisted. "If you'd give me time to show you how—"

"Fuck!" He swung around. His haunted expression cut off her words. "I *told* you this would happen. I said good sex can—"

"I loved you *before* we had sex, you big idiot." Her heart hammered so hard her ribs ached. "Why do you think I kept insisting *you* be the one to take my virginity?"

"No." He shook his head. "You just think it's love because you're innocent and inexperienced and—"

"Don't." She pointed at him. It was a good thing she excelled at self-control, or her right fist might have found a home in his left eye socket. "Don't belittle me or what I feel just because I was a virgin until twelve hours ago. I love you, Mason. It's not puppy love or lust masquerading as love. It's *love*. And if you don't love me back because…" She shook her head and left the sentence unfinished before adding, "Well, that's one thing. But don't for one minute think I'm going to—"

"What I feel or don't feel for you doesn't have anything to do with *you*, Alex." His chin was tipped down, and his voice was so low she had to strain to hear him.

Her brain turned over his words and then ground to a halt. "How can what you feel for me have nothing to do with me? That doesn't make a damn bit of sense."

"It does when you realize there's something wrong with me," he said stiffly.

She eyed his naked form. All that tough skin and dark hair. Those thick muscles. The mesmerizing blue of his eyes that suddenly reminded her of icicles. He'd donned his mask, and it was impossible to read what was in his head.

"I don't see a thing wrong with you," she told him quietly, her anger morphing into compassion.

"That's 'cause you don't know me." He looked around like he was fighting to find the right words. "I'll never be the kinda man who can take his kids to Disney. When I'm in a crowd, I check everyone's hands for weapons and watch their eyes for ill intent. When I'm standing in line for coffee, I turn sideways so I can see who's coming through the door. I can't even take a leisurely sail without some shady motherfuckers coming along and trying to kill me."

His expression turned pleading. "Dontcha see? I'm not *normal*. Maybe I never was, but *if* I was, then the navy sucked it out of me. Sarah saw it happen. Saw me change from someone who coulda had a regular life into someone who…" He swallowed. "I can't be what you want me to be. What you need me to be."

She opened her mouth to argue, but before she could get out a word, a loud *bang* echoed up through the floorboards. It was followed by the sound of Meat barking his fool head off.

"What the fuck?" Mason's brow wrinkled.

He immediately swiped his swim trunks off the floor, reminding Alex of how she'd tugged them off him and tossed them over her shoulder two hours earlier.

Pressing a hand to the tape surrounding his bandage—some of it had come loose during the Fantastic Elevator position—he stomped over to the dresser and picked up his walkie-talkie. His face immediately blanched of color.

"What is it?" A sick feeling landed in the bottom of Alex's stomach.

"Dunno," he gritted between his teeth. "It's dead. Fucking piece of nonmilitary-grade shit."

He bent to grab his Colt. But before he could lay a hand on it, the door opened a fraction and a short black tube appeared in the breach.

For a full two seconds, Alex's brain tried to reason out what the object could be and who could be out there wielding it. Then, her misfiring synapses sparked.

Gun!

She screamed at the same time Mason said something under his breath that wasn't fit for inexperienced ears.

Chapter 26

ALEX LOVING HIM GOT FILED DIRECTLY UNDER LEAST of My Worries when an AR-15 nosed through Mason's bedroom door.

It wasn't conscious thought. It was more instinct that had him grabbing the barrel of the weapon and yanking the man attached to it into the room. With his free hand, he slapped his palm against the butt of the rifle, effectively twisting it out of his assailant's grip and breaking the ass clown's finger against the trigger guard in the process.

The *snap* of the bone was obscenely loud as it reverberated above the sound of Meat's growls and snarls downstairs. But it wasn't as obscene as the high-pitched squeal the man made when he cradled his mangled hand to his chest. His face was covered by a black balaclava, but the whites of his eyes were stark with pain.

That's gonna feel like a hand job from an angel compared to this!

Mason spun the rifle, fit the stock against his shoulder, and took aim. But before he could squeeze off a shot, his bedroom door flew open so fast and hard the doorknob buried itself in the drywall.

"Drop it!" a heavily accented voice screamed from the darkness.

Mason squinted. He could barely make out the silhouette of another man dressed head to toe in black. But he had no problem seeing the hole that stared at him from the end of another assault rifle. It was a deeper shadow among the shadows. A thing he'd learned to recognize early in his career because it ate all light.

How the fuck did these motherfuckers make it ashore?

There was only one way. One or more of Mason's friends, his brothers in every way but blood, had to be dead. And if they'd managed to call in a Mayday, he'd missed it because his fucking walkie-talkie had gone tits up.

The rank taste of remorse mixed with the sour flavor of rage on his tongue. Every cell in his body wanted to rant and rave and leave nothing but carnage in its wake. But good sense prevailed.

Good sense and the need to figure out what he was dealing with so he could save Alex and the others.

Speaking of… What the hell happened to Uncle John? His room was across the hall. Surely, if he'd been in there, he would've come out to see what the commotion was about. And what about Chrissy? She'd been on the trundle bed last Mason knew.

Too many unknowns.

Instead of doing as he was told and dropping the AR-15 to the floor, Mason allowed his mouth to curve into a mockery of a smile. "Dunno who you motherfuckers are. But let me tell you who I'm *not*. That's some run-of-the-mill chickenshit whose eyes go all pie plate at the sight of a loaded weapon pointed my way." Venom dripped from his tongue. It matched the poison pumping out of his heart.

He wasn't one for words, but he found he couldn't stop talking. "You can sure as fuck put one in me," he told the man in the hall. "But not before I decorate the wall with fifty shades of your friend's gray matter. So, if I were you, I'd put that rifle on the floor, nice and slow, and then kick it my way. I'll give you to the count of ten before I pull the trigger. Fair warning, though, I'm starting at six."

A hoot of laughter echoed around the hall. It was caustic, hitting Mason's ears like acid. Before he could blink, the evil black eye of the assault rifle slid from his chest to aim into the room behind him.

He heard Alex gasp like she'd been slapped. All the blood drained from his head, leaving him dizzy, because…

Game over.

He'd never had an Achilles' heel before.

He had one now.

Her name was Alexandra Merriweather. And despite all the reasons why she shouldn't, she loved him. He'd never be able to live with himself if something happened to her on his watch.

With a harshly whispered "Fuck!" he lowered the AR-15 to the wood-plank floor.

The prick whose finger he broke snatched it up. Using his good hand, the man awkwardly aimed it at Mason's head, the barrel weaving and swaying.

"Careful," Mason warned the guy. "Wouldn't want that to go off." He glanced from one masked man to the next. "I'm assuming you want me alive or else I'd already be dead."

"You are not ours to kill," Shadow Man growled.

"Oh, goody." Mason's tone was bored and sarcastic, but his mind was a hurricane, swirling with a million and one thoughts. The topmost being *Can I reach my Colt? Probably not before I take a round*, he decided.

If it were just him, he'd risk it. But it wasn't just him.

"Get dressed, woman," the man in the hall snarled. "Then come with us."

Mason bent to grab the tank top and pajama shorts she'd worn to his room, and Shadow Man barked, "Do not move!"

He slowly lifted his chin. His eyes were mere slits, but he hoped the asshat could read the truth in them. "You'll hafta kill me before I'll letcha make her get dressed in front of you."

For a couple of seconds, silence reigned. He could tell both men would've liked nothing better than to take him up on his challenge. Eventually, however, Shadow Man dipped his chin and Mason tossed Alex her clothes.

She caught them one-handed, using her other hand to keep the sheet pulled up to her chin. Her gaze never left his. *Her* eyes *were* pie-plate round, and the skin over her cheeks was so tight he could see the blue of her veins snaking beneath.

"It's okay, babe." He infused his voice with more certainty than he felt.

He'd do anything to take away even a fraction of her terror. And given the chance, he was going to kill both balaclava-clad bastards for making her suffer one moment of fear. Well, he'd kill them for that and for whatever they'd done to his friends.

Devastating grief threatened to wash over him like a tidal wave. So he pushed the thought to the back of his head.

Mourning was something a man did *after* the danger passed and the innocents were safe. Until then, he had to keep his head in the game, his eye on the prize, and wait for an opening that would allow him to gain the upper hand.

It probably wasn't the smartest move, but he kept his back to the intruders while Alex dressed. Partly because he wanted to make sure she could wrestle into her sleepwear while staying concealed beneath the sheet. The idea of anyone, but especially these cocksuckers, seeing her intimate flesh filled him with a fury so hot it made his lungs burn. But mostly because she seemed to need the reassurance in his eyes.

"Quickly!" Shadow Man shouted impatiently.

"I'm done!" Alex scooted from beneath the covers, and then stood demurely beside the bed, chin down, hands clasped behind her back.

"Come forward!" the man commanded from the hall. Obviously, he was the one in charge. Mason filed that bit of information away for future use.

Alex did as instructed, stopping only when she pulled even with Mason. He turned so they both faced their assailants, and the move had his arm brushing hers.

It broke his heart to find her skin clammy and cold, to

feel her fingers stiff with fear when she clasped his hand to...

Those aren't her fingers, he realized with a start as she stealthily transferred the KA-BAR knife he kept on his nightstand into his hand.

She must've palmed it while she was holding up the sheet to get dressed. Trust her to keep her head about her even with a full-auto pointed her way.

Beautiful, brilliant woman, he thought, pride filling his chest.

If he wasn't in love with her before, he fell a little in love with her right then and there.

"Come out!" Shadow Man commanded. "Slowly. No sudden moves."

Mason concealed the KA-BAR knife along the length of his forearm by cupping the hilt in the tips of his fingers. He kept his entire arm pressed close to his side, hoping their attackers would mistake his stiffness for fear.

When they made it into the dark hall and down the stairs without the balaclava twins spying his weapon, he heaved a sigh of relief. Shuffling onto the porch, glad to hear Meat still going crazy somewhere close because it meant that his dog was alive and kicking, he watched and waited for one of his enemies to make a false move.

There was a saying in the spec-ops community. *The more you sweat in training, the less you bleed in combat.* He wasn't as good as Wolf when it came to knife play. But after hundreds of hours of practice, he could certainly hold his own. All he needed was—

The thought screeched to a halt when they were

escorted down the front steps and the scene by the hammock met his eyes.

Now he knew what had happened to Uncle John and Chrissy. Two men had taken them hostage. They were on their knees in the sand, arms dangling at their sides, eyes round and reflecting the moonlight as they stared at him in fear.

A thin line of blood trickled from a cut on Uncle John's forehead.

"Y'okay?" Mason asked, any optimism he'd harbored that he could single-handedly take out their assailants slowly leaking from his ass.

Two against one was doable. But four against one?

He'd spent most of his life weighing the risks and playing the odds. Which meant he knew both were stacked against him. *Way* against him.

Hell is empty and all the devils are here, he thought, the grip of the KA-BAR no longer a comfort in his hand.

"Gettin' dumped out of the hammock and held at gunpoint isn't my favorite way to wake up," Uncle John said. "But, yeah. I'm fine."

Mason turned his gaze to Chrissy. All she seemed to be able to manage was a jerky nod.

Alive and mostly unharmed. That's something.

"On your knees!" Shadow Man ordered, jabbing the end of his rifle hard into Mason's kidney. Beside him, Alex squeaked when the same was done to her. Mason would swear red edged into his vision.

"Dontcha fucking hurt her!" he snarled, even as his knees hit the cool sand.

"Or what?" A voice sounded from the shadows of the porch.

Craning his head around, Mason watched a fifth man slowly make his way toward the group. Maybe it was the eerie light from the nearly full moon, but Mason would swear there was something strange about the way the guy moved. It was careful. Deliberate.

Injured? Mason wondered. *Or...old?*

The new arrival said something to the asshole from the hallway. Mason didn't speak Farsi, but he recognized it when he heard it. A chill streaked down his naked back despite the sweat dewing his skin.

As soon as he'd seen the nose of the AR-15, he'd assumed the intruders were more Iranians. Now, he knew for sure.

What the fuck is this?

He had a feeling he was about to find out. And an even *stronger* feeling he wasn't going to like what he learned.

"Where are the others?" the fifth man inquired with a slight tilt to his head.

"What others?" Mason asked.

"We took out the one patrolling the island's perimeter. But you left Key West this morning with two more. My man says they are not in the house. Where are they?"

They'd only taken out *one* man? Which meant two of his teammates were alive! If Mason could bide his time, the two remaining SEALs would make themselves known to him, and the odds would be far more in his favor.

"They stopped here to get more clothes, and then

they went back to Key West." He wasn't one for untruths, so the lie felt greasy on his lips.

The fifth man's eyes narrowed as he stared out at the lagoon. "The floatplane is still here."

"The one you say you took out flew them to Key West before coming back."

Again, the men reverted to Farsi and Mason tried to judge from their intonation whether or not they believed him. If he was forced to put money on it, he'd say they *didn't*.

Expecting more questions about his two missing friends—and maybe a little torture to try to get the truth from him—he was caught off guard when the fifth man pointed to Alex and said, "Is this your woman?"

For tonight. And if I were someone different, I'd make her mine forever.

Of course he admitted none of this aloud. Were they hoping to use her against him? Torture *her* so he'd be forced to admit the truth?

"She was in his bed," Shadow Man answered and Mason's fingers twitched around the hilt of the blade in his hand. One swift strike and he could sever the asshole's femoral artery. It would be so satisfying.

It would also be the dead last thing he did on this earth. *Dead* being the operative word.

"Interesting." The fifth man tapped a finger against his chin. "I had not considered making you watch while I kill those you care about. But the idea has merit. An eye for an eye."

A cold fingernail of horror scraped up Mason's spine. *This is about me*, he realized.

"Who are you?" His voice was little more than a dull rasp.

The fifth man slowly peeled back his balaclava. Dark skin. Hate-filled stare. And hair that had been black at one point, but was now a steely gray.

"I am Commodore Izad Bagheri." The man held his chin high so he could stare imperiously down his nose at Mason. "I am father to Arman, Basir, and Kazem. I am husband to Hettie. Because of you, they are all dead."

Mason shook his head, trying to make sense of the old man's words. He'd done his share of killing in the name of the flag and freedom. But he'd never harmed a woman.

He told Bagheri as much. Then he added, "And if your sons were the ones on the boat yesterday, I'm truly sorry for your loss. I didn't want any of that. They attacked *us*."

Surely, as a military man, Bagheri could understand there was nothing ignoble about self-defense.

"You mistake me." Bagheri shook his head. "Only one of my sons was on the boat yesterday. He was there to avenge his older brothers. To avenge his mother, who died of a broken heart when she heard there was nothing left of her boys to bury because *you* blew them into a thousand pieces!" Bagheri's voice rattled with fury.

"I have *never* killed anyone who wasn't trying to kill me," Mason swore between clenched teeth, feeling the atmosphere growing more volatile with each passing second.

"Lies!" Bagheri sliced a hand through the warm night air.

That one syllable cracked like a whip, and Alex jerked

beside him. Covertly, Mason pressed the back of his hand against hers. She immediately rubbed her pinkie finger along his.

It was a small move. And yet it told him she was grateful for his touch and understood he could do no more.

Bagheri pointed a finger at Mason's nose. "My sons were *not* trying to kill you! You boarded *their* ship! *You* detained *them*! And then you set your charges and condemned them to the sea!"

A memory swirled to the surface of Mason's mind. "The Gulf of Aden. What was that? Ten years ago?"

"So you *do* remember?" Bagheri's eyes were feverish now, brimming with a killing light.

Mason wished he was better with words. As it was, he thought hard about what he wanted to say and how he wanted to say it. "My team was tasked with a VBSS mission." When Bagheri scowled, he clarified. "Visit, board, search, and seizure. The ship your sons were on was a Syrian vessel suspected of smuggling antitank and antiaircraft weapons to Hezbollah."

"In the righteous fight against the Zionists!" Bagheri hissed, and the missing piece of the puzzle clicked into place for Mason.

It hadn't been a Syrian ship. It'd been a renamed Iranian ship flying the Syrian flag. Which meant, unbeknownst to him, Mason *had* been involved with the Iranians. His entire team had been.

Fuck!

"Politics aside, that ship and those weapons were in violation of sanctions and international law," he replied carefully, remembering how deeply dangerous the work had been. His team had been ordered to sneak up on the suspicious vessel in their fast boat and then get on board without the ship's crew being any the wiser.

"Our job wasn't to kill anyone," he continued in the same calm, even tone. Hoping it would help Bagheri hear. Hoping it would help the man *see*. "We were just supposed to verify the cargo and then disembark and let a joint task force of American and British destroyers seize the vessel. But the sailors on board discovered us. They refused to surrender despite being outnumbered and outgunned. They barricaded themselves on the bridge, and once my team breached their fortifications, they opened fire."

"Lies!" Bagheri yelled again.

"No, Commodore," Mason calmly contradicted him. "It's the truth. What's also the truth is that I wasn't there for the gunplay. I was in the cargo hold verifying the shipment. By the time I made it topside, the entire crew— your sons included—was already dead."

"If that's true, why would you blow up the ship? Unless it *wasn't* as you say. Unless it was an unsanctioned massacre and you were trying to conceal—"

"No." Mason shook his head, figuring he should interrupt before the commodore followed his theory down the rabbit hole. The man was grasping at straws now. "In the confusion, the vessel drifted into Iranian waters. It's true I was the one to set the charges. My specialty is demolitions. But I didn't do it to kill your boys. They were already dead. And I didn't do it to get rid of any evidence.

My team gave every last man on board that ship a chance to surrender."

Bagheri was pacing now. Shaking his head.

Mason pressed on. "I set the charges because our navy has no operational jurisdiction in your sovereign waters. There was no way the destroyers could take the ship. And those of us left on board couldn't allow the cargo to be reclaimed by our enemies. It was *war*. It *is* war, Commodore, even though our two nations will never openly admit it." Mason specifically used the man's rank, hoping to cement in Bagheri's mind that they were both sailors. Cut from the same cloth and bound by the same sorts of oaths.

"You can kill me for taking part in the mission," he continued quietly. "But I don't think that, knowing what you know now, my death will taste as sweet. And I *know* you don't wanna involve innocent people in something that should remain between us fighting men."

"Why should I believe you?" The whites of the old man's eyes were snaked with blood veins that looked black in the moonlight. "Why should I believe a word out of your filthy mouth?"

"'Cause it's the truth." And then a thought occurred. "How did you find me? How did you even know I was involved in that mission?"

The commodore turned his head slightly, his mouth curving into a hint of a smile. "I have a man on the inside. An American, like you. Someone with his own ax to grind. It seems you have many enemies."

Mason racked his brain, wondering who would have

a reason to sell him out, and came up empty. As far as he knew, throughout his military career he'd comported himself with honor and dignity. He'd stabbed no one in the back. He'd made no promises he hadn't kept.

"Enough talk," Bagheri declared. "Whether you personally killed Arman and Basir matters not. Just as it matters not if you were the one to personally kill Kazem yesterday. The fact remains: you are a cog in the American machine that thinks to impose its will on this world. And you will pay for it."

Bagheri took a step toward him.

Where are *you guys?* Mason silently implored his missing friends. *Now would be a good time to show your fucking faces!*

Bagheri reached behind his back, and Mason fully expected to see the man pull out the weapon that would end his life. Glancing at Alex, he let his eyes tell the truth his lips could not speak.

I love you.

A second later, the air was ripped by the sound of gunfire.

Chapter 27

THE AWFUL SOUND OF WEAPONS FIRE HAD ALEX instinctively covering her ears and squeezing her eyes shut.

Mason! Her heart screamed his name even as a great and terrible sob shook her chest. *No! No! No!*

She couldn't look. She never wanted to look. As long as she kept her eyes closed, she wouldn't see him lying lifeless beside her. And surely, any minute now, Bagheri would send a bullet into her and the choice of whether or not to look wouldn't matter. She'd be dead.

But seconds passed and she experienced no sudden punch of pain. No gruesome-sounding *crack* as a deadly projectile broke the sound barrier.

In fact, the only noises were coming from Meat and Li'l Bastard. The poor dog was going crazy on the back porch. And the rooster, ever sympathetic to Meat's emotions, crowed like it was first light on the last day of the world.

Cautiously lifting her head, a quick glance assured her Mason wasn't on the ground next to her. The wave of relief that washed through her was so enormous, it left her dizzy.

Of course, that relief was instantly replaced by the

hot burn of bile when she saw the two men who'd been aiming their weapons at Chrissy and Uncle John lying dead on the ground. The contents of their heads leaked through the fabric of their masks and what remained of their skulls.

"Don't," she heard Mason snarl, and lifted her chin to find his arm around the commodore's chest in a steely grip. The edge of his blade was pressed tight to the old man's neck. "I swear if you so much as twitch, I'll slit his throat from three to nine."

Alex tracked the direction of Mason's gaze and found the masked man from the hallway was now behind her, the barrel of his weapon a mere inch from her head.

"Same goes for you," Mason added, and Alex carefully turned her head to discover that the man whose hand Mason had broken with his crazy kung-fu, Jedi, ninja move had transferred his aim to Chrissy and Uncle John.

Holy hell. This is a tinderbox. One wrong move will be the spark that has this whole thing going kaboom!

"Tell whoever is in the trees to come out slowly with their hands up, or we kill your friends," Hallway Guy hissed.

"Do it!" the commodore shouted. "Kill them all!"

"No!" Mason bellowed. "Haven't we had enough of that to last us a lifetime? No one else needs to die here today. No one else needs—"

Alex didn't hear what Mason said next because Broken-Hand Man pulled the butt of his weapon tight against his shoulder. It was a small move, but she recognized his intent. Apparently, the remaining Deep Six guys did too—just *two* remaining. *Oh god.* She couldn't think of that now. She'd have to think of it later.

Before Broken-Hand Man could squeeze off a round, muzzle flashes glowed from the shadows of the mangrove forest. Blood sprayed as bullets slammed into him. He hit the ground, wheezed once, and then made a terrible gurgling sound that had Alex longing to cover her ears again.

"No!" Hallway Guy roared, turning to aim into the trees. He got off a handful of rounds, the *bwarrr* of his automatic sounding enormous as it echoed over the lagoon.

Something warm and wet sprayed Alex's face a second before Hallway Guy stumbled. He went down on one knee, a hand pressed to the open wound in his chest. Another *crack* came from the direction of the forest. And right in front of her eyes, a neat hole opened up in Hallway Guy's right cheek.

He tumbled backward, dead before he hit the sand.

Her gorge rose. Unfortunately, she had no time to indulge in the esophageal eruption she so richly deserved because Mason cried, "No! Hold your fire!"

She spun to see the commodore had wiggled from Mason's grip and now stood in front of him, breathing heavily.

"Please don't, Commodore," Mason pleaded with the man when the commodore pointed a matte-black handgun at Mason's chest. "The only way outta here for you is a body bag unless you lower your weapon. And haven't enough died already?" He gestured to the carnage of corpses littering the ground.

Alex's knees ached where the grains of sand dug into

her flesh. She thought if she squinted, she could see the air vibrating between the two men.

"I knew this island would be the death of me," Bagheri said in his thick accent.

"It doesn't hafta be." Mason's expression was imploring.

"Oh, but you see…it *does*." An expression of fatalism drifted across the commodore's face. "I long to be reunited with my wife and children. But first, if there is a hell, I must see you in it."

The light of the moon cast the tendons in Bagheri's hand in stark relief as he began to squeeze his trigger. Alex's mouth stretched wide over a silent scream. But before a round could belch from the end of the commodore's weapon, gunfire once again blasted from the tree line.

The old man grunted when two bullets plowed into him. Slowly, almost gracefully, he sank to his knees, his weapon slipping from his lax fingers.

"Hettie," he wheezed and then whispered something in Farsi before toppling sideways into the sand.

This time, Alex couldn't contain herself. Leaning over, she retched onto the ground.

"Fuck!" Mason bellowed. "Fuck! Fuck! *Fuck!*"

Wiping the back of her hand over her mouth, Alex looked up to find him standing over the commodore's lifeless body. His face full of anguish.

"Mason…" She jumped to her feet and ran to him.

"Do you see now?" He waved a hand at the dead men. "Do you understand now that this is my life?"

The shattering heartache in his eyes cut her to the core. She reached for his hand, but he pulled it away to run agitated fingers through his hair.

"None of this is your fault," she told him quietly.

"Isn't it?" His tone was packed with misery and self-loathing. "No matter what I do, no matter how long I'm out, death and violence follow me." His voice cracked on the last word, and Alex felt a small fissure open up in her heart.

"You can't be guilty of something you can't control," she assured him quietly. "As for death and violence following you…it follows *all* of us. Just ask the victims of mass shootings. Ask anyone who's been mugged or raped or beaten for being a little different. It's a violent world, Mason."

"Those things you're talking about are different," he insisted, his voice full of misery.

"How so?" she challenged. "Innocent people get targeted by evil men with diabolical axes to grind every day. Just because you spent most of your adult life fighting for your country doesn't mean—"

That's as far as she got before a bloodcurdling scream rent the air, raising every hair on Alex's head. Whipping around, she saw Chrissy stumbling toward the trail that snaked through the trees toward the back of the island. Wolf's name was a desperate cry on her lips.

Alex blinked and then quickly realized Doc and Romeo had materialized from the tree line. Which meant…

Oh god! Oh, no!

"Chrissy!" she shouted, breaking into a sprint after the woman, her heart broken at the thought of what must have happened to Wolf.

Alex wasn't professionally trained in the nuances of the human brain and how it dealt with trauma, but she knew Chrissy would be better off never seeing whatever awaited her at the back of the island.

Thud, thud, thud! The sound of the men's footfalls on the sand as they quickly fell into step behind her matched the pace of her lungs as she ran after Chrissy.

"Chrissy!" she screamed again. But Chrissy didn't miss a step, kicking up great plumes of sand as she continued to dodge and dart up the trail.

"We put out a Mayday the moment we heard the first shot. Didn't you hear it?" Doc demanded of Mason.

"My fucking walkie-talkie died," Mason replied, sounding as if he was hot on Alex's heels. "We gotta get better comms."

"Damn." Doc panted with exertion. Then, "Sorry we didn't help sooner. By the time we were halfway to investigating the shot, we saw the masked ass clowns skulking toward the house. Once they started rounding up everyone in the front yard, we figured we should wait until—" He cut himself off. "Jesus, none of that matters now. Wolf, man." His voice broke. "*Wolf.*"

"I know," Mason chuffed, and Alex couldn't bear it.

To hear these men, the toughest sonsofguns she'd ever know, choking back tears was too much. Her own eyes filled.

Stepping to the side of the trail, she pressed a hand to the stitch in her side. "Go!" she told them. "Stop her before she sees him!"

Chrissy had legs like a gazelle. Alex's little stumps had no hope of catching her.

Doc blasted past, his strides eating up the trail. Romeo was almost as quick. But Mason stopped to place a hand on Alex's shoulder.

Sweat slicked his forehead. "Y'okay?"

"Fine," she assured him around the Texas-sized lump in her throat. "Go. I'll catch up."

He hesitated. Then, with a determined dip of his chin, he gave her arm a squeeze and sprinted up the trail.

Once she caught her breath, she jogged the remaining distance. The entire time, she thought of Wolf. His cheesy quotes. The way he sang the wrong song lyrics. How he'd made her laugh the first time she caught a fish and was too scared to take it off the hook.

Such a good man, she thought, wetness making her vision swim.

She stumbled to a stop when she reached the end of the trail and saw her friends not crouched around Wolf's body, but huddled behind a stand of trees. Her chin jerked back in consternation when Mason stepped onto the beach, the AR-15 and handgun he'd snatched off the dead Iranians both held high in the air.

What in the world?

Scrambling up behind the group, she touched Doc's elbow. Just his elbow since his rifle was up and at the ready as he sighted down its length. "What's he doing?" she whispered.

"Either something very dumb or something very brave." Doc's reply came from the side of his mouth. "I'll let you know which once it's all over."

"Once *what's* all over?" The note of desperation in her

voice matched the hard kernel of fear that had put down roots in her heart.

"Oh, Alex!" Chrissy clasped her wrist in a desperate grip. "He's alive! Wolf's alive!"

"What?" Alex ducked so she could see under Doc's arm. The scene that met her eyes sent a knife's blade of horror slicing through her chest.

A rubber dinghy sat in the surf. Standing in front of it was another masked man who held a barely conscious Wolf. Moonlight slanted off the barrel of the pistol pressed tight against Wolf's skull.

It looked like Wolf had lost a gallon of blood from the wound near his temple. It stained his entire tank top, his swim trunks, and dripped from the tips of his fingers onto the sand at his feet.

Then there was Mason...

He lowered his weapons to the ground and continued to walk slowly toward the dinghy with his hands in the air. Looking for all the world like he was ready to sacrifice himself to save Wolf.

Alex's heart plummeted and one desperate word slipped past her lips. "No."

———

1:13 a.m.

"There's one of you and three of us!" Mason yelled to the balaclava-covered bastard who held Wolf like a human shield. "All the friends you brought with you are dead!

So why dontcha let *my* friend go and we'll talk about next steps!"

"No fucking way!" Masked Man hollered without a hint of an accent.

Ah, Mason thought. *The American Bagheri spoke of.*

He didn't recognize the voice. It sure as fuck didn't belong to anyone he knew, so *why* had this sonofabitch sold him out?

"The second I drop your friend," the asshole continued, "those dickheads in the trees will drop *me*! I'll just keep your friend with me until I'm in the dinghy and well on my way!"

"Don't think he's gonna be much help backing your play!" Mason tipped his chin toward Wolf, whose head was bobbing on the end of his neck, making the gun pressed to his temple slip in his blood. "You'll end up dropping him the minute you try to step into the dinghy, and my guys in the trees will put one clean through your brainpan! So how about you take me instead?"

"No!" A shout came from the tree line. Mason hated the anguish in Alex's voice. He hated causing her one more moment of alarm or fright. But he had to do this.

"I'll come to you unarmed!" He lifted his hands higher in the air to illustrate his point. "I'll cooperate in any way you tell me to!"

Masked Man hesitated, and Mason counted each of his heartbeats. Finally the guy shouted, "Deal! You keep walking this way nice and slow!"

There were still a million and one ways this shit show could go pear-shaped, but at least now there was a chance to get one thing right. There was a chance to save Wolf.

Accustomed as Mason was to adrenaline, he welcomed the burn of it through his veins. It heightened his senses. Made the moon brighter. The earthy smell of the mangroves stronger. The *shush-shush* of the waves lapping against the sand louder. But most importantly, it bunched his muscles in readiness.

Doc liked to tease him by saying, *Most times you're slower than a Sunday afternoon. But when push comes to shove, you got a little quicksilver in you.*

Agreeing to go with this traitorous masked cocksucker was agreeing to a dance with death—no doubt the douche canoe planned to waste whoever came with him. But Mason's ability to strike fast and hard had saved him more times than he could count. He was banking it would be enough to save him this time too.

Once he was two feet from Wolf, he allowed himself three seconds to assess his friend's condition. Two was all he needed to decide Wolf was in worse shape than he'd feared.

A bullet had grazed Wolf's skull, tearing away a chunk of scalp. The loose skin flapped over his ear, and his eyes bounced around like pinballs. Thick, sticky blood oozed from the wound and trickled down his neck.

"How you doin', Wolfman?" Mason hoped the horror he felt wasn't evident in his tone.

"Peassshhhy fuckin' keen," Wolf slurred, and the urgency Mason felt increased tenfold.

Head wounds were always a bitch. But one like this

could kill a man faster than he could spit. Wolf's brain could be swelling inside the tight confines of his skull even now.

"Tell them to toss their weapons onto the beach where I can see them," Wolf's captor snarled. "Then tell them to step out with their hands up."

Mason turned his chin slightly to relay the orders. There was a brief pause, and he knew his teammates loathed the idea of giving up their guns. But eventually two Colts flew out of the darkness to land with a pair of resounding *clacks* on the beach. In the semidarkness of the night, they looked like little more than a pile of dark sticks.

A second later, Romeo and Doc stepped from the shadows. Doc's shaggy blond hair reflected the starlight. And Romeo's dark eyes penetrated the distance that separated them, telling Mason without words *I hope you know what you're doing.*

That makes two of us. Mason dipped his chin in answer.

"Tell the others to come out too," the masked man demanded.

"What others?"

"Don't fuck with me." To emphasize his point, the douchebag pressed his pistol harder against Wolf's temple. An involuntary grunt of pain sounded at the back of Wolf's throat, and Mason clenched his fists.

"By my count, there should be two women and one old man," Masked Man said. "Now, tell them to come out with their hands up."

It went against everything in Mason to ask the ladies

to move away from the safety of the trees. But Wolf's jaw was beginning to sag. Time was of the essence.

"Alex!" he hollered over his shoulder. "Chrissy! Come out and join Doc and Romeo on the beach, please!"

"And the old man too."

"Uncle John didn't come with us to this side of the island," Mason told the masked man. "My guess would be he's on the satellite phone or marine radio calling in a Mayday as we speak. The Coasties will be swarming this whole place soon. Which means if you're hoping to make a clean getaway, you better get the fuck on it."

He could see the asshole's jaw clench even through the fabric of the balaclava. But the guy took Mason's advice and yelled over Wolf's lolling head, "Everyone move twenty yards up the beach! Hands where I can see them the entire way!"

Glancing over his shoulder, Mason saw his friends trudging through the sand. Alex caught his gaze, her eyes wide and pleading with him to be careful.

There'd been a dull ache in his chest ever since she confessed to loving him. But seeing her now, maybe for the last time, made it grow sharp.

Someone had cut his heart in half. He feared that someone might be himself.

She wanted to know what his one do-over would be? It would be to go back in time to the moment she said the three most beautiful words in the English language. And instead of getting all bent out of shape and telling her she was too young and inexperienced to know what she was talking about, he would thank her for honoring him with such a sweet and wonderful gift. Then he would gently explain once again why she shouldn't.

"Push the boat out and get in. Then, start the engine," Balaclava Buttmunch commanded. "Do everything nice and slow, or your friend here gets what's left of his head blown off."

Mason did as instructed, pushing the dinghy into the warm, frothing surf and clambering aboard. The pull-motor took two tries, but eventually the diesel engine sputtered to life.

As soon as it was humming, the masked motherfucker unceremoniously let go of Wolf. He immediately turned to point the malevolent mouth of his pistol at Mason's chest, and with a clenched jaw, Mason watched his friend crumple to the sand unconscious, his blood loss finally getting the better of him.

The hollow end of the Beretta never wavered as the ass clown climbed aboard the dinghy. Mason felt its sinister intent as surely as he felt the moisture in the night air.

Hitching his chin toward the horizon to the west, Masked Man said, "Head that way. Nice and easy."

Mason engaged the engine and pointed the dinghy toward the speedboat he could see bobbing some distance out. For what seemed like a very long time, but in actuality could only have been a couple of minutes, he concentrated on piloting the little craft over the waves. Once they were past the surf, he turned back to see his friends on their knees, huddled around Wolf's form. Doc whipped off his shirt and wound it around Wolf's head.

Come on, Doc, Mason silently implored. *Here's where all that schooling comes in handy.*

"How the hell do you sonsofbitches do it?" Masked Man broke into his thoughts.

"Do what?" Mason frowned as the dinghy plowed over a wave. When he braced himself, his foot brushed up against a towel that'd been left in the bottom of the boat.

"Come out on top every damn time," his captor growled.

Mason lifted one shoulder. "Overabundance of training, I guess."

"I was overabundantly trained, too, but you and yours have still bested me and mine twice now."

Mason stared hard into the man's icy green eyes. "Who the fuck *are* you?"

An oily smile stretched thin lips. With his free hand, the man peeled back his balaclava, and the face that was revealed wasn't one Mason had ever met in person. But neither was it one he was likely to forget.

It was the face of one Rory Gellman. An Army Ranger turned high-priced mercenary. The man the FBI had discovered was partially responsible for the assault on Garden Key and the subsequent events that followed.

Gellman had been a ghost since that night, eluding the government agencies that'd been tasked with finding him. And the guys of Deep Six had all but forgotten he existed. But apparently, Gellman was the type to nurse a grudge.

Mason knew the glare he leveled at Gellman's nose

was stony. His tone was even stonier when he said, "I'll be goddamned."

Gellman laughed. "Oh, most certainly."

"Why the fuck do you keep turning up like bad breath?" Mason's grip tightened on the tiller. "Did my team do something to piss you off at some point?"

The merc snorted. "Please. I didn't even know you cocksuckers existed before that bad business that went down on Garden Key. I was hired to do a job there. A job that ended in the deaths of my entire crew and left me without a way to earn a living."

"So that's why you fell in with the commodore? For greed and revenge?"

"Don't give yourself so much credit," Gellman scoffed. "I had no idea when I answered Bagheri's ad on the dark web that I'd run into you dickholes again. But low and behold, the men responsible for the deaths of his sons also happened to be the men responsible for the deaths of my guys. I guess it was fate." He shrugged. "Or dumb luck that brought us back together."

Mason shook his head as the little dinghy continued to skip across the surface of the sea toward the waiting vessel. The closer they got to the boat, the closer he knew Gellman was to making his move.

"Fucking mercs," he growled.

"Oh, come on," Gellman sneered. "You're no different. You hide behind the facade of valor and patriotism, but you were paid to kill just like I'm paid to kill. The only difference is that my employers pony up a lot more cash than old Uncle Sam."

The merc's words hit too close to home. Played too much into Mason's 2 percent theory. And yet he was quick to draw a distinction between them.

"But you're leaving out the part where you *like* it."

"Big talk from a guy speeding away from an island strewn with dead bodies."

A muscle twitched in Mason's jaw as the dinghy hit a wave and salt water sprayed over the side. Both men wore the mist on their faces. Neither of them lifted a hand to wipe it away.

Tension pulsed in the air, making it feel electric. Mason would swear the wind around them smelled of burned ozone. The second one of them moved, it would be on.

"You tell yourself whatever story you hafta to make your life choices set right in your mind," Mason managed despite his clenched jaw. "But I know when you get still and quiet on a cold, dark night, you think about the lines you were never supposed to cross."

Gellman's nostrils flared, proving Mason had scored a direct hit. Still, the merc argued, "You delude yourself by standing on imaginary principles. Nothing truly matters in this world but doing what you need to do to make your time on it as comfortable as possible. And speaking of time…" Mason saw the muscles in Gellman's gun hand bunch. "Yours is up."

Orange fire blinked out of the end of the merc's pistol, but Mason was already lunging to the side. Despite his catlike reflexes, it was still a close thing. The round passed so close to his cheek that he felt the air it displaced.

Snagging the towel in the bottom of the boat with his toes, Mason kicked it into Gellman's face at the same time he brought the hard edge of his palm down on the bundle of nerves in Gellman's gun wrist. Involuntarily, the merc's grip went lax. The pistol slipped from his grasp to land in the quarter inch of water wetting the bottom of the dinghy.

Gellman ripped the towel away from his face and flung it at Mason before lunging for the weapon. Because the merc was closer to the pistol, he was able to get his hands around it first.

It was instinct more than anything that had Mason quickly grabbing the ends of the towel and twirling it into a rope that he used to wrap around Gellman's forearm. One hard twist and the bones in the merc's wrist snapped like dry twigs under combat boots.

As he howled in pain, Gellman's hand relaxed helplessly. Only this time, instead of the pistol landing in the bottom of the boat, it hit the side of the rubber dinghy and bounced overboard.

Mason leapt, but before he could tackle the merc, Gellman tossed himself overboard too.

After the pistol? Is he crazy? He'll never find it in the water.

Mason glanced around and quickly realized what had prompted the bastard to abandon ship. The dingy was barely ten yards from the bobbing speedboat, and the distance was closing fast.

Fuck!

Mason dove for the tiller and was able to whip it hard

left. The rubber boat banged a tight U-ey, its engine showering the speedboat in propeller wash as it passed within inches of the other vessel's hull.

"Come on, you cocksucker!" Mason throttled down, slowing the dinghy to a crawl so he could search the water for Gellman. "Show yourself!"

But he barely had time to do one quick scan of the sea around the speedboat before Doc yelled from the bank. "Mason! We need that damned dinghy! Now!"

"Fuck!" he hissed, taking another second to scan the drink for the injured merc. Then he laid on the gas and sped to shore.

It rankled to let Gellman escape. But the desperation in Doc's call was impossible to miss. Wolf was running out of time.

Chapter 28

Thirty-six hours later

WHY IS HOSPITAL FURNITURE SO DAMN UNCOMFORTABLE? Alex thought as she squirmed on the small, rock-hard love seat pushed against the far wall of Wolf's assigned room.

As if reading her mind, Romeo, who'd been in an equally small and equally rock-hard chair positioned next to Wolf's bed, jumped to his feet and bent side to side. "That's it. Can't stand sitting in that torture device a second longer. Headed to Caroline's Café to grab some chicken wings. Anyone need anything while I'm out?"

Both Alex and Chrissy—who was in the chair on the opposite side of Wolf's bed—shook their heads. But Wolf sat up a little straighter.

After Chrissy tenderly plumped the pillow behind his back, he said to Romeo, "Grab me some condoms. I might get lucky tonight and need protection." He waggled his eyebrows—or rather his one good eyebrow—at Chrissy.

"Don't confuse friendly concern for something more," Chrissy told him with a roll of her eyes.

"Yeah." Romeo nodded. "Plus, I think your face is protection enough."

"That bad?" Wolf pressed a hand to the thick bandage

wrapped around his head and under his chin. The entire side of his face was swollen. His left eye was so puffy, you couldn't tell if he had eyelashes.

"It's not that bad," Chrissy assured him. "Once the swelling goes down, you'll be as pretty as ever. And all the ladies will be chasing after you again."

"Who says I want that?" Wolf pasted what passed for a scowl on his lopsided face.

"Please," Chrissy scoffed. "Every man with a pulse wants that."

"Not me." Wolf shook his head and then winced like the movement hurt. Instant concern clouded Chrissy's eyes.

The woman wasn't fooling anyone. What she felt for Wolf went far beyond friendly concern. And that made Alex smile.

The expression felt good. It'd been a while since she'd donned it because, at many points over the last day and a half, things had been touch and go.

Despite his best efforts, Doc hadn't been able to stanch the blood pumping from Wolf's head. Turned out that was because the bullet that'd grazed Wolf's skull when he turned his back on his post *for five seconds to take a piss*—emphasis was Wolf's when he finally regained consciousness and could tell them the story—had sliced clean through his temporal artery.

"We have to get him to a hospital. *Fast*," Doc had growled that night on the beach, his hands flying as he examined the wound.

"Let's carry him to the floatplane," Romeo had said,

grabbing Wolf's shoulders, only to have Doc stop him with a bloody hand on his forearm.

"No time." Doc had jumped up to yell for Mason to bring in the dinghy, and Alex had been left with nothing to do but watch in horror while the scene in the water played out.

It'd been awful seeing Mason tussle with Gellman. Worse even than when she'd watched him take a knife to the gut, because she'd been so helpless. So completely useless to offer any assistance.

She'd dragged in a huge breath of relief when Gellman jumped overboard. But it was short-lived. Because Doc's face had told her that while Mason had come out on top, it looked very likely that Wolf might not.

The fact was Wolf *wouldn't* have made it if it hadn't been for Mason. Not only had Mason raced to shore so they could pile inside the dinghy in a classic Keystone Kops free-for-all and speed around the island to the waiting floatplane, but he'd also been the one to step up to the plate to donate blood when Doc determined on the flight to Key West that Wolf wouldn't make it otherwise.

Alex had objected to the plan, scared Mason hadn't the blood to spare after his knife wound. But she'd soon learned it was him or no one. He was the only universal donor.

Doc had quickly set up what he termed a *battlefield transfusion*, and Alex had sat on the floor of the floatplane holding Mason's hand and feeling it grow colder and clammier as the minutes ticked by and the blood he so desperately needed drained out of him and into Wolf.

Between the events on Garden Key and what'd happened with the Iranians, she'd known true fear. But nothing had terrified her more than when Mason lost consciousness and slumped beside her.

She'd screamed his name.

What happened after was nothing more than a blur of landing, loading into the waiting ambulance Romeo had called for over the plane's communications system, and racing to the hospital where Wolf had been rushed into emergency surgery, and Mason had been laid on a gurney in the emergency room to receive two bags of blood.

Watching Mason nearly bleed out to save Wolf was the most selfless, heroic thing Alex had ever seen. And was further proof why she loved the very bones of him.

Put simply, he was the best man she'd ever known.

As if thinking of him conjured him, she heard his deep voice in the hallway. The hospital had released him this morning, and she'd tried twice to pull him aside to talk about things between them. But each time he'd claimed to need to go take care of something.

No more excuses, she thought as she stood from the apparatus for pure torment that was masquerading as a love seat. She had things she needed to say—set the record straight, so to speak—or she'd never forgive herself.

Heading for the door, she stopped in her tracks when she heard Agent Fazzle's voice join in the hallway conversation. It was lowered to a conspiratorial whisper. Which, of course, had her leaning against the doorjamb so she could eavesdrop.

1:45 p.m.

"Rory Gellman escaped. We lost his trail in the Bahamas."

"*Fuck!*" Mason hissed, then winced when the big-haired nurse at the nurses' station gave him a disapproving scowl.

Sorry, he mouthed to her, before turning back to Fazzle. "Shoulda killed the rat bastard when I had the chance."

Doc, who was huddled up close with them, snorted. "And left Wolf to bleed out? Right."

Ignoring Doc, Mason demanded of Fazzle, "How the hell did Gellman find out we were part of the op that killed the commodore's sons? Can you at least tell me that?"

A look of disgust passed over the FBI agent's face. "Unfortunately, yes. Turns out one of Gellman's former Army Ranger buddies now works for the Pentagon. When Gellman approached him about your old op, he didn't think twice before using his security clearance to dig into the classified files in the naval archives. He confessed the whole thing when we questioned him. Said Gellman paid him ten grand for the file."

"Sold his soul to the devil for a measly ten G's?" Doc shook his head. "Pathetic."

"Apparently those Pentagon jobs don't pay much." Fazzle shrugged. "And this joker has a gambling problem to boot."

"Fuck," Mason said again. Only this time he was careful to keep his voice low so that Nurse Ratched didn't try to murder him with her eye daggers.

"I'd say that about sums up this entire case." Fazzle nodded. "It's the damnedest thing I've come across in my twenty years with the Bureau. I mean, an Iranian commodore. Here. In the good old U. S. of A."

"Speaking of Bagheri," Doc said, "you federal boys are playing your cards close to your vests, aren't you? Not a word of what happened on Wayfarer Island has come across my CNN News feed. Uncle John said a bunch of Men in Black came by, loaded up the bodies, and flew away without so much as a by your leave."

"Keeping things quiet was an order from on high." Fazzle made a face. "Seems the president doesn't want the bad press this would generate. Especially during an election year. And especially since she's claiming she used her first term in office to tighten up our borders and make it impossible for our enemies to breach our shores."

"Damn politicians," Doc cursed and then looked chagrined when the nurse glowered his way. A wink and a flash of that big Montana grin and Nurse Ratched's stone-cold heart melted. She blushed and glanced demurely back to her computer screen.

"Works out for you guys, though," Fazzle said. "You won't have the press crawling up your ass looking for interviews. It'll be like it never happened."

"Ya-huh." Mason nodded. "And I'd stomach that just fine if Gellman wasn't walking around a free man. If Madam President is trying to sweep this whole thing under the rug, how's that gonna affect the search for the fuckface?"

Fazzle's irritated expression said it all.

"She's not gonna put a task force on this, is she?" Mason's tone was laced with disgust.

Reluctantly, Fazzle shook his head.

Mason felt a hard jolt of anger, but it was quickly replaced by certainty. He knew what he had to do. It was the *only* thing to do to make sure everyone on Wayfarer Island could sleep securely in their beds at night.

"And what would Madam President say if one of us were to go after him? 'Cause I gotta feeling if Gellman's not stopped, he's gonna find a way to fuck us over again. It's personal now. I saw that in his face."

"Gellman isn't in the States. And what happens outside our borders?" A wily grin played with the corners of Fazzle's lips. "Well, she doesn't have any say over that, now does she?" Then he sobered. "If you catch him alive, call me. I'll make sure he's held accountable. If you don't catch him alive..." Fazzle let the sentence dangle and pinned a look on Mason. "Then I don't want to know about it."

Mason nodded his understanding and then took the hand Fazzle offered him. "Stay out of trouble," the fed said.

"We try." Doc shook Fazzle's hand as well. "But the damn stuff follows us."

"So it would seem." The FBI agent spun on his heel and started up the hallway toward the bank of elevators.

After Fazzle disappeared behind the sliding silver doors, Doc said, "I'm coming with you, of course."

"You don't hafta."

"But see?" Doc gently cupped Mason's cheek. "I do. Because you complete me."

"Fuck off." Mason shook Doc's hand away.

Doc laughed and then his eyes landed on something beyond Mason's shoulder. "Baby Bear."

Mason stiffened, not wanting to turn but unable to help himself.

Alex headed toward them, her short legs eating up the distance, her eyes firmly—and frightfully—fixed on his. He looked around for an escape route. She'd been trying to corner him all day. And he knew damned well why.

She wanted to pick up the conversation they'd been having in his bedroom before the shit went down. Which was the dead *last* thing in the world *he* wanted to do.

He already hated himself for who he was, the sort of man who'd never be what she needed or deserved. But if he saw that hurt look in her eyes one more time, he might just be tempted to eat his own M4 for dinner.

"Doc, if he tries to run," Alex called, having accurately read Mason's expression, "tackle him to the ground."

Doc obediently placed a restraining hand on Mason's shoulder and leaned over to whisper close to his ear, "Despite your willful pursuit of ignorance on the matter, I think you know, deep down, that the pain we suffer for love is always worth it."

Bitter cold washed down Mason's length.

Doc knew.

Well, of *course* Doc knew. Because they'd been friends and teammates and partners for the better part of a decade. And because they'd been through countless battles together, which had a tendency to suck all the gray out of anyone's personality and leave only the black and white behind.

For instance, Mason knew when Doc got that far-away look in his eye, he was thinking about his dead wife. And when Doc said he *needed to go see a woman about a horse*, he wasn't really looking for sexual gratification, but instead seeking a little comfort in the arms of a stranger.

So, yeah. It wasn't a surprise that Doc could read Mason as easily as Mason could read Doc.

"It's not *my* pain I'm worried about," he hissed from the side of his mouth, and then straightened because Alex now stood in front of him, flame hair wild around her face, hands planted firmly on her hips. She looked like a little tyrant.

Since they'd arrived in Key West in swim trunks or, in Alex's case, a sexy-without-trying-too-hard set of sleep shorts, yesterday Romeo had made a round trip to Wayfarer Island to pack a bag for each of them. Typical of Romeo, he'd managed to find the hottest outfit Alex owned. A little sundress that molded to her pert breasts and hugged the nip of her waist.

Fucking Romeo, Mason thought uncharitably as a million and one images of Alex naked and writhing beneath him assaulted his brain. As if he wasn't tortured enough already.

"Have I told you how much I love that dress on you, Baby Bear?" Doc crooned at Alex while covertly digging an elbow into Mason's side.

She blinked down at her dress. When she glanced up, her expression was one of genuine confusion. "Really?" Her green eyes were guileless behind the lenses of her glasses.

On any other woman, Mason might have thought it an act. But Alex truly had no idea how beautiful she was.

And oh! How he loved her for that. Well, that and about a million other things.

"You look hot, little momma." Doc waggled his eyebrows.

Before Mason realized his own intent, he slammed a retaliatory elbow into Doc's side. "Fuck on out of here, why dontcha?" he growled.

Doc smirked and tipped an imaginary hat. "That's my cue."

A little line appeared between Alex's eyebrows as she watched Doc saunter down the hall and disappear into Wolf's hospital room. When she turned back, there were shadows in her eyes.

That M4 is looking tastier and tastier.

"You're going after Rory Gellman," she said, and Mason released the breath he hadn't been aware he'd been holding. At least this subject wouldn't break his damned heart.

He nodded. "Gellman has to be stopped."

She didn't argue, simply continued to frown. "When will you leave?"

"Today." He wanted so much to smooth the line from between her eyebrows. And then smooth her eyebrows so he could feel once again how silky soft those arches were.

"So soon?" If he wasn't mistaken, there was a hitch in her voice.

His own was a little scratchy. "Can't let his trail get cold."

She swallowed and nodded her understanding. "How long will you be gone?"

"As long as it takes."

A long breath slid from her. She opened her mouth but he lifted a hand, hoping he could adios her plan to resume their previous conversation.

Time away would be good for her. *And* for him. It would clear their heads. Without their undeniable chemistry clouding their minds, she'd quickly come to see he wasn't what she wanted. Not really.

"I know what you're gonna say," he told her. "And I wish you wouldn't. I like you so much, Alex. I respect you so much."

He didn't tell her he loved her so much, but he wondered if the truth was in his eyes.

"I don't wanna hurt you," he continued. "I've hurt you enough already. So please, *please* let's leave things where they are. Let's quit while we're ahead."

For a drawn-out moment, her eyes searched his. There was a point in there when he thought he'd won. Then, crossing her arms, she tilted her head and demanded, "Are you finished?"

The hand he ran through his hair was shaky. He hadn't succeeded in heading her off at the pass, and he braced himself for what would come next. His nod was slow, a mere dip of his chin.

"Good." She dipped her chin too. "Now, I think your excuses are bullshit."

He opened his mouth, but in true Alex style, she plowed right ahead. "You've convinced yourself there's something wrong with you that precludes you having a 'normal life.'" She made air quotes. "But what the hell is normal, anyway? You claim 2 percent of the population are natural-born killers? Yeah, well, 2 percent of the population has green eyes, did you know that? Also, 2 percent of the population are redheads. My point being no one thinks a thing about that because 2 percent is still a shit-ton of people, meaning it's not actually that rare and is, in fact, quite normal for the human race."

Again he tried to argue. Again she talked over him. "You claim the navy changed you. Well, *of course* it did. No one can see the things you've seen or do the things you've done without being changed. The change means you're human. It means you're normal. And if you really want to know what I think?"

Like she hadn't been telling him what she really thought for the last two minutes?

"I think your ex-wife gaslighted you. I think she couldn't take the blame for her infidelity and, instead, placed it on you by telling you *you* were the one at fault. Which is just awful and sad, and I'm so sorry she did that. But I'm even more sorry you seem to have *believed* her."

He had nothing to say to that. Mostly because his mind was spinning around, trying to find a flaw in her logic.

"The simple truth is I didn't know you before," she continued. "I know you *now*. And I love you now. Just as you are. A man who'd rather grunt and growl than have a conversation."

He found a place to jump in. "I talk more to you than I do to anyone."

She ignored him. "A man who likes to sit in a quiet spot and paint pictures of the sea and sky. A man who hates crowds but loves dogs. A man who understands how dangerous the world can be and is always ready to guard himself and everyone else around him against it. Somehow you've convinced yourself this last thing is a bad thing. But I don't see it. What I see is *you*, Mason. *All* of you. The good parts, the bad parts, and the parts you think aren't worthy. And I'm here to tell you I love it all."

Her words landed like hand grenades on his heart, hard and hot and painful.

There's a flaw in her logic. Find it, a voice whispered through his head. Only this time, he thought he might recognize it as his ex-wife's.

Was it possible Alex was right?

No. No, she couldn't be. He wasn't—

Before he could finish the thought, Alex lifted her chin and added, "You go on and do your thing. Find Gellman. And while you're out chasing the bad guy, I want you to think about what I've said. Then when you come back home, if you're still convinced you don't want to take a shot on seeing where this thing between us will go, fine. We'll find a way to be friends. But if you *do* feel like taking a shot, then I'll be there. Waiting. Hoping. Get it? Got it? Good."

With a decisive dip of her chin, she turned and strode down the hall, leaving him standing there like a spare prick.

For a couple of seconds, he didn't move. He *couldn't* move. There was too much confusion in his head. Then, without conscious thought, his feet began inching forward of their own accord. They carried him down the hall to the elevators.

When he stepped out of the hospital three minutes later, he couldn't feel the brush of the breeze through his hair or the warmth of the sun on his skin. He couldn't feel the beat of his own heart inside his chest or the rush of air through his lungs.

He couldn't feel anything because Alex's words had stunned him, leaving him completely numb.

Chapter 29

Eight days later

"This car is a POS," Doc grumbled. "It couldn't outrun a dairy cow."

From his position behind the wheel, Mason glanced over to find Doc's haggard face covered in a week's worth of beard stubble. His hair was lank and listless from the wind and salt spray. And his nose was peeling from the sunburn he'd received the first day of their hunt when they'd landed in the Bahamas and spent twelve hours in the subtropical sun running from one boat rental shop to the next until they'd finally found the one Gellman had used to rent a forty-foot catamaran.

Since that first day, they'd barely stopped to eat. They'd slept in shifts. And the islands they'd visited while closing in on Gellman's trail were so numerous they were nothing but a blur.

In short, they were running on fumes. And Mason felt as bad as Doc looked.

Probably look as bad too, he thought, and then winced when he tried to shift into third gear and the transmission on the little Nissan hatchback they'd rented from the guy in port put up a fight. After a few seconds of grinding, he found the gear and told Doc, "Not like we had a lotta choices. Beggars can't be choosers."

"Mmph" was all Doc allowed before pointing. "Hang a left. The bar the dockhand said he told Gellman to hit should be on the next corner."

Mason did as instructed and was gifted with a view of the mountainside. Pastel-painted houses climbed up the incline. They looked cool and crisp compared to the dirty streets and brightly colored umbrellas shading the carts of the street vendors lined up and down the avenue in downtown Port-au-Prince.

The last time Mason had been in Haiti, he'd still been in the navy and working a security detail for the president. Apparently, there'd been rumors of an assassination plot and the Secret Service had called in the big guns, a.k.a. the Navy SEALs.

"Place hasn't changed much," Doc observed as Mason found an open spot near the curb and parallel parked the Nissan.

"In my experience, most places don't," Mason said before pushing out of the car. The door hinges screamed as if in agony.

Once he was on the street, he was accosted by the smell of frying plantains and car exhaust. Making sure his tank top covered the small of his back where his handgun rested against his spine, he joined Doc on the curb and headed toward the run-down watering hole on the corner.

The neighborhood wasn't one for tourists. He and Doc got plenty of curious looks from the locals, but their expressions succinctly stated that any questions would not be welcome.

"What d'you suppose the chances are of him still being here?" Mason asked wearily, feeling every single one of his missing meals.

"That dockhand said he sent Gellman this way barely two hours ago. Maybe we'll get lucky this time."

Mason grunted. They'd been hoping to get lucky for over a week. And for over a week, they'd come up empty-handed. He was starting to lose hope.

He blinked after pushing through the open front door of the bar. When his eyes adjusted to the dimness, he took a quick glance around and then cursed low and long beneath his breath.

There were two dozen people lining the plywood bar and sitting at rickety tables. But none of them was Rory Gellman.

Beside him, Doc sighed tiredly. "Let's head to the bar for a nip or two and see if maybe Gellman was here. If he was, maybe he let slip to the bartender where he plans to head next."

Mason figured it was an exercise in futility but followed Doc to the bar nonetheless. The bartender took one look at them and then asked in heavily accented English, "What will you have?"

Mason didn't pay attention to what Doc ordered. He was too busy using the mirror behind the bar to keep an eye on the door. It was habit. One he knew he'd never break.

He downed the drink the bartender set in front of him, and then coughed and fought the tears that pooled in his eyes. Whatever was in the shot glass burned all the skin off the roof of his mouth.

He turned to Doc to ask what the fuck he'd just put down his throat. Before he could get a word out, however, the door to the bathroom opened and out walked the man of the hour.

Rory motherfucking Gellman.

Doc spotted him at the same time Mason had. A split second later, Rory spotted *them*. For a couple of interminable moments, no one moved. No one dared breathe.

Mason felt the weight of his pistol against his back, the metal warm from being next to his skin. But he didn't dare pull it. Not in a bar full of Haitians. He was many things, but dumb as a Maryland stump wasn't one of them.

A muscle twitched beside Rory's left eye.

Mason knew what came next and felt his own muscles tense in response. "He's gonna rabbit on us," he told Doc from the side of his mouth.

"Yep. There he goes." Doc nodded when Gellman leapt over a table where two men were smoking and playing cards. Three more steps, and the former Army Ranger dove headfirst through the open front window. "I hate it when they make me run," Doc added.

Even as he was finishing the sentence, Doc was sprinting for the door. Mason was hot on his heels, noting that the locals looked on with only mild interest. Apparently, squabbles between foreigners didn't concern them much.

Out on the street, they turned on the speed and rounded the corner in time to see Gellman dart into an alley a block and a half ahead. Mason had no hope of keeping up with Doc's long-legged strides. But then an elderly woman wearing a head scarf and pushing a shopping cart suddenly appeared from out of nowhere and landed right in Doc's path.

Mason was able to skirt the front of the cart with a Heisman Trophy–worthy juke move, which meant he was the first into the alleyway. That also meant he was the first to see Gellman's fatal mistake.

It was a dead end. The trash-strewn back street was closed off by a ten-foot chain-link fence. And while Gellman was doing his best to climb the sucker, the cast on the arm Mason had broken while they fought in the dinghy was slowing him down. Also, the fence was old and rusty. Every time Gellman got a good foothold, the metal gave way and he fell back to the ground.

"End of the road, Gellman!" Mason yelled as he skidded to a halt six feet from the asshole. He could feel Doc, who had managed to navigate the shopping cart, come to a stop behind him.

Gellman reached into his front waistband, and ice ran through Mason's veins. Despite the heat of the day, angry goose bumps erupted along the back of his neck.

He took two steps forward. His voice was low and deadly when he said, "Only assholes keep their guns in their front waistbands. You know how I know this? 'Cause the only way you'd be walking around without fear of blowing your cock off is if you keep the safety on or don't have one in the chamber. Either way, there's no way you can draw and fire before I punch you so hard you'll be eating your own fucking teeth."

Gellman, proving himself a complete idiot, didn't

heed Mason's warning. He pulled his pistol and Mason
balled up his fist, letting it fly with all the hard-packed
muscle he had in him.

The sound of Gellman's front tooth cracking off was
wickedly satisfying. So was the blood that poured down
Gellman's chin when he stumbled back, his shoulder
slamming into the chain-link fence, which acted as a
trampoline and propelled him straight back into Mason's
arms.

Caught unaware, Mason barely had time to catch the
fucker before he felt Gellman's pistol—which the asshat
had somehow managed to hang onto—poke into his gut.

"Use it or toss it away," he growled into the merc's
bloodied face. "I don't have time for your indecisiveness."

"Jesus, Mason!" Doc yelled, but Mason ignored him.

He saw the truth in Gellman's eyes. He'd been right
about the mercenary's gun chamber being empty. And
Gellman knew as well as he did that Mason's first punch
was nothing compared to what would come next should
Gellman pull the trigger.

"How the hell did you find me?" Gellman panted,
the whites of his eyes shot through with blood veins. He
looked worse than Mason and Doc. Which wasn't sur-
prising, considering the only thing more exhausting than
chasing down an asshole was being an asshole on the run.

"Easy." Mason smiled, but it was all teeth and no feeling. "Every slug leaves a trail."

"Fuck you," Gellman snarled as Mason twisted the
pistol from his grip and tossed it to Doc.

"Speak another word and I'll hafta hurt you," Mason

growled, spinning Gellman around and shoving him face-first into the fence. Mason pulled a plastic zip-tie from his pocket and quickly cuffed the merc's one good hand to his cast.

Gellman glanced over his shoulder, his expression confused. "Why hog-tie me if you're just planning to kill me? Why not get it over with? It's not like the folks in this neighborhood will stop you."

"Death is too good for you," Mason muttered. "You're a disgrace to your country and to the uniform you once wore. You gotta stand in front of a jury and face that." Turning to Doc, he said, "Watch him, will you? I gotta call Agent Fazzle."

Doc traded places with him. But before Mason could pull out the burner cell phone he'd bought back in the Bahamas, he heard Gellman let loose with a banshee cry. He turned back in time to see Gellman headbutt Doc's chin.

Dumbass, Mason thought because Doc barely stumbled back a half step.

"You little cup of piss," Doc snarled, driving his fist into the middle of Gellman's face. The sound was loud and echoed down the alley. A second later, Gellman crumpled to the ground, out cold.

"Damn, that was satisfying." Doc grinned, flexing the fingers on his hand before using them to test his jaw. "Now, get Fazzle on the horn. Chasing this merc's sorry ass all over the Caribbean for the last week has me tired, hungry, and ready to go home."

"Me too," Mason agreed, dialing Fazzle's number.

Although, on second thought, he wasn't so sure about that last thing. Alex was back home. And he still hadn't decided what the hell he was supposed to do about her...

———

Twelve hours later

"You assholes look like shit on a stick, eh?" Romeo said over his shoulder as he went through the preflight check in the seaplane's cockpit. Then he grinned. "Which means it must've been one hell of a good hunt."

"If we look like shit on a stick it's 'cause we *feel* like shit on a stick," Mason grumbled wearily, stretching his legs toward the bulkhead that separated the passenger cabin from the pilot compartment. He'd aged eight years in the last eight days.

Or at least he felt like he had.

The one boat ride and two flights it'd taken them to get from Haiti to Key West certainly hadn't helped things.

When he'd called Fazzle, the FBI agent had given him instructions to take Gellman to the Toussaint Louverture International Airport on the edge of Port-au-Prince Bay. Ninety minutes later, the merc had been loaded onto a military transport, headed back to the States where Fazzle promised Gellman would stand trial. Not for his role in what happened with the Iranians—Madam President hadn't been kidding about keeping that on the DL—but for the part he'd played in what happened that night on Garden Key.

But since Mason and Doc had had no "official" part in Gellman's capture, they'd been left to find their own way home.

Home.

Where Alex was waiting for him. Where she'd ask if he'd thought about what she said, which *of course* he had, but—

"What are you going to do, my man?" Doc cut into Mason's swirling thoughts as Romeo piloted the Otter toward the runway.

"What d'you mean?" Mason had to raise his voice above the little plane's engines revving in preparation for flight.

"About Alex!" Doc shouted because Romeo had pulled back on the throttle and the floatplane raced down the runway.

Mason always hated this part, when the g-forces pushed him against his chair and he felt powerless over his fate.

Alex did that to him too. Made him feel powerless. Powerless to resist those dancing green eyes. Powerless to resist that laughing smile.

The thought of the eventual crash was too terrible to contemplate.

"You're in love with her!" Doc kept on. "And she's in love with you! You know that, right?"

For a couple of minutes, as the plane lifted into the air and the engines screamed, Mason said nothing. It was only after Romeo leveled them out, and the sound in the fuselage dimmed from a deafening roar to a low hum that he turned to Doc.

"She only *thinks* she loves me 'cause she's sweet and idealistic and has never been hurt before," he admitted wretchedly. "She hasn't developed the emotional scars or the sixth sense for self-preservation that would let her see me for what I really am."

A line appeared between Doc's eyebrows. "And what are you?"

Something snapped in Mason. His voice cracked when he said, "Broken! The rest of you just slid into this civilian life with no problem, but no matter how hard I try, I can't!"

Doc was shaking his head before Mason finished speaking. "So you've got a little PTSD? Good. Great. Join the club, asshole."

Mason's chin jerked back. He knew his face showed his astonishment when he asked, "You?"

"Yeah, me. Me and Romeo and Bran and *all* of us. War is *war*. Killing is *killing*. There's no coming back from it. But that doesn't mean we all can't still have a *life*."

Mason clung to his denial like a life raft. "It does for me," he grumbled low. "I couldn't do that to Alex. Inflict myself and all of my baggage on her. She deserves something good and sweet and unbroken."

"For God's sake." Doc rolled his eyes. "Here you sit, reeking of hearts and flowers and good intentions, willing to sacrifice yourself and your shot at happiness, and for what?"

"For Alex!" Mason's temper erupted again. Doc had scrambled his brains, which made him have doubts. And for whatever reason, those doubts brought hope with them.

"You've been carrying your past around like a disease for years now." Doc's voice was annoyingly even in the face of Mason's outburst. "But I'm here to tell you that you *can* make peace with it. That you *deserve* to make peace with it. And if you'll allow her, Alex will help you with that."

Mason opened his mouth to argue, but Doc pressed ahead. "I care about Alex. If even a tiny part of me thought for one minute you couldn't be everything she needs, I'd be the first to tell you to screw off and leave her alone. And yet here I am telling you to go for it."

Mason stubbornly shook his head. "My scars are too deep."

"You only get scars when you've healed." Doc snorted. "What you have, my friend, are wounds. If you pull your self-sacrificing head out of your ass, Alex will help you heal them."

Mason once again opened his mouth, but Doc lifted a staying hand. "Nope. I've said my piece and have no interest in listening to more of your chin music." Closing his eyes, Doc reclined his seat and folded his hands over his flat stomach.

Mason turned toward the window, his eyes blind to the cerulean waters stretched endlessly toward the horizon. His mind was filled to the brim with doubts. And hot on their heels?

Ya-huh. You guessed it.

Hope.

Terrible, terrifying, torturous hope.

Is it possible Doc is right?

Alex worked the easternmost section of the underwater search grid. Using a venturi pump—basically an underwater Dirt Devil—she sucked sand from one location and deposited it somewhere else.

It was taxing work, made more strenuous by the watery environment and the constant push and pull of the waves as they piled up against the reef. But she didn't feel the burn of her muscles or the pressure in her lungs.

Because her mind was on Mason.

She'd had butterflies in her belly ever since Romeo begged off dive duty so he could fly to Key West to pick up Mason and Doc. All she could think was *Today is the day I find out if my bruised and beaten heart gets broken once and for all.*

Suddenly, a dull flash of black appeared in the void created by the venturi pump. Adjusting her mask, she waved away the swirling sediment. A gentle kick of her swim fins and she was floating two feet above the object.

She flapped her hand, creating currents that further revealed the dark mass. It was covered in crustaceans, making it impossible to discern what it was or if it was of any importance. Nonetheless, goose bumps broke out over her arms.

After clipping the pump to the grid so it wouldn't catch a current and tumble away, she kicked toward the surface. Once there, she pulled out her regulator, popped her goggles atop her head, and put her fingers between her teeth. Her whistle was shrill and piercing. It immediately drew LT's gaze.

Their fearless leader stood on the deck of the salvage ship. Alex knew they would need one of its cranes to bring up whatever she'd found. Because it was big. But also because the ship came equipped with a laboratory where they could house artifacts in saltwater tanks.

One of the challenges of bringing things up that'd spent centuries underwater was that exposure to air caused them to dry out and crumble like old parchment paper.

She waved at LT and then pointed to the water below her. He turned to yell something to Bran, who was piloting the vessel. Then he whistled to Chrissy, who was floating in the dinghy a little further down the search area.

Lifting her hand to shade her eyes, Chrissy followed the direction of LT's point and nodded when she spotted Alex bobbing at the surface. Two minutes later, Alex tossed her fins into the bottom of the rubber boat and handed her tanks to Chrissy.

"What have you got?" Chrissy asked as Alex hoisted herself aboard, dripping salt water over everything.

"Something big," Alex told her, her heart thudding with excitement. "Something metal. We're going to need the crane to—"

The sound of a floatplane's engines revving in the distance cut her off.

Lifting a hand against the glare of the sun, she watched as Romeo expertly piloted the Otter in. The pontoons missed the exposed reef by inches before touching down in the still waters of the lagoon. And then, like a duck coming in for a landing, the plane skied to shore.

When Alex lowered her hand, it was to find Chrissy watching her closely. "Are you going to do it?" Chrissy asked.

"Do what?" Alex frowned, those butterflies in her belly going buck wild now that Mason was home.

"Tell him you love him?"

Alex let loose with a long, beleaguered breath. "Already did that the night the Iranians came. It just sort of slipped out."

Chrissy snorted. "That's why I do Kegels."

"Gross." Alex wrinkled her nose, but felt a smile tugging at her lips.

Chrissy's grin melted when she tentatively asked, "He didn't return the sentiment?"

"He did *not*." Alex twisted her lips. "He got all flustered and started listing a bunch of excuses for why I *shouldn't* love him."

Chrissy looked toward the beach where Doc, Mason, and Romeo hopped out of the seaplane. Alex followed the direction of Chrissy's gaze, and the minute her eyes landed on Mason's big, brawny back, she felt a tug at her heart that echoed down into her belly, exacerbating the butterflies.

"So what are you going to do now?" Chrissy asked, the warm breeze playing with the ends of her ponytail.

"Guess I'm going to go face my fate." When Mason disappeared inside the house, Alex turned to Chrissy. "Mind giving me a ride to shore?"

Five minutes later, she climbed the wide, wooden steps on the front porch. But she didn't go inside the house. Instead, she took a seat atop the top tread and waited.

He would come to her. She knew he would. Mason was many things, but a coward wasn't one of them.

For what felt like hours but could only have been minutes, she watched the whitecaps giggling and spraying as they slammed into the reef. Listened to the *crackle* and *hiss* of the palm fronds blowing in the breeze. And then the squeak of the screen door told her he'd arrived.

She didn't need to turn around to know it was him. She'd always been able to feel when he was near. And her heart, which had already been pounding a mile a minute, somehow found a way to lay on more speed. So much so, she was dizzy by the time he sat beside her, his big shoulder brushing hers.

She breathed in his scent, that wonderful combination that was uniquely Mason. But she couldn't bring herself to look at him. She knew the answer to her question would be in his eyes, and she wasn't ready to see it. For a moment more, she wanted to live in the wonderful gray area of not knowing. Of having hope.

"Welcome home," she whispered quietly, her eyes trained on the hammock as it gently swayed with the wind.

"Thanks. It's good to be home."

She closed her eyes when his deep voice slid through her, warm and welcome as the memory of a hot island night.

"Gellman?" she asked after opening her eyes, but still not looking at him.

"Getting his just deserts even as we speak."

She nodded. "Good. I'm glad. And your wound?"

"Healing up. Yours?"

"Same."

For a while after that, they sat in silence. She would swear she could hear the solid *thud* of his heart. Or perhaps that was simply the rush of blood between her own ears.

"You should keep this, Alex," he finally said.

She glanced over to see the Big Papi baseball in its brand-spanking-new display case. She'd had her parents ship both items to Chrissy's house, and then had brought them to Wayfarer Island to place on Mason's bed.

She'd wanted him to see them first thing so he'd know she was a woman of her word. So he'd know that, no matter what his answer, she *would* continue to be his friend.

"It means more to you than it will ever mean to me," she told him. "I want you to have it."

A sigh whooshed from the depths of his chest. "You make it impossible. You know that, right?"

She studied her bare feet. Water had sluiced off her bathing suit and down her legs to create wet marks on the wooden tread. "Make what impossible?"

"Everything!"

That had her glancing into his eyes. Those bluer-than-blue eyes that could be ice cold or as hot as blue flames.

He looked awful. As Doc would say, *Like ten miles of*

bad road. And yet she thought him the most beautiful man she'd ever laid eyes on.

"I'm not good with words," he said quietly. "I never know what to say or how to say it. And the truth is, I didn't have any great epiphanies or sweeping changes to my personality while I was gone." Alex felt the first tingles of warning. This wasn't going to go the way she'd dreamed it might. "But I did think about you all the time."

And just like that, the warning tingles turned into sparkles of hope.

"No." He frowned. "That's not right. 'Cause that would imply I was actively doing something. I wasn't. You were just *there.*"

"Like an annoying gnat," she supplied helpfully.

"More like the air in my lungs or the heart in my chest."

Okay, and it was official. Hope. Sparkles and sparkles and sparkles of hope.

"Then Doc said something to me that made me start to wonder if it's possible I could have the life I want for myself."

Sparkles and sparkles and *sparkles* of hope!

"I do love Doc," she managed, even though her breath had strangled in her lungs. "He's great at cutting through the crap. What did he say?"

"That I'm not as fucked up as I thought I was." Mason shook his head as if that wasn't quite right. "Or that maybe I am, but it's normal given all I've been through."

"It *is* normal," Alex assured him.

Mason went on as if she hadn't spoken. "I think I wanna try, Alex. I wanna try for that life."

Her. World. Stopped. Spinning.

"What *exactly* are you saying, Mason?"

"I'm saying I want you, Alex." His eyes searched her own. "I'm saying I want you to be the last thing I see when I close my eyes at night, and the first thing I see when I open them in the morning. I'm saying—"

She didn't care what *else* he had to say because he'd already said enough. Besides, the heat and hint of desperation in his eyes told her more than words ever could.

Bright, shiny, incandescent joy filled her up until she was surprised rays of light didn't shine out of her eyes.

He wants me! The mighty Mason McCarthy wants me!

It was all she'd ever wanted, and more than she'd ever dreamed. With a squeal of unfettered happiness, she jumped into his lap. Straddling him, she grabbed his face—registering the rough scrape of his beard stubble against her palms—and slammed her mouth over his.

If someone had asked her what she was thinking in that moment, she couldn't have said. Maybe for the first time in her life, her head was completely hollow. But oh! Her heart was full.

Full in a way she'd never felt before. Full in a way she hoped to feel until her dying day.

At first, Mason's kiss was tentative, as though the man who hated talking actually had more he wanted to say. Then a low groan sounded at the back of his throat, and wrapping his arms around her, he kissed her until they were both panting.

"Upstairs?" he asked in that deliciously gravelly snarl

she'd come to recognize as his *I'm hard and achy and I need you* voice.

"Yes, please." She nodded enthusiastically and then squeaked when he hoisted her into his arms and raced inside to take the stairs two at a time.

Once they were in his bedroom, he tossed her atop the coverlet. She would have bounced except he immediately threw himself over her, pinning her to the mattress.

When he reclaimed her lips, she had a vision of their future. Of adventures and arguments. Of amazing moments sprinkled in with the mundane. And through it all, she was falling in love with him.

Was that possible? To *continue* to fall in love with one man for an entire lifetime?

By god, she was going to give it her best shot.

———

10:27 a.m.

Mason had said it before; he would say it again. Alexandra Merriweather was a damned prodigy.

He'd never really been a fan of the sixty-nine position. Had always felt it was too difficult to concentrate on two things at once, what *his* mouth was doing and what *her* mouth was doing. But somehow, Alex had set up a give-and-take rhythm that'd made the act so fucking hot he'd lost his damn mind.

Thankfully, if her squeals and squirms were anything

to go by, she'd lost hers too. And now they lay side by side, sweaty and replete.

"So?" She twirled her fingers in his chest hair. "Are you going to say them or not?"

"Huh?" His brow furrowed as he once again proved how articulate he was *not*.

"You know, those three little words."

He ducked his chin so he could look at her. Her green eyes sparked with mischief. But there was also a hint of uncertainty there.

"If memory serves, I wasn't done talking outside on the front porch," he informed her. "But you attacked me. Couldn't keep your hands off me a second longer."

"True." She nodded, and he loved the silky slide of her hair against his shoulder. "But now I'm all ears."

He opened his mouth, but to his great annoyance, nothing came out. He realized that was because the words were so big in his heart, he was struggling to get them past his throat.

After swallowing, coughing, and rubbing a hand over his chest, he managed, "I love you, Alex."

Her eyes crinkled at the corners. She could see how much it cost him to say the words aloud. But they were all the more meaningful because of it. "I love you too, Mason," she assured him in a whisper.

With his heart full, his head turned to other matters. "It occurs to me that I've never even taken you on a proper date."

"True." She frowned. "We seem to have skipped that part. Unless you count the picnic."

"Do *you* count the picnic?"

She shrugged. "Seems in order to be counted as a true date, we should have more than BLTs and brownies. I'm thinking candlelight, fresh caviar, and expensive French wine."

His chin jerked back. He wasn't a fancy guy. Never had been, never would be. She knew that, didn't she? "Are you serious?"

Her grin was impish. "No. What I seriously want the next time we're on Key West is chicken wings, a cold beer, and not less than four orgasms."

His smile stretched his lips tight. "That's my girl."

Her smile was just as wide. "And you're my guy. Forever. Has a certain ring to it, doesn't it?"

He couldn't stand it a second longer. He had to claim her Kewpie-doll lips. She welcomed his kiss with the same enthusiasm she'd welcomed his love. With open arms and a heart so fierce and sweet that he knew he would spend the rest of his life proving himself worthy of her.

Just when things were turning from romantic to erotic, a hard knock sounded at the door. "Cover yourselves!" Romeo's voice boomed through the solid wood. "I'm coming in!"

Alex scrambled to lift the sheet to her chin before the door burst open and revealed Romeo on the threshold. His dark eyes sparkled so feverishly that alarm instantly filled Mason. "What the fuck's happened now?" he demanded.

"It's a cannon." Romeo's voice was hoarse.

"What is?" Mason blinked in confusion when, from the corner of his eye, he saw Alex scramble for her glasses on the bedside table.

After she slipped them on, she stared hard at Romeo. "And?"

Romeo nodded jerkily. "Verified against the log books."

"Oh my god!" Both Alex's hands flew to cover her mouth. She shook her head in disbelief.

"What?" Mason looked between them. "What am I missing?"

"I uncovered a cannon on my dive earlier." Alex's voice was so breathless she could barely get the words out. "It's from the *Santa Cristina*. Oh my god, Mason! We've found her!"

With a shout, she tackled him back onto the mattress and covered his face and jaw with biting little kisses.

He'd like to say he was thrilled about the prospect of the ghost galleon's riches. But the truth was, with his woman all warm and willing and gloriously naked atop him, all he could manage to think about was the blood pooling in his cock.

"I'll…uh…leave you to it, eh?" Romeo quietly closed the door behind him.

Mason flipped Alex onto her back and settled himself between her legs. Claiming her mouth, he was once again hit by the image of a little girl with red hair and laughing blue eyes. Only this time, the vision didn't frighten him.

Thanks to Alex. Who had freed him from his past. Freed him from fear of the present. Freed his soul while making him long for all that would be in their future.

"Wait, wait." She grabbed his face so he was forced to release her lips. "What kind of breakfast cereal do you like?"

He blinked at her in confusion. "Um...Raisin Bran?"

Her grin was secretive. "Oh, good. Mine's Rice Krispies."

Before he could wonder what breakfast cereal had to do with anything, she sealed their lips and kissed every thought from his head.

Epilogue

June 23, 1624

BARTOLOME VARGAS SCANNED THE OCEAN BEYOND THE reef. The black water was unbroken, save for the silvery moonlight reflecting over the tops of the waves.

No prying enemy eyes. No one around to know their secrets.

Good, he thought and dropped his spyglass so he could check on his men.

After liberating the Santa Cristina of her precious riches, they had waited nearly a week for an ultra-low tide. But even with the water pulled away from the reef by the magnetic force of the Mother Moon, the crew still struggled against the waves as they worked tirelessly to secure the treasure in its new home.

Again, Bartolome felt a punch of pride at the sight of them. They were starving and thirsty and weak from living outdoors. And yet they toiled on. Because they believed in the mission the same as he did. Because they—

A cry made the hairs on the back of his neck stand on end. It came from Alejandro, one of his older deckhands.

Alejandro gripped his chest as his lips peeled back in a gruesome grimace. He tried to say something, but his eyes rolled back in his head and he fell into the surf face-first.

Bartolome raced toward the drowning man, but Rosario

beat him there. His midshipman jumped into the sea and came up seconds later with Alejandro's limp body.

Bartolome knew Alejandro was dead before Rosario managed to drag him atop the reef.

Thirty-three, *Bartolome thought.* Thirty-six of us survived the hurricane, but already we are down to thirty-three.

With grim determination, he looked to the heavens and implored, Dear Father, please, I beg you. Have mercy. Do not take us all before we can finish our work.

HELL
ON WHEELS

Available now from Sourcebooks Casablanca

Jacksonville, North Carolina
Outside the Morgan Household

THOSE SCREAMS...

Man, he'd been witness to some bad shit in his life. A
great deal of which he'd personally perpetrated but very
little of which stuck with him the way those screams were
going to stick with him. Those soul-tearing, gut-wrench-
ing bursts of inconsolable grief.

As Nate Weller, known to most in the spec-ops community simply as "Ghost," gingerly lowered himself into
the Jeep that General Fuller had arranged for him to pick
up upon returning CONUS—continental U.S.—he figured it was somehow appropriate. Each vicious shriek was
an exclamation point marking the end of a mission that'd
gone from bad to the worst possible scenario imaginable,
and a fitting cry of heartbreak to herald the end of his best
friend's remarkable life.

Grigg...

Sweet Jesus, had it really been just two weeks since they were drinking raki in Istanbul? Two weeks since they'd crossed the border into Syria to complete a deletion?

And that was another thing. Deletion. *Christ*, what a word. A ridiculously euphemistic way of saying you put a hot ball of lead that exploded with a muzzle velocity of 2,550 feet per second into the brainpan of some unsuspecting SOB who had the appallingly bad luck of finding himself on ol' Uncle Sam's shit list.

Yep, two lines you never want to cross, horizontal and vertical.

"Get me out of here," Alisa Morgan choked as she wrenched open the passenger door and jumped inside the Jeep, bringing the smell of sunshine and honeysuckle with her.

Ridiculously pleasant scents considering Nate's day had begun in the seventh circle of hell and was quickly getting worse. Shouldn't that be the rotten-egg aroma of sulfur burning his nose?

He glanced over at the petite woman sitting beside him, stick straight and trembling with the effort to contain her grief, and his stupid heart sprouted legs and jumped into his throat. It'd been that way since the first time he'd met Ali, Grigg's baby sister.

Baby, *right*.

She hadn't been a baby even then. At seventeen she'd been a budding young woman. And now? Over twelve years later? Man, now she was *all* woman. All sunny blond hair and fiercely alive, amber-colored eyes in a face guaran-damn-teed to totally destroy him. Oh buddy, that face was a real gut check, one of those sweet Disney princess-type deals. Not to mention her body. Jesus.

He wanted her now just like he'd wanted her then. Maybe more. Okay, definitely more. And the inner battle he constantly waged with his unrepentant libido whenever she got within ten feet of him coupled with his newly acquired, mountainous pile of regret, guilt, and anguish to make him so tired. So unbearably tired of…everything.

"What about your folks?" he murmured, afraid to talk too loudly lest he shatter the tenuous hold she seemed to have on herself. "Don't you wanna be with them?"

He glanced past the pristine, green expanse of the manicured, postage-stamp sized lawn to the little, white, clapboard house with its cranberry trim and matching shutters. Geez, the place was homey. So clean, simple, and welcoming. Who would ever guess those inside were slowly bleeding out in the emotional aftershock of the bomb he'd just delivered?

She shook her head, staring straight ahead through the windshield, her nostrils flaring as she tried to keep the ocean of tears pooling in her eyes from falling. "They don't…want or…n-need me right now. I'm a…a reminder that…that…" she trailed off, and Nate had to squash the urge to reach over and pull her into his arms.

Better keep a wrinkle in it, boyo. You touch my baby sister and you die. Grigg had whispered that the day he'd introduced Nate to his family and seen the predatory heat in Nate's eyes when they'd alighted on Ali.

Yeah, well, *keeping a wrinkle in it* was impossible whenever Ali was in the same room with him, but he hadn't touched…and he hadn't died. Grigg was the one who'd done that…

Christ.

"They want you, Ali," he assured her now. "They need you."

"No." She shook her head, still refusing to look at him, as if making eye contact would be the final crushing blow to the crumbling dam behind which she held all her rage and misery. "They've always been a pair, totally attuned to one another, living within their own little two-person sphere. Not that they don't love me and Grigg," she hastened to add as she dashed at her tears with the backs of her hands, still refusing to let them fall. "They're *great* parents; it's just…I don't know what I'm trying to say. But how they are together, always caught up in one another? That's why Grigg and I are so close…" Her left eyelid twitched ever so slightly. "*Were* so close…*God!*" Her voice broke and sympathetic grief pricked behind Nate's eyes and burned up the back of his throat until every breath felt as if it was scoured through a cheese grater.

It was too much. He couldn't stand to watch her fight any longer. The weight of her struggle compounded with the already crushing burden of his own rage and sorrow until all he could do was screw his peepers closed and press his clammy forehead to the backs of his tense hands. He gripped the steering wheel with fingers that were as numb and cold as the block of ice encasing his heart. The one that'd formed nearly a week before when he'd been forced to do the unthinkable.

A barrage of bloody images flashed behind his lids before he could push them away. He couldn't think of that now. He wouldn't think of that now...

"Nate?" He jumped like he'd been shot when the coolness of her fingers on his arm pulled him from his brutal thoughts. "Get me out of here, okay? Dad...he shooed me away. I don't think he wanted me witnessing Mother's breakdown and I think I can still hear her..." She choked.

Uh-huh. And Nate knew right then and there those awful sounds torn from Carla Morgan's throat weren't going to stick with just him. Anyone who'd been within earshot would be haunted forever after.

And, god*damn*it, he liked Paul Morgan, considered him a good and honest man, but *screw* the bastard for not seeing that his only daughter needed comfort, too. Just because Ali put on a brave front, refusing to break down like her mother had, didn't mean she wasn't completely ripped apart on the inside. And damn the man for putting Nate in this untenable situation—to be the only one to offer Ali comfort when he was the dead-last person on Earth who should.

He hesitated only a second before turning the key and pulling from the curb. The Jeep grumbled along, eating up the asphalt, sending jarring pain through his injured leg with each little bump in the road. Military transports weren't built to be smooth rides. Hell no. They were built to keep chugging and plugging along no matter what was sliding under the wheels. Unfortunately, what they gained in automotive meanness, they lost in comfort, but that was the least of his current problems. *His* pain he could deal with—brush it aside like an annoying gnat. He was accustomed to that, after all. Had trained for it and lived it over and over again for almost fifteen years.

Ali's pain was something else entirely.

Chancing a glance in her direction, he felt someone had shoved a hot, iron fist straight into his gut.

She was crying.

Finally.

Now that she didn't have to be strong in front of her parents, she let the tears fall. They coursed, unchecked, down her soft cheeks in silvery streams. Her chest shook with the enormity of her grief, but no sound escaped her peach-colored lips save for a few ragged moans that she quickly cut off, as if she could allow herself to show only so much outward emotion. As if she still had to be careful, be tough, be resilient.

She didn't. Not with him. But he couldn't speak past the hot knot in his own throat to tell her.

He wanted to scream at that uncaring bitch, Fate. Rail and cry and rant. But what possible good would that do them? None. So he gulped down the hard tangle of sorrow and rage and asked, "Anywhere in particular y'wanna go?"

She turned toward him, her big, tawny eyes haunted, lost. "Yeah, okay." He nodded. "I know a place."

After twenty minutes of pure hell, forced to watch her struggle to keep herself together, struggle to keep from bursting into a thousand bloody pieces that would surely cut him as deeply as they cut her, he nosed the Jeep along

a narrow coast road, through the waving, brown heads of
sea oats, until he stopped at a wooden fence. It was gray
and brittle from years spent battling the sun and weather-
ing the salt spray.

He figured he and that fence were kindred spirits.
They'd both been worn down by the lives they'd led until
they were so battered and scarred they no longer resembled anything like what they'd started out being—and
yet they were still standing.

Right. He'd give anything to be the one reduced to an
urn full of fine, gray ash. Between the two of them, Grigg
had been the better man. But on top of being uncaring,
Fate was a *stupid* bitch. That's the only explanation he
could figure for why he'd made it out of that stinking,
sandy hut when Grigg hadn't.

A flash of Grigg's eyes in that last moment nearly had
him doubling over. Those familiar brown eyes...they'd
been hurting, begging, resigned...

No. He shook away the savage image and focused his
gaze out the windshield.

Beyond the fence's ragged, ghostly length, gentle
dunes rolled and eventually merged with the flat stretch
of a shell-covered beach. The gray Atlantic's vast expanse
flirted in the distance with the clear blue of the sky, and
the boisterous wind whipped up whitecaps that giggled
and hissed as they skipped toward shore.

It just didn't seem right. A day like that. So sunny, so
bright. Didn't the world know it'd lost one of its greatest
men? Didn't its molten heart bleed?

He switched off the Jeep and sucked in the familiar

scents of sea air and sun-baked sand. He couldn't find his usual comfort in the smells. Not today. And, maybe, never again. Hesitantly he searched for the right words.

Yeah, right. Like there *were* any right words in this God-awful situation.

"I won't offer y'platitudes, Ali," he finally managed to spit out. "He was the best man I've ever known. I loved 'im like a brother."

Talk about understatement of the century. Losing Grigg was akin to losing an arm. Nate felt all off-balance. Disoriented. More than once during the past week, he'd turned to tell Grigg something only to remember too late his best friend wasn't there.

He figured he wasn't suffering from phantom-limb syndrome, but phantom-*friend* syndrome.

"Then as a brother, tell me what happened…what *really* happened," she implored.

She'd always been too damned smart for her own good.

"He died in an accident. He was cleanin' an old gas tank on one of the bikes; there was a spark; some fuel on his rag ignited; he fell into a tray of oil and burned to death before anyone could get to him." The lie came out succinctly because he'd practiced it so friggin' often, but the last word still stuck in his throat like a burr.

Unfortunately, it was the only explanation he could give her about the last minutes of her brother's life. Because the truth fell directly under the heading *National Security Secret*. He thought it very likely Ali suspected Grigg hadn't spent the last three-plus years partnering with a few ex-military, spec-ops guys, living and working in Chicago as a custom motorcycle builder, but it wasn't *his* place to give her the truth. The truth that Grigg Morgan had still been working for Uncle.

When he and Grigg bid their final farewells to the Marine Corps, it was only in order to join a highly secretive "consulting" group. The kind of group that took on only the most clandestine of operations. The kind of group whose missions never made the news or crossed the desk of some pencil-pushing aide at the DOD in a tidy little dossier. They put the *black* in black ops, their true identities known only to a select few, and those select few were *very* high up in government. *High*. Like, all the way at the friggin' top.

So no. He couldn't tell her what *really* happened to Grigg. And he hoped to God she never found out.

She searched his determinedly blank expression, and he watched helplessly as the impotent rage rose inside her—an emotional volcano threatening to explode. Before he could stop her, she slammed out of the vehicle, hurdled the fence, and raced toward the dunes, long hair flying behind her, slim bare legs churning up great puffs of sand that caught in the briny wind and swirled away.

Shit.

He wrenched open his door and bounded after her, his left leg screaming in agony, not to mention the goddamned broken ribs that threatened to punch a hole right through his lung. *Blam!* Wheeze. That quick and he'd be spending another day or two in the hospital. Fan-friggin'-tastic. Just what he didn't need right now.

"Ali!" he bellowed, grinding his teeth against the pain, running with an uneven, awkward limp made even more so by the shifting sand beneath his boots.

She turned on him then in grief and frustration, slamming a tiny balled-up fist into the center of his chest. *Sweet Christ...*

Agony exploded like a frag grenade. He took a knee. It was either that or just keel over dead.

"Nate?" Her anger turned to shock as she knelt beside him in the sand. "What—" Before he knew what she was about, she lifted the hem of his T-shirt, gaping at the ragged appearance of his torso. His ribs were taped, but the rest of him looked like it'd gone ten rounds with a meat grinder and lost.

"Holy shit, Nate!" He almost smiled despite the blistering pain that held him in its teeth, savage and unyielding as a junkyard dog. Ali never cursed. Either it was written somewhere in her DNA or in that contract she'd signed after becoming a kindergarten teacher. "What happened to you?"

He shook his head because, honestly, it was all he could manage. If he so much as opened his mouth, he was afraid he'd scream like a girl.

"Nate!" She threw her arms around his neck. God, that felt right...and so, so wrong. "Tell me! Tell me what happened to you. Tell me what really happened to Grigg." The last was breathed in his ear. A request. A heartrending plea.

"Y'know I can't, Ali." He could feel the salty hotness of her tears where she'd tucked her face into his neck. Smell, in the sweet humidity of her breath, the lemon tea she'd been drinking before he knocked on her parents' door and told her the news that instantly blew her safe, sheltered world apart.

This was his greatest fantasy and worst nightmare all rolled into one. Ali, sweet, lovely Ali. She was here. Now. Pressed against his heart.

He reluctantly raised arms gone heavy with fatigue and sorrow. If Grigg could see him now, he'd take his favorite 1911-A1 and drill a .45 straight in his sorry ass. But the whole point of this Charlie Foxtrot was that Grigg wasn't here. No one was here to offer Ali comfort but him. So he gathered her close—geez, her hair smelled good—and soothed her when the grief shuddered through her in violent, endless waves like the tide crashing to shore behind them.

And then she kissed him…

Acknowledgments

A million thanks to my family for being a constant source of encouragement and support. These past two years have been a roller coaster, but you all stayed strapped in beside me, laughing with me during the highs and crying with me during the lows. I love you all to the moon and back again.

A shout-out to Amanda Carlson, sci-fi author extraordinaire. You've been a confidante, a shoulder to lean on, and a true and loyal friend. I couldn't have written this book without our daily check-ins. You made this story possible.

Huge bear hugs to Dan and Mary Somers. Thanks for sticking with me through thick and thin. Your friendship means the world to me.

And last but not least, kudos to all the folks at Sourcebooks who work so hard to take the dirty lumps of coal that are my manuscripts and polish them up to make them shine like diamonds. I appreciate you more than words can convey.

About the Author

A *New York Times* and *USA Today* bestselling author, Julie Ann Walker loves to travel the world looking for views to compete with her deadlines. And if those views happen to come with a blue sky and sunshine? All the better! When she's not writing, Julie enjoys camping, hiking, cycling, fishing, cooking, petting every dog that walks by her, and…reading, of course!

Be sure to sign up for Julie's occasional newsletter at julieannwalker.com.

To learn more about Julie, visit her at julieannwalker.com. Or follow her on Facebook at facebook.com/julieannwalkerauthor and Instagram @julieannwalker_author.

THE DEEP SIX

Get ready to dive in! *New York Times* and *USA Today* bestselling author Julie Ann Walker takes you to the fabulous Florida Keys, where finding a sunken treasure is only the beginning...

Hell or High Water

Former SEAL Leo Anderson and CIA agent Olivia Mortier race to recover uranium lost on the ocean floor before the attraction burning between them ignites...

Devil and the Deep

When socialite Maddy Powers is kidnapped, Bran Palladino will stop at nothing to rescue her and prove that they're both stronger together.

Ride the Tide

Former SEAL Mason McCarthy is determined to avoid the fairer sex, but he can't ignore historian Alexandra Merriweather...

"Hot men, hot action, and hot temperatures make for one hot romance!"

—*BookPage* for *Hell or High Water*

For more information, visit: **sourcebooks.com**

BLACK KNIGHTS INC.

New York Times and *USA Today* bestselling author Julie Ann Walker brings the heat with elite ex-military operatives who will ignite all your hottest fantasies.

Hell on Wheels

He's the bad boy Ali Morgan's always wanted, but Nate "Ghost" Weller has been keeping a terrible secret...

In Rides Trouble

Daring and dauntless, Becky "Rebel" Reichert isn't afraid of anything...except not knowing the heated touch of Frank Knight.

Rev It Up

Jake "The Snake" Sommers has spent most of his life as a soldier. Now his biggest mission is to win back the woman who stole his heart.

"Edgy, alpha, and downright HOT, the Black Knights Inc. will steal your breath...and your heart!"

—Catherine Mann, *USA Today* bestselling author, for *Hell on Wheels*

Also by Julie Ann Walker

Way of the Warrior (anthology)